THE UPPER CRUSH

EVIE ALEXANDER

First Published in Great Britain 2024 by Emlin Press

ISBN (eBook) 978-1-914473-30-2

ISBN (Print) 978-1-914473-31-9

ISBN (Audiobook) 978-1-914473-45-6

A CIP catalogue record for this book is available from the British Library.

www.emlinpress.com

For Diana Hayward

ALSO BY EVIE ALEXANDER

THE KINLOCH SERIES

Highland Games

Hollywood Games

Kissing Games

Musical Games

Wedding Games

Christmas Games

❧

THE FOXBROOKE SERIES

One Night in Foxbrooke

Love ad Lib

An Unholy Affair

The Upper Crush

The Love Position

Christmas off Script

One Night Only

Righting Mr Wrong

Under the Influencer

Foxbrooke Extras

❧

By Evie Alexander and Kelly Kay

EVIE & KELLY'S HOLIDAY DISASTERS SERIES

Cupid Calamity

Cookout Carnage

Christmas Chaos

Get Evie's books in all formats as well as special offers, early releases, and exclusive deals direct from her website:

www.eviealexanderbooks.com

Saturday December 2nd - Seven-twenty p.m.

There were no last thoughts or words from Lady Estelle Gloria Elizabeth Foxbrooke as she plummeted towards certain death. No scream. No swearing. No internal cry at her own carelessness. Just a gasp, then whooshing panic as she toppled over the banister and headed straight for the tiled floor of Foxbrooke Manor's entrance hall, thirty feet below.

Ten minutes earlier

'Oh, no,' Estelle muttered as the sound of barking dogs echoed towards her down the corridor. It was the night of the revamped Winter Ball at Foxbrooke Manor and her family couldn't afford to have anything go wrong. Thanks to her wayward father, Arthur, the Duke of Somerset, the estate was on a financial precipice, and it only needed one more cock-up to send it over the edge.

The guests had arrived and were making their way from the bar areas to the two dining rooms. The corridor of her family home was empty, so Estelle tried to run towards the noise she knew could only spell trouble. However, her long legs were constrained by a tight turquoise dress that felt a size too small, and her feet were in heels that belonged in hell.

Both had been gifted to her by her aunt, Simone, a famous American fashion designer who'd settled in Paris thirty-five years previously. Lady Estelle Foxbrooke may have had the height and looks of a model, but she had no interest in following her mom onto the catwalk, or restricting her calories until she reached the required weight.

Up ahead, the barks were now interspersed with excited growls.

Kicking off her heels, she yanked the skirt of her dress to the top of her thighs and sprinted forward. Her stockinged feet slid on the tiles of the entrance hall and she grabbed at a coat rack to steady herself.

Dad! No!

Arthur Foxbrooke owned two black hellhounds: Caligula, a Great Dane, and Borgia, a Labrador Retriever. Both animals were more unmanageable than their master, which was saying something, and were now enjoying an orgy of destruction as they attempted to fight, eat, or shag each other, as well as all the decorations running up the stairs.

'Heel!'

Her tone may have worked on her own dogs, as well as most people, however Caligula and Borgia were having none of it. They took one look at Estelle, then bounded up the stairs and away.

Clenching her hands into fists, she let out a cry of frustration. Despite her twin brother, Henry, returning to the family home a few months ago to help run the estate, their father always seemed to find a way to undo their good work. Neither she nor Henry could babysit Arthur or his pets twenty-four-seven and so, in a few brief minutes, two uncontrollable dogs had destroyed a day's worth of work.

What a mess...

Winding up the banisters had been metres of lights, winter foliage, garlands of fragrant dried fruit, and loops of popcorn threaded on gold string. It had been a magnificent feast for the eyes as well as the nose, but now everything lay in tangled tatters.

Should I get Jack?

No.

Jack, one of her oldest friends, had just moved back to Foxbrooke and had spent the last few weeks helping to organise the Winter Ball. During that time, he'd also fallen in love with Eveline, Estelle's best friend, and tonight was their first official outing as a couple. Estelle didn't want to disturb them, or any of the staff who were rushed off their feet preparing for dinner. She could clear this up on her own.

Hands on her hips, she surveyed the scene. If she ignored the confetti of popcorn, leaves, and oranges studded with cloves that littered the floor, most of the decorations were still intact—just not in the right place. She glanced at her watch. Twenty minutes until dinner was served. She could do this.

Dashing to the bottom of the stairs, Estelle began disentangling the lights from the greenery, popcorn and fruit garlands. The bulbs had gone off, but she didn't care about fixing them. She just needed to get the overall appearance back to how it was and hope people were drunk enough not to notice.

And this is why I did a final check, she thought as she made her way up the stairs, looping the decorations around her arms. As with most matters relating to her family and their home,

Estelle could never truly relax. It was like keeping an eye on a delinquent toddler centipede—having to be on constant alert as you waited for one of the hundred shoes to inevitably drop.

Tonight was meant to be the moment where everything came together and they made a decent profit. A night where she could relax and let her hair down. But no. Here she was, cleaning up her father's mess, whilst he chugged champagne and partied with her two mothers elsewhere in the house.

Estelle paused and briefly closed her eyes as her throat tightened. Her three parents were still happily in love after over thirty years, Henry was smitten with his girlfriend, Libby, and now Eveline had found her perfect man in Jack. Despite her public protestations to the contrary, Estelle's love life was non-existent and had been that way for years.

And no surprise. There's no room or time for a boyfriend.

As well as managing the estate, Estelle ran a livery. Until Henry had returned, she'd been working fourteen-hour days, seven days a week, for years without a break. She had more time to herself now her twin was back, but the only man she was interested in didn't seem interested in her.

Isaac Hayward was a brilliant yoga teacher, kind, and extremely hot. He had dark curly hair, emerald green eyes, seven-day-stubble, and the body of a gymnast. Yet despite Estelle inviting him to every event she could, he always declined.

No-one else makes me—

Another man's face came to mind, sending a wave of heat crashing through her.

No, no, no. A thousand times no! NOT him!

Turning back to the miles of lights, she looped more around herself and staggered up another step like an overloaded Christmas tree. There was no way in hell she was going to let her treacherous body and mind think of, or react to, the man who was her brother's worst enemy: James Hunter-Savage.

Estelle had known about James for years, but had only met him in person twice. From Henry's description, she'd always pictured an ogre with the social skills of a cocky troll. James was definitely overflowing with attitude, but his self-confidence was not misplaced. Six foot four, a body that rowed Oxford to victory in the Boat Race and looks that would make a male model feel insecure, James had been the most successful broker at Conqueror, the company Henry had worked for in London. He was now living on the other side of the Foxbrooke river which bordered her family's estate.

The first gong for dinner rang, signalling everyone to move to their tables. *Shit!* Estelle was almost at the top of the stairs, but her decision to wrap every piece of decoration around her body was slowing her progress.

Forget doing all of it. There's no time. Just start mending it and work your way back down.

By now, the loops of lights were almost at her eyeballs. She stumbled, reaching for the support of the wooden banister. *Be careful!* She was barely able to move her arms under the weight of decorations and they were heavy around her neck, making her unbalanced.

Staggering forward, she managed to unhook the first loop of lights and tie it to a railing with one of the wires the dogs had ripped off earlier. It was going to take forever. Pushing a garland of dried fruit to her forehead, she leaned over the support to work out if she could fix it any quicker.

Suddenly, there was the sound of barking behind her and the rumble of feet.

She turned to fend the dogs off, but one of them jumped up, hitting her in the chest. Tangled and weighed down by decorations, her feet left the floor and she toppled backwards over the railing.

Pivoting, she flailed her arms, her fingers making contact with a branch. Time seemed to slow as she gripped it, pain searing into her palm from the holly leaves.

For a brief second, she hung, suspended in air. Then the branch snapped, and she plunged towards a painful and inglorious death. There was no time to think, scream, or brace herself for impact. One moment she was falling, and the next she'd landed.

However the floor was no longer flat and felt very much like someone's arms.

'I've got you,' a man's voice murmured.

She shook with adrenaline, her breath coming in shaky gasps.

'Shhh. It's okay. I've got you,' he repeated.

Estelle opened her eyes. All she could see were strands of lights and leaves.

'You saved my life,' she stammered.

'I don't know about that. I think I saved a Christmas tree. You just happened to be hiding inside it.'

A nervous laugh burst out of her. The man's voice was deep and confident. It held her fractured mind together with the same assurance as his arms held her body.

'Are *you* okay?' she asked.

'Me?' He sounded surprised. 'Never felt better. Why?'

'Well, you've just caught me and enough decorations for an average-sized house. That's quite a weight.'

His arms shifted, as if he were flexing his muscles. 'I've benched far more without breaking a sweat.'

A giggle slipped from her lips, and she mentally slapped herself. *Stop it!* She was being as ditsy as her youngest sister, Summer.

'Should I get down?' she asked.

'I wouldn't advise it just yet. I presume the lights are plastic, but a lot of them are broken. I want to make sure they don't hurt you as we take them off. How do you feel?'

My heart's pounding and there's a tingling in my pants, but I think that's mostly down to you…

'Are you in pain anywhere?' he continued.

Estelle took a deep breath. She may not have been able to see her rescuer, but—*oh, my god*—could she smell him. His scent was hot, spicy, and woodsy, cut with something citrus. Her mouth watered.

'What are you wearing?' she blurted.

There was a pause. 'Clothes,' he eventually replied. 'Are you disappointed I'm not also festooned in baubles and garden clippings?'

Another giggle bubbled out. *Stop it!* 'No, I mean, what aftershave or cologne do you have on?'

'Is it too much?'

She shook her head and the lights rattled. 'It's really nice.'

Another pause. 'So are you.'

Her pulse rocketed. 'You don't know who I am.'

'Yes, I do. Even though you're ninety-nine per cent Christmas tree, I'm still one hundred per cent sure I'm holding Estelle Foxbrooke.'

A flash of panic and arousal slammed through her. Was this *James?*

'What's your name?'

He cleared his throat. 'When I was born, my parents christened me Kevin.'

Her body relaxed, but she wasn't sure if it was with relief or disappointment.

'Kevin?'

'Uh-huh.'

'Oh.'

'You don't like it?'

Estelle tried to arrange her thoughts. The name 'Kevin', didn't seem to fit the voice, or the size, of the man who held her.

'No, that's not it. It just doesn't seem to go with you, that's all.'

'Hmm. And what do you think *should* go with me then?'

Er, me? 'A name like "Atlas", or "Thor".' *Or James…*

He laughed, and the vibrations rumbled out of his chest into hers.

'Well, I think *your* name suits you perfectly.'

'Estelle?'

'Yes. You're a star.'

Oh, my god. Was this mysterious stranger coming onto her?

She swallowed. 'In what way?'

'You shine brighter than everyone else.'

A lump formed in her throat. Had anyone ever said anything like that to her before?

'Are you flirting with me?' she whispered.

He huffed out a short breath. 'I'd like to.'

'Are you married?'

'No. I'm ninety-nine per cent single.'

'And the other one per cent?'

'Has a crush on a Christmas tree.'

Laughter burst out of her, free and unrestrained. She was alive, and in the arms of a sexy stranger, who—thank god—was *not* James Hunter-Savage.

The sound of the second gong for dinner sounded.

She sighed. 'I really should get back.'

'Can we have a drink together after the meal?'

Excitement rippled through her, and she nodded.

'I want to get to know you,' he continued. 'But I also need to talk to you about some things.'

Excitement veered off track into nervous-land. 'What things?'

'Business-related stuff.'

She froze in his arms. Had he followed her into the hall? Waited for her to tumble before making his move? *Don't be ridiculous!*

He lowered her feet carefully to the ground. 'Let me help get you free of all this first. Don't move and I'll untangle you.'

Standing stock still, her eyes squeezed shut, Estelle allowed him to unwind the decorations from her arms. As soon as they were free, she shuffled the loops from her waist, down and off her legs, then tugged the hem of her dress back to her knees.

The man stayed behind her, lifting the final strands over her head.

With the decorations gone and her shoes still in a corridor, Estelle felt naked. She could feel the heat of him behind her, her own heart hammering inside her chest. She'd gone from fear to excitement to dread.

'Estelle?' His voice was low.

She slowly turned and opened her eyes. They confirmed what her gut already knew.

James Hunter-Savage.

Hurt, anger and confusion fought for her attention. She'd been vulnerable with him. She'd let her guard down. And what had he given her in return?

'You lied to me,' she whispered.

He shook his head, a muscle twitching in his jaw.

'You *lied* to me!' she shouted.

'No! Estelle, I didn't.'

He reached his hand towards her and she recoiled.

'Don't touch me.'

Shaking, she bent to lift the pile of lights and foliage, but it was too much and half of it dropped back to the floor.

'Let me help,' he said behind her.

'No.' She ran the bundle to a side door, opened it, and threw the decorations inside.

'Please, can we talk?'

Returning for the rest of the pile, she carried as much as she could, kicking the rest in front of her.

'I need to tell you something,' he continued.

'I'm not interested in anything you have to say, *Kevin*,' she spat. 'I don't care how you managed to wheedle your way in here tonight, but I'm going to make sure you never darken our doors again.'

'Darken your doors?' His tone sharpened. 'I'm not a vampire.'

'No, you're the antichrist.'

Furious with herself for falling prey to his charms, and livid that tears were threatening to spill, Estelle turned on her heels and ran.

❦ 2 ❦

Blinking sweat out of his eyes, his heart pounding at the edge of VO2 max, James pushed himself to the limit on the rowing machine. His movements were robotically precise, his gaze glued to the small screen monitoring his progress. Despite the pain wracking his body, he would not allow even half a second to drop off his pace.

James Hunter-Savage was a self-made man. From the age of seven, he was made to understand that his name, his voice, his appearance, his likes and dislikes could all be broken down or discarded, and remodelled into something better. The same went for friends. The people with whom one associated were a reflection of your social status and power. If they elevated you, they stayed. If they threatened your standing in any way, they were cut without a second thought.

No-one worked harder to create and maintain James Hunter-Savage than the man himself. Building and sculpting his powerful physique, still Olympic standard even at the age of thirty-three, required a single-minded focus.

At the start of the year, his life had been ninety-five per

cent on track. He was the most successful, and highly paid, broker Conqueror had ever produced, was in the best shape of his life, and could bed any woman who took his fancy.

Now, twelve months later, everything had gone to shit. He'd lost his job in the worst possible circumstances, was currently barred from working in the City, and hadn't had sex in nearly a year.

James Hunter-Savage was used to holding life by the balls, but it had turned around and kicked him in the nuts.

His body screamed at him to stop rowing, but his mind had a point to prove. Maintaining his physical strength was the only thing left he had control over, so he kept punishing himself until his guts led the final rebellion. Dropping the rower handle mid-stroke, he grabbed a bin from the floor beside him and threw up into it, feeling a perverse sense of satisfaction and relief, even as his chest and stomach heaved.

There was a knock at the door, and a woman in her late fifties entered, carrying a plastic cleaning caddy. Her white-blonde hair was arranged in a donut bun on the top of her head, and her eye and lip liner had been heavily applied. Dressed in a pale pink cleaning tabard over a leopard print top and matching leggings, her feet were in python print Gucci sliders, and her toenails were painted red. James knew her fingernails matched, however her hands were currently inside yellow rubber gloves.

'Babe,' she began, her nose wrinkling, 'you've done it again, haven't you?'

Crossing the room, her free arm extended as if to take the bin from him.

He stood. 'I'll do it.'

'You don't want to be dealing with that. Give it to me.'

James held it aloft. 'No, Mum.'

His mother glanced at the bin, a frown on her face as if

calculating the possibility of jumping to reach it, then took a bottle from her caddy and sprayed it liberally over the rowing machine.

'Well, I'll do this then.' She vigorously rubbed the wet surfaces with a microfibre cloth.

'Mum—'

'Honestly, babe. For the life of me, I don't know why you do it to yourself. It ain't right.' She tugged at the machine to move it.

'Let me.' James pulled the rower back to its original position—no longer facing the wall, but a window that looked out onto a rose garden.

'And why stare at the wall? If you don't want to look outside, there's the telly.'

James glanced around the home gym, filled with state-of-the-art equipment he was sure only ever got used by him.

'I don't need the distraction.'

She slapped his chest with her cloth. 'You need to make it fun. I've been bingeing *The Real Housewives of Chelsea*. You should watch it.'

'I'd rather have a full-frontal lobotomy.'

His mother laughed. 'I dunno what that is. Sounds naughty to me.' She went to the treadmill and began spraying.

'Mum, I've already wiped it down, and we've got cleaners for that.'

'They don't do a good enough job, babe. I only keep them on to please your dad.'

James tied a knot in the plastic bin liner and removed the bag. There was no point in arguing. Beverley Hunter-Savage could never rest until every surface in her house sparkled and shone. Her clothes may have been designer, but nine times out of ten they were hidden under an apron.

'Go take a shower, babe, then find your dad. He wants to see you.'

'Okay.' James bit back a sigh and left the room, carrying the results of his exercise session.

STRIDING THROUGH THE GROUND FLOOR CORRIDOR TOWARDS the kitchen, James's skin itched with irritation. His father should never have bought this Georgian pile. It was far smaller than Foxbrooke Manor, but still impressive enough to have come with a seven-figure price tag.

Overpriced pile of shit. Damp was already showing through the freshly applied paint, and without modern insulation, James knew the fuel bill to heat it over winter would be astronomical.

Earlier in the year, his father had decided the Hunter-Savage family's progression up the ladder of the British social classes should skip a few rungs. Step one involved consolidating their holdings and buying Shoscombe Manor, a Palladian mansion set in four hundred and eight acres of rolling Somerset countryside. Step two involved ingratiating themselves with the local nobs. However, once James discovered which members of the aristocracy lived on the other side of the river to the mansion house, he'd put a stop to that plan.

Henry fucking Foxbrooke.

James was fifteen when Henry, two school years younger than him, had started at Eton. Lord Henry Foxbrooke was a viscount, his father a duke, his biological mother a glamorous Black American movie star, and his other mother a wild and beautiful Irish woman. Henry's family were infamous and exciting, and James expected the heir to the Foxbrooke estate to be cut from the same cloth.

He wasn't.

Shouldering open the stiff kitchen door, James stamped on the bottom bar of an industrial-sized bin to lift the lid, then dropped the bag he was carrying inside.

He's a pathetic little dweeb.

What Henry Foxbrooke had been handed on a plate, James had been forced to fight for every day of his life. But despite being born into money and the top tier of society, Henry was meeker than a mouse and appeared embarrassed by his title. That had annoyed James beyond belief. However, analysing exactly *why* Henry riled him so much would mean a journey of introspection James wasn't prepared to take. So instead he needled Henry, hoping to provoke a reaction.

It had taken him seventeen years to get one.

Stalking to a cupboard, James took out a tub containing a post-exercise recovery powder he'd created himself, then glanced around the kitchen for his blender.

Fuck's sake!

It was sitting, unwashed by the sink.

Again.

Running the hot water, he scrubbed at the flecks of dried green with a brush. What *was* this shit? Kale? Spirulina? Pond water? And why the fuck couldn't she just clean it up after she used it?

As if summoned by the power of his thoughts, the kitchen door opened and a woman entered. Blonde, beautiful, and adventurous in bed, Elyse Kirwin should have been a perfect match for James Hunter-Savage. One night three years ago, she'd approached him in a City bar, and they'd had a two-week fling before James had ended it.

Elyse hadn't accepted his decision.

Her eyes scanned his body, her gaze a calculated mix of amusement and desire. 'Hard?' she asked with a smirk.

He turned back to the sink. 'My workout, or cleaning your smoothie off my blender?'

She giggled. 'Sorry, I forgot.' Coming to his side, she leaned against the counter, watching him. 'There's a restaurant in the village called The Colour Palate that's meant to be good. Wanna go tonight?'

He shook his head. When they'd briefly dated, it hadn't taken long for James to twig that Elyse wasn't someone he wanted to spend any time with outside of the bedroom. He'd been upfront and honest with her, but she'd insisted they kept meeting to 'talk things through'.

He'd indulged her a couple of times, but stopped returning her calls when she wouldn't accept whatever they'd had was over. After six months of her pestering, she went quiet. Three months later, his dad introduced him to his new PA—Elyse.

'Oh, come on,' she continued. 'It'll be fun. For old time's sake.'

Shaking his head again, he twisted the cleaned blender back onto the base unit and measured out scoops of powder. Avoiding Elyse when he worked at Conqueror was easy enough, but now? She even lived in the same house as he did. His parents thought the sun shone out of her arse, and hoped their son would get together with her.

Been there, done that, not going back.

'Do you believe in fate?' she asked, standing too close to him.

'No,' he replied, sloshing raw milk into the jug. No matter what Elyse asked him, the answer was always a negative. He hoped if he kept shutting down every conversation, she might finally leave him alone.

She curled a strand of hair around a finger. 'But look at us... We're now living—'

James turned the blender on, drowning out the rest of her

sentence. When he reluctantly switched it off, Elyse held out a cup.

He twisted the jug off the base. 'I'll take this with me.'

'Your dad wants to see you.'

'I'll find him in a bit.'

James went to the door and yanked it open.

'Enjoy your shower,' she called after him.

He didn't reply, already starting down the corridor.

'Think of me...' she continued, the words slipping through the closing door and sticking to his skin.

BACK IN HIS BEDROOM, JAMES WENT TO THE TALL WINDOW that looked out over the formal gardens, gulping his recovery drink.

The small box hedges surrounding the rose bushes had been immaculately trimmed when his parents had bought the house, but without constant upkeep, the garden was beginning to unravel.

Just like my life.

His dad had employed one gardener, but even in the winter it wasn't enough for a place this size. James wanted to be rich, but he was also pragmatic. What was the point in buying a lifestyle you couldn't afford to maintain?

He glanced around his bedroom: a chintz palace, where every possible eyesore was hidden by the same flowered fabric. The tops of the curtains were tucked behind upholstered pelmets, the bottom of the bed was obscured by a frilly valance, and the pillows and duvet were hidden by a coverlet as if they'd just died. Even the radiators were tidied away inside wooden boxes with lattice fronts to let the heat out. The wallpaper had the same pattern of blue roses as the soft furnishings, and the overall effect of the room was that of being suffocated by a rich grandmother.

James finished his drink and took the jug into the adjoining bathroom, rinsing it out in one of the two sinks, then tossed his clothes to the marble floor and stepped into the shower. This was the best part of the house: hot water that came out with more power than a herd of stampeding elephants. He let the droplets batter his muscles, releasing some of the tension that seeing Elyse had overlaid on top of the stress of everything else.

I need to get back to London.

But how? His flat was rented out to cover lawyers' fees and most of his savings were gone. Everything he'd worked so hard for had disappeared because he couldn't keep his big mouth shut.

Now he was living with his parents and his ex in the arse end of the country, and had taken on a job he had no clue how to do.

Resting his forehead against the back wall of the shower, he let out a breath, his thoughts returning to last Saturday night.

Estelle Foxbrooke...

If meeting Henry when they were at school had been a surprise, then meeting his twin sister had been an even bigger one.

Estelle was fire, light and energy. Power crackled from her into him, turning on every cell in his body from his brain to his cock.

Even during their first brief meeting on Foxbrooke high street, a few months ago, the force of Estelle's personality had met his and given it a kicking. '*I know exactly who you are... And if you know what's good for you, you'll stay away from my family.*'

A smile spread across his face and his dick sprang to life. He'd savoured every word she'd hurled in his direction and had replayed the meeting each and every time he'd brought himself off since. Now, that first encounter had been superseded.

Reaching down, James gripped his shaft. He'd blagged himself an invitation to the Winter Ball at Foxbrooke Manor so he could see her again. Thanks to his father's machinations, he needed to talk to her, but he also wanted another hit. A kick to his heart to keep going when everything else in his life was falling apart.

Catching sight of Estelle across one of the rooms on Saturday night had jolted his heart with electricity. Tall, curvaceous, and devastatingly beautiful, she'd been wearing an iridescent turquoise dress he wanted to rip off with his teeth.

Closing his eyes, he stroked his hard length, sensation shuddering up his body as he imagined her full lips parting with pleasure, her eyelids fluttering in bliss as he slowly fucked her.

Last Saturday, standing at the bar with Henry and the local vicar, Estelle had, once again, sent him packing. But before dinner, he'd searched for her.

His hand stilled around his cock as blinding panic shot through him, his mind replaying the moment when Estelle tumbled off the balcony. He'd never experienced terror like that before.

Thank god I was there.

And after catching her, she hadn't realised who he was. It was a blessing and a curse. A blessing because he got to see a different side of her, the one he knew she gifted to her family and close friends. And a curse, because he'd been so blinded by her charms that he'd flirted with her, then fucked everything up.

Letting go of his cock, he turned the shower icy. Time to wake up and smell the cold cup of coffee sitting in the chipped mug of reality. Estelle Foxbrooke didn't want him, and he couldn't be chasing someone that hot to handle when he needed her onside.

Ten minutes later, James knocked on a door downstairs and pushed it open.

'Jamesy-boy!' his father cried. 'Grab a seat.'

Elyse sprang up from behind a desk. 'Let me get it.'

'No,' James replied, taking a chair and positioning it across from his father. He sat, staring at the bottom of his dad's loafers.

Kevin Hunter-Savage was leaning back in his leather chair, his feet on the desk in front of him, playing with a fidget spinner. His hair, once naturally black, was now approximately the same shade as before, but with a blue hue to it, courtesy of the dye he used. He was wearing a garish Versace patterned shirt, the top buttons undone to show off a multitude of gold chains, and a pair of Gucci jeans a size too small.

'Elyse, babe,' his dad said. 'Give us five, would ya?'

She nodded. 'Of course, Kev.'

He gave her a wink. 'That's my girl.'

She smiled at him and left the room.

'Why won't you make a move?' his father hissed the moment the door was closed. 'What's wrong with you? She's like family.'

James sighed. 'She's *not* family.'

'She is to me and your mum—'

'I'm not going to change my mind.'

Kevin flicked the fidget spinner. 'She fancies you.'

James didn't reply.

'Elyse,' his father continued, as if James didn't know who he was talking about.

'I don't give a fuck.'

The spinner fell to the desk with a crash.

'You *should* give a fuck,' his father snarled, pointing a finger encircled with heavy gold rings at James. 'She's a nice girl and your mum wants grandkids. Do it for her if you won't do it for yourself.'

James let out a bitter laugh. 'You want me to impregnate your assistant just to make Mum happy?'

'Impreg-what? Don't use your fancy words with me, Jamesey-boy. Just marry her and make babies.' He flicked his hand at his son. 'I give you my blessing.'

'Thank you so much,' James replied, his voice laden with sarcasm.

'She's nice,' his dad continued.

'So you keep saying.'

Kevin picked up another fidget toy, this one a poppet in the shape of a dinosaur, and started playing with it. James wasn't sure if he'd prefer his father scrape his nails down a miniature blackboard.

'You wanted to see me?'

'Yeah, yeah,' his father replied, depressing the silicone circles with his thumbs so fast it sounded like he was making popcorn.

'Dad!'

Kevin tossed the toy to the desk and picked up the fidget spinner again. 'We've got a bit of an issue.'

James's heart sank. *What now?*

'We're going to have to relocate the company I bought for you.'

'Where?'

'Here.'

'No.' James stood. 'Absolutely not.'

His dad flicked the spinner and balanced it on the end of his thumb. 'No choice, son. If we're paying rent on that place in Bath then there's no moolah left to pay for the gig next year.'

Christ. 'How long have we got?'

'Gotta be out at the beginning of next week.'

'What?' James felt like he was watching what little was left of his life disappearing down a plug hole. 'It's buying this shit hole that's done it, hasn't it?' he yelled, gesturing to the house around them.

His father stood. 'Watch it, son.'

'They saw you coming, didn't they?'

'I got this pad for a steal,' his father blustered.

'Bullshit. It was on the market for months. You should have got it for a quarter of what you paid.'

'Your mum wanted it.'

'You still could have got the price down!' James ran his hands through his hair. 'I'm not doing this. I'm walking away.'

'You can't.'

James stalked to the door. 'Watch me.'

His dad ran after him. 'Son, if you do that, we'll lose the house.'

'What are you talking about?'

Kevin looked away, his hands now fiddling with loose change in his pockets. 'Our businesses have taken a hit over the last couple of years, and you're right, I overextended getting this place. I can just about scrape together enough to pay for what we promised in the contract, but if you can't make the event next summer turn a profit, then your mum and I are out on our arses.'

James took out his phone and fired off an email.

'What are you doing?'

'Telling our only surviving member of staff to cancel the meeting on Monday with our business partner.'

His dad's shoulders relaxed. 'So, you'll do it? You'll stay?'

'I'm doing this for Mum, not you. And you know what you have to do. Anyone connected with the new business, whether stakeholders or the guy who delivers pizza after hours, they *never* see you.'

James held his father's gaze as the terms of a bargain struck twenty-six years ago were aired once more.

'Deal?'

His father sighed and held out his hand. 'Deal.'

❧ 3 ❧

One Week Later

Life is good, and the future's going to be even better.

Striding up Milsom Street in Bath, Estelle had just the right amount of adrenaline running through her veins. It was enough to make butterflies dance excitedly in her stomach, but not enough to turn it.

She was within touching distance of her dream of staging a music and arts festival at Foxbrooke Manor, but needed outside help and investment to make it happen. After successfully securing both through a partnership with Excelsior Events the previous month, the company had, unexpectedly, been bought out. Now she was on her way to meet the new owner.

Please let them be nice. Not some cocky arsehole or society queen who looks down her nose at me.

Crossing the road, she checked her appearance in the windows of a shop filled with Christmas decorations. She'd swapped her usual wardrobe of jodhpurs, jeans and jumpers for a plum-coloured cashmere coat her mom had given her. Underneath, she'd crammed her curves into a tight pencil skirt and cream silk blouse that complemented her brown skin.

Her feet, usually in riding boots or wellies, were now squeezed into uncomfortable designer boots. The added height took her to just over six feet tall and helped her fake the confidence her parents had down to their bones.

Pausing at the window, she ran her fingers through her curly black hair and frowned at her reflection. Should she have worn make-up? Rummaging in her handbag, a gift from her aunt, she pulled out a vanilla lip balm and swiped it over her lips.

Why did they specify we have to work together in the same office?

The butterflies in her tummy flapped their wings faster. The new owner had honoured the original contract she'd signed with Excelsior, but with a few amendments, one of which was that Estelle had to work directly with whoever now ran the company.

Are they using me to get to Mom and Dad? Mammy?

A year after becoming the Duchess of Somerset, Estelle's mom, Vivienne Camille Boucher, had fallen in love with a single mother from the village and brought her into the marriage. Arthur, Vivienne, and Dervla Foxbrooke's unconventional relationship, as well as the sex parties they hosted at the manor, were a source of embarrassment for their six children, as well as gleeful gossip-rag fodder for the wider world.

Growing up, the eldest Foxbrooke siblings—Estelle, her twin brother, Henry, and their adopted brother, Connor—had borne the brunt of the public's fascination with their family. Even though Estelle loved her parents deeply, she also wished they were a little more normal.

Letting out a long breath, she squared her shoulders.

Come on. You've got this. After thirty years dealing with Mom, Dad and Mammy, there's nothing you can't handle.

She continued on through the crowds of tourists enjoying the Christmas market, refusing to allow them, or her tight skirt and pinching boots, to slow her pace. Bath may have been small, but she was used to the rural quiet of Foxbrooke and the company of her dogs, horses, and small circle of family and close friends. Here, jostled by strangers, she was aware just how much of an adjustment it was going to be commuting from her comfort zone into the city.

Just breathe. The new owner is just one person. How bad can it be?

Half way up Bartlett Street was the address she'd been emailed for the new offices of Excelsior Events, now called 'BDE Entertainment'. As she was about to ring the buzzer, a man exited the building and pulled the sign for the company from a frame to the right of the door.

'Excuse me,' she began.

He turned. 'Yes?'

She nodded at the sign in his hand. 'Are they still here?'

'Till the end of the day. Then they're out.'

What? Her tummy prickled with anxious confusion. 'Why?'

He shrugged. 'They haven't paid their rent.'

Estelle's mouth opened, but her brain was in freefall and all words had been lost to the wind.

'Do they owe you money, too?' the man asked.

Only a few hundred grand to pay for the festival... She swallowed, her mouth drier than a desert.

He punched numbers into a keypad and opened the door for her. 'First floor. Go on up. They might not let you in otherwise.'

Stammering her thanks, she entered, taking the carpeted stairs slowly, as if doing so would order the thoughts flapping inside her skull like headless chickens. She'd already spent so much of the estate's money on the festival; securing acts, putting down deposits, building a website. There was no money left if they didn't have the events company footing the rest of the bill.

Fuck, fuck, fuck, fuck, fuck! Pausing on the first landing, sweat beading on her brow, she undid her coat to let in some air. She'd only met the previous owners, Colin and Deborah, once before and they'd seemed straight down the line. Surely they were staying on for a transition period?

Just speak to them. Everything will be fine. They signed a contract. Remember?

Jogging up the rest of the stairs, she stopped and stared at a sign stuck to a door. It had the words 'Big Dick Energy Entertainment' printed on it, with a logo consisting of an eggplant emoji being struck by a bolt of lightning.

This was BDE Entertainment?

Heart hammering, she knocked.

The door opened inwards and a man in his twenties appeared, dressed in a plaid shirt and navy jeans. His eyes gleamed as he gazed at her, as if she was Santa arriving with presents. Or a strippergram. She re-tied her coat.

'Lady—' he began.

'I told you to take that *fucking* sign down,' a man yelled from inside the office. 'Twice.'

Estelle couldn't see who was shouting, but the voice was deep, powerful and angry. She took a step back.

The young man rolled his eyes. 'Bear with,' he said to her under his breath. '*Someone* hasn't had enough coffee yet.' He held out his hand and she shook it. 'I'm Max, we met briefly a couple of months ago.'

'Who is it?' the voice from inside snapped.

Max winked at her and closed the door slightly. 'Lady Foxbrooke,' he said over his shoulder. 'Your ten o'clock.'

Silence.

The anxiety that had been pricking at Estelle's stomach now turned stabby. She had no idea what was going on, and Max seemed to be taking perverse delight in riling whoever he was talking to.

'I told you to cancel her,' the man hissed, still loud enough for Estelle to make out every word.

'No, you didn't,' Max replied calmly.

'Yes, I *did*. We're not doing this now. Apologise and tell her we'll re-arrange.'

Max turned back to her. 'Lady Foxbrooke—'

'*Estelle* Foxbrooke, and no.'

'No?'

'We're not re-arranging anything.'

Max smirked. 'Of course.' Opening the door, he stepped back, bowing slightly as he extended his arm into the office. 'Lady—*Estelle* Foxbrooke. Welcome to Big Dick Enter—*Energy* Entertainment.'

Summoning all her courage, Estelle marched into the room, then stopped dead.

No, no, no, no, no, no, no.

Perched on the edge of a desk, surrounded by boxes, was James Hunter-Savage.

Memories from ten days ago at the Winter Ball winded her. She was once again tumbling through the air towards certain death. Only this time, a duplicitous stranger with a silvery tongue wouldn't be there to catch her. Her angel was in clear sight, his mask gone, revealing exactly who he really was: Lucifer.

'*You...*' she choked out.

Even though James's posture was relaxed, she recognised a tightness around his eyes and jaw.

He opened his palms. 'Me.'

'I don't understand.'

Pushing upright, he held out a hand. 'I'm the CEO of BDE Entertainment.'

Estelle's fingers curled inward to form fists.

You shine brighter than anyone else…

Had he *really* murmured those words in her ear?

Dropping his arm, he glanced over her shoulder at Max. 'Go to the nearest decent café and get us—' He broke off and frowned. 'No, safer to find a Starbucks. Double espresso for me and make sure it's in two cups to keep it warm.' His attention came back to Estelle. 'What would you like?'

You to turn back into Kevin? Disappear in a puff of smoke? Spontaneously combust?

She shook her head. 'Nothing.'

James kept his gaze on her as he spoke to Max. 'Cappuccino?'

Surprise rippled through her like an electric shock. *How did he guess right?*

His nostrils flared at her reaction, as if scenting victory. 'And make it a double shot.'

Her mouth fell open. She quickly snapped it shut again.

A dangerous smile spread across James's face. 'No sugar. She's sweet enough.'

'Screw you,' she spat, attempting through the force of will alone to summon lightning bolts from her eyes.

He raised an eyebrow, and a traitorous flame of arousal flickered low in her belly. She stamped it out.

'Screw me?' he replied casually. 'Is that an invitation?'

Estelle's mind immediately flashed an image of James's naked body above her, and desire shot from her belly to her chest. She sucked in a breath.

His expression darkened, then he glanced at Max. 'Go on, then. Use the company card.'

'No,' she said.

'No to...?' James let the question hang in the air.

Shut this down. Now. 'Coffee. You. Everything.'

He paused. 'I'm really not as bad as you think.'

'I know. You're worse.'

Something that looked like vulnerability flickered across his features. 'Will you at least give me a chance to prove you wrong?'

'When hell freezes over.'

The look disappeared and he shrugged. 'Apparently the climate is changing.'

She gave him her frostiest glare in return.

He didn't break eye contact. 'Max, why are you still here?'

'Um—' Max began.

'He stays,' Estelle interrupted.

'Do you feel unsafe around me?' James asked.

Only because my stupid lips want to kiss your stupid face.

The intensity of his stare was making her tummy swoop.

Think! 'You attacked my brother.'

'I did? Which one?'

'*Henry*, of course. Connor and Leo know to avoid you like the plague.'

James stepped behind the desk and sat. 'Please, take a seat.'

She didn't move. Despite the unsettled rage, she didn't trust herself not to lurch straight into his arms like an out-of-control robot fuelled by sex hormones.

'Look,' he began. 'Much as I would rather believe your version of what happened back in June, the truth, and you know it, is that your delightful brother punched *me*, not the other way around.'

'You were coming onto Summer.'

James steepled his fingers as his dark eyes held hers. 'So,

talking to a woman during the day in a public space warrants an unprovoked attack and a broken nose?'

'You stole Henry's girlfriend,' she blustered.

'No, I kept Elizabeth company after your brother stood her up.'

'He didn't stand her up.'

'Oh, yes, of course,' James replied, his voice dripping with sarcasm. 'He was just an hour and a half late for their date.' He glared at Max. 'Leave.'

Estelle turned. 'Stay.'

Max was glancing between them, a smirk back on his lips.

She faced James. 'And you also stole Henry's client, the deal he was working on, and his commission.'

He gave her a half shrug. 'So, hitting me was justified?'

Estelle hesitated. She knew it wasn't, but right now the overwhelming urge to kiss James was nicely balanced by the urge to punch him.

He eyeballed her.

She stared back. *Do not break. Do not even blink.*

'Er...' Max began.

'Go,' James snapped, at the same time she said 'stay'.

'Estelle—' James began.

'Do *not* call me that,' she hissed at him.

His eyes widened as if genuinely surprised.

Shit! She'd spoken without thinking. The sound of her name on James's lips felt far too intimate, but she knew she'd just set herself up for something far worse.

'Would you prefer "Lady Foxbrooke"?'

She shook her head, her cheeks heating in anticipation of what was coming next.

'*Foxy lady?*'

'No! There's no need to address me as anything, because this is the last time we're ever going to meet.'

James leaned back in his chair and put his hands behind the back of his neck. His pose was at ease, but he had the alertness of a tiger preparing to pounce.

'You know that's not true.'

'But—'

'We need to have a conversation about the festival,' he interrupted. 'And in private. If you won't have it here, then we'll go outside.'

She strode out of the office, running down the stairs as fast as her skirt would allow.

James caught up to her at the front door and leaned forward to hold it open.

Pushing past him into the street, Estelle welcomed the drop in temperature, but wished she was in jeans and riding boots so she could run away.

'Where are you parked?' he asked.

She didn't reply, keeping her gaze fixed forward as she navigated the meandering crowds.

'Estelle, please can we have a civilised conversation about this?'

Civilised? The word felt like a punch to the guts. Her whole life she'd endured the media describing her family as the polar opposite. She walked faster.

'Can you afford to put the festival on without the financial backing of BDE Entertainment?' James continued.

Of course we fucking can't! She pressed her lips together as if to permanently seal them shut.

'Do you have the money to pay the penalty clauses if you cancel?'

No! she internally howled.

'Do you believe you can find another events company this late in the day to invest *and* pay BDE Entertainment for breaking the contract?'

Oh, god. Oh god, oh god, oh god. What am I going to do?

There was a pause, then he sighed. What was he going to say next? Tell her she was a star? That he wanted to flirt with her?

'Want a hot sausage? Some roast nuts?'

She glanced at him in shock.

He gestured to a Christmas market stall. 'Bratwurst? Chestnuts? Glühwein?'

'Are you trying to be funny?'

'Not particularly, but we need to have a proper conversation, so I'm trying to lighten your mood.'

Stumbling to a halt, she pointed at him, her finger stopping a centimetre from his chest.

'*My* mood?'

James was far too close for comfort and now she could also smell him. The scent was irresistible, like a love potion crossed with a superconducting magnet.

'Yes. You're all thunderbolts and lightning.'

'Very, very frightening?' she added sarcastically.

'I wouldn't say I was frightened...'

'What are you then?' she asked, before immediately wishing she hadn't.

His gaze flicked to her mouth and she swallowed.

He paused before speaking. 'Challenged... I think we're going to work well together.'

'We're not going to be doing *anything* together,' she snapped.

'I disagree.'

'We are never going to see each other again. Ever.'

James took a card from his pocket and held it out. 'Re-read the contract you signed, then give me a call.'

She snatched it from him and tried to rip it in half.

However, it was laminated in plastic and wouldn't tear. She dropped it to the pavement.

'Littering? Really?'

Dammit! Bending to pick it up, her face took a whistle-stop tour of James's perfectly formed body. Despite the December cold, she was burning up. Stalking to a bin, she threw the bent card inside, then headed down Stall Street towards Southgate car park.

He followed.

'What are you doing?' she spat.

'Enjoying your scintillating company?'

'Fuck you,' she muttered.

'Anytime, foxy lady.'

She whirled around. '*Don't* call me that.'

'Then what *can* I call you?'

The question hung in the air.

'Star?' he finally asked, his voice low, as if the word was for her and her alone.

A wave of emotion flooded Estelle's chest. She shook her head, hitched her skirt up under her coat, and ran.

❆ 4 ❆

Fuck.

James stood, his focus entirely on the curls of Estelle's hair as she dashed away. It was only when she finally disappeared from view that he allowed the rest of the world to re-enter his sphere of awareness.

To his right, Day-Glo horses cantered around an antique merry-go-round to chirpy organ music. To his left, stallholders with rosy cheeks and beaming smiles made eye contact with the public to entice them closer.

Every sound grated on James's nerves. He needed peace and quiet to think, and he couldn't do it in the middle of this bullshitmas-fest.

He stalked back up Stall Street, heading for the office he and Max had to vacate by the end of the day.

Max...

James didn't need to check his phone to know his sole employee had received *and* read the email he'd sent to cancel the meeting with Estelle, but had blatantly ignored the directive.

Gaslighting little shit.

If James wasn't already up to his neck in it, then he would have kicked him out on his ear a month ago.

Unfortunately, Max, with his two years of experience working for Excelsior Events, not only possessed the shovel to dig James out of the hole he was in, but also the knowledge of how to use it.

Thanks, Dad… James swallowed the bitter taste of anger and frustration souring his mouth. His father was reckless with business dealings, risk-taking with the hope of more successes than failures. Buying Excelsior Events was a knee-jerk reaction to a catastrophic fuck-up and an expensive apology gift to his son.

However, it had happened too fast and without due diligence. Kevin Hunter-Savage hadn't included a non-compete clause, so before the ink was even dry on the contract, all members of staff, bar Max, handed in their notice and buggered off to the newly formed 'Excalibur Events', taking all of their clients, except for Estelle, with them.

To add insult to injury, his dad hadn't even kept the company name, changing Excelsior Events to Big Dick Energy Entertainment because he thought James would find it funny.

James didn't.

So, now he was left with one member of staff, who was clearly so disliked by his former colleagues they didn't ask him to join their new company, and one client, Estelle Foxbrooke.

The music and arts festival had to go ahead, and it had to work. Just as it would cost the Foxbrookes to pull out, it would cost him and his family just as much, if not more. James had no plan B, and he doubted Estelle did either.

Estelle. She would be in her car by now. No doubt steaming mad and on her way home to whine to her brother about him.

James wasn't worried. Henry Foxbrooke was about as threatening as a damp paper bag.

What should I do now? He shook his head. *Nothing. Just get out of the office on Bartlett Street, then make a plan.*

❧

'WHERE ARE YOU GOING?' ESTELLE ASKED, HER HEART RATE rising as Henry strode across their shared office, an expression of murderous resolve on his face.

'To the gun room,' he replied, yanking the door open with such force it slammed back against the inside wall.

Panic smashed into Estelle's chest. Her brother was one of the most mild-mannered men she knew and had only ever hit one person before. Now, however, it seemed he was about to up the ante.

'Henry! Wait!'

But he was gone.

Following him into the main body of Foxbrooke Manor, Estelle tugged her skirt back to the top of her legs so she could catch up with him.

'Henry!'

He didn't stop.

'Big Dick Energy?' he muttered. 'Well, at least I know where to aim once I find him.'

Estelle was glad she'd swapped her designer boots for wellies otherwise she would never have kept up with her brother's pace.

'Henry, wait up—'

'First Elizabeth, then Summer,' he spat. 'I know you're not blonde, but—'

'What's that got to do with anything?'

'Elizabeth had blonde hair, like Summer. I don't know if

he's got a type, but I'm not taking any risks.'

They were almost at the gun room. Estelle was strong, but her brother was stronger. She wouldn't be able to physically stop him. *Please let it be locked!*

'So you're going to shoot him?' she cried.

'Isn't that what you want to do?'

'Of course, but I'm me and you're you!'

He sped up. 'Meaning?'

'You're the nice twin. The calm one. The yin to my yang or whatever.'

Reaching the door, Henry grabbed the handle and rattled it.

'Why's it locked?' he growled.

'It's a gun room.'

'You keep a loaded shotgun by your bed at the livery.'

'Yes, but like I said, I'm *me*. And anyway, numpty tourists don't visit my house looking for a free souvenir.'

'Where does Dad keep the key?'

Estelle crossed her arms. 'Henry, if anyone's going to shoot James, it's me.'

'But this is my fault.' He strode off, yelling for their father.

'How?' she cried, running to catch up to him.

'That man has made it his mission since school to make my life miserable. It's like some kind of sick game. And I guess he hasn't forgiven me for punching him.'

They reached the bottom of the main stairs and Henry took them two at a time. 'Dad! Where are you?'

Estelle followed him up and along the first-floor corridor towards their parents' room. A sock hung on the door knob.

'Dad!' Henry yelled, battering the door with his fist. 'Get out here!'

It opened slightly and their mother glided out of the room, tying a red silk dressing gown around her.

'Where's the key to the gun room?' Henry demanded.

Vivienne ignored him, staring at Estelle's skirt. 'Honey, you do know it's not meant to be worn like that?'

'I know, Mom,' Estelle muttered, pulling the hem back to her knees.

'And rain boots? What happened to the Louboutin's I gave you?'

'I can't walk in them. They're too uncomfortable.'

'Fashion isn't meant to be comfortable, darling.'

'Mom,' Henry interrupted. 'The key?'

The door opened and their father now appeared. He'd made an attempt at decency by wearing a frayed gold silk dressing gown, however had forgotten to do it up.

'What's going on?' he asked. 'There was a bally sock on the door handle! You know that means *Do Not Disturb*. Is the house burning down?'

'No,' Henry replied. 'I need the key to the gun room.'

'Burglars, is it?' Arthur ran his hands through his salt-and-pepper hair. 'Why the devil can't they come at night?'

Dervla, their third parent, now entered the corridor in a tie-dyed silk robe.

'Burglars?' she cried, pushing her messy blonde fringe out of her eyes. 'Have you rung the police?'

'There aren't any burglars,' Henry replied through gritted teeth.

Arthur harrumphed. 'Then what y'doing disturbing our quiet time?'

'It's Monday morning!' Henry shouted. 'You should save—' he waved his hand at the three of them '—*this* for the weekend.'

'Rot!' Arthur retorted. 'We were all too exhausted after Eveline's wedding. And anyway, you need to take a leaf out of our book. You and Libby should be at it like rabbits, not bloody pandas. With your attitude, we'll never get any grand-children.'

'Do you want me to make you some of my special tea?' Dervla asked. 'To help with your libido?'

'No!'

'Mom, Dad, Mammy,' Estelle interrupted. 'I need you to help calm Henry down.'

'I've got a herbal mix for that as well,' Dervla said.

'Why should we do that?' Arthur interjected. 'It's nice to see a bit of fire in his belly.'

'Because he wants to shoot James Hunter-Savage!'

Their mom turned to Henry. 'But why, honey?'

'Because—'

'He's the new CEO of the company footing the bill for the festival next year,' Estelle interrupted.

'Ooh! What fun!' Dervla exclaimed.

Estelle gasped. 'Fun?'

Vivienne's eyes were alight. 'Yes, such an interesting and *sexy* young man.'

'*What?*' she and her brother yelled in unison.

'Humph,' Arthur said. 'Not as sexy as me.'

'Never,' Vivienne replied, kissing his cheek.

'Mom!' Estelle cried. 'This is a disaster. I can't work with him.'

'Why not?'

She threw her hands in the air. Why couldn't their parents see what she and Henry did? 'Honestly, where do I even start? It seems he's pissed off ninety per cent of the staff so they've all left. He's being kicked out of his office because he hasn't paid the rent—'

'He could work out of the manor?' Arthur suggested.

'No!' Estelle shouted. 'And to top it off, he's re-named the company "Big Dick Energy Entertainment"!'

There was a short silence, then all three of their parents started laughing.

'Ho, ho, ho!' Arthur chortled. 'How wonderful!'

'No, it's not,' Estelle replied. 'The bloody logo is a lightning bolt striking an aubergine!'

Dervla giggled. 'He's such a gas.'

Estelle stared at her parents, then turned to her brother. The fight seemed to go out of him and his shoulders sagged.

'Come on,' she said, 'let's put our heads together and try to find a way out of this.'

He nodded.

'Crisis averted?' Arthur asked. 'Jolly good. Now, off you both trot. Your mothers and I have unfinished bedroom business to attend to.'

ESTELLE AND HENRY MADE THEIR WAY BACK TO THE GROUND floor of the manor, through wood-panelled corridors lined with ancient oil paintings.

Inside their office, her brother went straight to a coffee machine that sat on a table near the window. 'Let me make you a cappuccino. Double shot?'

Estelle gave him a resigned nod. She wasn't going to change the way she drank her coffee just to prove James wrong.

Henry turned the machine on. 'While I make this, why don't you grab the contract? We can look for a loophole.'

Pushing herself away from the door, she went to her desk. Where Henry's workspace was minimalist in the extreme, with only a framed photo of his girlfriend, Libby, a laptop, pad of paper and pen on the top, hers looked like it housed the aftermath of a fight between a stationery cupboard and a gift shop. Moving empty mugs and ornaments off piles of paper, she searched for the contract she'd signed.

'I just don't understand any of it,' Henry continued, taking a bottle of milk from a small fridge. 'He's a broker, not an event organiser. How on earth did he get the job? And why?'

Estelle shrugged, picking up a stress ball in the shape of an angry Friesian cow and squeezing. 'He told me he was the CEO. Could he have bought the company?'

Her brother ran a hand over his head, scratching at the tight curls. 'God knows.' He glanced at her. 'Don't you have a digital copy you can check?'

She huffed. 'Yes, I do. I'm all over the place right now.' Sitting at her desk, she moved a foot-tall wooden letter 'E' out of the way and flipped her laptop open. 'I'll send it to you now.'

Henry frothed the milk, then poured it into her mug. 'What about the members of the team at Excelsior that are still there? Could you work with them and ignore him?'

'How can I ignore someone that big and cocky?' Estelle grumbled as she searched through her emails. 'You spent the best part of seventeen years trying and failing. And anyway, there's no-one left.'

'Huh?'

'The only member of staff there, apart from Beelzebub, was some young dude named Max, who seems to hate his boss almost as much as we do.'

'What?'

'And didn't you hear what I just told our folks? They're getting kicked out of their offices at the end of the day because they haven't paid their rent.'

'Jesus Christ!' Henry rubbed at the lines on his forehead as if trying to remove them, then carried her cappuccino over. Estelle tossed a notepad to the floor to create room, and he placed it down. There was a perfect pattern of a leaf created in the foam.

'Thanks, little brother.'

He squeezed her shoulder. 'Anytime, big sister. And don't worry. I'm a contract whizz. I'll find a way out of this.'

ESTELLE SLAMMED THE DOOR OF HER LAND ROVER Defender shut behind her and breathed in the smell of hay and horse shit, a smile spreading across her face.

Home.

The knot of tension in her stomach eased a little as she gazed at the livery stables. This was her world, and James Hunter-Savage had no claim on it.

At the sound of loud barking she dropped to her knees. A small, fluffy black dog dashed forward and barrelled into her arms, his tail a wagging blur.

'Who's my Chester-chops? Who's a good little doggie? You miss me?' she cooed as the dog attempted to lick every part of her he could reach.

An English Setter trotted around the corner to join Chester in saying hello.

'And Joy-dog. You missed me too?'

Joy barked.

'Well, I missed you more, my gorgeous girl,' Estelle replied, scratching behind Joy's ears. 'Shall we go and find Molly?'

The dogs bounded off and Estelle followed, pulling her irritating skirt up to mid-thigh so she could walk at an almost normal pace.

At the far end of one of the stable blocks was an office. Photos of horses were stuck to the dusty wooden walls, along with rosettes, a calendar from *Horse & Hound* Magazine, and handwritten names and numbers for the vet, feed suppliers, and livery clients.

The room was dirty but serviceable, and as familiar to

Estelle as the manor where she'd grown up. It used to feel like she lived here, but slowly, over the last ten years, when she became more heavily involved with running the estate, she'd ceded day-to-day management of the livery to Molly.

Molly glanced up from her laptop as Estelle entered, a smile on her freckled face. 'How did it go?'

She grimaced. 'Don't ask.'

Hooking a chair with the toe of her riding boot, Molly pulled it forward. 'Come on now, you can't say "don't ask", and not expect me to want to know more.'

The knot in Estelle's stomach tightened. She could hardly admit even to herself that part of her fancied James, and the last thing she wanted to do was explain who he was and why this situation was such a nightmare.

So she shrugged. 'It's all a bit up in the air again. The company has been re-structured and they're also moving offices.'

'But it's still going ahead? The festival next year?'

Estelle puffed out her cheeks. 'Well, if it doesn't, the estate is going to be in real trouble.'

'Shit. Is there anything I can do to help?'

'Just keep this place going for me. Anything happen today I need to know about?'

'Nah, we're all good. I've got a couple of new girls starting, but you don't need to worry about any of that. You going to take Duke out?'

Estelle nodded. 'Just as soon as I've got this stupid skirt off.'

Molly grinned. 'You do know it's not meant to be worn like that?'

'Bugger off. I've already had the fashion police onto me.'

'Your mom?'

'Yep. And even Henry asked if my skirt was at the "functioning length" when I went for my meeting.'

Molly snorted. 'Your brother cracks me up. He's such an English gent.'

'From the seventeen hundreds...'

'True. I can't believe how different you are.'

Estelle nodded, even as a tiny pang of insecurity pricked at her heart. Did *everyone* see Henry as polite and well-mannered, and her as the loud-mouthed, abrasive one?

'Hey,' Molly began, leaning forward and squeezing her hand, 'you're the best, Estelle. Whatever happened today, you'll sort it. I know you will. Now go and put on some proper clothes and go for a ride. It'll make you feel better. I promise.'

SWINGING HERSELF INTO DUKE'S SADDLE, A BOW AT HER back and a quiver of arrows at her hip, Estelle whistled for Chester and Joy and set off out of the livery yard into the Foxbrooke estate. The air was cold enough to make the going firm, but not so cold as to make the ground too uneven for Duke. Nudging her beloved horse forward, he broke into a canter, whinnying with delight as he carried her up the grassy incline, the two dogs bounding along beside.

She wanted to speak to her best friend. But Eveline was on a short honeymoon and the last thing Estelle wanted was to disturb her friend's happiness with her problems. Two days ago, Eveline had married Jack, one of Estelle and Henry's oldest friends. Their wedding was overflowing with love and happiness, and those warm feelings had still glowed inside Estelle like a wood fire in winter when she'd set off that morning for Bath.

Discovering James Hunter-Savage was the owner of BDE Entertainment had immediately doused the happy flames.

Duke reached the top of the incline where the land flattened out and Estelle had set up targets attached to straw bales. She'd been practising mounted archery for over a year now and was almost ready to enter her first competition. The sport required intense strength, skill, focus, and an almost telepathic relationship with one's horse. Despite the long hours she'd been working trying to save her family's estate from her father's idiotic business ideas, she'd still managed to find a couple of hours a week to practice.

'Chester, Joy, sit,' she commanded, pointing to a straw bale safely behind her. They jumped to the top and sat, their tongues lolling and tails wagging as they waited for the action to start.

Clicking to Duke, she let the reins drop, steering him with her thighs and verbal instructions. He trotted to the far end of the course she'd set, and exhilaration rushed through her as she lifted her bow and notched the first arrow into position.

Raising her face to the wintery sky, Estelle let out a wild cry that carried with it every emotion from the day. Frustration, fury, fear and now freedom on the back of Duke.

Her horse took off at a gallop. Gripping with all her might to stay level and balanced, she let the first arrow fly, whooping as it thudded into the straw bale. Duke's hooves thundered along the grassy track as she let arrow after arrow go. Some missed, but most hit their targets.

When the quiver was empty, she whistled to Joy and Chester, who collected the arrows lying on the ground. The rest she pulled from the bales, then set everything up for another run.

The midwinter sun was close to the horizon when she finally stopped, out of breath and euphoric. For the past hour, her mind had been focused, and blissfully blank. Now, however, as her breathing quietened, thoughts of James woke, demanding attention.

She glanced away from the direction of the livery. The estate James's parents had bought was only a few fields away. Before she could second-guess herself, she whistled to Chester and Joy and nudged Duke in the direction of the house.

Trotting forward, Duke brought her to the top of a small hill that overlooked the back of the manor.

Standing for two hundred and fifty years, Shoscombe Manor was built at the height of interest in Palladian architecture and was simple and elegant. The formal gardens at the rear of the building were based around geometric patterns, with box hedges and gravel paths in between.

Lights were on in the house, but Estelle couldn't see inside. Curiosity getting the better of her, she nudged Duke down the hill to get a better look.

Less than fifty yards away, a man stepped out from behind a tall yew hedge and gazed at her.

James.

With dusk falling, and the lights from the building behind him, Estelle couldn't make out his face.

He lifted his hand in greeting.

Chester growled, and Duke's ears pricked up.

Estelle raised her bow and fitted an arrow, aiming for James's chest.

He stepped fully into view and stood, his legs apart and both arms away from his body, giving her a bigger target to hit.

Arrogant fucker.

Dipping the bow ever so slightly, she let the arrow fly. It thudded into the ground, right between his feet.

James didn't flinch.

Wheeling Duke around, she urged him to a canter and took off up the hill, Chester and Joy barking at her side.

❧ 5 ❧

From: James Hunter-Savage
    To: Estelle Foxbrooke
    Subject: Moving forward

Dear Ms Foxbrooke,

I'm emailing to request a meeting at your earliest convenience to discuss a road map for the partnership between yourself, on behalf of the Foxbrooke estate, and BDE Entertainment.

As of tomorrow, BDE will have moved from Bath to Shoscombe Manor. This is where you will be working from the start of next year.

You can contact me via this email address or the mobile number below. Please do not arrive at the manor house without prior warning. There has been an incident with a local warrior, and we need to ensure the area is secure before you visit.

Kind regards,
James Hunter-Savage

• • • •

FROM: JAMES HUNTER-SAVAGE

To: Estelle Foxbrooke

Subject: Meeting up before the Christmas break

Dear Ms Foxbrooke,

In accordance with the season and the spirit of goodwill to all women and men, I would like to arrange a meeting with you in the next couple of days. I hope this will reassure you our relationship going forward will be mutually beneficial. You can reach me via email or the number below.

Festive greetings,

James

FROM: JAMES HUNTER-SAVAGE

To: Estelle Foxbrooke

Subject: Your contractual obligations

Dear Ms Foxbrooke,

I presume by your continued silence, my emails are accidentally sitting in your spam folder, the letter I wrote to you at the livery failed to arrive, or you have been unable to find a way out of the contract you freely signed with BDE Entertainment. Kindly get in touch, so we may move forward.

Yours,

James

FROM: JAMES HUNTER-SAVAGE

To: Estelle Foxbrooke

Subject: Your holiday

Dear Ms Foxbrooke,

I visited the livery today in the hope of speaking in person with you, but was informed by your stable manager that you were abroad. When questioned, Ms Kenyon seemed unsure as to your exact location, so I hope you are well, wherever you are.

I also hope your two extremely excitable dogs are being cared for in your absence. I'm particularly concerned the smaller of the two is adequately fed, as he presented a dead rat to me on my arrival. Is this his normal diet?

Safe travels,

James

'UGH,' ESTELLE MUTTERED, BEFORE SHOVING THE PHONE into the back pocket of her jeans.

'Everything okay?' Eveline asked, as she bent to open the oven door.

Estelle dashed forward, elbowing her out of the way. 'I'll do that.'

Grabbing a double-ended pot holder from the rail by her head, she pulled out a large tray of sizzling sausages.

'I know I'm not as strong as you,' Eveline said behind her. 'But I'm perfectly capable of doing that myself.'

'Yes, but I promised Jack I wouldn't let you do any heavy lifting,' Estelle replied, putting the tray on a rack by the side of the stove. 'You might be carrying the second coming.'

Eveline rolled her eyes. 'It's only been two weeks since our wedding. I'm not expecting a miracle.'

'Well, you should. You're a vicar, so God's on your side. And anyway, the rate at which you two have been banging, I expect twins in nine months.'

'Shush!' Eveline hissed, her cheeks turning pink as she glanced around the empty kitchen.

Estelle grinned. 'You're too easy to wind up. Is this the last tray?'

'Yes, we took everything cold over first thing this morning,'

Eveline began, tearing off a strip of tinfoil and covering the tray. 'And Jack took the rest of the sausages just before you arrived.'

'Cool. Well, I'll take this and you can lock up behind me.'

'So what's up, then?' Eveline asked, as Estelle carried the deep tray from the rectory towards Saint Saviour's church, across a tarmacked area filled with parked cars. 'Is it Mr Hunter-Savage?'

Estelle huffed. 'Of course it is. He sent me an email this morning informing me of a hurricane in the Caribbean and "expressing his concern" that I might have been caught up in it.'

Eveline giggled. 'You could just talk to him?'

Estelle didn't reply.

'And you know what Henry said about the contract being watertight?'

She let her silence continue.

'I thought you'd reconciled yourself to this?'

Estelle shrugged. She knew there was no way of getting out of it, but James unsettled her in a way no person, no *man*, had ever done before. It was as if she'd spent her life sailing the seven seas, dealing with squalls and tempests, but now, just as she'd thought she'd got control of her ship, it had been pirated by a sea monster and steered into uncharted waters.

It felt safer to ignore James and pretend the next year wasn't actually going to arrive, even though it was less than two weeks away.

Eveline opened the small wooden gate that led into the churchyard. 'And he's been pleasant in his communications?'

'He's a snake with a forked tongue.'

'A forked tongue? Now that *does* sound exciting.'

Estelle nearly dropped the tray she was carrying.

'Eveline Newton! I can't believe those words just came out of your pious little mouth! What *has* Jack done to you?'

Her friend gave her a cheeky grin. 'Many, *many* things...'

'Oh, my god! I want to wash my ears out with soapy water!'

Eveline giggled. 'We *are* married, you know.'

'Humph. Well, anyway. Enough of the sexy talk from you, Missy. From now on, the only kind of sausage you're allowed to refer to are the pig-related ones.'

'Deal,' Eveline replied, pulling the heavy church door open so Estelle could carry the tray through.

Saint Saviour's usually smelled of old wood and incense, but once a month it was filled with the aroma of sausage rolls and hot dogs. On 'Sausage Saturday', Eveline used the pork she reared in her back garden to feed anyone who came by. If you were struggling financially, everything was free. If you weren't, you could make a donation and the money was given to a local food bank.

Jack was already inside, along with Henry and his girlfriend, Libby, by a row of trestle tables. As soon as Jack saw Eveline, his eyes lit up. He stepped forward as if it had been half a life-time, not half an hour since he'd last seen her.

A sudden stab of loneliness pierced Estelle's chest, but she covered it with a smile. She strode towards her brother with the tray. 'This is the last one.'

'Thanks,' he replied, taking it from her and placing it on the table, perfectly aligned with all the others.

Estelle leaned forward and nudged it out of place.

Henry sighed and moved it back.

Reaching out, she pushed at the corner.

'Stelle...' came Jack's voice behind her.

'What?' she asked, turning to him.

He gave her a look. 'Stop winding him up.'

Eveline was nestled into the side of his body as if Jack was her love-duvet. The sight made Estelle's eyes prickle with emotion. She was so happy for her friends, but it was a visceral reminder of what was missing from her own life.

'Okay, okay,' she huffed, turning back to the emotional safety net of annoying her brother.

However, in the short amount of time her attention had been elsewhere, Henry and Libby had started kissing.

Fuck's sake! Estelle moved down the table, making minute and unnecessary adjustments to paper plates and napkins. All through school, and most of life, she'd never felt like she fitted in. And right now, with her closest friends and family so loved up, she felt like a clunky fifth wheel.

God, I know we don't speak much, but please deliver me from this love fest. I invited Isaac to come today, so can you make him show up? For me? Please?

The sound of the door creaking open echoed around the empty church.

She closed her eyes with relief. *Thanks, God. I owe you one…*

'Oh, shitsticks,' Libby said under her breath.

Estelle glanced up in surprise to see Libby's mouth open and Henry's pressed tightly shut.

Huh? Turning, she saw the reason for her twin's displeasure.

James was standing in the doorway.

Eveline was the first to move, breaking away from Jack and going towards James, her hand outstretched. 'Mr Hunter-Savage! What a lovely surprise!'

'What the fuck is *he* doing here?' Henry growled.

'Hey!' Jack whispered sharply. 'Don't make a scene.'

'Chill out, Sir Protect-a-lot,' Estelle muttered. 'She's not up the duff yet.'

Libby's gasp filled the sudden silence, and shame shot through Estelle. She wanted to apologise, but her jaw was quivering with emotion. Turning, she ran to the back of the church and the privacy of the sacristy.

Entering the small room, she sat at the wooden table, sinking her head into her hands.

Fuck, fuck, fuck, fuck, fuck.

Jack had every right to be protective. Three weeks ago, Eveline had almost died. The arrival of James today was inconsequential in comparison. *You thoughtless idiot!* Even with three wayward parents and working two jobs, Estelle always felt some semblance of control. But now? With James? It was like trying to juggle with jellyfish.

There was a knock, and she glanced up.

Henry poked his head around the door. 'Can I come in?'

She shrugged.

Sitting across from her, he took one of her hands in his. 'You don't have to do this.'

She didn't reply.

'You don't have to work with Hunter-Savage.'

'I do,' she whispered.

'No, you don't. I've spoken to Libby and we've decided.'

Huh? 'Decided what?'

'We're putting the renovation of our cottage on hold indefinitely and I'm selling my flat in London.'

Estelle froze. 'Why?'

'The money will pay the fees to get you out of the contract with BDE Entertainment, and should leave enough to run a pared-down version of the festival next year.'

Pulling her hand from Henry's she gripped the edge of the table.

'No way. You can't do that.'

Her brother's gaze was filled with compassion. 'It's the least I can do. For the last decade, you've managed our parents *and* the estate and allowed me the life I had in London. Buying your freedom is nothing in comparison.'

'But—'

'The cottage isn't going anywhere and we're happy to keep living at the manor. I'm just annoyed with myself for not thinking of this solution sooner. I'm sorry, Estelle.'

'Henry, you can't.'

'Yes, I can. You're my sister, and there's no way in hell you're spending another moment in that arsehole's company.'

There was a knock at the door and Eveline entered.

'Sorry to disturb you both,' she began, 'but quite a lot of people have just shown up. Would you be able to come and help?'

Estelle got to her feet. 'Yes, of course.'

'Has he gone?' Henry asked.

Eveline hesitated. 'No, but everything is in hand. Would you be able to suffer him in silence for the next couple of hours?'

'Sorry. I'll conduct myself properly. I promise.'

'Thank you, that is most appreciated.' Eveline gazed at Estelle and raised an eyebrow.

'I'll behave,' she mumbled to her friend.

'Marvellous! Let's go and get started then.'

ESTELLE FOLLOWED EVELINE OUT INTO THE MAIN BODY OF the church, her feet leaden. There was already a queue of people waiting to be served. Libby and Jack stood at one end of the line of trestle tables, James at the other.

Estelle caught Jack's eye and mouthed *'sorry'*.

He smiled. *'It's okay'*, he mouthed back.

'Nearly there, everybody!' Eveline called out. 'Just mustering the rest of the troops!'

Estelle's fingers itched for a weapon.

'Okey dokey!' Eveline continued. 'Henry and Libby, can I put you with the sausage rolls at one end? Jack, you meet and greet with me, and Estelle, come this way and you can help James with the hotdogs.'

Before Estelle could argue, she was dragged to James's side, like a child on the way to the naughty step.

Eveline's enthusiasm was unrelenting. 'Righty-ho! I haven't made them up in advance as the sausages are still hot, however the rolls are sliced halfway through. Estelle, you're in charge of them. Take one, open it nice and wide, and then James, you can stick your sausage in.'

Excuse me? Estelle stared at her best friend's guileless face, but Eveline just beamed at them both and continued.

'Then hand it over and the customers can select their own condiments from the table over there. Okay?'

James cleared his throat. 'I will follow your instructions to the letter.'

'Estelle?' Eveline asked.

'Does this give me a free pass to heaven?'

'It doesn't work quite like that.'

'Or a smiting voucher?'

Eveline laughed. 'That's *definitely* not on the cards.'

'Shame. What's the point in having a direct line to God if there aren't any perks?'

'*This* is one of the perks,' Eveline replied, gesturing to the people standing at the other end of the table. 'Isn't it wonderful how many people have come?'

'You're too lovely for your own good,' Estelle grumbled.

Eveline gave her a quick hug. 'Thank you so much. *Both* of you. And don't forget to "glove up". It's important to use protection!'

Seriously?

'Have fun!' Eveline dashed off to the start of the line of people, shaking hands and smiling as if eternally grateful they'd made the time to come to eat delicious free food she'd spent months rearing and the past two days preparing.

'What an incredible woman,' James murmured, stretching a pair of vinyl gloves onto his large hands.

An unpleasant sensation stabbed Estelle's stomach. 'And what's *that* supposed to mean?' she asked sharply, tugging her own gloves on. 'She's married. Not that it would stop you. Horn dog.'

'Hot dog?'

She glanced up. James was addressing a smiling man.

'Yes, please, I'll take two,' the man replied.

'Excellent,' James said to him. 'My charming assistant—'

'Boss.'

'*Colleague*, will prepare your rolls, then I'll slip the sausages in.' James turned to her. 'Ms Foxbrooke?'

Estelle grabbed a roll and wrenched it apart with so much force, the two sides separated.

For heaven's sake!

'Unfortunately,' James began, 'my colleague—'

'Indentured servant,' Estelle muttered.

'Is a very powerful woman, and isn't always aware of her own strength. Plus—' he lifted his gloved hands, '—these do rather reduce sensation.'

I should have aimed higher with my bow last week.

She took another roll and held it open for him.

Using a pair of tongs, James placed the sausage inside and wiggled it up and down until it was firmly seated inside the bread.

'Doesn't that look good?' he asked.

Estelle's cheeks pricked with heat. She handed the hot dog over and grabbed another roll, refusing to meet James's eye.

James was affable and polite as he greeted people, but Estelle was a robot powered by a thunderstorm. When the first flurry of customers had passed, she turned to him, her gaze fixed on the middle of his chest.

'What are you doing here?' she demanded.

'Looking for you. How was your holiday?'

'Not long enough.'

'Where did you go?'

'Up Uranus.'

'Est—*Ms Foxbrooke*—'

'Don't call me that.'

He sighed, then started taking his cashmere jumper off.

She took an involuntary step back. 'What are you doing?'

He paused, the top around his broad shoulders. 'I'm hot.'

Her gaze flicked over the expanse of his chest, the white t-shirt stretched over his pecs, the tantalising glimpse of skin where the bottom had become untucked from his jeans. James was right. He *was* hot. But that didn't mean she was going to go anywhere near him.

'May I?' he continued.

She shrugged, wanting to look away but being betrayed by her eyes, which appeared to be glued to his body.

He pulled the jumper off and tossed it onto a chair behind him. 'If I can't call you by any derivative of your name, then what *can* I call you?'

I don't know! she internally screamed, whilst her traitorous subconscious supplied the word *Star*...

'Look,' he began, 'we have to work together, so I'm trying to make the experience tolerable for both of us.'

Tolerable? And no, thanks to Henry, now we don't *have to work together*.

'You think you know me—'

'I *do* know you,' she interrupted. 'You're the bully who

punched my brother on the arm each time you passed him at school. You're the one who encouraged others to call him "Viscount Nob-end". And you're the arsehole who said Mom and Mammy were—' She broke off.

James ran a hand through his hair. 'I don't remember saying anything about your—'

'You called them "posh slags",' she spat.

He flinched.

'Remember now?'

James shook his head. 'But it does sound like the kind of thing I might have said. Look, kids are twats—'

'Henry wasn't.'

'That wasn't really me—'

Estelle put her hands on her hips. 'Who was it then? Mr Hyde? *Kevin?*'

Emotion flickered in James's eyes, but she couldn't work out what it signified.

'I've changed—'

'No, you haven't. You've been an unwanted guest in our lives since I was thirteen. I know you.'

He folded his arms across his chest. 'Really now?'

She mirrored his stance. 'Yes.'

'Favourite colour?'

'Black. Like your soul.'

'Food?'

'Babies.'

He rolled his eyes.

'Or the trampled remains of your enemies,' she continued.

'Drink?'

'Double espresso. You need the extra caffeine to keep your cold, dead heart beating.'

The corner of his mouth twitched up. 'Favourite music?'

'The "Imperial March" from *Star Wars*.'

'Number?'

'Six-six-six.'

He smirked. 'Middle name?'

'Beelzebub, Lucifer, Satan.'

'Wrong, wrong, wrong. See, you *don't* know me. Give me a chance to prove I'm not who you think I am.'

Estelle stared James down. After today, she didn't need to spend any time with him ever again thanks to her brother's generosity.

'Is everything okay?'

She jumped. Henry was standing on the other side of the table, a frown on his face. Libby was by his side, holding his hand as if to prevent her boyfriend from launching himself at James.

Estelle's heart squeezed as she gazed at them. Libby was the only woman Henry had ever brought home and Estelle was desperate for their relationship to work. Forcing them to continue living in the manor with her and Henry's bonkers parents might end up being the kiss of death. Even though Henry was bigger than her, she was intensely protective of him, and ashamed to be contemplating their offer. It would mean them giving up their dreams just to save her from six months of working with James.

'Fine,' she replied, forcing a smile. 'I was just telling James how much I'm looking forward to partnering with BDE Entertainment next year.'

Out of the corner of her eye, she saw James's shoulders relax.

'Estelle!' Henry cried. 'You don't have to do that anymore! We—'

'James,' Estelle interrupted. 'If you expect to see me on January the fourth, you need to leave. Right now.'

He didn't hesitate, giving them all a brief nod, then striding away and out of the church.

'You don't have to do this,' Libby said as soon as he was out of earshot. 'Honestly, we're happy to help.'

Estelle smiled. 'I know, and I love you both to the moon and back for offering, but don't worry. I have a plan.'

'Should we be worried?' Henry asked.

'No, but James should. I give it a week before he hands BDE Entertainment's money over to me and begs me to bugger off and run the festival on my own.'

Libby narrowed her eyes. 'What are you going to do?'

'I'm not entirely sure,' she replied, then glanced at the chair where James had left his jumper. 'But I've got a few ideas...'

❧ 6 ❧

January 4th

Icy rain relentlessly carpet-bombed the gravel driveway as James peered out of the window, waiting for Estelle to arrive. He shivered, his nose so close to the thin glass he could practically feel the cold gusts as the pane rattled in the wooden frame.

Overpriced dump, he thought for the millionth time.

Shoscombe Manor was a listed building, so his family wasn't allowed to replace the single-paned windows with triple, or even double-glazed ones. As such, the manor leaked heat like boiling water pouring through a sieve, and the bill to bring the inside temperature slightly above freezing was currently running at over a thousand pounds a week.

His father had always played fast and loose with his finances, but this was the first time in his life James had seen him on the back foot. The money for the music and arts festival had been ring-fenced in BDE Entertainment's account, but it wasn't as much as they'd promised to invest. So now

James had to find ways to cut corners and hope Estelle never found out.

Estelle.

A flush of heat moved across his skin. He hadn't seen or spoken to her since their meeting in the church, but he'd thought about her constantly. She was like a racehorse; strong, powerful, beautiful... and skittish. He had no desire to tame her, he just wanted to harness and direct all that wild energy towards him.

Rein it in.

If Estelle lived in London instead of this damp and dreary backwater and he was still the highest earning broker at Conqueror. *If* she wasn't related to Henry and James's parents were different, then maybe...

Shut up. It's never going to happen.

It wasn't just one obstacle he had to clear to reach her, it was an entire course of them. Pits lined with sharpened stakes, netting electrified by two hundred and forty volts, and sheer walls topped with razor wire.

He let out a sigh of frustration, his breath fogging up the glass. Contracts could be broken, and by the way Henry had talked to Estelle at the church, it was clear her family were trying to get out of the one she'd signed with his company. James hadn't wanted to push his luck, so had left her alone, crossing his fingers she showed up this morning.

His heart beat faster as a Land Rover Defender roared into the drive and skidded to a halt in a shower of gravel.

Right on time.

Pulling open the manor's heavy front door, he dashed to the driver's side of Estelle's car carrying a golfing umbrella. As she got out, he clocked her battered, moss-green Barbour jacket and Le Chameau wellies. Both were clues to the fact that the only people above her in the British class system were the King and his immediate family.

'Welcome to Shoscombe Manor,' he said, the words sounding stiff and formal.

'Thank you, Jeeves,' she replied with a smirk, shunting the strap of a large bag to her shoulder.

Holding the umbrella out to protect Estelle from the rain and from having to stand too close to him, James extended his arm towards a long, single-storey wing of the house.

'This way. The offices are here.'

She strode towards the building and he followed, trying to gauge her mood. However, her stunning face was also alarmingly impassive. Having Estelle Foxbrooke all thunderbolts and lightning felt far easier to handle than this. She was currently calmer than a day without a whisper of wind and it was unnerving.

He opened the door to the building, and she passed through into a bare entry room, the walls lined with coat hooks and low shelves for shoes.

'This is to accommodate temporary staff nearer to the event date,' he said.

There was a door to the right that led to the offices, and one to the left with a sign on it reading 'No Entry'.

Estelle nodded again, tugged off her wellies, and took a pair of slippers from her bag. Each one was twice the size of an adult head, and in the shape of a demented, Day-Glo unicorn. She fiddled with something inside, and the googly eyes lit up, cycling through a rainbow of colours.

James bit his tongue to stop a comment from escaping.

Putting the slippers on, she gestured at the door to their left. 'What's through there?'

'My parents and their staff.'

She turned the handle. 'It's locked.'

'And will remain that way.'

'Where's the key?'

'There's no reason for you to pass through.'

'*Pass through?* Is it a portal to another dimension? One where Kevin lives?'

His heart rate quickened. *You don't know how right you are, foxy lady...* Even though anxiety prickled in his belly at the thought of her being so close to his family, so too did a frisson of excitement. This was the Estelle he wanted around, the sassy one that delighted in needling him.

'May I take your jacket?'

She took a step backwards and one of the slippers whinnied then made a sound like it was galloping away.

'No, thank you,' she replied, unzipping her coat.

James wasn't sure what he was expecting to see underneath, but was disappointed to discover a shapeless jumper over baggy jeans.

Her eyes narrowed. 'What? Expecting a stupid tight skirt?'

'I was hoping for Xena, Warrior Princess.' The words spilled out of his mouth before he could stop them. *Shut-up!*

Her nostrils flared slightly, and her cheeks darkened.

Electricity tingled at the base of his cock, and he moved back. 'Let me show you around.'

Holding the door to his right open for her, she walked through, one slipper whinnying and clip-clopping, the other making a jingling sound that reminded him of a revolting pink plastic wand his little sister used to wave about.

'Well, that's not annoying at all,' he muttered, before realising he'd just vocalised his thoughts. *Again.*

'What was that?' she called over her shoulder, above the sound of a fairy being trampled to death by a horse.

'Nothing,' he replied, forcing his jaw to relax. 'On the left here, we've got bathrooms for men and women.'

She pushed the door to the ladies open, revealing three stalls on one side, and a shower cubicle and a bank of sinks on the other. 'Ooh, fancy. Are the tampons and sanitary towels free?'

'Help yourself to whatever you want.'

'I want that hairdryer. Check out the diffuser on that bad boy.'

James didn't reply. He'd stocked the bathroom thinking of Estelle.

Shutting the door, she glanced around the corridor, her nose wrinkling. 'Has it just been painted?'

He nodded, putting his hands behind his back in case any flecks of paint remained on his skin. There'd been no money to pay for a decorator, so he'd done it himself over the Christmas break.

The next door had a pane of glass in it, and Estelle gazed through into the small kitchen.

'Then we've got two offices for general staff,' he said, moving away from her. 'And a small conference room. Our office is at the end of the hall.'

'Where's Max?'

'Next door to us. He'll be arriving shortly for our first meeting.' James had made sure Max wouldn't turn up until half-nine, giving him a chance to show Estelle around and check out her mood without an audience.

She twinkled and whinnied down the hall, then laid her hand on the last door on the left. 'Is this us?'

'Yes.'

Pushing it open, she stepped through. James followed.

The room was bright and spacious, with a set of full-height windows on the far side that overlooked the rose garden. In front of the window was a pink velvet chaise longue his sister hadn't wanted, framed by two tall house plants in glazed pots.

On the left of the room was a desk containing a computer screen, with an office chair behind it. On the right was an identical set-up, but with James's laptop hooked up to the screen and his jacket over the back of the chair.

He watched Estelle taking it all in, trying to read her expression. Both she and her slippers were silent. He didn't want to ask her if she liked it, as they were still, unofficially at least, at war. However, he hoped she did.

She skipped to the chaise longue, the sound of her slippers already grating on his nerves, and sat, jamming her fingers down the sides.

'Looking for loose change?'

She shrugged. 'That or a winning lottery ticket.' Her eyes lit up, and she pulled out a folded piece of paper. 'What have we here?'

Crossing the room, James held out his hand. He didn't know what it might be, but he didn't want her knowing *anything* about his family.

'Give that to me,' he said, his voice more commanding than he'd anticipated.

She held the paper to her chest.

'It could be confidential or proprietary information,' he continued, fully aware he was sounding like an utter twat.

One corner of her mouth twitched up. Opening the piece of paper, she skimmed it, then smirked.

'Oh, Mr Hunter-Savage, this is *quite* the dilemma.'

Fuck. What had she found?

'"Who I love, and why",' she read out loud. '"Oliver Simmonds, because he has a nice smile and gave me his pencil in Latin. He is a nice boy".' Estelle glanced up. 'How terribly *nice…*'

James folded his arms across his chest and lifted his chin an inch.

Estelle gave him a bored once-over. 'Your power stance could do with a bit of work. Try manspreading your legs more.' She turned her attention back to the piece of paper. '"Blaise Ponsonby-Urquhart"—good grief. And there was me thinking "Hunter-Savage" was posh—'

'So says *Lady* Estelle Foxbrooke,' he interrupted before his filters had a chance to spring into action.

She ignored him. '"Blaise Ponsonby-Urquhart, because he is tall, dark and handsome, and asked to copy my prep, so he knows I am clever. But he's a bad boy".' Estelle sighed. 'Who did you choose in the end? And did they love you back?'

Striding forward, James snatched the piece of paper out of her hand, scrunched it in his fist, then dropped it into the wastepaper basket by his desk.

Estelle sniggered. 'Oh, don't be like that. Love is love. You should never be ashamed of falling for someone called Blaise Ponsonby-Urquhart. Even if he is a bad boy.' Putting her feet up on the chaise longue, she rested her hands behind her head. The movement made the fabric of her jumper ride up and frame her breasts.

James looked away.

'I wonder if he's still a bad boy,' she mused. 'Does he park his Bentley across the disabled bays at the supermarket? Fail to recycle?' Her tone hardened. 'Or simply steal his colleague's client and commission?'

His gaze snapped to hers. She was smiling at him, but there was no warmth behind it.

'Boss-man!'

James jerked his head as Max entered the room carrying a laptop, then knocked on the inside of the door.

Irritation flared in James's gut, but he dampened it down.

'Hi, Lady Foxbrooke,' Max continued with enthusiasm.

His words emptied a full can of petrol on the smouldering embers of James's annoyance.

'Max—'

'Just my first name please,' Estelle interrupted, getting to her feet and going to shake Max's hand. 'Did you have a good Christmas?'

He stared at her noisy slippers, then glanced at James, a smirk on his face. 'Yes, thanks. I'll make sure to call you Estelle from now on. It's just that Boss-man insisted I use your full title.'

No, I fucking didn't. 'Really?' James replied, his tone artificially pleasant. 'And there was me thinking I requested you do the exact *opposite*.'

Max shrugged. 'How about we get started?' he said to Estelle, then took a spare chair from beside James's desk and carried it across the room to hers. He sat, placing his laptop down and flipping it open. 'James,' he continued, addressing the screen as he tapped in his password. 'Why don't you pull up a chair, buddy?'

Why don't you go fuck yourself? Buddy...

'We'll use the conference room,' James replied, grabbing his laptop, stalking to the door and leaving the room without a backwards glance.

Entering the corridor, he took a long, slow breath, filling his lungs with the headache-amplifying smell of fresh paint.

Just stay calm. This is your only option right now.

The sound of Estelle, Max, and a herd of unicorns heading his way made him continue towards the kitchen.

'I'll get us coffee,' he called over his shoulder.

'Nice one, Boss-man,' Max said. 'I'll have a—'

Entering the kitchen, James body-slammed the slow-closing safety door behind him. Flipping on the ludicrously expensive coffee machine that had once sat in his London flat, he rested his hands on the edge of the countertop and dropped his head.

Fuck. My. Life.

He'd once had the world at his feet, but now he was in the arse-end of nowhere, waiting hand and foot on an obsequious little wanker who undermined him at every turn, and a goddess who despised him.

Six months. That's as long as your sentence needs to be.

He just had to make the event at Foxbooke Manor turn a profit. Then his mum could keep her dream life in the sticks and he could get back to civilisation. He didn't give a shit about his dad. Hunter-Savage senior could do whatever he liked with BDE Entertainment once the festival was over.

But until that glorious moment when James could drive out of Somerset without a backward glance, he had to find a way of working with Estelle and Max *and* keeping his sanity intact at the same time.

Going to the fridge, he pulled out the carton of 'soylmond milk' that Max insisted was the only thing his stomach could tolerate in coffee. Well, that and a pump each of vanilla, caramel, white mocha, toffee nut, toasted coconut, and peppermint syrup, plus cinnamon powder, monk fruit extract, stevia and cold foam. James had studied chemistry at Oxford and the concoction Max had created turned his head as well as his stomach.

He made Max's coffee-like substance as quickly as he could, then left it on the side whilst he prepared Estelle's cappuccino. The part of him that wanted to show off demanded he create a pattern in the foam. As well as hearts, leaves and ferns, he could also do a swan, a peacock, and even a horse.

Could I try a unicorn?

Brow furrowed in concentration, he gave it a go. The attempt was passable, but not up to his exacting standards, so he rubbed it out with the tip of a spoon, shook a blend of cocoa powder and coconut palm sugar over the top, then made himself a triple espresso.

HOLDING THE DRINKS ON A TRAY IN ONE HAND, JAMES pushed the door open and entered the conference room. Max sat at the end of the long table, his attention on his laptop. Estelle was beside him, trying to see over his shoulder.

Max raised his hand, but not his head. 'Cheers, buddy, chuck it down over there. I won't be a sec.'

James sat on the same side as Estelle, placing the tray between them and out of Max's reach. Working for years at Conqueror, one of the City's top brokerage firms, he was used to facing off against Ivy-league-educated alphas, men who'd arrived in London from New York with balls even bigger than their pay packets. He'd outwitted and out-alpha'd them in the boardroom *and* the bedroom and wasn't going to let Max take control.

He passed Estelle her drink. 'How would you like me to address you?' he asked, his tone mild.

Her eyes darted away from his, then settled on the coffee. 'Estelle would be fine, thank you.'

The tension in his stomach eased a little. Nodding, he flipped open his laptop. 'We'll spend today getting you up to speed with our intranet, so we're all using the same systems and sharing information.' Max glanced up and James continued, his voice a little firmer. 'Over this week we'll discuss big-picture stuff, like confirming the artists, then allocate tasks. Is there anything in particular you'd like to take the lead on?'

'Well—' Max began.

'Estelle?' James interrupted, not allowing any of his focus to shift from her face.

She also appeared to be tuning out Max, her deep brown eyes holding his. 'I'd like to continue with scheduling the stages and liaising with artists.'

'But—' Max interjected.

'Agreed,' James said. 'This festival is your baby, and thanks to your efforts, UberGraft are headlining. BDE Entertainment is here to support you. Isn't that right, Max?'

Reluctantly breaking Estelle's gaze, James stared at the younger man. Of course Max wanted the fun jobs. After being abandoned by his former colleagues, the most exciting reason to stay on at BDE was the chance to arselick famous people. James didn't care about any of that. He viewed everything over the next six months as a marathon to be endured, not enjoyed.

'Thank you,' Estelle said.

His gaze flicked back to her. She seemed surprised he'd agreed so readily to her request. Her expression seemed softer, more real. Another tingle began at the base of his spine.

Glancing away, she took a sip of her drink. A speck of foam clung to her soft lips. He wanted to lick it off.

There was a tentative knock at the door and he leapt up, urgent alarms going off inside him.

'Stay here,' he growled at Max and Estelle, then went to the door and opened it a crack.

His eyes briefly closed at the sight of his mother, holding a plate of shop-bought cakes.

'How's it—' she began.

Shaking his head to cut her off and using his body as a shield, he slipped into the corridor.

'Mum,' he whispered urgently. 'You and Dad have got to keep to your side of the house.'

Taking her arm, he ushered her away.

'But it's your first day with Lady Foxbrooke, babe.' She held the plate up. 'I bought you your favourites.'

Memories flashed through his mind, as clear as the day they were formed. There was a time in James's life when Mr Kipling's French Fancies were the very definition of 'posh'. The appearance in the house of the pretty little sponges covered in coloured fondant icing had signified his mother was trying to impress someone, and James had always hoped there would be one left over for him. On his seventh birthday, as well as having a cake in the shape of a football pitch, James had been allowed to eat a French Fancy for every year of his life, and it had seemed the ultimate treat.

However, by the time he turned eight, he'd learned 'chav cakes' were as naff and lower-class as the people who bought them.

Still, his mouth watered at the sight.

'How's it going?' his mum continued.

James propelled them both through the door marked 'No Entry' into the main house.

'It's been less than half an hour,' he ground out.

'Is it clean enough for Lady Foxbrooke? I ran the hoover around first thing, but she showed up in wellies. Shall I wash them for her? Give the cloakroom floor a quick mop?'

'No!' He took a breath, trying to control his irritation. 'Mum, please. The cleaners who do the main house are going to do the offices as well.'

'But they don't do a good enough job,' she fretted, the skin around her heavily made-up eyes creasing. 'And she's so posh!'

'Mum, Estelle lives at a stables. She's surrounded by horses, dogs, rats—'

'Rats? Oh, my Christ, babe. You serious?'

He nodded, remembering the smaller of her two dogs carrying a rat as long as it was.

Beverley Hunter-Savage rearranged her shocked features

into a reassuring smile. 'Well, they must be classy rats then. What with her being a lady and all that.'

James resisted the urge to roll his eyes. 'Mum, I appreciate the concern, but you know what we agreed. Please, can you stick to this side of the house?'

For a second, her smile slipped, then it was back. 'Of course, babe.' She held the plate up. 'One for the road?'

His mouth controlled his hand before his brain could catch up, selecting a pink one and popping it whole into his mouth. As his teeth sank through the fondant icing and his tongue found the vanilla buttercream hidden underneath, he hummed with pleasure.

Beverley beamed. 'You sure you don't want to take these back with you?'

He shook his head as he chewed. The Honourable Lady Estelle Foxbrooke wasn't a Mr Kipling kind of woman.

'Okay then, I'll take them to Elyse and your dad.' Raising onto her tiptoes, she planted a kiss on his cheek. 'You've got this, babe. We're so proud of you.'

James swallowed the cake and a feeling of unease. He could do this. He was James Hunter-Savage. Nothing could crack the façade he'd created.

7

Hurt prickled inside Estelle's tummy the moment James re-entered the conference room. She hid it by putting two fingers in her mouth and wolf-whistling.

He frowned at her and retook his seat.

'Who was that?' she asked.

'No-one you need to concern yourself with.'

The prickle turned into a blade, slicing open the box containing his words from the Winter Ball. The ones where he said he wanted to flirt with her, have a drink with her. Henry was right, James was a manwhore who couldn't be trusted. He didn't even care enough about his latest shag to give her a name or introduce her to them.

Max sniggered.

'Is something funny?' James snapped.

'Not at all, boss,' Max replied, lowering his head, the smirk still in place.

Estelle took a packet of Wonder Woman tissues from her

bag and held it out. 'It would appear that "No-one" wears some pretty bright lippie.'

James rubbed his cheek, then stared at his stained fingertips, his mouth a tight line.

Taking a tissue from the packet, Estelle handed it over.

Snatching it from her, he wiped his face, as if attempting to remove a layer of skin along with the lipstick.

'You're making it worse,' she said. 'Now it looks like half of you is auditioning for the role of Bashful in *Snow White and the Seven Dwarfs*.'

Both his cheeks coloured.

'And now you're one hundred per cent in character!' She scrunched up her features as if in deep thought. 'Although maybe Grumpy would be a better part for you to go for in this year's pantomime... Max, what do you think?'

James shot him a look that could cut through steel. 'Let's keep this environment professional, shall we?' His fingers jabbed at the keyboard of his laptop.

'Absolutely!' Estelle replied, channelling the eternally sunny enthusiasm of Libby. 'So, no more passionate trysts in the stationery cupboard then? Heated glances over the water cooler?'

He glared at her.

'Hang about. I didn't know we even *had* a stationery cupboard. Do I have to pass my probation before I find out where it is? Or work my way down to the seventh layer of hell?'

James slammed the lid of his laptop shut, stood, then turned to Max. 'Set Estelle's laptop up and go through our systems with her.' He stalked to the door.

'Where are you going?' she asked.

'To my office,' he replied, not looking back. 'I've got work to do.'

Yanking the door open, he strode into the corridor.

'Don't you mean *our* office?' she called after him.

He didn't reply.

Estelle waited until the door closed, then turned to Max.

'So who *was* at the door?' she asked, unable to stop the question bubbling out.

Max leaned back in his chair, a smug and secretive smile on his face. Estelle immediately wished she'd kept her mouth shut. Max was more slippery than a bagful of eels.

'Well,' he began. 'I haven't met his family, but I have seen a woman coming and going. Blonde hair, slim, pretty.'

Estelle's stomach tightened. That sounded like a description of Henry's ex, Elizabeth, who James had stolen from her brother.

Max cupped his chin and glanced up and to the left, frowning. It was as if he'd been practising expressions at drama club, and this one was entitled 'recalling a piece of information from the past of utmost importance'.

'Younger than you,' he continued. 'Maybe late twenties?'

Bugger off! I only turned thirty last summer! Estelle tried to keep calm, but every one of Max's words made her hackles rise. He wouldn't have known James made a play for Summer, her youngest sister, another blonde, however his words described a woman who was the physical opposite of Estelle.

'She's always dressed in pencil skirts and heels,' Max said, as if he were in court and it was imperative he remembered every detail. 'Her make-up—'

'I get the picture. Can we get on with setting up my laptop now?'

Max's eyes lit up, as if he knew he'd found another of her weak spots. 'Yes, Lady—*Estelle...*'

. . .

Estelle stared out of the window at the formal gardens as Max fiddled with her computer. The winter solstice had been and gone, but the land was still sleeping under a blanket of frost and the unbroken expanse of clouds had turned everything into a palette of greys.

Just like my mood...

But isn't this what you wanted? The little voice in her head sounded exactly like Eveline. *To have more reasons to dislike James?*

Yes, but he smells so good. It's like the man equivalent of chocolate, Chelsea buns and horses.

He smells of horses?

Course he doesn't! Jesus. I can't believe I'm having this conversation.

You're not. I'm you.

Shut up.

Estelle forced her gaze back to her laptop. She used to wholly despise James, but the percentage of her dislike had slipped from one hundred down to ninety-seven, which was dangerously low. She needed to stop him wearing whatever it was that made him smell like an attractive human, and force him to use a cologne that revealed his true nature.

Her toes curled as she relived the sensations of him sitting so close to her—the heat, the scent. The attraction was clearly sorcery on his part. Re-crossing her ankles, one foot made a supposedly magical sound and she swallowed a grin. When Willow had asked what she wanted for Christmas, Estelle said she wanted the most garishly offensive slippers her sister could find.

James clearly hated them, but the noises they produced each time she took a step also irritated the hell out of her. Still, it wouldn't be for long. She was giving it a week before he begged her to work from home.

She pushed her chair back. 'I need the loo. Can you just crack on without me?'

Max nodded. 'Sure.'

OUTSIDE, THE CORRIDOR WAS EMPTY. ESTELLE PASSED BY THE bathroom, straight to the entrance hall and the door through to the main house.

Still locked.

She wasn't naturally nosy, but the masochistic part of her needed to know who the woman was that had kissed James.

Don't go there! You don't like him, remember?

Turning around and going to the bathroom, she avoided her reflection in the mirrors, instead focusing her attention on a wicker basket filled with toiletries. They were high-end, mostly organic, and had never been used before. Had the 'beautiful blonde' selected them? Estelle sighed. If she had, then the woman could also add 'has impeccable taste' to her long list of attributes.

Going through the products, she found a small glass bottle without a label. It was intricately cut crystal, with the letter 'E' incorporated into the design. Her heart fluttered. Was the 'E' for Estelle?

Pulling off the cap, she held it to her nose.

Nothing.

She sprayed it into the air and wafted her hand through the fine mist. Suddenly, every nerve ending in her nose and brain lit up, as if the perfume was the perfect key to activating the essence of her. She sniffed again, her nostrils flaring to take in more of the scent. It was earthy and spicy but at the same time utterly feminine, with light floral overtones.

Depressing the top twice more, she moved through the spray. An image came to her of riding at dawn through fields of flowers, the air holding the scent of early morning dew and damp earth, but also the murmurs of brightly coloured petals as they woke up and reached towards the rising sun. It contained the spice of cedar and the warmth of beeswax, with bold base notes and delicate top ones.

Breathing it in, the corners of her eyes prickled with emotion. The perfume felt like the truest representation of her, in all her complexity. Estelle knew she rubbed people up the wrong way, but the scent seemed to recognise that under her ballsy exterior, she could be just as nurturing as Willow, as sweet as Eveline, and as sunny as Libby. She'd never worn perfume before, but this seemed to become effortlessly part of her, something that would complement and amplify both her and the smells she loved from her daily life.

She stared at the bottle, wondering who 'E' was. She wanted to meet her as much as she didn't. And which other mysterious woman had written the note she'd found stuffed down the side of the chaise longue? Surely not the same person. Did James have a sister?

Estelle sprayed more of the scent on the inside of her wrists, rubbed them together, then onto each side of her neck. Maybe she could 'borrow' the perfume and take it home? Apply it before her next yoga class? Would it be the magic that made Isaac respond to her advances?

Ugh. It was easier to break a wild horse than get Isaac Hayward into bed. No matter what she tried, he remained professionally aloof. Why couldn't she just listen to Eveline and let it go?

Because he's the only hot man in the village, and he's also really nice.

She let out a heavy sigh. Unlike James, who may have been hotter than the devil, but had a far less attractive personality.

Spraying the perfume one more time into the air, she walked through it.

Come on. Just follow the plan, then soon Beelzebub will be out of your hair.

'HEY, CO-WORKER,' ESTELLE SAID BREEZILY TO JAMES AS SHE re-entered their office. 'My laptop's all set up now, so I'm good to go.'

James was staring at his computer screen, his hands steepled in front of him as if he was posing for the cover of *Mafia Today* magazine.

Estelle could see how tight his jaw was, so did a turn of the office, making sure each step was small, to increase the amount of noise coming from her feet.

'Do you mind?' he spat through gritted teeth.

'Mind what?' she asked, standing in the space between their desks and doing star jumps.

'What are you doing?' he growled, his gaze finally flicking up to meet hers.

'Exercise,' she replied, her feet continuing to impersonate Genghis Khan and his horde invading fairyland. 'Getting the blood flowing.'

James's blood seemed to be pooling in his temples. 'Do you normally do this?'

She changed to jogging on the spot. 'I usually do yoga.'

'But today...?'

'I don't have my mat. I could bring it tomorrow?'

'That would be preferable,' he replied, his gaze returning to the screen in front of him.

'Can I bring some more things from home?' she asked, picking up the pace. The noises from her feet were grating on her nerves, however James's nerves looked frayed to the point of tearing so she wasn't going to stop.

'What kind of things?'

'Personal items. For my work environment.'

He stood. 'Bring whatever you need.' Picking up a piece of paper from his desk, he held it out. 'The code for the main door, so you can come and go as you please. You have my number if you need to reach me outside of work.'

She stopped running and went forward, taking it from him. His gaze was fixed on a point an inch above her head, but suddenly his nostrils flared and his eyes snapped to meet hers.

Her breath stuttered in her throat at his expression. She saw surprise, something that looked like victory, then dark heat.

Oh, shit. The perfume! Do I remind him of whoever 'E' is? Turning, she dashed back to her desk.

By the time she took her seat, James was at the door. 'I'll leave you to it for a bit. If you need me, ring my mobile.'

Then he was gone.

Estelle put her hand to her heart. It wasn't the star jumps or running that was making it race out of control. It was James.

Hold it together until the end of the day, then it's time to put phase two into action.

Henry: I know I don't need to worry about you but I can't help it. Please ring me when you can and let me know you're okay X

Libby: How was your first day with the Big Bad Wolf? Did you blow his house down? XXX

Eveline: I have complete faith that today will work out perfectly but you are still in my thoughts and prayers xxxx

Finn: Have you served James his balls on a plate yet?

Willow: How's it going? What did he think of the slippers?????

Jack: My wife is calmly confident you're absolutely fine, but Henry is fretting. So could you message him when you get a chance and get him off our backs? Ta x

Connor: Been thinking of you today and hope it went well. If Eveline's right and James does fancy you, then it should make things easier? Big hugs xxx

Leo: Your favourite brother here. Henry says I need to be worried about you working with this James bloke. I told him not to get his knickers in a twist and you'd eat James for breakfast. Speaking of food, when are you next coming over for dinner? X

Estelle: I'm creating this group chat and entitling it 'The Destruction of James Hunter-Savage'. Here are the headlines from today

I'm alive!

Unfortunately, so is JHS…

The slippers are GENIUS torture. James HATES them. I did star jumps and ran on the spot in front of him and he nearly popped a vein. I'm aiming for an aneurysm by Friday

Eveline, I'm sorry my darling, but you were WRONG about him liking me. Someone came by but JHS didn't let us see them. Five mins later he comes back with lipstick on his cheek. Apparently, there's a 'beautiful blonde' living with him and his folks

Leo, I'm too busy in the evenings making sure the stables are doing okay, but I'll come over as soon as I can. It needs to be Sunday through Thursday though, and Dad has to make onion bhajis. I want to be able to fart at will the next day. Maybe I could gas JHS to death?

Love you all xxx

Eveline: I'm so glad your first day went well! However, the blonde lady might be his sister? And maybe you could think about changing the name of this group chat from 'the destruction of James-Hunter Savage' to 'the befriending of James Hunter-Savage'? He seemed perfectly pleasant when I met him xxxx

Henry: Estelle, I'm so glad you're okay. Eveline, you're far too kind and forgiving. Trust me, that man doesn't deserve it

Connor: How about the 'ignoring' of James Hunter-Savage?

Libby: The 'mindful acceptance' of JHS?

Estelle: Ugh. No way. I'm thinking of changing 'destruction' to 'annihilation'

Leo: Is he really that bad you want to inflict Dad's onion bhaji farts on him?

Henry: YES!

Estelle: YES!!!

Finn: How about 'the boning of James Whatisface'?

Estelle: EXCUSE ME?

Finn: Well, the line between love and hate…

Estelle: Fuck off, Finley, then fuck off some more

Henry: Really not helping, Finn

Finn: LOL. Stelle and Savage, sitting in a tree…

Estelle: I'm going to kick you out of this group if you don't shut up

Finn: K-I-S-S-I-N-G!

Finn has been removed from the group.

Estelle: Right. That's Finn gone. Anyone else want to side with Savage?

Leo: I'm not saying a word. This is top quality weekday night entertainment and I've got a ringside seat

Henry: We're here for you, Estelle. Whatever you need

Estelle: Thanks bro X

Willow: So, what's the plan for tomorrow? Xxx

Estelle: I'm gonna spice up his life...

Leo: With bhajis?

Estelle: No, the girls are coming with me to work...

❧ 8 ❧

The sun still hadn't risen when Estelle brought the Defender to a careful stop outside Shoscombe Manor the next morning. A couple of lights were glowing from inside the main house, but the offices were dark. Using the torch on her phone, she inputted the code, then propped the door open so she could bring things in.

James and Henry may have had wildly different personalities, but their desks were identically spartan.

Estelle's was not.

When working, she needed to see everything at the same time, and also have reminders of the people she loved around her. These weren't photos, but knick-knacks she'd been given, everything from mugs to ornaments to stress balls. Henry couldn't stand the clutter and Estelle was hoping James hated it even more.

It took three trips to get everything from the car, including some extra additions she'd collected from the livery and bought from a gift shop in the village. Her slippers remained turned off. Despite what she was going to pretend to James later, she not only hated the sounds they made but also any noise when she worked.

By half-past eight, the room was set, and Estelle was ready for the first coffee of the day. The winter sun had finally risen and shone weakly into the corridor as she made her way towards the kitchen. Up ahead, golden light was spilling out from under the door to the ladies' bathroom. Was it 'E' getting her perfume back?

She pushed the door inward to see a woman cleaning one of the sinks.

'Oh, my Christ!' the woman yelled, leaping back and crashing into the hand drier.

Estelle held her hands up in a gesture of defence. 'Sorry! I didn't mean to startle you!'

The woman was gasping for breath, her kohl-rimmed eyes wide. She was wearing rubber gloves and a coral-pink tabard over a zebra-striped jumper, and was clutching a neon-green cleaning cloth to her chest.

Smiling, Estelle held out her hand. 'Hi, I'm Estelle.'

The woman stared at it as if it were a box of chocolates suspended over a bear trap, then turned, grabbing spray bottles and jamming them in a cleaning caddy.

'You're not meant to see me,' she muttered, giving the already spotless sink another quick once-over with her cloth. 'I shouldn't be here.'

'Why not?'

The woman hovered, her eyes flicking to the door behind Estelle as if desperate for escape.

'Promise you won't tell him you saw me?'

Estelle's stomach lurched. Did she mean James? His dad?

'Tell who?'

The woman swallowed. 'James.'

She froze. How evil *was* James for his staff to be this terrified of him?

Drawing her shoulders back, she nodded. 'I won't say a word. Your secret is safe with me.'

The woman's face relaxed a fraction. 'Thanks, babe.'

Estelle moved to the side and opened the door. The woman glanced around the bathroom with a frown, as if she couldn't bear to leave without finishing her job.

'It's so clean I could eat my dinner off it,' Estelle said to her.

'You sure, babe?'

'Yes!'

'Do you want me to wash your wellies for you?'

'What?'

'They're a bit muddy.'

Estelle swallowed her smile. 'You *really* don't need to do that. I live at a stables, so they're always filthy.'

The woman's forehead creased again, as if she was working out how she could keep the whole of the countryside dirt free. Then she nodded and went into the corridor.

Estelle followed her to the door that separated the office wing from the main house. The woman opened it and peeked through. There was a big key in the lock on the other side.

'Do you like French Fancies?' she whispered to Estelle.

'The cakes?'

'Yes.'

'Love them. Why?'

The woman shook her head. 'I've got to go. Thanks for not saying anything. You're a doll.'

Slipping through the door, she closed it behind her. Estelle heard a key being turned, then the faint sound of footsteps as the woman ran away.

Going back into the bathroom, she stared at her reflection

in the wall of mirrors, sadness sitting heavy in her stomach. Each time a tiny part of her hoped she'd been wrong about James, some other nasty fact came crawling out of the woodwork to remind her just how rotten he really was. Yesterday it was the girlfriend he didn't want to acknowledge, and today it was discovering just how petrified his cleaner was of him.

Estelle hardened her expression and her heart. Her, Henry, and Connor, the eldest Foxbrooke children had grown up fiercely protective of each other and their younger siblings. Estelle was used to fighting tooth and nail for the underdog, and right now she wanted to tear a strip off James for being such a bully.

Reaching for E's perfume in the basket, she sprayed it on. She didn't give a shit it was someone else's. The scent felt like it belonged on her skin, making every facet of who she was shine even brighter. And this morning she was a badass who was going to make James Hunter-Savage beg her to work somewhere other than Shoscombe Manor.

TEN MINUTES LATER, ESTELLE'S HEART QUICKENED AS SHE heard heavy feet running down the corridor. They slowed as they reached the office door and she quickly flicked on both her slippers.

James strode in. Water dripped off the ends of his jet-black hair onto his collar, and his pressed white shirt clung to his skin, as if he'd pulled it on without having had time to dry himself properly.

Estelle leaned back in her chair and stretched. 'Morning, colleague!'

James's eyes darted around the room, as if checking no-one else was inside, then his gaze fell to her desk.

'Can you be a love and make me a cappuccino?' she continued. 'That coffee machine is complicated as fuck and I couldn't find a manual.'

'What time did you get here?'

She shrugged. 'Dunno... Seven-thirty? Why?'

He cleared his throat. 'Did you... Was there anyone else around?'

Estelle tried to look innocent. 'No, there wasn't. Should there have been?'

He shook his head.

Silence.

'So... Coffee?'

He gave her a curt nod and left.

James soon returned, carrying a cappuccino.

He stood by her desk. 'And where am I meant to put this?'

Estelle leapt to her feet, her slippers coming to life. 'Let me clear a space.'

Moving some papers to one side, she found a coaster that read 'Coffee. Because adulting is hard'.

James was silent, his gaze on the mug as he placed it down.

Estelle breathed in deeply, filling her head with the incredible scent of him. Whatever cologne he was wearing seemed to be half pheromone and half tractor beam, pulling her into the heart of the Death Star. She held her breath, but the smell was already inside her, making hot, dirty love to every cell.

No, no, no, no, no!

James's chest rose and his nostrils flared.

Oh, shit. He can smell his girlfriend's perfume. Quick! Do something!

She jumped on the spot, activating her mood-killing slippers.

'Thanks for the coffee!' she enthused, lifting it up. 'Did you attempt a pattern in the foam?'

Turning abruptly, James went to his desk, standing by it with his back to her.

'You've covered the top with cocoa powder,' she continued. 'But underneath it looks like you've tried to create something, then given up and rubbed it out with a spoon.'

If he'd been still before, now it seemed he'd been turned to stone.

Bingo! 'There's no shame in trying.' She tried to sound kind, and not gleefully smug that her hunch had been right. 'It took Henry at least a week before he mastered it.'

James huffed, then went around the side of his desk, sat, and flipped his laptop open.

Estelle hid her grin inside her mug as she took a sip. *Oh, my god, that's good.* Tapping the foot that jingled, then the one that whinnied and galloped, she tried to work out from James's micro-expressions which one irritated him the most.

His eyebrows were drawn together, his fingers hammering at the keyboard.

'What are you doing?'

He ignored her.

Putting her coffee down, she clip-clopped around her desk and made her way over to his.

His fingers moved faster, then he punched the return key and slammed the lid down before she could see what he'd been doing.

She pouted. 'Aww, you're no fun.'

His gaze flicked to her desk. 'And you're Comic Sans all the way.'

'*Comic Sans?*' she spluttered. 'What's that supposed to mean?'

'It looks like a joke shop got burgled,' he replied, his dark eyes glittering. 'And *that* was what the thieves couldn't bear to steal.'

She stamped her feet.

'You're the kind of person who has a sticker on the back of their car which says, "My other car's a Ferrari",' James continued.

'My other car *is* a Ferrari,' she blustered.

'No, it's not.' He leaned back, eyeballing her. 'It's a broom.'

Estelle stalked back to her desk. 'You're just jealous no-one loves you enough to buy *you* presents.'

'Ah yes,' he replied, his voice laced with sarcasm. 'How I wish someone would give me a giant letter J in case I forget the start of my own name.'

Snatching her moody cow stress ball, she turned and threw it at him.

He caught it with one hand, then squeezed it until the head appeared about to pop.

'Careful!' Estelle cried. 'That's a present from Eveline.'

'The lovely vicar?'

Fury punched her in the gut. 'She's *married*.'

'So you keep telling me,' he said, still squeezing the cow. 'That doesn't stop her from being one of the nicest people I've ever met.'

And I suppose you think I'm the opposite?

Isn't that the point? You're not trying to make him like you!

James stared at the cow's frowning face. 'Did this come with a manual?'

'What?'

'These are meant to relieve stress, not be used as a weapon.' He tossed it back to her as if bored with it.

Catching it, she felt the residual warmth from his hand. She put the toy down and took another gulp of her coffee.

'Speaking of the vicar...' James began.

Her heart rate spiked. 'The one who's off-limits.'

'Can you ask her something from me?'

Estelle turned with a jerk, coffee spilling out of the mug onto the saucer.

James smirked. 'She's got an item of my clothing and I'd quite like it back.'

It was impossible to compose herself when her mind was flashing images of James naked with Eveline. Estelle wanted to vomit.

His eyebrow raised. 'My jumper? I left it at the church after you gave me my marching orders last year.'

Breathe! She attempted a nonchalant shrug, but it was so vigorous, the cup and saucer rattled. 'I'll ask her.'

'Thanks. And don't worry, she's not my type.'

'Not your *type?*' Estelle hissed, all composure gone as she thought of her youngest sister. 'We all know what your type is.'

'You do?'

'Yes. Your girlfriend is a perfect example of the kind of woman you go for.'

James dipped his chin and levelled her with a stare that stopped her heart. 'I don't have a girlfriend.'

Her heart restarted with a jolt, half relieved at his words, and half horrified he was treating 'E' so badly.

He gestured to the wall behind her. 'I like it.'

Huh? 'The Spice Girls?'

The corner of his mouth twitched. 'The map.'

'Oh.'

James rolled back his chair then stood, completely in control of the game unfolding between them. Estelle felt like she'd dropped the ball five minutes ago.

'Although I have nothing against the Spice Girls.' He moved around his desk towards the life-size cut-outs of the band she'd propped against the wall. 'I enjoyed their company multiple times during my adolescence.'

'You're a pig.'

'No, just honest.' He stroked his chin. 'Staring across the office at them over the next six months is going to rekindle so many happy memories.'

Estelle's face heated at the thought of James 'rekindling' his memories, and she moved further away from him.

He turned his attention from contemplating her favourite girl band to the satellite photos of Foxbrooke Manor and the surrounding area. Estelle had enlarged them, printed them out, then stuck them to the wall, covering a three-metre squared area.

'I've seen the site plan on a screen before,' James continued. 'But this is a far better way to understand the festival. We need copies of this for the conference room and the other offices.'

'And you expect me to do that?'

His gaze stayed on the wall. 'No. Just tell Max where you got this done and he can organise it.'

She didn't know how to reply, so ran her finger around the smooth edge of a mug with a picture of a cockerel on it, and the words 'Rise & Shine, Mother-Cluckers!'

James glanced out of the window. 'No rain is forecast today. How about we visit the site this morning?'

'You want to come to Foxbrooke Manor?'

He shrugged. 'It would be good to walk the grounds and check the layout works before we set it in stone.'

'It's fine. I designed it.'

'And Estelle Foxbrooke is never wrong.'

She bit the inside of her mouth, remembering the Winter Ball. She'd been spectacularly wrong about James that night, falling into his arms and then for his charms.

He moved closer, picking up another mug from her desk and reading aloud. 'I'm not opinionated; I'm just never wrong.'

'You can have that one,' she muttered, breathing through her mouth so she didn't fall prey to the power of his scent.

'What do you think, Max?' James asked.

Estelle whipped around to see Max standing just inside the door. *When had he come in?*

'Hey boss, hi Estelle,' he replied, a guileless smile on his face. 'Great idea. When are we going?'

'Now,' James said. 'I'll drive us.'

Estelle itched to know what car James drove, but didn't want to be in an enclosed space next to him.

She grabbed her jacket. 'I can drive us over.'

James went to his desk and picked his keys up. 'I know where to go.'

'I'm not getting in your car.'

'Thank you for your consideration,' he replied, moving to the door.

'Meaning?'

'I like to keep her clean.'

Her? 'And I'm dirty, am I?'

His lips twitched and her stomach did a somersault.

'I know your *boots* are...'

Oh. 'Well then, Max, you can either go with James in whatever crass overcompensation for personal shortcomings he drives, or come in the Defender with me.'

She stomped to the door and the two men let her pass.

Estelle: Urgent! On way to manor with JHS to check out the site. Release the hounds!

Henry: On it

Willow: Did you mean to send that to the group chat?

Estelle: Fuck! No

Libby: Delete your messages before Eveline sees them

Estelle: Deleted message

Estelle: Deleted message

Eveline: Before I see what?

Estelle: It's a surprise. I'll see you later xxx

A LOUD AND AGGRESSIVE CAR HORN MADE ESTELLE JUMP AND drop her phone into the footwell.

'Fuck's sake!' She bent to retrieve it, then glanced through the window towards the garage. One of the wooden doors was open and a black Ferrari exited, the number plate reading 'JHS 1'.

'Now there's a surprise,' she huffed as the car growled across the gravel towards the main road.

'Oh, no you don't,' she growled back. '*You* follow *me*, sunshine.'

Slamming the Defender into gear, she swerved to cut him off, assuming James wouldn't want his shiny toy getting into an argument with her beat-up Land Rover.

She was right, and he came to an abrupt stop.

Smiling, she eased onto the road, knowing exactly how she was going to drive James to the edge of reason during the short journey to her family home.

❊ 9 ❊

James's fingers tapped the leather steering wheel impatiently, his gaze flicking to the speedometer on the dashboard.

'She's a very careful driver,' Max said from the passenger seat.

James didn't reply. They'd been tailing Estelle for a couple of miles, travelling at exactly ten miles per hour *below* the speed limit, and he was thrumming with frustration. Living in the back of beyond was bad enough, but not being able to take advantage of the Ferrari's handling and performance on these country roads was like forcing a sprinter to perform tied to a donkey.

He couldn't put his car through its paces in London, but it did come with other advantages. No matter what women may have claimed, they swarmed to it, then him, like bees to black honey. His Ferrari was the one possession he refused to part with when everything went tits up. However the only females who could currently see his car didn't give a shit. They were either in fields chewing silage, or driving in front of him slower than a tractor.

Six months. That's all.

Coming up was a short stretch of dual carriageway. James dropped a gear as they approached. Estelle must have anticipated his move as she floored the Defender, shooting forward.

Never take a knife to a gunfight…

Slamming his foot down, the car accelerated with a joyous roar, the sound almost entirely covering Max's yelp of fear. A smile spread across James's face and he gave Estelle a salute as the Ferrari cruised past her.

She flipped him the bird in response.

Once the dual carriageway ended, James slowed to exactly one mile per hour *above* the speed limit, and gave most of his attention to the rear-view mirror, his eyes finding Estelle's furious ones.

Being in separate cars felt in some strange way like normal rules didn't apply, as if they were on different planets and he could ignore the professional guidelines he'd forced himself to adhere to. Before he could stop himself, he winked at her.

The change in her expression was dramatic—her eyes widened and her lips parted.

He grinned.

Slamming her mouth shut, she fixed her gaze on the road ahead, ignoring him completely.

James didn't care. If he could get under her skin with just one wink, then he'd put up with all the childish games she could throw at him.

D RIVING BETWEEN THE ENORMOUS STONE PILLARS THAT flanked the entrance to Foxbrooke Manor, James's grip on the steering wheel tightened. The grandeur of the place was yet another reminder of how different he was from the Foxbrookes. James had had to fight for his position, but Henry and Estelle had grown up as Lord and Lady Foxbrooke and afforded every privilege that class and money could buy.

Easing the car to a stop, he got out, going to the driver's side of the Defender and opening the door for Estelle.

'Thank you,' she said as she exited, moving quickly away and staring at the sandy ground.

'Shall we begin?' he asked. 'Estelle, why don't you run through how it's going to work from the start of the festival?'

She nodded, put more distance between them, then addressed Max.

'The festival begins on Friday, but we'll be setting up for at least two months before that. There are three entrance points for punters—through the main gates here, and through the parkland to the side and rear of the house. There's enough room there not only for the main stage but also camping facilities and temporary hard-standing for cars.'

'Security?' James asked.

'A four-metre-high fence with a forty-five-degree overhang, built from aluminium planks and a captive joint system so there are no nuts and bolts. It's the same one used at Glastonbury.'

And really fucking expensive. 'Isn't that overkill?'

She shrugged. 'If we can't keep people safe and numbers within our prescribed limits, then we'll never be allowed to run another festival. And the headline act on Sunday is insanely popular.'

And also stupidly expensive. American electronica act, Uber-Graft, were the biggest draw and James couldn't understand why they'd agreed to perform at such a small-scale, and brand new, festival.

'How did you get them?'

Estelle frowned at her phone, then put it back in her pocket, still refusing to meet his gaze.

'Mom met them in LA last year and pitched the idea. They're headlining at Glastonbury the weekend before, so they'll be in the country, anyway. And apparently MisTee likes Shakespeare, so wants to check out the production we'll be doing in the gardens at the same time.'

'Hmm.' Of course, there had to have been a back-door route in. The band, made up of a real-life couple, were notoriously difficult to deal with.

'What?' she said defensively. 'You know how it works. It's just like what you did in London.'

'Me?'

'Yes. Bringing the client onside and getting to know what they like. We're doing Macbeth so I bought a facsimile copy of the first folio and sent it to MisTee with a hamper of produce from the estate. She rang me to say thank you and agreed to perform.'

'You actually spoke to her?' Max interjected. 'What was she like?'

'Really nice. Quiet. Not like how she comes across on stage.'

Digging his fingernails into his palms, James tried to hide his stress. 'I still don't think we need that level of fencing. We should go for a cheaper spec.'

'I've budgeted for it.'

'We need a contingency.'

'We've got one.'

No, we haven't. 'We need a bigger one.'

'In case the fence fails and we need to hire a bunch of thugs to kick out another bunch of thugs?' she asked sarcastically. 'Or we could just do a proper job the first time around?'

He crossed his arms. 'All payments have to be approved by me.'

She copied his stance, standing with her legs wider than his currently were. 'Says who?'

'The contract. The one you signed.'

She stared him down.

He stared right back, revelling in the chance to dive deep into her dark eyes.

A loud barking broke the moment and panic cracked through his heart like a lightning bolt. The last time he'd heard those dogs, Estelle had almost died.

'Shit!' Max yelled, running back to the cars as Caligula and Borgia came bounding towards them.

James dashed forward and grabbed their collars as they leapt at Estelle, using every ounce of his strength to yank them away.

'No!' he snarled. 'Down!'

They immediately obeyed. Borgia started whining, and Caligula shook himself as if drying off after a dunking.

'Sit,' he continued, his voice now resonating at extreme-alpha frequency.

They complied. Then, as if seeking further approval from their master, lay down.

When he was certain they wouldn't move, James turned, crossing the short distance to Estelle.

He took her hand. 'Are you okay?'

She seemed flustered, her gaze flitting around like a grasshopper on hot coals. James breathed in deeply, powerful pride rushing through his veins as he caught the smell of her perfume, now richer and more complex than when he'd smelled it on her earlier. The combination of chemicals was only part of the picture. Estelle had taken the scent and made it her own. Touching her skin, it had become something else, something as utterly intoxicating as she was.

'Is everything alright?' a voice called out from the side of the manor.

Estelle froze, then pulled her hand from his and went forward.

Viscount Nob-end. Fucking brilliant. James turned to see Henry striding towards them, his familiar frown in place.

'Fine, thanks,' Estelle said. 'The dogs must have got out. Can you take them back in? We're just here to look over the site.'

'I didn't think they would go for you,' Henry said to her. 'I'm so sorry.'

'Well, what can I say?' She fake-laughed. 'Hahaha! I'm clearly the most attractive member of the team.'

Without question...

Max came forward from his hiding place, holding his hand out to Henry.

'Lord Foxbrooke, I'm Max.'

Henry took it. 'Just Henry, please.'

'Sure thing, buddy. You gonna give us the tour?'

Estelle stiffened.

'Er—' Henry began.

'I don't think that will be necessary,' James interrupted. 'Seeing as Estelle is the one who's planned the festival, as well as having lived here for most of her life.'

Henry nodded. 'Absolutely. It's her baby, not mine. I'll leave you to it.' He turned to the dogs, still lying on the drive. 'Caligula, Borgia, come on.'

They looked up at James as if seeking permission to move.

'Heel!' Henry shouted.

Neither James, nor the dogs, moved a muscle.

Henry pulled on their collars, but they were dead weight.

Max snorted.

James felt a kick to the back of his leg and snapped his head around. Estelle was glowering at him.

He winked at her, then whistled at the dogs. 'Go on, boys.'

They lumbered to their feet, giving him one last look before trotting off after a fuming Henry.

'Now *that's* Big Dick Energy, Star,' James murmured under his breath. 'You've either got it or you haven't.'

'My arse,' she hissed in return. 'You know what they say about men who drive cars like yours?'

James was feeling far too smug to moderate his words. 'Rich, good-looking, and the lay of your life?'

'No. Really fucking tiny penis.'

He laughed.

'What was that?' Max called over.

'Estelle was—'

'About to go over the rest of the plans,' she interrupted. 'Starting with the fact we still don't yet have permission to run the festival.'

'We don't?' Max asked.

'No. My family have had a, er, *complicated* relationship with the local authority over the years and it's up to us to prove that working with SDE Entertainment will be a different experience. They need to know they can trust us to deliver what we've promised.'

'SDE?'

'Keep up, buddy,' James said. 'It's what Estelle's renaming the company. It stands for Sexy Dick Energy. I'm going to fill out the forms with Companies House to get the name changed this afternoon. Maybe add another lightning bolt to the logo.'

Estelle ignored him. 'Max, can you please set up a meeting with the local councillors approving our application for the week after next? That should give us enough time to finish our plans and cover all bases.'

'Yeah, sure, no worries.'

'Thank you,' Estelle said, then gestured at the long drive in front of them, with large areas of lawn either side. 'With all vehicles in the park, this is where the outside caterers will go for everyone attending events inside the manor and gardens. There'll be another food court in the park near the main stage.'

'Have you booked anyone yet?' James asked.

'Provisionally, yes. I've spoken to Leia and Ben, who run The Colour Palate restaurant in the village. They're going to help me coordinate local suppliers.'

'Get a deposit from them now.'

She frowned. 'They're not paying to be here.'

'What?'

'We're not charging any of the concessions to sell food at the festival.'

Anxiety nipped at James's heels. 'Why not?'

'Because they always overcharge for what they sell.'

'Not our problem.'

Estelle's hands were now planted on her hips as she faced him down.

'Yes, it is. We want the festival to be affordable, and that's not going to happen when you're being charged fifteen quid for a portion of soggy chips.'

I don't give a rat's arse. Without extra money coming in, there wasn't even going to *be* a festival.

'So, by not charging, you expect them out of the goodness of their little hearts to put their prices down?'

'It'll be a requirement. Leia and Ben will be working with me and all suppliers to set prices and portion sizes that are fair for everyone.'

'Except for us! Who's paying for the electricity to run their stalls?'

She hesitated. 'I'm sure we can come to an arrangement.'

'Yes, one that involves them handing us cold, hard cash for the privilege of being here.' He shook his head. I'm sorry, Estelle—'

'You're not sorry at all.'

He paused. 'You're right. I don't give a shit if someone pays fifteen quid or fifty for a portion of chips. It's all about the bottom line.'

Her mouth dropped open. 'Don't you want to create something good here?'

'No.' He crossed his arms, as if it would hold back the fear and fury. 'I don't care if punters show up to see UberGraft or take part in some stupid Morris dancing workshop. The only thing that matters is making a profit.'

Silence.

Estelle's face hardened. 'And this month's award for "coldest heart in hell" goes yet again to Mr James Hunter-Savage. Once more he's knocked Scrooge, Stalin, and John D. Rockefeller off the podium.' She pointed her finger at him as if it were a weapon. 'I *do* care about making a profit, but unlike you, I want to create something so good that next year's festival makes *more* money because people actually want to come back.'

James didn't give a toss about next year. By the end of the summer, he wanted to be back in London with everything in Somerset firmly behind him. *Especially* thoughts about Estelle Foxbrooke.

'And another thing, you opinionated arsehole,' she continued. 'Morris dancing is *not* stupid. It's an ancient cultural practice that goes back over seven hundred years. And it's not costing the festival anything to put on because my father is running the workshop for free.'

Fuck.

'Estelle—'

'Max, if you'd like to follow me, we can go around the back of the manor and I can show you where the open-air theatre will be, as well as the tents for the silent disco, acoustic sets and spoken word performers.'

She didn't wait for a reply, but strode off, her boots crunching on the hard ground.

Jamming his hands in his pockets, James followed. How had he ever thought this was going to work?

'It's never going to work,' Estelle huffed as she stomped through the back door of the rectory a few days later.

'It's only been a week,' Eveline replied. 'You can't expect a miracle.'

Estelle fixed her best friend with a look. 'That's blasphemy coming from you. Have you forgotten your boss made the whole bloody universe in less time than I've had to convert Hunter-Savage into an actual human being?'

Eveline rolled her eyes. 'Come into the kitchen. Jack made a chocolate fudge cake earlier.'

'Ooh! Yum!' Estelle followed her through the ground floor into a large room which was in the process of being modernised. New taps sat above the butler sink and the doors were missing from the cupboards. 'Where is your domestic god, anyway?' she asked, going to the kettle and flicking it on.

'At Wickes, buying paint and looking at cabinets.'

'Sexy stuff. I see you're still in the honeymoon phase.'

Eveline blushed. 'He's just perfect in every way.'

Estelle bit back a retort. Her friends had found true happiness with each other and she didn't want to keep raining on their parade just because she was single and grumpy. Pulling out several items from her bag she'd bought from a craft shop earlier, she laid them on the table.

Eveline gazed at what she'd brought. 'What are you making?'

'A present for the antichrist.'

'Half of that sentence sounded nice. What is it?'

Estelle held up a giant wooden letter in one hand and some neon-pink fake fur in the other.

Eveline glanced between them, a frown creasing her forehead, before realisation struck and her eyebrows hit her hairline.

'Estelle!'

'What? Beelzebub expressed an interest in the letter E that Leo got me, so I'm making this for him,' she replied with a smirk.

Eveline shook her head, cut two slices of cake and brought them to the table.

'This smells like heaven,' Estelle said, her mouth watering. Taking a fork, she sliced off a piece and popped it into her mouth. 'Uck ee, at's ood,' she moaned as her mouth and brain simultaneously orgasmed.

Eveline grinned. 'Why don't you take some with you to give to James?'

'Uck off!' Estelle cried, then started coughing as a crumb went down the wrong way.

A glass of water appeared in front of her. 'I think God wants James to have a piece of cake.'

Estelle gulped from the glass. 'Never. He doesn't deserve it.'

'He can't be that bad, really?'

'He's so horrid to his cleaner that she's literally terrified of him. He claims he doesn't have a girlfriend, but a 'beautiful blonde' smothered his cheek with her lippie—'

'You don't know—'

'He drives a Ferrari with a personalised number plate—'

'Jack owns an Aston Martin—'

'Which is stylish and classy and also a *British* company—'

'It's still a very expensive sports car.'

'It's not the same. Anyway, Jack is lovely, but James is...' Estelle wanted to say that James also smelled amazing, made the perfect cappuccino, and perhaps had a sense of humour hidden under the tightly tailored shirts. But if she did that, it would become clear that her feelings towards him were *complicated*.

'And you haven't driven him mad yet?'

Estelle shrugged. 'He's hiding it well. He tends to come in first thing, make me a coffee, stick a pair of headphones on when I play the Spice Girls, then bugger off to the conference room when I start singing.'

Eveline visibly winced.

'Oh, come on. My voice isn't *that* bad.'

Her friend deflected. 'He makes you coffee?'

'Yeah, the machine looks like NASA designed it, and the display's in Italian, so I don't want to press the wrong buttons and break it.'

'It sounds like he's being more than accommodating to you.'

Estelle crammed another chunk of cake in her mouth to avoid answering.

'And have you asked him if you can work from home?'

She swallowed. 'No, that's too obvious. The suggestion has to come from him. But I did ask if I could bring Chester and Joy with me to work next week.'

'Oh, that sounds nice.'

'Yeah, their training is almost complete.'

Eveline frowned in confusion. 'What training?'

'Um...' Estelle dropped her gaze to the table, where it fell to one of Eveline's romance novels. This one was entitled *A Cornish Christmas at the Fluffy Puppy Therapy Café on Starfish Cove.* 'I'm training them to be therapy dogs.'

'Really?' Eveline didn't sound convinced. 'And what does that involve?'

'Making them friendlier.'

'How?'

'You know, exposing them to lots of different smells, sounds, and so on.'

'Oh.'

Estelle took a tube of glue and a pair of scissors from her bag. 'Anyway, enough about me. How are you? Got a bun in the oven yet?'

Eveline's cheeks pinked.

'Holy shit! You have?'

'We don't know yet,' she replied hurriedly. 'But I am a few days late, so...'

'Have you done a test?'

She shook her head. 'Jack's going to pick one up this afternoon.'

Estelle's heart squeezed and her eyes pricked with emotion. She knew how much her friend wanted to be a mum.

'How are you feeling?'

'Apart from head-over-heels in love, I feel exactly the same. I've never been pregnant before, so I don't know what to look out for.'

'I remember when Mammy was pregnant with Summer, she was knackered all the time. But then again, it was her fourth, and Summer was as demanding in the womb as she is out of it.'

Eveline laughed. 'You have to make a lot of noise if you're the youngest. How's she getting on in France?'

'According to her, she's a "social media sensation". But as far as I can tell, this mainly involves being photographed constantly, going to glitzy parties and accumulating "followers". Henry and Willow worry about her, Dad, Mammy, Connor and Leo say she'll be fine, and Mom's over the moon that Summer's living the life she wanted for me and Henry.'

'And you?'

Estelle let out a sigh. 'Despite how full of herself she is, I do miss having her around. But right now, I'm happy the English Channel is between her and Hunter-Savage.'

'He only talked to her once, and apparently it was innocuous?'

'Summer's blonde, pretty, young and loves attention. I wasn't there when James tried it on with her, but it must have been bad for Henry to lose his shit like that and break his nose.'

Eveline's hand covered her heart. 'Oh, my goodness!'

'It's fine. His face could do with a small imperfection.'

'He *is* rather handsome.'

'Mmm—I mean NO! He is absolutely *not* handsome. He's a troll who got hit several times by the ugly stick.'

'That's not true, and more importantly it's not kind.'

Estelle slumped back in her chair, angry tears building in the back of her throat. She knew she was being a cow, but it felt the safest thing to do rather than admit she fancied a man who seemed to use and discard women as if they were utterly inconsequential.

Reaching across the table, Eveline took her hand. 'My darling friend. It's okay to find a man you dislike attractive. And you're also allowed to like someone even if your twin despises them.'

'I *don't* like him,' she mumbled.

Eveline gave her hand a squeeze. 'Would you like another slice of cake?'

She nodded.

'Okay, I'll get it for you. You concentrate on creating your gift for James.'

Eveline: Just letting you know that the test came back negative. Don't worry about me, I'm fine. I didn't think it was likely to happen that quickly, especially as I'm considered 'geriatric' xxx

Estelle: WTAF? Geriatric? Down with the patriarchy! I'm so sorry, sweetheart xxx

Eveline: Honestly I'm okay X

Eveline: You know, you don't have to give your 'gift' to James…

Estelle: Do you want it?

Eveline: Absolutely not

Eveline: I do hope he sees the funny side of it

Estelle: Well, if he doesn't, then he can be consoled by the best therapy dogs in Somerset…

'WILL YOU BEHAVE!' ESTELLE SHOUTED OVER HER SHOULDER as she left the livery for Shoscombe Manor the following week. 'We talked about this, didn't we? Huh? *Huh?*'

Chester was on the backseat of the Defender, growling and holding Joy's leg in his jaws as he attempted to engage her in a game of rough-and-tumble.

Joy was ignoring him, barking instead at Estelle.

'I know we've been planning this since before Christmas, but the two of you have got to be chill. Okay?'

Chester let go of Joy's leg and leapt into the front of the car, down into the passenger footwell, where he proceeded to tear receipts Estelle had left there to shreds.

'For heaven's sake!'

Swerving to a stop in a layby, she grabbed Chester and went to the back of the car.

'Time out, Mister. You can go full Berserker when we get there, but right now you need to calm down.'

She opened the boot, then the crate in the back.

Chester started whining.

'Oh, don't be like that, little man.' She kissed his fluffy head.

He licked the end of her nose, his tail wagging against her arm.

Raising her eyes to the wintery clouds, Estelle let out a huff. 'Okay, okay, but that was your last warning.'

Returning Chester to the backseat with Joy, she restarted the car.

It was less than a ten-minute drive to the manor but it was enough time to send her pulse rocketing. Each time she knew she was going to see James, her tummy swooped and dipped a little more as if she was graduating to higher and higher roller coasters. But now, with her gift for him wrapped in a bag beside her, and Chester and Joy hyped up and ready for action, she wondered if she'd gone too far.

And would her plan even work? Caligula and Borgia were the most uncontrollable dogs she'd ever known, but two words from James had them still and silent at his feet. Would he have the same effect on hers? Even after she'd spent weeks training them to attack his jumper?

She glanced at the clock on the dashboard. *Late.* She hated running behind for anything. Getting into the office before James meant that she could compose herself and her sassy game-face. Now all the witty remarks she'd carefully prepared had seeped from her skin and were mingling with the sweat trickling down the back of her neck.

Coming to a stop outside Shoscombe Manor, Estelle clipped leads to Chester's and Joy's collars. It was a new place, and she knew they'd want to explore. However, the last thing she needed was to be running after them as they chased anything that moved.

Did James's parents have a cat? He hadn't mentioned anything about one when they'd discussed bringing her dogs to work. *Shit.* If they did, she hoped it was the size and temperament of Henry and Libby's cat, Mr Pussy, who was an evil bastard to anyone but his owners.

Inside the office entrance, she kicked off her boots, her nose twitching along with Chester's and Joy's. The cloakroom held the incredible scent of a freshly-showered James. He was here already.

Both dogs barked loudly, their ears pricking up.

Was this a bad idea? Or a fucking terrible one?

Chester and Joy were now straining against their leads, desperate to head down the corridor towards the smell they'd been getting to know since Sausage Saturday the previous year.

'I've changed my mind,' she hissed at them. 'We're going home. Now sit whilst I put my boots back on.'

The dogs complied.

'Stay.'

They did.

She dropped their leads and grabbed her boots.

The office door at the far end of the corridor opened, and James stepped out.

Oh, shit.

'Stay!'

They didn't, hooning off towards him like Greyhounds with an acute case of the zoomies.

She ran after them, but it was too late. They'd reached him, and were—*oh, god.*

'No!'

Chester was humping James's right leg with the energy of a jackhammer, and Joy was vigorously humping his left. His gaze went from one dog to the other, then travelled up to meet hers.

'Um...' she began.

He smirked. 'Want to join in?'

'Chester! Joy! Heel!' she growled.

They ignored her.

'Dammit!' Grabbing their collars, she yanked them away.

James extended his arm towards the open door. 'After you.'

She dragged them inside the office, but it was challenging when their heads were turned almost one hundred and eighty degrees so they could still see James.

He shut the door behind them, crossed to his desk and leant against it, his arms folded across his broad chest as he watched her.

'Chester! Joy! Sit!' she yelled.

Joy's tail was a blur, and Chester was jumping and yipping as if he'd been promised a walk with unlimited squirrel-chasing opportunities.

'They're very...' James began. '*Enthusiastic*...'

His voice was deep with sexual innuendo, and Estelle's body heated.

'I didn't expect them to be like this,' she replied through gritted teeth before turning back to her dogs. 'Calm down!'

'Did you hope they would attack me instead?'

She didn't reply.

James whistled, and the dogs stilled.

Pushing himself upright, he came to Estelle's side. She stared at his chest, breathing in deeply and luxuriating in the warmth radiating out through the crisp white cotton of his shirt.

'Sit,' he commanded the dogs.

Estelle forced her own body not to obey as both Chester's and Joy's backsides hit the floor.

'Good girl,' James murmured.

Her thighs involuntarily clenched.

'Good boy,' he continued.

Estelle let go of her dogs' collars but couldn't move, trapped between the hard edge of her desk and the even harder expanse of James's body.

She held her breath, the scent of him filling her lungs and diffusing into her blood.

James stepped back. 'Coffee?'

She nodded.

He went to the door.

Chester and Joy followed.

'Stay,' he said to them.

They did.

James gave them a dazzling smile then left the room.

Estelle let out her held breath, then turned to her pets. 'What was all that then?' she hissed. 'That was *not* the plan.'

They ignored her, sniffing around James's desk.

'Come here. Get away from the dark side.'

James's mobile rang and Chester barked. Estelle crossed the room and picked him up, glancing down at the phone screen. Someone called 'Char' was calling. *Charlotte? Charlie?* The temptation was strong to answer it, so she went back to her own desk and plonked down her bag containing James's gift. *Is this a mistake, too?* Undecided, she put the bag on the floor behind the desk and sat, flipping her laptop open.

Five minutes later, James returned. Her dogs acted as if he was the second coming bearing gifts of marrow bones.

'Chester! Joy! Leave him alone!'

James placed her cappuccino down on a small space she'd cleared, then called the dogs to heel.

Staring at the froth, once again Estelle was convinced he was trying to make a pattern in it. But of what?

'Do they have beds?'

Huh? Her head snapped up.

'Your dogs.'

'Yes, in the Defender, but it doesn't mean they'll use them. I'll get them in a moment.'

James's eyes fell to Chester. 'What have you got there, boy?'

She stood to look over the desk. Chester was dragging her bag over to James.

'No!'

The bag fell open. 'A present?'

'It's not for you.'

He picked it up and read the back of the gift tag. 'Do you know another James Hunter-Savage?'

'Er...'

He traced the patterns on the sparkly wrapping paper. 'Maybe one who's going through a "unicorn phase"?'

'Um...'

'How did you know it was my birthday?'

'It is?'

'In eight months' time.' The corner of his mouth lifted. 'I appreciate how—' his gaze fell to the mess of her desk '—*organised* you are.'

Heart thudding in her chest, she took another sip of her perfectly-made coffee.

'I wonder what it is.' James gently squeezed the package, a pensive look on his face. 'It feels soft, but at the same time, very, very hard...' The tip of his finger slid under the edge of the wrapping paper. 'May I?'

Estelle stared, her eyes unable to break away from their locked position on his hands as he slowly undressed her gift. The fact he was taking so much care not to rip the paper just made the situation in her pants even worse. Yes, he was objectively hot, but his sinfully sexy personality was a siren call her body didn't want to ignore.

Placing the wrapping paper to one side, he held her present in his hands, his forehead furrowed.

'My name doesn't start with the letter Q.'

'I know,' she replied, trying to sound cool, even though everything inside her was anything but.

Running his fingers over the fur, he inspected her handiwork. His hand stilled as he found an uneven edge. 'You *made* this?'

She shrugged.

His smile was broad. 'You made this for *me*.'

Estelle forced her lips to stay shut. This was not how she thought this would go down. Eveline had been right. The amount of time and effort she'd put into creating the fur Q had demonstrated just how much she'd been thinking about James.

He placed it carefully on his desk, then held her gaze. 'Thank you. I'll think of you every time I look at it.'

Oh, god. She swallowed. *Quick! Think of something cutting to say!*

His phone rang. Not breaking eye contact, he reached to pick it up, only glancing at the screen when it was in front of him.

His expression immediately changed.

Pushing off the desk, he moved towards the door. 'I've got to take this.'

Chester and Joy went to follow.

'Stay,' he said to them.

James went into the corridor, closing the door behind him, but not before Estelle heard him say the word 'Char'.

❧ II ❧

'Hey, hey, it's alright. Just tell me what's going on so I can sort it,' James said into his phone as he strode towards the door to the main house.

Max stuck his head into the corridor. 'Boss-man!'

James held up his hand, his fingers splayed to indicate he needed five minutes, and continued on.

'Hang on, let me find somewhere quiet,' he said into the phone.

The door to the main house was unlocked.

Fuck's sake. Was it his mum? *Elyse?*

Taking the stairs two at a time, he made his way to his room. There were women's clothes on the bed.

'Char, don't go anywhere,' he said into the phone before pressing it into his chest and calling out, 'Elyse?'

Elyse wandered out of his bathroom, her hair in a turban and a tiny towel barely covering her modesty. 'Hi, I thought you were done.'

'What are you doing here?'

She shrugged. 'Your shower's better than mine.'

'You can't use it.'

'Why not?'

'I need to take this call.'

'Don't mind me.'

James stalked out, slamming the door behind him. Was there nowhere to hide from Elyse? He knocked on his parents' bedroom door.

No reply.

Going in, he sat on the bed and lifted the phone back to his ear.

'Sorry about that, Char. Go on.'

As she relayed the details of her drama, his head sank lower. If a bucket of confidence had been shared between the Hunter-Savage siblings, he got most of it and his sister had been left with the dregs at the bottom. James believed she was settled and happy, but now it appeared everything had fallen apart.

'So I'm going to come home for a bit,' she finally finished.

'What, here?'

'Where else can I go?'

Shit. The last thing he wanted was her living in the same house as Elyse. And no matter how much he loved his sister, he didn't want Estelle meeting her, either. He wanted to keep his business and personal life separate, and his family firmly away from the Foxbrookes. If only he had access to his London flat, Char could have moved in there. But his tenant had signed a year's lease, and James needed the money.

'Have you spoken to Mum?'

'No, I wanted to speak to you first.'

He rubbed his forehead. 'Whatever you need, you know I'm here for you.'

'Thank you.'

'Promise you'll ring Mum?'

He could hear her sniffing back tears.

'Char?'

'I'll ring her now.'

JAMES THUNDERED DOWN THE STAIRS AND INTO HIS FATHER'S office.

'Elyse has got to go.'

His dad glanced up from the computer screen, his dinosaur poppet toy in one hand. 'What you talking about?'

'She can't live here. She's currently upstairs, using my bathroom.'

Kevin shrugged. 'So what? You've got the best shower.'

'Dad! This is a family home. Elyse is an employee. She needs her own place.'

'Jamesy-boy, I need her around.' He tapped his head. 'This never sleeps. If I've got an idea, she's got to be on hand to write it down.'

'Why can't you do it? If you don't want to write, just type it out.'

'Nah, she's quicker. When I'm riding my seam of conscience, I need her holding the steering wheel.'

'It's a *stream* of *consciousness,* Dad,' James spat. 'And I can't live with her. She has to leave.'

His father dropped his poppet and picked up a fidget spinner. 'Not going to happen. This is my manor, not yours.'

'I don't give a shit. Thanks to you, I don't have a job *or* a home. I'm stuck here saving your arse and the very least you can do is keep your staff out of my personal space.'

His dad sighed, his gaze on the spinner as it whirled on the end of his thumb. 'I'll speak to her.'

'No, Dad. You're going to tell her to get her own place. Today. Anyway, Char just rang—'

'Don't call her that.'

'Things have gone tits up with Marcus, so she's coming to live here for a bit.'

'What?'

'She needs Elyse's room.'

He shook his head. 'There's more than enough space here for everyone.' Dropping the spinner, he picked the poppet back up. 'Does your mum know?'

'She's talking to her now.'

'Okay, good. Good.' Kevin stared off into the middle distance, the only sound in the room the rhythmic pop-pop-pop as he played with his toy.

'Dad—'

'I know what you need,' his father interrupted, leaping to his feet and going to a pile of boxes. 'These arrived yesterday and I forgot to show them to you.' Opening the top of one, he pulled out a folded white t-shirt and threw it at his son. 'This'll cheer you up.'

James opened it out, coming face-to-face with an aubergine emoji being struck by lightning.

'Got a great deal on them. Thought we could give them to punters at the festival.'

James stared at the ridiculous logo, printed on cotton so cheap and thin he could practically see through it.

'Why couldn't you have spent the money on something useful?' he growled. 'Like a budget for decent staff?'

'You'll make it work, son.' Kevin rummaged in the box and pulled out another couple of t-shirts. 'Give these to Lady Foxbrooke and that Max bloke. They'll love them.'

'No, they—'

'Morning Kev!' trilled Elyse as she entered the room. 'Ooh, aren't the t-shirts great, James?'

He threw the one in his hand back at his dad, gave him a

pointed look and left the room, slamming the door like a petulant teenager.

'BOSS-MAN!' MAX CALLED OUT AS JAMES LOCKED THE DOOR to the main house behind him.

James nodded in reply as he strode up the corridor.

The corners of Max's mouth turned down, his eyebrows drew together, and his head dropped to the side in a pastiche of concern. 'Everything okay, buddy?'

'Fine. What's up?'

'I've got the shortlist of candidates for you.'

The Spice Girls started playing from his office at the end of the corridor.

'Good. Let's go through them now.'

Following Max into the room, James took a seat at an empty desk and a pile of CVs were placed in front of him. These were for the key positions, the people who would report directly to him and Estelle, and oversee areas of the festival, from stages to logistics. At least half of them should have come with the company when his father bought it, so now James was starting from scratch.

His mood was already soured by Elyse and his father, plus his sister's situation, so it didn't take much to tip him over the edge.

'What the fuck is this?' he asked, dropping the papers to the desk.

'The candidates?'

James lifted one and read aloud. 'I organised the school prom.' He picked up another. 'Ran the welly-wanging stall at the village fête. Is this a joke?' He leafed through the CVs again. 'And why have they all got photos attached? I don't give a rat's arse what they look like.'

'This is what people do nowadays.'

'It's not a fucking beauty pageant. They're all women with an average age of twenty-two. How did this happen?'

Max crossed his arms. 'That's ageist and sexist.'

'No, it's a statement of fact. And here's another one for you. None of them are even remotely qualified for any position. How the hell did you decide this lot was the best fit for the job? Swiping right?'

'The salaries you're offering aren't high enough.'

James was silent. He knew that was true, but it still didn't explain why the candidates looked like a young man's dating wishlist.

He stood. 'Re-advertise. And all applications go through me.' Picking up the pile of CVs, he dumped them into the recycling bin. There was no way Estelle could see them. She was already convinced he was a blonde-obsessed horn dog, and these résumés would only confirm those assumptions.

There was no sound when James entered the corridor, but the moment he closed the door behind him, 'Spice Up Your Life' started playing. He rolled his eyes. Despite being a member of the British upper-classes and ballsy as fuck, Estelle also had an innocence about her. Her pranks were childish and rather sweet. He tried to imagine her in a corporate setting in London and felt a sudden surge of protectiveness. She'd be eaten alive by women like Elyse; corporate queens who ate low-carb nails with semi-skimmed blood for breakfast.

He smiled to himself. Estelle would go ballistic if he ever described her as 'sweet'. Would she shoot another arrow at him if he did? The prospect was far too tempting.

Pushing open their office door, he was confronted by three

dogs—two actual ones, and one downward one as Estelle's magnificent backside presented itself to him.

His dick immediately sprang to life and he dashed to his desk, Chester and Joy following.

'Hi!' Estelle called out. 'Just doing a bit of yoga.'

'Do you always do it to the Spice Girls?'

'Usually, yeah. They're very spiritual.'

'They are?'

She stood, raising her arms to the ceiling. She'd swapped her baggy jeans and jumper for a light grey Lycra vest top and leggings, and the fabric stretched deliciously over her ample curves.

'Yes,' she replied. '"2 Become 1" is about dissolving duality in the search for union with the divine.'

Folding at the waist, she placed her hands on the mat by her feet. James's mouth watered and his hands itched to pull her onto his rock-hard cock.

'And "Mama" is about honouring Gaia, the personification of the earth.' She jumped back into a plank, lowered to the floor, then pushed into another downward dog.

As if tuning into his raging sexual need, Chester and Joy attempted to shag him again.

'Down,' he growled.

'What, me?'

'No,' he replied, shifting to get comfortable. 'Your sexually incontinent dogs.'

She grinned at him from under her armpit. 'Maybe they're picking up on your unmet needs.'

You have no idea... Jamming his earbuds in, he selected a track of white noise, then opened up his laptop and went to an online store. If Estelle wanted to exercise in front of him, then two could play that game.

Chester barked, and he glanced up. Estelle was standing in front of him.

He pulled out an earbud. 'Yes?'

'What are you listening to?'

Changing the track, he routed it through the speakers of his laptop.

Her face lit up. '"The Imperial March" from *Star Wars*! I was right!'

'It would appear so.'

He held her gaze.

She broke first, turning her attention to the fur Q, and running her fingers through the pink pile. 'Have we had any CVs in?'

He turned off the music, leaving only the sound of the Spice Girls. 'No.'

'Oh.' She frowned. 'That's not good. There's already too much to do.'

His stomach knotted. Their workload was only a small part of the problem. The lack of money was a far bigger issue, and one she could never find out about.

'Well, maybe yoga could wait till outside of work hours?' he asked.

'Why?'

'So you've got more time to, I don't know, do your job?'

'It's helping my creativity. And anyway, you do personal stuff as well.'

'I do? What?'

'Who's Char?'

He tensed. He didn't want to give Estelle anything, but at the same time a stupid part of him wanted her to know Char wasn't a secret girlfriend.

'Is she the woman whose lips your cheek crashed into last week?'

'No.'

'Oh, so another one then. Charlotte? Charlene? Char-maine? Charcuterie? Chargrilled Chicken?'

'She's my sister.'

Her eyebrows raised. 'Oh.'

James dipped his head towards his laptop, starting programmes to give him something to do other than go through the can of worms he'd just opened up.

'What's she like? Is she nice?'

He ignored her.

'What's "Char" short for?'

His fingers tapped faster.

'Is she older or younger than you?'

James felt like he was a closed window, and Estelle was a fly repeatedly bashing herself against him, hoping he would open up.

'Can I see a picture? Does she live here?'

His frustration was mounting. 'Don't you have something you need to be doing?'

'We're bonding.'

James bit back a sigh. He'd stipulated Estelle had to work with him because he knew it would piss Henry off, and because he fancied her. But their relationship was never going to be anything more than colleagues, and he was never going to let her see the side of his life he'd so successfully hidden for the last twenty-five years.

'Is she blonde?'

He snapped the lid of his laptop shut. 'No. She's not. And my personal life is none of your business.' He stood. 'I'm going to work with Max today.' Grabbing his laptop, he strode to the door. Chester and Joy followed him. 'Stay,' he said to them, then left the office.

'What's happened to your hand?' Eveline cried as she opened the back door of the rectory for Estelle the next week.

'James Hunter-Savage,' she muttered.

Eveline's hand flew to her chest. 'Are you okay? Did you hit him?'

'I wish,' she replied, following her best friend through into the kitchen.

Jack was at the Aga, an apron over his clothes. 'Morning, Stelle,' he said over his shoulder. 'Bacon sandwich?'

'Yes please, and a cup of tea, and a slice of cake if you've got one. Failing that, a custard cream.'

'Darling,' Eveline said to him. 'Look what James did to Estelle!'

Jack's gaze fell to her bandaged hand and the spatula he was holding dropped with a clatter. 'What the hell did he do?'

'Nothing! James didn't do anything,' Estelle replied quickly, before Jack escalated the issue to Henry levels.

'Then what happened?'

'I was making him another gift and accidentally cut myself.'

'Oh, thank goodness you're alright,' Eveline said.

Jack went to his wife. 'Sit down, angel.' He guided her to a chair and knelt by her side, holding her hand, his thumb making circles across the back of it. 'Just breathe. Estelle's fine, okay? Nothing to worry about.'

Estelle narrowed her eyes. Jack was being even more attentive to her friend than usual.

'So, er, how did you hurt yourself?' Eveline asked her.

Both she and Jack were staring at her with concern. Estelle suddenly felt very foolish.

She sat at the table. 'I borrowed Finn's angle grinder and was cutting up forks,' she mumbled. 'And one of them pinged off and cut my hand.'

'Have you been to the doctor?' Jack demanded.

'Yes, I did. I promise it's okay.'

In the silence that followed, Estelle knew all of them were thinking about the time last year when a cut on Eveline's arm had become infected and she'd nearly died.

'So!' Eveline said, with tension-diffusing enthusiasm. 'What were you making with all the forks?'

'An enormous letter U.'

'I don't understand. Why a U? And why out of forks?'

'Angel...' Jack began.

Estelle watched the penny drop.

'Oh... A fork U...'

The corner of Jack's mouth twitched, and Estelle knew he was trying not to laugh.

'Did James like the last gift you made for him?' Eveline asked.

She shrugged, not wanting to admit that he'd seemed delighted.

Getting to his feet, Jack went back to the Aga, whistling 'Love is in the Air'.

'Bugger off, Newton,' Estelle muttered at him.

Eveline reached across the table and gave her unbandaged hand a squeeze. 'Do you think it might be time for you to bury whatever hatchet you and Henry have been wielding since you were children, and make an effort to get on with James?'

'It's pointless.'

'How come?'

Estelle threw her hands in the air. 'Because he doesn't want that either! Whenever I ask him anything personal, he shuts me down. He's like a professional tombstone.'

'But surely that's a good thing? It means you can just get on with the job?'

'It's miserable. I don't know if he lo—likes or hates me.'

Jack changed the tune he was whistling to the Beatles song 'He Loves You, Yeah, Yeah, Yeah.'

Estelle ignored him.

'So, you're unhappy because you can't get a rise out of him?' Eveline asked.

'I dunno. I can't get a handle on him. Sometimes I think a tiny part of him might actually be nice, but then he blows it by being an arsehole.'

'In what way?'

'Saying we have to have cheap and crappy burger vans feeding people at the festival. Making me run every tiny expense past him. Not giving me any updates on hiring staff. Hiding his girlfriend—'

'I thought he told you he didn't have a girlfriend?'

'Then who's the "beautiful blonde" living next door?'

'Have you actually seen her?' Jack asked, placing a pile of bacon sandwiches on the table.

'No, but Max has.'

'This is the bloke left behind when the rest of the Excelsior staff ran away?' Jack continued. 'The one who you said was, and I quote, "shifty AF".'

'I actually said "shifty as fuck". If you're going to quote me, Newton, get it right. Although props for not swearing.'

Jack rolled his eyes.

'The point is, my lovely friend,' Eveline said, 'you have no way of knowing she actually exists. And why does it matter if he has a girlfriend or not? You're there to work with James, not date him. Isn't that the case?'

Estelle took a huge bite of a bacon sandwich to avoid answering.

Jack brought mugs of tea to the table, then dropped a kiss on Eveline's head and sat next to her.

Eveline gazed at him as if he'd just cured all known diseases and all future ones as well. 'Thank you.'

Jack's smile was so broad, Estelle thought it might split his face in two. She glanced between the two of them as they stared at each other, their eyes becoming liquid.

Holy shit. She placed her sandwich down. 'You're pregnant.'

Eveline turned, her eyes sparkling with happy tears, and nodded.

'Oh, my god, congratulations!' Estelle leant over the table and grabbed them both into a hug. 'I'm so happy for you! When are you due?'

'It's very early days. So we aren't getting our hopes up.'

'And we're not telling anyone,' Jack added.

'You know I won't say a word,' Estelle said, sitting back down. 'How are you feeling?'

'The same,' Eveline replied. 'I can't quite believe it's actually happened.'

A lump filled Estelle's throat. This was her friend's dream come true—a handsome, doting husband and a baby on the way. She took another bite of her sandwich and tried to chew, but her jaw clenched tight with pain as she tried to hold back her own emotion.

Giving up the attempt, she pulled a tissue from her pocket and rubbed the tears away. 'Ucking ell!' She swallowed her mouthful of food. 'You know I don't do tears.'

Eveline took her hand and Jack reached across the table to squeeze her shoulder.

'Circle of trust, Stelle. We'll never let on that our baby's godmother cried when she found out Eveline was pregnant.'

'Godmother? *Me?*'

Eveline beamed as she nodded. 'If you'll accept?'

Don't cry, don't cry, don't fucking cry!

Her lower lip was trembling as she took a breath. 'I'd be honoured,' she whispered.

Eveline's face lit up as if her answer had not been a foregone conclusion. 'Thank you so much!'

Estelle blinked rapidly, but her facial muscles were not powerful enough to hold back the flood of tears.

'For fuck's sake!' she cried.

Jack's smile was as big as his wife's. 'We love you, Stelle.'

'Shut up, Newton! I can't cope.'

Eveline laughed. 'You've got the biggest heart, Estelle. If anyone can handle love, it's you.'

'Bollocks,' she mumbled, then blew her nose. 'I'm going to have to pretend I've got hay fever this morning, so Hunter-Savage doesn't see through my armour.'

'You could let him see this side of you?' Eveline suggested.

Estelle shook her head. 'When hell freezes over.' She glanced at Jack. 'You need to take me to work now before I start skipping down the high street, singing about rainbows and kittens.'

Eveline giggled. 'That's quite an image.'

'Yeah, and one that will live in your imagination only.' She picked up her sandwich and stood. 'Come on, Daddy Newton, let's go.'

'WHAT TIME SHOULD I PICK YOU UP LATER?' JACK ASKED AS he drove Estelle down country lanes towards Shoscombe Manor.

'Four-ish? Alan is going to ring me when they've finished working on the Defender, so I'll let you know. As long as I get her before the garage shuts at five, it'll be okay.'

'Cool.'

'Thanks for doing this. I didn't want to ask Henry in case he caused a scene with James.'

'Any time, Stelle.' Jack indicated and turned left. 'Henry's not calmed down then?'

Estelle huffed. 'No. It's like he's been saving all the anger up since he was thirteen and now can't stop it coming out. He's exercising even more at the moment, as if he's preparing for some kind of twatty CEO cage fight.'

'That doesn't sound good.'

'It's not. Thank god he's got Libby to talk some sense into him. Can you stop here?'

Jack eased to a halt at the side of the road. 'You don't want me to drive you in?'

She shook her head. 'I'll walk the rest of the way. I need the time to get my game face back on.'

He grinned, then started singing the theme tune from *Rocky*.

Estelle rolled her eyes, got out of the car, and closed the door behind her. 'I'll ring you later,' she called through the window.

Jack gave her a wave and pulled away.

. . .

Lifting her chest and taking a deep breath of wintery air, Estelle strode along the muddy verge towards the entrance to the manor. She loved all seasons, but now January was nearly done, she yearned for the first signs of spring.

But as each day passed, it brought them closer to the festival. Despite her ideas and all the planning she'd done the previous year, it still felt like they were light years away from making it happen.

She passed through the stone gateposts towards the house. The garage doors were shut and she couldn't see Max's car. Letting herself into the office wing, she found it empty. She'd emailed James and Max the previous day, letting them know she would be late. Were they out at a meeting?

The office she shared with James felt unnaturally quiet without him or her dogs. His desk was immaculately tidy, the fur Q sitting in the middle behind his closed laptop. Hers was its usual mess, but a manilla envelope, labeled 'CVs', was resting on her chair.

Had James finally found some good candidates?

Sitting, Estelle opened it up and flicked through them. Confusion and anger swirled inside her like the start of a storm. *This* was who James thought was suitable? A load of completely inexperienced pretty girls, all under the age of twenty-one?

Fucker.

Shoving them back inside the envelope, she left it on her desk and strode to the kitchen. It was ten o'clock, and a headache was brewing from caffeine withdrawal. She stared at the coffee machine, the instructions still in Italian, and pressed a few buttons, but nothing happened.

Before she could stop herself, she left the kitchen, went to the door leading to the main house and knocked.

No reply.

Trying the handle, the door opened.

Oh, my god. Adrenaline spiked through her. It was like discovering the back of the wardrobe was no longer solid, but now led to an unknown land.

'Hello?' she called hesitantly through the crack. 'James?'

Silence.

Still standing on her side of the door, Estelle pushed it open and stared down the corridor. The parquet floor was old but clean, and the walls were white and empty. Used to panelling, paintings, and suits of armour cluttering her family home, this one looked naked.

'Hello?' Her voice echoed back to her.

Feeling like a naughty schoolgirl, she stepped across the threshold, half expecting to be met with a siren, a poisoned dart, or a rockfall.

'James?'

Continuing forward to the first door, Estelle knocked. When there was no reply, she poked her head in. It was a living room; the sofas upholstered in animal print fabric, the low tables made from glass and polished chrome. It was the absolute opposite of what she imagined James's taste to be. Was this what his mum chose? His not-girlfriend?

Back in the corridor, she noticed the door at the far end had an inch gap at the bottom, revealing lino. Was this a kitchen? Would they have instant coffee? A machine in English?

Pushing open the door, Estelle entered a large kitchen. The room was a mismatch of styles, as if previous owners had taken a kitchen from the nineteen sixties, and turned half of it into an industrial one. The cupboards were plain beige, with stains around the handles from age and use, but the cooker was five-foot wide and stainless steel, and the fridge big enough to grace an American McMansion.

Going to the kettle, she flicked it on, then opened the nearest cupboard. Inside were glass jars of instant coffee, instant hot chocolate, instant tea granules and Ovaltine. Repressing a shudder, she pulled out the coffee. It would taste like shit, but it would do the job. Beside the kettle was a wooden mug tree with identical leopard-patterned, gold-rimmed mugs hanging off it.

Resisting the urge to snoop any further, she stared at the kettle as it came to the boil, her eyes unfocused as her thoughts returned to Eveline.

'Oh, hello.'

Whipping around, Estelle's hand jumped to her chest. 'Jesus Christ!' she gasped as her conscious mind attempted to reassure her unconscious one that the figure was not a threat.

A blonde woman stood just inside the door.

Estelle blinked as rumour, conjecture and myth converged into flesh and blood.

'I'm Elyse,' the woman said, her heels clacking on the floor as she came forward with a manicured hand extended.

So, this is the mysterious 'E'... Estelle tried not to stare as she took in everything about Elyse, the perfectly straight blonde hair that grazed her shoulders, the pressed white shirt and pencil skirt that revealed just how slim she was, and her beautifully symmetrical face.

She took the woman's hand, hoping her own nails were clean. 'I'm Estelle.'

'I know. Do you need anything?'

Estelle's cheeks heated. She'd broken into this woman's home and was helping herself to her stuff without asking.

'I wanted a coffee, but I don't know how to use the machine in the office. The door was open. Sorry.'

Elyse smiled and went to the fridge. 'It's not a problem at all. Milk?'

'Yeah, thanks.'

'I know what James is like about that coffee machine. He doesn't like anyone touching it. I tried to use it once at the flat in London and he got very cross.' Elyse rolled her eyes. 'Men, eh?'

How long have they been together?

Opening a drawer, Elyse took out a teaspoon, then went to Estelle's side and scooped coffee granules into the mug. 'Sugar?'

'No, thanks.'

'Oh, yes. I should have remembered.' Elyse grinned at her. 'He said you're sweet enough.'

Estelle tried to smile but her stomach was turning over. Elyse seemed to know everything about her. Did she and James discuss her in bed at night? Was she some kind of joke to them?

'Is he around?'

'Not at the moment,' Elyse replied, making Estelle's coffee, then putting the dirty spoon by the side of the sink. 'Can I get you anything to eat? We've got some pain au chocolat.'

'No, thank you.'

'Green smoothie? I was about to make myself one.'

'I should really get back.'

Elyse smiled. 'It's lovely to finally meet you.'

Estelle didn't think she could hate James any more than at this moment. Elyse seemed really nice. Why did he have to deny her existence?

'How long have you been together?' she blurted.

Elyse's face froze, then cracked to reveal a core of desolation. 'We're on a break,' she whispered, her gaze falling to the floor.

Without thinking, Estelle reached out to touch her arm. 'I'm so sorry.'

Elyse raised her head, her pale blue eyes glistening like the surface of the sea. 'No, I'm sorry.' She sniffed. 'I've only just met you and I'm blubbing like a baby.'

Estelle was torn between wanting to hug her, and finding James so she could immediately run him over with a combine harvester. 'It's fine, honestly. I've got five siblings and at any given moment, at least one of them is crying.'

'Thank you. It's been really hard, especially as we're still living together.'

'What happened?'

'Our relationship has always been very intense. Very sexual...'

Estelle's stomach turned, as unbidden images of James and Elyse in bed together jabbed at her mind's eye.

'But he can be very cold,' Elyse continued. 'And he said—' She broke off, her lower lip wobbling, 'he wanted us to cancel our future, er, *plans*...'

Did that arsehole break their engagement?

'And that we should see other people...' Elyse took a gulping breath. 'But I don't want to. I only want to be with him. I love him.'

Estelle's heart squeezed at the sight of Elyse's tears. Despite knowing how low James could go, this behaviour was scraping the bottom of the bastard barrel in hell.

Oh, god, the CVs. Was James using the festival as a way of finding new women to screw, then screw over?

Elyse's eyes widened. 'Don't worry, you're safe. He would never go for you.'

Estelle knew that, but the masochistic side of her still

wanted Elyse to voice the reasons why James Hunter-Savage wouldn't touch her with a barge pole. 'Why not?'

Elyse's face turned a delicate shade of pink. 'You're very attractive... But James has a type...' She twisted a strand of blonde hair around her finger as if to emphasise the difference between the two of them. 'And I'm it.'

Grinding her teeth, Estelle nodded. 'I'm really sorry, Elyse. Please, let me know if there's anything I can do.'

'Thank you,' she whispered. 'That means so much.' Her eyes became liquid again. 'There is one thing...'

'Cut off his balls with a pair of rusty shears?'

Elyse gasped. 'Oh, no!'

'Sorry! I was only joking.' *Kind of...* 'Go on, what can I do?'

'Please don't tell James you saw me. He can get very...'

Estelle's blood ran cold. 'Are you in danger? Has he threatened you?'

'Not in so many words. He's never hurt me.'

'Jesus, Elyse! You need to go to the police! Why are you still living here?'

She shrugged, helplessly. 'I have to. I work for his father.'

'What is this? The fucking mafia? Do you need money? A place to stay? Come and live with me. We can leave right now. I can help you find another job. I'll ask my best friend about charities that deal with modern slavery. We'll make sure you're safe.'

Elyse shook her head so fast, her face was a blur. 'No, I'm fine, I promise. Kevin is lovely.'

'*Kevin?*'

'James's dad. He's a bit rough around the edges, but he's very sweet. James and I will keep trying to save our relationship, and if we can't, then I only have to wait till the beginning of July, then he'll be gone.'

'Gone? Where?'

'Back to London. He doesn't want to organise the festival. He's only doing it to help his dad. And he hates Somerset.'

Estelle's blood went from ice to thermonuclear in the time it took her to draw breath. James had made Henry's life hell, he'd not told her he owned BDE Entertainment until she'd signed the amended contract, he didn't give a shit about making the festival a success, and now he didn't even *like* Somerset?

Elyse clutched Estelle's hands. 'Please don't say anything to him! For me?'

'I won't, I promise. But if you need to get out, come to the livery. If I'm not there, then ask for Molly. Okay?'

Elyse nodded. 'You'd better go. He might be back now.'

Estelle looked longingly at the cup of instant coffee. If she took it, then James would know she'd been in the main house. Going to the door, she peeked around it into the corridor. Still empty. Nodding at Elyse, she slipped through. She wouldn't say a word to James about meeting her, but she was going to make him wish he'd never been born.

❧ 13 ❧

Despite her power walk, Estelle's feet made no sound as she strode towards the end office she shared with James. Because she'd come via the garage and rectory that morning, she'd worn a pair of clean trainers and hadn't bothered to take them off.

Hearing a voice inside the room, she paused at the closed door and leaned in to listen.

'Here? In bumfuck nowhere?' James's voice was louder than normal, as if he was on the phone. 'Somerset's a pussy desert, mate. Drier than your girlfriend on date night.'

Bile rose up into Estelle's throat.

James laughed. 'Fuck you? You're not my type.'

Her head pounding, Estelle didn't know whether to keep listening or barge in.

'The women are alright if you like them in wellies with straw in their hair,' James continued, 'but I'd stick to London skirt if I were you.'

Estelle's fingers raked through her curls. A few days ago,

she'd come into work with a piece of straw stuck in them. Was he talking about her?

'Nah, I'm not here long, just gotta help the old man out for a few months. I'll be back by the close of Wimbledon. Get me a ticket for the women's finals, would you? Give me something to look forward to apart from banging your mum.'

Shaking with rage, Estelle shouldered open the door. It bashed against the inside wall.

James leapt to his feet, immediately cutting the call. 'Estelle—'

'You utter, *utter* bastard.'

His face was pale. 'That's not me.'

She advanced on him. 'Really? Well, who was it then? *Kevin?*'

'It's just an act.'

She gave him a slow handclap. 'And the Oscar goes to... James Hunter-Savage.'

'It's not what you think.'

Her blood pressure was rising and her heartbeat pulsed in her temples. 'Do you think I'm hard of hearing? Stupid?' She made a show of looking around the room and under the desks. 'Yep, just as I deduced from outside the room, there's only one "person" I could have heard being such a total wanker, and that's you.'

James ran his hands through his hair. 'Can you let me explain?'

Estelle crossed her arms, trying to contain her fury. 'Go on.'

'It was just someone from Conqueror. That's how we are at work—'

'Henry's not like that.'

James let out a terse breath. 'It doesn't mean anything. It's not who I really am.'

'Bullshit. It's exactly who you are. You use and abuse everyone.' She grabbed the envelope containing the CVs, stalked across the room and slapped it against his chest. 'And because Somerset is such a "pussy desert", you're using the festival and your position as boss of Big Dickhead Entertainment to catfish unsuspecting young women. It's the most disgusting abuse of power and takes sexual predation to another level.'

He took the envelope from her and opened it. Her fight-or-flight reflex was now leaning towards fleeing. She'd never felt scared around James before, but after what Elyse had said, she was now very much aware he had a good six inches on her and considerably more muscle. The door was still wide open and she was closest to it. She tensed, getting ready to run.

James tore the pile of CVs in half. 'This had nothing to do with me.' Going to the recycling bin by the window, he threw them in. 'It was Max.'

'Bullshit.'

'He showed me his selection last week. I chucked them out and told him to re-advertise. That's the last straw. I'm sacking him immediately.'

Estelle forced herself to stay put between James and the door. 'You can't do that. He's the only one of us who's ever done this before.'

'I don't give a fuck. He's a backstabbing, underhand little shit and—'

'Oh, that's rich coming from you!'

'Meaning?'

'Stealing Henry's clients at Conqueror, letting me sign the contract with your company not knowing you were behind it, horn-dogging your way across the county and breaking people's hearts—'

'What on earth are you talking about?'

'I've never met anyone as soulless as you in my entire life.'

James crossed his arms. 'And you're so perfect? With your

complete lack of professionalism and childish pranks? I've had arseholes beeping me all week before I realised you'd slapped a sticker that says "overcompensating" on the back of my car.'

Estelle paused, her mind whirling. She'd completely forgotten she'd done that.

'It's ruined the paintwork. Do you know how much it's going to cost to get fixed? No, of course you don't, because *Lady* Estelle Foxbrooke has never had to worry about money before—'

'You don't know the first thing about me.'

'And you've got me all figured out.'

'Based on *your* words and *your* actions. You don't even want to do the festival and can't wait to leave once it's over.'

'Well, for once you've got something right. The last thing I ever wanted was to have anything to do with your family. And I'd rather spend six months in a salt mine in Siberia than holed up in Somerset trying to pull this shit together. The only reason I'm still here is because I've got no fucking choice.'

'And you think I do?' she yelled.

A movement in the doorway caught her eye. She whipped around to see a couple in their sixties, dressed in dark suits, standing just inside the room. Max was behind them, a smirk plastered on his face.

No!

'Max, you're sacked,' James snarled. 'Get the fuck off the property.'

Max's grin faltered for a second, then he flipped James the bird and left.

'Can I help you?' James asked the couple, his tone still harsh.

The man drew himself up. 'I'm Councillor Mark Pensford, from the district council licensing committee, and this is

Councillor Sarah Hughes. We were invited to discuss your plans for a music and arts festival at Foxbrooke Manor.'

James turned to Estelle. 'Did you know about this?'

She shook her head, reaching for the side of her desk as her knees buckled. *It's over. Everything's over.*

'Please excuse us,' James said to the councillors, his mouth forced into a smile. 'It's been a bit of a morning and tempers have become a little frayed.' He moved forward, his hand extended. 'James Hunter-Savage.'

Mark and Sarah stepped back.

'Shall we go to the conference room?' he continued. 'Estelle, why don't you see the councillors through and I'll fire up the coffee machine?'

'No, thank you,' Mark said. He turned to Sarah. 'I think we've seen and heard enough?'

The woman nodded. 'Despite my previous experiences dealing with your family,' she said to Estelle, 'I came to this meeting with an open mind. However, the unpleasant scene my colleague and I have just witnessed reinforces my opinion that your event should not go ahead.'

'We can't speak on behalf of the rest of the committee,' Mark added, 'but we'll be recommending they join us in voting to reject your application.'

'But you haven't seen our plans,' James argued.

'I can't see how that would make any difference,' Sarah said. 'If the principal stakeholders can't even be civil to one another or respect their staff, then what hope do you have of pulling off a three-day event?'

The councillors turned and left the office.

'Wait up,' James said, running after them and closing the door behind him.

Estelle stumbled to the chaise longue and sank her head into her hands, her nervous system whining in her ears like a swarm of mosquitos. She'd spent the last decade trying to save Foxbrooke Manor from her father's crazy schemes, and now her own idea was going to sink the estate in one fell swoop because she'd lost her temper at the worst possible time.

Her phone buzzed from her back pocket and she pulled it out.

Henry.

'I've fucked up!' she stammered as she accepted the call. 'Henry, I've totally fucked everything up.'

'What's happened? Are you okay?'

Adrenaline was making her body shake as if she was sitting in an ice bath. 'I screamed at James in front of two of the councillors from the licensing committee and now they won't back our application. The festival's over.'

'What about the other committee members? When's the vote? Can you appeal?'

'It won't work, Henry. They all hate Dad. They shoot down in flames almost everything he tries to do. I hoped it would be different because the festival is me, not him, but I lost the plot in front of them. It's all my fault.'

'It can't be. What about James?'

'I started it, Henry. It doesn't matter what he said. I'm the one who kicked off.' She took a shuddering breath. 'God, Henry. All these years I bad-mouthed Dad, and now we could lose the estate because of me.'

'We won't. I promise—'

'I'm so sorry. I'm so fucking sorry.'

'Hey! It's all going to be okay. Come home and we can talk to Dad, try and brainstorm a way forward.'

'I can't. The Defender's at the garage.'

'I'll come and pick you up. I need to have words with Hunter-Savage, anyway.'

'Jesus! No, Henry, it'll just make everything worse!'

'Estelle. You tried to make it work, and it hasn't. He needs to hand the money over and walk away.'

She went to the door and peeked into the corridor.

Empty.

'Look, you know I don't like to admit I was wrong,' she said into the phone. 'But this morning's cock up is sixty per cent on me.'

Going down the corridor, an engine roared outside. Looking through a window onto the drive, she saw James's car accelerate away, the back wheels spinning on the gravel.

'He's just left, anyway.'

'James?'

'Yeah.' Estelle ran a hand into her hair, tugging on the roots as if it would help ease her headache. 'I'm going to walk through the fields back to the livery and spend the rest of the day shovelling shit. I think it's an apt metaphor for how much crap I've landed us in.'

'Please, come for dinner tonight? We can talk it through then.'

'Maybe. I'm so sorry.'

'Don't be. We'll sort it. I'm going to fill Dad in now.'

'If you think that would help?'

'We'll see. At least he'll know which of the councillors might be on our side when we appeal.'

AFTER GETTING OFF THE PHONE TO HENRY, ESTELLE WENT around the back of the manor, through the formal gardens, and into the park behind. It was at least an hour's hike through the fields to the livery and she needed the time away from everyone to process what had just happened.

The clouds were low and angry, the air filled with drizzle. It clung to her clothes as she made her way up the steep slope, coalescing into cold drops that found their way under her collar to run down her neck.

She forced herself to walk faster, her anger at James, and herself, fuelling her pace. She knew she'd been unprofessional in her outburst, but meeting Elyse, then hearing James's words on the phone, had made the red mist descend until she was choking with rage.

The festival was her baby. Finally, something for the estate that was nothing to do with her parents. She'd been so excited to work with Excelsior, but now she was more miserable than she'd ever been.

'You shine brighter than anyone else.'

She kicked a clod of earth with her muddy shoe as she remembered James's words to her at the Winter Ball. In that moment, she'd fallen just a little bit in love with the nameless, faceless stranger who'd saved her life and held her so confidently in his arms.

'Somerset's a pussy desert, mate.'

Raising her face to the prickling cold of the rain, Estelle let out a scream of frustration. *That* was the real James, the one Henry had warned her about, the one who'd treated Elyse so badly, the one who lied, manipulated and bullied at every turn.

BY THE TIME ESTELLE GOT TO THE LIVERY, THE EXERCISE had done nothing to take the edge off her anger. Changing into her wellies, she went to work, shovelling the heavy clods of dung and straw out of the stables until her arms and back screamed at her to stop.

'Bad day?' Molly asked as she arrived with a steaming cup of coffee.

Estelle took it. 'Thanks, and yes. Even shittier than what's in this wheelbarrow.'

'Want to talk about it?'

'No.'

'You do know we've got a load of young girls desperate to do this job? You really don't have to do it.'

'I needed to.'

'You could take Duke out?'

Estelle eyed Chester and Joy, who were sitting on the other side of the stable door, waiting patiently for her to do something more interesting that they could join in with.

'Yeah, you're right. I should have done that first.' She slurped as much hot coffee as her stomach could stand, then tossed the dregs down the drain. 'Thanks, Moll.'

Molly took the empty mug. 'Anytime. Now leave the rest of this and get going.'

Estelle nodded and went to the tack room, whistling for her dogs. She wanted to keep exercising until she was so tired that an immediate and dreamless sleep was guaranteed.

An hour and a half later, Estelle trotted back into the yard on Duke, sweating and streaked with mud from when she'd fallen off after losing her balance.

Molly dashed out of the stables. 'You've got to ring your brother.'

'Which one? What's happened?'

'Henry. He said it was an emergency.'

Estelle pulled her phone from her pocket. She'd had it on silent and had missed several calls from Henry, one from Jack and two from Alan at the garage.

'Fuck!' She glanced at her watch—six thirty. 'I've totally forgotten about picking up the Defender.'

'Are they still open?'

'No, they closed at five.'

'Do you need me to take you anywhere?'

'I don't know. Let me ring Henry and see what he wants.'

The call to her brother connected immediately.

'Estelle? You need to get over here. Now. Dad's gone and done something catastrophically stupid.'

'What?'

'He's invited the Hunter-Savages for dinner. They're arriving in the next five minutes.'

❧ 14 ❧

Dropping down a gear, James pressed on the accelerator pedal and the Ferrari shot forward. Swerving across the middle lane into the inside one, he undertook the morons holding him up, then back across to the outside lane of the M4 heading east.

After the councillors had refused to see reason, he wanted to get as far away from Somerset, and Estelle, as possible. He could have gone north, but instead, like a homing pigeon, got on the motorway towards London.

What on earth had Estelle been on about, accusing him of horn-dogging his way across the county? *If only*. It had been fifteen months since he'd last had sex and it felt like fifteen years.

His stomach tensed as he remembered the conversation Estelle had overheard. *Fuck*. He'd distanced himself completely from his former colleagues at Conqueror. None of them knew why he'd left, and he wanted to keep it that way. But if anyone could help him find a way back to his London life, it was the well-connected Sebastian Mayfield.

So, on the phone, he'd slipped back into the skin of an alpha City-boy. It had been a persona he'd crafted and honed since the age of eight, and the crude banter was second nature. Most of the time he didn't think twice about it, but around his family, or women, he left it at the door like a dirty coat.

Swallowing a swell of nausea, he relived what Estelle had heard him say. Her car hadn't been in the drive that morning, so he'd had no idea she was in the building. He knew full well he'd sounded like an arsehole. It didn't matter that he hadn't meant any of it or that the words had sounded bitter in his mouth. He'd said them and she'd heard them. How did he come back from that?

And if that wasn't bad enough, Max had detonated two hate bombs that morning. The first by retrieving the CVs from the bin and giving them to Estelle. And the second by not informing either of them of the meeting with the licensing committee, then bringing the councillors in for front row seats to their argument.

Fucker.

Hands clenched around the leather steering wheel, James's right foot itched to slam to the floor. He forced it to remain still as the average speed check signs appeared by the side of the road. *Screw smart motorways.* What a waste of a high-performance car.

Signalling left, he pulled onto the slip road for a service station. He needed coffee, and he needed to think.

TWO HOURS LATER, JAMES WAS PARKED UP OUTSIDE HIS London flat and no closer to a solution. Even if he walked away from the festival, and his parents, he couldn't come back here. Until his tenants' lease was up, he had nowhere to live, and even if he found somewhere to crash, he had no job prospects.

Flicking through the contacts on his phone, he assessed each one for potential. There was no time to retrain, so he'd need a job he could wing. Sales? *That* he could do. But what? And where?

And even if he stayed in Somerset and tried to save the festival, surely it was now dead in the water? James hadn't spent much time there, but he knew how small-minded and parochial people could be. The councillors had heard him slagging off their home county. That was on par with telling them their children were ugly or deliberately running over their cat.

Getting out of the car, he started down the busy street, weaving around people shouting into their phones, breathing in the polluted air as if it were perfume, and letting the sounds of sirens soothe his frayed nerves. His stomach growled, but he couldn't go to one of his usual haunts. He didn't want to be seen, nor have to field questions he couldn't give an honest answer to.

He found a pub he'd never been to before, ordered food and a beer, then sat at the back to try and work out what to do.

By mid-afternoon, every idea he'd scrawled on the back of a napkin had been crossed out. Estelle still hadn't given him her mobile number, so he couldn't even call her to attempt to make amends.

He fired off an email.

From: James Hunter-Savage
    To: Estelle Foxbrooke
    Subject: Moving forward (again)
    Estelle,
    We need to talk about what happened this morning. I apol-

ogise for leaving so abruptly. I felt it necessary to prevent saying things that would further inflame the situation. I do not have your mobile number, however mine is below.

Please call me at your earliest convenience,

James

AS HE STARED AT HIS PHONE, IT RANG.

Mum.

He picked up the call. 'Hi—'

'Babe, where are you?'

'London. Why?'

'London?' his mother screeched. 'What are you doing there? You need to get home! Now!'

James sighed. He'd had enough drama for one day. 'Why?'

'The Duke of Somerset's invited us all for tea!'

'What?'

'He rang the house half an hour ago. Said there'd been an almighty eff up and we had to get together to sort it out.'

'No. That's not happening. I'll deal with it.'

'But your dad said yes! And now I'm in a state 'cos I don't know what to wear!'

James stood. 'You're not going. I'm driving back now. Put me on the phone to Dad.'

Striding out of the pub with his phone clamped to his ear, James heard his mother's feet as she ran, then her voice. 'Kev, babe, James is in London and he said we're not to go.'

'Bollocks to that,' his father shouted in the background.

'Mum, give the phone to Dad.'

There was a short silence, then his father was in his ear. 'Jamesy-boy, you and Lady Foxbrooke have right cocked this up. I don't give a monkey's how we've done things in the past. It's not just your rep on the line, it's our home.'

'What do you mean, babe?' his mother cried.

'Nothing, Bev, babe,' his father said to her. 'Just a turn of speech.' There was the sound of a door closing, then Kevin's voice was back, growling in James's ear. 'Your mum wanted this house and to be friends with nobs. You're not losing both of them for her, Jamesey-boy. Got it?'

'You won't. I can sort it.'

'Starting with being on time for dinner. They want the three of us there at six-thirty. Don't be late.'

'Dad—'

But his father had ended the call.

'Fuck!' James sprinted down the road. Thank god he had a fast car. He could just about get there in time and stop this from happening.

As soon as he saw flashing lights in his rear-view mirror, James pulled into the middle lane.

Unfortunately, the unmarked police car followed him, signalling him to pull over.

Two minutes later on the hard shoulder, James realised he wasn't going to get back in time to stop his parents from leaving Shoscombe Manor.

Turning off Foxbrooke High Street, James followed a battered Vauxhall Corsa down Church Lane towards Saint Saviour's and Foxbrooke Manor. He didn't know who was in the car in front, but was grateful they were also driving ten miles an hour over the speed limit.

The Corsa accelerated through the stone pillars that marked the entrance to the manor, along the drive, then squealed to an emergency stop right outside the front doors. The passenger door opened and Estelle dashed out.

James slammed his car to a halt and followed her.

'Did you know about this?' she snapped at him over her shoulder.

'A couple of hours ago,' he replied, moving forward to open the door for her.

She shouldered past him into the house. 'And why didn't you stop it?'

'I tried. But I was in London.'

Stopping, she stared at him, a look of disbelief then contempt flashing across her features. 'Doing what?'

'Trying to think of a way to save the festival.'

'And you had to go to London to do that?'

He shrugged, then his gaze left her flushed face and travelled down her body. It looked like she'd fallen off a horse into a muddy ditch.

'I sent you an email,' he said, trying to keep his tone even. 'I would have called, but you refuse to give me your number.'

She opened her mouth, then shut it again.

'Could I ask you for five minutes of privacy?'

Her eyes widened. 'For what?'

'I don't want you to meet my parents.' He hesitated. What lie could he tell her? 'They're not like me. They're extremely quiet and reserved. Can you wait somewhere else, *anywhere* else, while I remove them from your family home?'

Her eyebrows nearly hit her hairline.

'Please?'

'Er, okay. I'll—'

'Estelle!'

James turned to see Henry rushing along the corridor towards them. As he approached, he slowed, his posture rigid.

James widened his stance and lifted his chin.

Estelle stepped between them. 'Henry, James was just about to collect his parents.'

Henry's forehead creased. 'But they've only just got here.'

'It doesn't matter,' James replied.

'Okay. But, er, do you think they'll want to leave?'

'I don't care. I just need to get them out of here.'

James's house of cards was tumbling down. He'd kept his family away from every other aspect of his life for over two decades and now Henry Foxbrooke, the man he'd despised for so many years, knew who they were. James tensed, his hands forming into fists, waiting for Henry to make the slightest joke at their expense.

'Henry,' Estelle said. 'I said I would wait in the kitchen whilst James took his parents home. Why don't you join me?'

'Why?'

'Because apparently they're very quiet and reserved and I think we're probably a bit much for them.'

Henry's mouth dropped open, then his gaze flicked to James.

James stared him down, desperate to have an excuse to punch away his own pain.

'Sweetheart!' Now Henry's girlfriend was running down the corridor. 'Hi Estelle! Hi James!' Libby gasped, her smile trying to cover up the fact she'd obviously run to find them. 'Why don't we all go to the dining room?'

Nobody moved.

'Your dad's decided we should play some games before dinner!' she continued, her smile utterly manic as her eyes bored desperately into Henry's. 'He wants to start with Twister!'

'Jesus Christ,' Henry muttered, his hand moving to his head as if to stop it exploding. He glanced at James. 'I'm sorry.'

Huh? Henry was apologising? For *his* parents?

Henry strode off down the corridor with Libby, and Estelle and James followed. Everyone's feet moved faster until they broke into a jog.

Laughter echoed from a room up ahead. This was it. The moment of ultimate mortification—when Lady Estelle Foxbrooke met Kevin and Beverley Hunter-Savage, née Skinner.

As James followed Henry, Estelle, and Libby through the door, his heart was pounding faster than when he'd been rowing for the line at the Boat Race.

'There they are!' a voice boomed out. 'Come in, come in!'

James's eyes shot to the end of the table where Arthur Foxbrooke was standing and beckoning them forwards. He was wearing one of the t-shirts Kevin had printed, with the aubergine emoji being struck by a lightning bolt.

Arthur pointed to his chest, then at his two wives sitting either side of him who were also wearing the t-shirts. 'Estelle! Look what we got! Aren't they wonderful!'

There was a choked gasp to his right, but James didn't turn to see Estelle's expression. The sight of supermodel and Hollywood actress, Vivienne Boucher-Foxbrooke, and her wife, Dervla, wearing something that belonged on a stag do was bad enough. He didn't need the true horror of the situation reflected on their daughter's face.

'Next time I'll bring more,' Kevin said. 'I didn't know how many Foxbrookes to fit.'

James dragged his gaze from the Duke of Somerset and his two wives, to his father, who was dressed as if wearing the wealth of an East End pawn shop. He had fat diamond studs in his ears and so many gold chains around his neck James was surprised he could remain upright. Every digit on his hand held at least two rings, and his Versace shirt resembled the baroque-style rug on the floor of the room. His mother's outfit was a mishmash of animal prints, as if she was sporting the results of a fashion designer's big game hunt.

'James!' Vivienne cried. 'We're so glad you and Estelle could make it.' She pushed back her chair and came to their side, Dervla following. Estelle's mom kissed James on both cheeks as he stood woodenly, incapable of performing even basic social functions.

Vivienne's nose wrinkled as she took in her daughter. 'Honey, is this the best you can do?'

As Dervla came forward to embrace him like a long-lost son, James risked a glance at Estelle. She looked like a storm cloud about to break.

'Mom,' she spat through gritted teeth. 'I only found out about this ten *minutes* ago.'

'Come and meet James's ma,' Dervla said, taking her arm and pulling her forward. 'This is Beverley.'

His mother stood to greet Estelle and the two women stared at each other. Estelle's eyebrows were drawn together as if trying to work out a complex puzzle. His mother was blinking rapidly, as if attempting to communicate an urgent message to Estelle using morse code.

James's stomach turned to ice. They must have already met.

'How lovely to meet you!' Estelle said warmly, holding out her hand. 'I promise it's clean, but I can't say the same for the rest of me.'

'You too, babe,' Beverley replied, the relief evident on her face. 'And that's my husband, Kevin, over there.'

Across the table, James's dad lurched to his feet with a clanking of chains and leaned across the china and silverware. 'Awright Lady F? Charming to meet you, babe.'

James knew enough about Estelle's body language by now to know she was making a herculean effort to hide the truth of whatever she was thinking or feeling. Her movements were stilted and her smile unnaturally big as she reached to shake his father's hand.

'Please, just call me Estelle,' she said, then glanced at the people sitting at the end of the table. 'Excellent,' she said forcefully. 'Everyone's here.'

James followed her gaze to see three people he didn't know, all staring at him warily.

'These are my other brothers, Leo and Connor,' Estelle said. 'And one of my sisters, Willow. Our other sister, Summer, is currently in France.'

James started towards them and they stood, their posture stiff, as if not knowing whether to punch him or shake his hand.

'I'm James,' he said, wishing he was in an alternate universe where they'd never heard his name before.

The man with blond hair was the nearest. 'I'm Leo. Good to meet you.'

Is it? Really? James took his hand and tried to smile, but his mouth was refusing to comply with the directive from his brain.

'Connor,' said the man sat at the end of the table opposite Arthur.

James shook his hand.

'And I'm Willow,' said a pretty woman with her blonde hair dyed blue and tied into two plaits.

Looking at her, James was suddenly reminded of Estelle's unicorn slippers.

Willow waved him over. 'You're here, between me and Estelle.'

James went around the table and sat as everyone took their seats. What was going to happen now, and when could they leave? He stared at the plate in front of him, wanting to be anywhere other than this living hell. His mother may have dreamed of sitting down to dinner with the Duke of Somerset and his family, but this was James's version of a nightmare.

'Can I get you a drink?' Willow asked him. 'Wine, beer, water?'

'Water, thank you,' he replied, his mouth feeling full of sand. 'I'm driving.'

She poured him a glass. Estelle reached for a bottle of red wine, sloshed it into a tumbler, then drained it in four large gulps.

'Ooh, look!' Leo said. 'Estelle's making an effort! She didn't drink from the bottle!'

His sister ignored him.

Arthur got to his feet, clinking the side of his wine glass with a knife. 'Let's have a toast! To the joining of our families!'

What the fuck? Across the table, Henry's eyes widened and his hands formed into fists. James glared at him.

'Dad!' Estelle hissed.

Arthur ignored her, raising his glass in one hand, the other waving through the air as if he were conducting a choir. 'To the joining of our families!'

James kept his mouth shut.

Pulling a walkie-talkie from a pocket, Arthur pressed a button, then shouted into it. 'Foxbrooke One to the kitchen, over!'

There was a burst of static, then a voice came back. 'Roger that, Foxbrooke One, Red Leader on standby, over.'

James glanced at Estelle. A muscle was twitching in her jaw.

'Roger, roger, jammy dodger, Red Leader. We're all present, correct, and ready for launch.' He gave everyone around the table a big wink. 'On my mark, deploy dinner!'

Estelle grabbed the bottle in front of her and poured herself another glass.

'In three, two, one, go!' Arthur yelled. 'Foxbrooke One over and out!' He waved the walkie-talkie at everyone. 'Can't believe I didn't think of this years ago! It was Libby's idea. Bally clever.'

Going to the door, Arthur opened it and a woman in her fifties entered, wheeling a cart filled with food. He helped her place the dishes on the table.

'Perry, our cook,' he said, 'also known as Red Leader, has prepared this dinner with Libby's and my assistance, in honour of our partnership with BDE Entertainment! It's got more big dick energy than you can shake a stick at. We've got horny goat masala, lady finger balti, aubergine, or as Vivienne would say, *eggplant*, madras, and tandoori bull testes!'

'Dad!' Henry hissed. 'What the f—'

'You don't have to eat it if you don't want to,' Arthur interrupted. 'Although I do recommend you give it a go. Might help you and Libby in the old baby-making department?'

'Arthur!' Libby said sharply.

He raised his hands. 'Sorry! Anyway, there's rice, raita, poppadoms, naan and pickles as well, so help yourself.'

Beverley turned to her left, where Henry and Libby were seated. 'Are you trying for a baby?'

'Definitely not at the moment,' Libby replied.

'More's the pity!' Arthur called out. 'I want grandchildren.'

'Me too,' Beverley said. 'I don't know if we're ever going to get any.'

James stared at his mum, but her attention was on Arthur.

'Jamesy-boy has never even had a girlfriend,' she continued. 'And S—'

'Mum!' James snapped. He felt everyone's eyes on him like ants crawling over his skin.

'Just like Henry until our Libby came along,' Arthur said. 'Well, James is a handsome chap, and my three gels are single, so—'

'Dad!' shouted all five Foxbrooke siblings.

On either side of Arthur, both Vivienne and Dervla placed a hand on his arm, as if telling him to be quiet.

Silence fell upon the table.

'Well, I don't know about the rest of you,' Connor said, 'but I'm starving and this smells delicious.' He stood. 'James, can I pass you anything?'

15

Estelle piled rice and curry on her plate, avoiding the tandoori bull's testicles. Her stomach was in knots, but she was also starving from the day's physical labour.

If she thought the day had been weird and stressful enough, she was still reeling from meeting James's parents. Nothing about them made any sense. James had been to Eton, then Oxford. He was a posh nob who worked in the City and drove a Ferrari. She'd imagined his mother would be as upper class as Gram-Gram, the Foxbrooke family matriarch. However, the last time Estelle had seen Beverley Hunter-Savage, she'd been in a cleaning tabard and wiping down a bathroom. And James's dad? Never in a million years would she have thought Kevin and James were related.

And why did his mum say James had never had a girlfriend before? Elyse bloody *lived* with them! Estelle took another mouthful of wine. The only way she was going to get through this evening was by being steaming drunk.

'So, Kevin, you're a self-made-man?' Arthur asked James's dad.

'Call me Kev, mate. Kevin's too formal.'

'And you can call me Bev,' Beverley added, reaching across and taking her husband's hand. 'We're Kev 'n' Bev.'

Kevin smiled at his wife. 'Dream team, innit babe?' He released her hand and turned to Arthur. 'Yeah, that's me. Self-made millionaire. Don't be fooled by the rocks I've got. I'm still Kev from the block. If the block were Stepney. Know what I mean?'

Out of the corner of her eye, Estelle saw James's knuckles getting whiter with every second as his hand clutched his fork.

'I do indeed, Kev,' Arthur replied. 'I had all of this given to me on a plate. Didn't have to do anything to get it other than be born with a penis. I admire a man like you. You not only had a penis but also enormous balls.'

To Estelle's left, Kevin visibly inflated. To her right, James seemed to shrink.

'On the money, Arthur. Bigger than a bull's. Had to take a lot of risks to get where I am today.'

'How did you start?' Arthur asked. 'And what line of business *are* you in?'

Estelle had a deep connection to her twin, and she sensed his energy across the table as he leaned forward slightly. This evening must have been even weirder for him, having known James since he was thirteen, but having had no idea who his parents were.

Kevin puffed out his cheeks. 'Bit of this, bit of that. Started out as a market trader when I was fourteen, buying and selling. Looking for the trends and jumping on 'em. Remember tamagotchis? Loom bands? I flogged them faster than shit off a shovel. Then I went to China, made some good contacts, and got into rebranded luxury goods.'

'Rebranded?' Vivienne asked.

Estelle tensed. Not only was her mother a model, her fashion-designer sister didn't look kindly on cheap rip-offs of her products, either.

'Yeah, they're not copies or anything,' Kevin replied. 'We take the concept and improve on it. Like what they do on the high street, but better.'

'Kev came up with this amazing idea,' Bev chipped in. 'He just adds a letter or changes it.'

'So, Chanel becomes Channel,' Kev continued. 'Burberry is Blurberry, Hugo Boss turns into Hugo Bass, Estee Lauder is Estelle Lauder—' He broke off and turned to Estelle. 'Like you, babe. And I changed Calvin Klein to Kevin Klein after me.'

'Ha!' Arthur said. 'Ingenious!'

No-one else around the table was talking. Everyone was riveted to the conversation between Arthur and Kevin. James's head was bowed as he stared at his plate.

'The latest thing is pheromones,' Kev said. 'Powerful stuff.'

'Ooh!' Arthur rose from his chair. 'I tried to make my own from fox glands. Sprayed them all over the manor before one of our sex parties. Thought it might help get people in the mood, but they stank the bally place out.'

'Nah, mate,' Kev said. 'Wrong animal. We use hamsters. They're at it even more than rabbits and rats. We've added pheromones to our entire range. It'll make anyone fancy you.'

Oh, my god. Was *this* what James was wearing to make him smell so good?

Kevin took a small purple glass bottle from his jacket, which hung over the back of his chair, and passed it left to Vivienne.

'It's our version of Dior's Poison. It's now called Door's Eau de Poisson. With two "s's".'

'Eau de Poisson?' Vivienne repeated, with the correct pronunciation.

Estelle froze. Did Kevin know he'd called his perfume 'fish water'?

'Yeah,' Kev replied. 'Jamesey-boy told me not to, but I'd already put the order for the bottles in. And anyway, who cares what it's called if it gets you laid?'

Vivienne took the stopper out of the bottle and waved her hand across the top. 'My goodness. That *is* powerful.'

Kevin grinned. 'Keep it.'

Vivienne passed it to Arthur, who dabbed it on his neck.

'What a complex bouquet!' he said. 'You're working with a very clever perfumier.'

'Well,' Kevin began, leaning forward as if about to impart a great secret, 'you'll never guess—'

'Dad!' James spat.

'Awright, awright,' Kev said. 'Keep your wig on.' He turned back to Arthur. 'Anyway, I made some good investments—'

James reached for his water glass and downed the contents.

'—and decided to move into the entertainment biz, buying Excelsior.'

Arthur chuckled. 'I love the new name. Big Dick Energy Entertainment. Priceless!'

'It was Jamesy-boy's idea.'

'No, Dad, it was not,' James said through his clenched jaw.

'But I first heard it from you—'

'As a phrase I'd heard around the office.'

'Well, I think it's a capital name,' Arthur said. 'And this logo is simply marvellous.'

'That was all me,' Kevin said proudly. 'I'm good at branding. I even rebranded our family.'

'You did?' Arthur asked. 'How?'

'We were Kev and Bev Skinner until little Kev was seven.

Then I made a mint and decided to upgrade us to Hunter-Savage.'

'Dad...' James said, his voice low and threatening.

'The Royal Family changed their surname from Saxe-Coburg-Gotha to Windsor during the First World War, so I thought to myself, if it's good enough for them, Kev me old mucker, then it's good enough for us. Skinner became Hunter-Savage, Kevin became Lord James and Char—'

'Dad! Shut the fuck up!' James shouted.

The table fell silent.

Holy shit. So James *had* been born Kevin. He hadn't lied. Estelle's brain was buzzing.

'*Lord* James?' Arthur asked, vocalising the question on Estelle's mind.

Kevin laughed. 'Yeah. Thought it would be funny. Lord James Hunter-Savage.'

There was a stunned silence, then Arthur started laughing. 'Love it!' he wheezed. 'I need to tell my older sister to change her name to "The Duke of Somerset". It's what she's always wanted.'

'But Jamesy-boy won't use it,' Kev continued. 'What a waste.'

Estelle could feel the anger radiating off James. She thought she knew who he was, but in the space of half an hour, every origin story she'd created had been ripped to shreds.

When Arthur's laughs petered out, the table once more lapsed into silence.

'How are you enjoying your meal?' Dervla asked Beverley.

'It's lovely, thanks, babe,' Bev replied. 'I was going to ask, how do you keep a place this size clean?'

'We don't,' Dervla said. 'It's impossible. We leave Bridget, our housekeeper, in charge of all that. Life's too short to be cleaning anything.'

Beverley frowned, as if she'd just been told the Earth was actually flat.

'There's a permanent cleaning staff of three,' Estelle said. 'And we draft in more when there's an event on.'

'Like the festival,' Bev replied.

Estelle managed to nod, as another silence fell over the rest of the table.

'So, Kev and Bev,' Arthur began. 'Let's put our heads together and see what we can come up with to save the festival.'

'Yeah, mate,' Kevin said. 'We need to take charge.'

'Unfortunately, I've had countless run-ins with the local council,' Arthur continued, 'and am not their favourite person.'

'That's because you always get permission for one thing, then do another,' Estelle said.

Arthur waved his hand dismissively. 'They're just a bunch of pen-pushing jobsworths.'

Kevin leaned forward, a piece of naan bread in his hand. 'I know the type, Arthur. We should just bribe 'em.'

There was a clatter as James's fork fell to his plate. Face tight with fury, he turned to his father. 'Dad!'

Kevin shrugged and held his hands up as if his suggestion were the most logical one.

'Kev's right,' Arthur said. 'But it won't work. Tried it umpteen times. I was even going to offer some of the lady councillors a night with me, but Vivienne and Dervla vetoed that idea.' He glanced at his wives with a fond smile. 'They didn't want to share.'

Dad, just shut up! Estelle caught Henry's eye. He looked in acute pain.

'Could we bribe them through the back door? Sponsor their kids' football team or summat?' Kevin asked.

'Take too long,' Arthur replied. 'We need this sorted now.'

'Estelle, James,' Connor said firmly from the end of the table. 'What do *you* both want to do?'

James glanced at her, his eyebrows lifting slightly as if asking the same question. Right now, all Estelle wanted to do was leave the table and run away.

'I don't know,' she said, hating how unsure her voice sounded. 'We need to show them the festival is different and we can work together.'

The tension etched on James's face since he arrived at the manor softened a little.

He nodded. 'Estelle is right. Perhaps we could invite the entire council, and others with unofficial sway in the community, to a night of entertainment to show the kind of event we want to put on?'

His words were addressed to everyone, but he didn't take his eyes off her. Estelle let herself be held by his gaze, as if he was a safe port in a storm of nonsense from both their fathers.

'And we could put it on here?' he suggested.

'We could display the maps and other information so they could see how far we've come?' she said to him. 'To show how serious we are?'

'Well—' Arthur began.

'That sounds like a fantastic idea,' Connor interrupted. 'Willow, fancy accompanying me on the piano for a few songs?'

'Yes, absolutely,' she replied.

Estelle glanced towards the other end of the table where her siblings sat.

'I can do a Shakespeare monologue?' Leo suggested. 'Or a scene with Mom?'

'And I can run a short Regency dancing workshop,' Libby said. 'If you'd like?'

Estelle's heart lifted. It might not sway the councillor's

minds, but it was a better idea than trying to bribe them or offer them sex.

Arthur waved his hand. 'And I can do something!'

'Dad,' Henry said forcefully. 'We all have to be on our best behaviour.'

'I can do that!' his father replied. 'Look at tonight. I'm wearing clothes, aren't I?'

Henry ignored him and turned to Estelle. 'Whatever you need, we can help.'

'Thank you. I think we have to move fast.' She looked from Henry and Libby to her other siblings, then ended up gazing once more at James. 'Do you think we could pull it together in a couple of weeks?'

He nodded. 'Yes. And I'm going to hand write apology notes to the two councillors first thing tomorrow.'

'Can I help?'

'Yes, I would appreciate your input.'

Something shifted between them, as if they'd slipped away from the solid ground of their animosity onto a moving sea, where anything was possible. It was unsettling, but her nerve endings thrilled with excitement.

'Ooh! And do you know what you should both do?' Arthur cried excitedly.

James tensed, as if waiting for a blow to land.

'Do we want to hear this?' Henry asked. 'Really?'

'Yes! It's your idea, anyway!'

Estelle shot a glance at her brother as he frowned at their father. 'Go on...'

Arthur's eyes were bright with excitement, like a small child desperate to show a parent what they'd made at school.

'The whole point of the evening is to show that Estelle and James can work together without any of the hoo-ha from this morning. Yes?' He didn't wait for a response, but ploughed on. 'So, they should pretend to be lovers!'

'What?' Estelle and James shouted at the same time, as Henry, Libby, Connor, Leo and Willow yelled, 'no!'

'It worked like a charm for Henry and Libby,' Arthur continued. 'Just look at them! The councillors can't argue with love.'

'Dad, for god's sake. That's the most ridiculous idea you've ever had!' Estelle snapped. 'What are we meant to do? Start snogging in front of them?' Her mind instantly supplied an image of James's lips on hers, and her body replied with a tingle in her pants.

Arthur raised his hands. 'No, no need to go that far. Just a bit of light hand-holding, a few—what did you call them in your contract with Libby, Henry?' He glanced at his first-born son. 'Loving glances?'

If Estelle was on the brink of disowning her father, Henry looked as if he was about to kill him.

Libby placed her hand over Henry's as he clutched his knife. 'Arthur—' she began firmly.

'Henry and Libby's love started with a fake relationship contract,' Arthur interrupted as he addressed Kev and Bev. 'Frightfully detailed, y'know.' His gaze switched to James. 'He could draw one up for you and Estelle.'

'That won't be necessary,' James growled.

Estelle jumped, and her nipples hardened as his voice rumbled through her.

'Oh! So, it's going to be real?'

'No. Our relationship, as well as the evening, will remain completely professional.'

'But—'

'Arthur,' Libby began with the tone of a primary school teacher addressing a non-compliant six-year-old. 'Why don't we play the "getting to know you" game?'

'The what?' Estelle asked.

'Ooh, yes!' Arthur cried. 'Such fun!'

Libby smiled at her. 'Don't worry, I've written the questions. It's just a gentle way for us to find out a bit more about each other whilst we have dinner.'

Arthur stood. 'I'll get what we need.' He turned to Dervla. 'Dee-dee, darling. Swap places with me so you and Vivi can partner with Kev, and I'll go with Bev.'

'Estelle and James,' Libby said. 'You go together. I'm going with Henry—'

'But you already know him!' Estelle protested.

Libby fixed her with a patient, but firm, smile. 'We've only been together since last summer. There's plenty we don't know about each other.' She turned to the end of the table. 'Connor, Leo and Willow, you'll be in a three.'

Arthur handed each group an envelope, pads of paper, and pens.

'The questions are all in order,' Libby continued. 'Some of them might involve writing or drawing. If you don't want to say the answers, you can always write them down.'

Estelle took the envelope from her father and placed it on the table. She couldn't look at James.

'Have fun!' Libby said.

Neither she nor James moved. The envelope lay between them like an unstable bomb.

'What's your favourite colour?' Arthur read aloud from the other end of the table.

'Black,' Estelle muttered under her breath.

'You or me?' James murmured.

She glanced up. One of his eyebrows was arched.

'You, of course.'

'Ah yes. Because you know me so well.'

She looked away, her cheeks heating.

'What's *your* favourite colour?' he asked.

'Does it matter?'

'Don't you want to play the game?'

Estelle didn't want to play *any* game with James, as she wasn't sure she could ever win.

'Brown,' she eventually replied.

'Why?'

'Duke is brown.'

'Your horse?'

'Yes, and earth is brown. And coffee, autumn leaves, my favourite riding boots, my skin.'

'Can I change *my* favourite colour?'

Heart jumping, she ignored his question and pulled the first two slips of paper from the envelope, discarding the first one. 'How do you take your coffee?' she read aloud. 'Easy. Double espresso—'

'Cappuccino, double shot.'

She took out another. 'Favourite music or song. 'The Imperial March' from *Star Wars*.'

'I thought we were meant to be answering for ourselves, not each other?'

She shrugged. 'It's quicker this way.'

'Well then, your favourite song is "When 2 become 1" by the Spice Girls.'

'It's *one* of my favourites.' She pulled out another question. 'Draw your first pet in less than a minute.' Still not meeting his eyes, she handed James a small pad of paper and a pencil, then started drawing Peewee, her first ever horse. When she'd finished, she handed it to him. He passed her his pad. It was blank.

She glanced up in surprise.

His expression was impassive. 'I've never had a pet.' He

looked at her drawing. 'What was your dog's name?'

'Peewee was a horse, you pillock,' she muttered, then paused. 'Did you ever want a pet?'

James didn't reply, instead taking another piece of paper from the envelope. 'What's your favourite form of exercise?' he asked, gazing directly at her.

'Riding,' she replied, her traitorous brain substituting James for Duke.

'Sounds fun. I might have to try it.'

She looked away and took out another question.

'It's rowing, by the way,' he said. 'My favourite form of exercise.'

'What's the coolest thing you've ever made?' she asked, her attention now on her glass of wine. Every time she looked at James, her heart raced a little faster, and her mind spun with everything she now knew about him and his family.

'I'll show you tomorrow.'

She looked at him in shock. 'Have you made me something?' she blurted before she could stop herself.

He cleared his throat. 'No, I made it for... others. But I hope you still like it.'

James had *made* something? Sort of for her?

'What's the coolest thing *you've* ever made?' he asked.

The answer stuck in her throat.

'The fur Q?'

She nodded.

He grinned. It was the first time that evening she'd seen him smile, and the sight of it stopped her heart for a beat.

'It's the coolest thing I've ever been given,' he said.

Now her heart was racing triple time.

James took another question and read it out. 'When was the last time you cried?'

'This morning,' she replied before thinking.

He frowned, the skin around his eyes pinching. 'I'm sorry.'

'Oh, it wasn't because of you.'

His gaze turned thunderous. 'Who hurt you?'

Estelle gasped as fantasies she didn't even know she had, charged through her body, weapons drawn, on their way to destroy her enemies whilst simultaneously delivering her multiple orgasms.

'It was, er, good crying,' she stuttered. 'Because I was happy. It was before I got to work.'

The anger left his expression, to be replaced with a questioning look.

'I can't tell you what it was. I can't tell anyone yet,' she continued.

His eyebrows raised even further.

'I'm not pregnant!' she hissed. *Shut up! Shut up!*

'Who's pregnant?' Arthur cried from the end of the table. 'Estelle?'

'Honey?' Vivienne added. 'Is there something we should know?'

'No one's pregnant!'

'Is it Eveline?' Dervla asked. 'She told me you were there this morning.'

'What wonderful news!' said Arthur. 'I wonder if she'll let me be a godfather? I'm very good at baby-sitting.'

'We must make sure she rests enough,' Vivienne said. 'Eveline works too hard as it is.'

'Mom! Dad! Mammy! For god's sake! Eveline is *not* pregnant and you *cannot* ask her if she is. Okay?'

Arthur winked theatrically and tapped his nose. 'Okey-dokey, Estelle. *Mum's* the word. Ha ha!' He glanced around the table. 'Okay, everyone, circle of trust. Eveline is definitely not pregnant and we cannot ask her if she is. Roger, roger?'

'Roger, roger, jammy dodger, Dad,' Leo replied with a grin.

Estelle growled and turned her attention back to James, who was smiling at her. 'When did *you* last cry?' she demanded.

His expression faltered for a moment. 'When I was seven.'

'What happened?'

He ignored her and pulled another question from the envelope. 'What do you wish more people knew about you?'

Long held feelings twisted inside her stomach. 'That I'm not just a loud, foul-mouthed arse.'

'Those are three of the characteristics I love most about you,' he replied quietly.

Forcing her gaze to stay down, butterflies took off inside her. Memories of the Winter Ball fluttered through her, but were chased away by visions of Elyse crying.

'What do you wish more people knew about you?' she mumbled.

He sighed. 'That I'm not a soulless bastard and a total wanker,' he said, repeating the words she'd thrown at him that morning.

Guilt gnawed at her. She'd been vile to him. 'I'm sorry.'

James didn't respond, instead taking out another question. He huffed out a laugh then read it. 'Do you believe that people can change?'

Estelle glanced up the table to her irrepressibly eccentric parents who weren't going to change for anyone, then at her brother, who'd come out of his shell after meeting Libby.

'I don't know. I think at their core, people don't really change.'

She forced her eyes to meet his.

'I changed everything about myself when I was seven,' he said.

Estelle tried to read his expression, but it was as if he'd pulled the shutters closed over his emotions.

Breaking her gaze, he took another slip of paper from the envelope. 'What was the scariest moment in your life so far?'

Estelle swallowed. 'There are two. The first was when I was seven, and the second was when I fell off the balcony.'

'What happened when you were seven?'

She'd given away far too much of herself and her family to her brother's mortal enemy already this evening, and that story was not one she was willing to share.

'What was the scariest moment in *your* life?' she asked, ignoring his question.

'When you fell from the balcony.'

Her body flooded with heat as she stared at him, remembering how she felt in his arms, his strength, the rumbling depth of his voice.

She took another question and read it aloud. 'What is your biggest regret?'

'Not knowing when to keep my mouth shut. You?'

She pulled a face. 'If I thought about how much I regret, then I'd never get out of bed in the morning.' She took another piece of paper out. 'Is there something you've dreamed of doing for a long time?'

James glanced away with a rueful smile.

'What is it?'

He shook his head.

Now she really needed to know. Nothing was more important than finding out what James Hunter-Savage dreamed of.

'Okay,' she said, 'I'll go first.' She lowered her voice. No-one apart from Eveline knew what she was about to say. 'I've always wanted to enter a mounted archery competition.'

His eyes met hers, surprise on his face. 'Why don't you?'

She shrugged. 'Not enough time. I can't leave the livery or the manor. And anyway, I'm not good enough.'

'Yet...'

He held her gaze. Unspoken words and feelings ricocheted between them. How well did she *really* know him?

'Go on then,' she said, feeling out of breath. 'What have *you* dreamed of doing?'

What looked like vulnerability flashed across his features and he shook his head again.

'Oh, come on now.' She lowered her voice to a whisper. 'No-one here knows my dream of competing.'

He stared at the envelope. 'I've always dreamed of falling in love,' he said quietly, then took another question and read it aloud as if he hadn't just bared his soul to her. 'How do you show people that you love them?' He sniffed. 'Easy. I do things for them.' He glanced at her. 'You?'

Her mind was racing. 'The same.' And it was true. She primarily showed her love by stepping up and trying to make the lives of those around her better.

Estelle grabbed another piece of paper and read the question out before thinking. 'When did you last have sex?' Her gaze snapped across the table. 'Libby! Seriously?'

'I most certainly did not include that question!' Libby retorted. 'Show it to me.'

Estelle held up the piece of paper.

'That is *not* my handwriting.' Libby turned to the end of the table. 'Arthur?'

'Ho ho ho!' he chuckled. 'I thought I'd liven things up a bit.'

Libby rolled her eyes. 'No-one needs to answer that question.'

'I don't mind,' Leo said. 'For Connor and Willow, it was sometime never, and for me, it was last week.'

'Bollocks,' Connor replied as Willow started baaing like a sheep.

'It was a woman!'

'Her name was Baabraa,' Willow said to the rest of the table. 'And it was only because she felt sorry for him.'

'Well, I don't care who he managed to shag as long as there's grandchildren,' Arthur said. 'Chop chop.'

'Lamb chop,' Willow added.

Estelle looked at James. She'd promised Elyse she wouldn't reveal she'd met her, but something wasn't adding up. Why would Beverley say James had never had a girlfriend before when Elyse was living with them and had told Estelle they'd only just broken up? If she managed to get James to answer this question, then it would be another piece of the puzzle.

'So then,' she began, trying to keep her tone light and breezy. 'When did you last have sex?'

James stared at her. 'Do you really want to know the answer to that?'

Estelle did, and she didn't. The thought of James having sex with another woman made an unpleasant sensation uncoil inside her that felt a lot like jealousy. But then how else could she corroborate what Elyse had told her?

She nodded.

'Fifteen months ago.'

Her mind stuttered. 'But...'

'I told you, I didn't steal Elizabeth from your brother,' he said, his voice dropping to almost a whisper. 'I kept her company at Imperium after he was late for their date, then took her for dinner. At the end of the night, we went our separate ways and I didn't see her again.'

'But she's your type,' she said, reiterating Elyse's words and Henry's convictions.

James frowned. 'My type?'

'You know, blonde.'

'I don't have a type. When was the last time *you* had sex?'

There was no way Estelle was answering that one. She

hadn't had sex for years. 'None of your business,' she said primly, then pulled out the next question. 'What has been your longest sexual relationship?'

'Four months,' James replied without hesitation. 'You?'

She stared at him. 'Four *months*?'

He nodded.

Huh? None of what James or his parents had said was tallying with what Elyse had told her earlier. But Elyse had seemed genuinely heartbroken.

'I know it's not very long,' James continued, his voice low. 'But I don't see the point in continuing a relationship if it's not right. It's not fair to the woman.'

'What do you mean?'

He let out a terse sigh. 'In my experience, men can keep a relationship going that they're not really committed to because they have easy access to sex. But most women want more than that and many of them want the opportunity to have kids. Men can father children throughout their lives, but women can't. So, stringing someone along when they could be looking for someone better, someone who really wants them, is unfair.'

Her mouth dropped open.

James pulled another question from the envelope and read aloud. 'What are you most excited about right now?' He looked tired as he gazed at her. 'I'm most excited about this dinner party ending.'

Estelle nodded. The day felt like it had been going for years and her emotions had been put through the wringer. First with Eveline's pregnancy, then meeting Elyse, then hearing James being a twat on the phone, the blow up in front of the councillors, meeting James's parents, and all the revelations of the evening. She was exhausted.

'Can I give you a lift home?' James asked. 'We could leave now?'

Estelle looked around the table. Everyone else was chatting, laughing, and seemed to be having fun.

She nodded. 'I just don't want to give my father more to crow about.'

'French exit? You leave now, as if you're going to the bathroom, and I'll meet you outside in a few minutes?'

'Thank you.' She glanced down at her clothes. 'But I'm all muddy. And your car is so posh.'

'There's a picnic blanket in the boot. I can put that on the seat if you'd like?'

She nodded again, then pulled the last piece of paper from the envelope. 'Final one. What is a fact few people know about you?'

'That I was born Kevin Skinner, and when I was seven, my dad changed my name to Lord James Hunter-Savage.' He gave her a tired smile. 'Now go, before the rest of them finish and your dad brings out the Twister board.'

Estelle took the pad of paper with her drawing of Peewee on it and the pencil, then left the room without a backward glance.

FOUR MINUTES LATER, JAMES STRODE OUT OF THE FRONT doors of Foxbrooke Manor, unlocked his car, and passed Estelle a picnic blanket from the boot.

She carefully laid it on the passenger seat and got in.

Easing slowly away, he kept the engine revs low until they reached the main road out of Foxbrooke.

Neither of them said a word to each other as he drove. Estelle was spun out from the day, and trying not to be excited about her first ride in a Ferrari and being this close to James.

When he drove into the livery, he turned right, stopping outside a small cottage.

'I presume this is where you live?'

She nodded.

He cleared his throat. 'Will I see you tomorrow? At the office?'

'I need to collect the Defender from the garage so it might be a little after nine.'

'Okay.' He got out of the car.

Before Estelle realised what he was doing, he was at her side, opening the door, his arm extended.

Despite every promise she would never willingly touch him, she took his hand and got out.

James stepped back, giving her space.

She held out a folded piece of paper.

'What's that?'

'A fact few people know about me.' Pressing it into his hand, she strode briskly to her house and entered, closing the front door behind her. She only moved when she heard the sound of his car driving away.

FIVE MINUTES LATER, HER PHONE PINGED WITH A MESSAGE.

> James Hunter-Savage: Thank you for giving
> me your number

❧ 16 ❧

Waking early the next morning, James lay on his back in the darkness. He'd spent a lifetime believing if his public and private lives met, his own personal universe would implode. Yet he was still alive, and no matter what the Foxbrooke family might have been thinking about him or his parents, they'd been unfailingly friendly.

Even after everything they'd heard about him over the years.

James's stomach tightened. He'd always been able to rationalise, excuse, or forget whenever his behaviour hadn't met someone else's standards. But the decision last year to steal Henry's client and deal at Conqueror had been misjudged.

Turning on the light, he got out of bed and prepared for the gym. He needed to give his mind something else to focus on besides whispering the negative mantra of 'you were wrong', over and over. Pulling on his trainers, he went to the door. Could he tell Estelle why he did it?

Shouldn't you be having that conversation with Henry? a tiny voice inside him piped up.

Fuck off, the rest of him automatically replied.

Making his way quietly through the silent house, James's head was filled with Estelle. It mattered what she thought of him. He wanted her to like him. Last night, she'd finally let the door to her soul open a crack and given him a glimpse of what lay inside. James already wanted to move in.

He huffed out a derisive laugh at his thoughts and entered the gym. As if Estelle would ever want that. Last night she'd been as wrung out as he'd been by their families meeting. That was the only reason she'd let her guard down.

But she gave you her number, his inner cheerleader reminded him.

As colleagues, his self-doubt replied.

Sitting on the rowing machine, he began his warm-up. The repetitive movement and rhythmic sound were relaxing, and allowed his mind to continue processing the previous day and evening.

Arthur Foxbrooke. If James had thought *his* parents were embarrassing, they were nothing compared to the Duke of Somerset. It was one thing reading about him online, or glimpsing him across a crowded room at the Winter Ball, but quite another to sit down for dinner with him.

James had always been envious of Henry growing up with such effortlessly upper-class parents, but last night his muscles involuntarily tensed each time Arthur opened his mouth. No wonder the local councillors didn't like him. Trying to bribe them and offering them sex? *Jesus Christ.* His dad had thought it hilarious and his mum had laughed along, but James didn't know if she'd meant it.

He kept rowing until he started to sweat, then moved onto the weights. Why had Estelle seemed so confused when he'd told her about his dating life? And why so obsessed with the belief he preferred blondes? Was it a subconscious attempt to keep him at arm's length? Or was it something, or some*one*, else?

Could she have met Elyse? It was clear Estelle had met his mother before, even after his attempts to keep them apart. After leaving the dinner party early and dropping Estelle back at the livery, James had driven straight home and gone to his room. He hadn't had a chance to ask his mother how she'd already seemed to know Estelle, and had avoided Elyse. She was watching television downstairs when he'd crept in, but had still managed to leave her damp towel and dirty clothes on his bed.

Fuck it. If the world hadn't ended after his work and personal life had finally met, then it was time to bring another secret out into the open.

'Babe!'

Beverley tottered down the corridor towards James in zebra-print wedge mules and a leopard-print silk dressing gown tied over her pyjamas.

'Come here, you beauty,' she cried, pulling him in for a hug.

'Hi Mum, how are you doing?'

She drew back. 'Peachy keen, babe.' Her eyes were shining. 'I still can't believe last night! Me and the Duke and Duchesses of Somerset! I was good though. I didn't ask for Vivienne's autograph or nothing. D'you know how much I could have got for it on eBay?'

'Mum—'

'And where did you skive off to with Lady Foxbrooke? Is there something you need to tell me?'

He shook his head. 'Where's Dad?'

'Office. Want me to make you some breakfast, babe? The Duke—*Arthur* gave me a pot of honey last night. He said it was biogangic or summat and good for your sex drive. Want to try some on a piece of toast?'

'No thanks, Mum, I've already eaten. But I need to speak to you and Dad about something.'

His mother's brow furrowed. 'Should I be worried?'

'No, it's fine. I just should have told you a couple of years ago.'

'Is it a secret baby?' Beverley asked as they walked together down the corridor.

'What?'

'From a one-night-stand? And the mother's been trying to track you down ever since.'

James stared at her. 'No.'

She wrinkled her nose. 'Shame.'

He rolled his eyes and opened his dad's office door for her.

His father was behind his desk, frowning at his laptop, a poppet toy in one hand and a fidget spinner whirling on the thumb of the other.

'Kev, babe,' Bev began. 'James wants to talk to us.'

Her husband's gaze snapped away from the screen and he leaned back in his chair. 'What happened to you last night? Did you pull? Your mum wants to know if you and Estelle have kids if they'll be an official Lord or Lady. D'you know?'

James bit back a sigh. 'No, and no.'

'You've lost your touch, Jamesy-boy. You should have closed the deal.'

For fuck's sake. 'Dad, I need to talk to you about Elyse.'

'Have you finally come to your senses?'

'I already have. Years ago.'

'You what, babe?' his mum asked.

'Three years ago, I met Elyse in a bar. We had a two-week

fling, then I ended it. She didn't take it well. She still wants to get back together. I don't.'

The whirr of the fidget spinner filled the silence as it slowed down. His father had even stopped playing with his poppet toy.

'But...' Beverley began. 'Why didn't you say something when she started working for your dad?'

'Because I didn't want you to treat her any differently. Or me.'

Kevin's mouth was hanging open.

'Dad, I told you she can't live here, and this is one of the reasons why. You said you'd talk to her, but nothing's changed. I can't go to my room and find her in my bathroom. You pay her enough. She can afford her own place.'

His dad's frown got deeper.

'Is Elyse even paying rent to live here?' James continued, his frustration rising. 'I'm not drawing *any* wage and yet I'm working seven days a week saving your arse after you landed mine in it.' All the stress from the past year was boiling inside him, bubbling its way to the surface. 'I can't do this anymore. I'm serious, Dad. Either she goes, or tonight I'm checking into a decent hotel in Bath and sending you the bill.'

Kevin dropped his fidget toys and held up his hands in a placating gesture. James already knew his dad wasn't going to do what was asked of him.

'Jamesy-boy—'

'No, Dad. I'm done. You can live with her, or me. Your choice.'

Going to the door, he wrenched it open.

Elyse was standing on the other side.

Great. Just fucking great. Side-stepping her, he strode away. It wasn't yet nine o'clock, and the day had already gone to shit.

· · ·

In his office, James started letters to the two councillors, with one eye on the clock as the minute hand ticked past the hour. He wasn't used to apologising, nor experiencing the prickles of nervous excitement in the pit of his stomach at the thought of seeing Estelle again.

How should he play it with her? Cool? Aloof? Honest? *Fuck off*. She knew enough about his life now. He wasn't going to start baring his soul and revealing the truth about why he was in Somerset. If Estelle knew, it would lay to waste whatever gains he'd made with her, and sour her opinion of his father permanently.

He glanced towards the window at the gifts he'd made. Were they a mistake? Was he turning into a sap like Henry Foxbrooke? He stood, thinking of where he could hide them. However excited barking and a thundering of paws coming down the corridor outside meant he was too late. Estelle had arrived.

James opened the door and braced himself as Chester and Joy tackled him.

'Sorry!' Estelle called out as she made her way towards him. 'I have no idea why, but they seem to think you're the most attractive human on the planet.'

'It could be my animal magnetism?'

She pulled a face, but he could tell she was trying not to grin. 'I think you're hiding treats in your pocket.'

He held his hands out to the side. 'Want to check?' *What the fuck? Shut-up! Stop flirting!*

For a brief moment, desire flashed through her eyes, then she let her attention be drawn to Chester, who was now making love to James's leg with extreme prejudice.

'Chester-chops! No!' She pulled him away and into the room. 'We do not hump people,' she scolded. 'Least of all him.'

Joy trotted to the window and barked.

'What is it?' Estelle asked. 'Oh...'

She'd seen them.

'Joy-dog, Chester-chops, look at these!' Crouching, she inspected the two porcelain water bowls which were decorated with her dog's names. 'How cool is that?' She glanced at James over her shoulder. 'These are incredible! Where did you get them from?'

The room was suddenly far too hot. James went back to his desk, tapping random keys in an attempt to appear nonchalant. 'The pottery place at the end of the high street.'

'The Creative Clay Café?'

'Yeah.'

He didn't look up, but the silence told him Estelle was putting two and two together.

'But they don't sell anything that's finished. Everything is blank for you to decorate yourself.'

He shrugged. 'I bribed them.'

She came to the side of his desk. 'What with? Money or sex?'

His gaze flicked up. One of her eyebrows was arched.

'Both?'

She pouted. 'And yet they still turned you down.'

He gave her a look. 'You don't believe me?'

Crossing her arms, she slowly shook her head. 'I don't think Barnaby or his mum are really your type, and even if you *had* persuaded them to paint those bowls, it's not in their style.'

Busted. He stayed silent.

'Thank you. You've done something awesomely thoughtful. Chester and Joy love them.'

Unfamiliar positive emotions were expanding inside James's chest. He was used to feelings of pride, but they were usually associated with victory at work or in rowing competitions.

These felt different because they were associated with doing something for someone else.

He stood. 'I'll make you a coffee.' Going to the door, he left as quickly as he could.

RETURNING FIVE MINUTES LATER, JAMES PLACED A cappuccino on Estelle's desk.

She peered at the pattern in the foam. 'Nice leaf. Your practising has been paying off.'

He didn't reply. It had been a piece of piss. It was the unicorn that still wasn't good enough to show her.

'I've made a start on the letters to the councillors. Do you want me to email them over?' he said, moving to his side of the office.

Still seated and holding her coffee, she rolled her chair out from behind her desk and over to his. 'No need. I'll look over your shoulder.'

James moved the laptop to the left and himself to the right. Whilst his body was demanding he be so close to Estelle that nothing was between them, even clothes, his head knew that to make his fantasies real was a bad idea. A very, *very* bad idea. She barely tolerated him at best, and at least one member of her family actively hated him. They had to make the festival work, but it was already teetering at the edge of the catastrophe cliff because he and Estelle couldn't rein in their tempers. After his last year of cock-ups, turning their already fragile business relationship into a sexual one would be a total disaster.

She leaned in closer, reading his draft letter.

Shit! She was wearing the perfume again. It was like a drug, amplifying her personality and drawing him in like a magnet.

Her hands reached forward. 'May I?'

'Knock yourself out,' he replied, letting Chester jump onto his lap as a canine cockblocker.

Her fingers moved over the keys confidently. James instantly imagined them on his skin.

Get a grip!

She glanced at him. 'There's no need to be so pissy. I'm not changing much.'

'What?'

'You huffed, and your face is all frowny.'

He attempted a smile.

'Now you look like a smartly dressed serial killer. Do you have any posh paper, or are we using what's in the printer tray?'

He opened one of the desk drawers and pulled out a sheaf of paper, matching envelopes, and a padded box containing his fountain pen.

'Smythson *and* Montblanc,' she exclaimed. 'Bloody hell, we are pulling out all the stops. Can I use it?'

'The paper?'

'The pen. I want to pretend I have a small penis and am signing a law on women's reproductive rights. That or a weapons contract.'

He internally winced at the thought of Estelle wielding it like a malfunctioning biro, scoring the nib so deeply into the paper it could be turned over and used as braille.

'Have you ever used a fountain pen before?'

'Once, when Gram-Gram let me use hers.'

'Did she let you use it a second time?'

She hesitated. 'I never asked again.'

'And that tells me everything I need to know.'

'Oh, go on. Don't you trust me?'

'No.'

Her eyes widened. 'Wow, that was pretty decisive.'

He gave a half shrug in return.

'But what if your handwriting is horrible? I bet it's all angular and angry.'

'And you dot your I's with hearts?'

She pulled a face. 'Who do you think I am? Eveline? Willow? Look, these need to be written by whoever can do the better job.'

James uncapped his pen and passed it to her, along with a piece of paper. 'Please don't press too hard.'

'You're trusting me?'

'I'm making a herculean effort to defy your expectations.'

Her eyes flicked from Chester on his lap to the dog bowls on the floor. 'You already are,' she muttered, then turned to the text on the laptop.

After she'd written a sentence, James let out the breath he was unconsciously holding. Estelle *was* being careful. Her handwriting, however, was loopy and chaotic. It started out passable, but as she continued, it bordered on illegible.

She put the pen down. 'In my defence, I never write anything anymore, I just type. But I bet you can't do any better.'

He took the pen from her, making sure their fingers didn't make contact, and laid a fresh piece of paper on the desk. Part of moulding himself into the archetypal upper-class man had involved attention to his handwriting. First learning calligraphy, then adapting what he'd learnt to create his own style.

He started at the top with the addresses of Shoscombe Manor and the council offices in Bath. By the time he'd written the second postcode, Estelle was sitting back in her chair with her arms crossed.

He glanced at her and raised an eyebrow. 'Should I continue?'

'Show off,' she grumbled, then cradled her coffee mug and sipped from it.

There was no reason for Estelle to stay sitting behind his desk, but she seemed in no hurry to move, and he was never going to ask her to. The back of his neck prickled with awareness as she watched him write. It was like being in an exam, one on the subject of 'impressing hot women'. James had always aced every academic test, but this was one he wasn't sure he could even reach the pass mark on.

The only sounds in the room were the pen scratching the paper and the occasional snuffle from Chester. Joy was lying on the floor beside him, her head resting on his foot. He was meant to be at work, but the scene was bizarrely cosy. All they needed was a coal fire and for Estelle to be darning his socks, and they would look like a poster-couple for the nineteen-fifties. Almost.

James took his time finishing both letters, privately noting that Estelle had made the contents of each one slightly different, then wrote the addresses on the envelopes.

'Should we hand deliver or send them first class?' he asked.

She blinked as she stared at him, as if she'd been lost in a daydream and was recalibrating her mind back to the present moment.

'I think we should drive them in today,' she replied. 'Along with handwritten invitations to every councillor asking them to save the date for the evening event. We need to get to as many as possible before Sarah and Mark have time to tell them what happened.'

'Agreed. I know it doesn't look good at the moment, but I don't want to put anything on hold. We don't have time to waste waiting for their decision. We have to move forward as if they'll say yes.'

She nodded. 'Do you want me to handle the evening event at the Manor? I can ask my friend Jack to help. He's the one who made the Winter Ball such a success.'

Memories from that night crashed into his mind, removing the ability to reply.

Her cheeks darkened and she glanced away, scooting herself back to her desk on the other side of the room.

'Yes,' he replied, still gazing at her, even though all he could see over her laptop was her curly hair. 'It'll be far quicker to have you do that. I'll focus on staffing. If that's okay with you?'

The top of her head moved up and down. 'Go for your life.'

'How about the Saturday after next? Will that give you enough time?'

'Yep.' Her fingers were tapping away at the speed of a professional touch-typist.

He sent her an email.

FROM: JAMES HUNTER-SAVAGE
To: Estelle Foxbrooke
Subject: Curious...
Are you typing actual words right now?
Kind regards,
James

TWENTY SECONDS AFTER HIS EMAIL WAS SENT, ESTELLE froze and her fingers abruptly stopped.

Then they started up again, much slower, but with the weight of a sledgehammer going through them onto the keys.

His heart jumped when her reply pinged in.

FROM: ESTELLE FOXBROOKE
To: James Hunter-Savage
Subject: Re: Curious...

Yes, I am. As opposed to staring across the office at my colleague.

GRINNING, HE PRESSED THE REPLY BUTTON.

FROM: JAMES HUNTER-SAVAGE
To: Estelle Foxbrooke
Subject: Wondering...
How can you type so fast?
Kind regards,
James
PS - I'm not staring, I'm contemplating.

FROM: ESTELLE FOXBROOKE
To: James Hunter-Savage
Subject: Re: Wondering...
I'm not a Rubik's Cube.

FROM: JAMES HUNTER-SAVAGE
To: Estelle Foxbrooke
Subject: Re: Wondering...
I know. You're far more interesting and complicated.
Would you feel more comfortable if I left the office?

THE MOMENT HE PRESSED SEND, HE REGRETTED THE decision. It seemed he was compelled to flirt with Estelle almost as much as his lungs compelled him to breathe.

Her fingers were silent. Clearly, she couldn't easily decide whether or not to send him packing.

The sound of footsteps in the corridor outside was followed by a knock at the door.

James leapt out of his seat to open it.

'Hey, babe,' his mother said, coming into the room. 'This arrived for you.'

He took a long box from her and she went to Estelle, holding out a plate of French Fancies.

'Ooh! Yum,' Estelle said. 'Thank you, Beverley. Are these all for me?'

'If you want, babe, but you might have to fight James for 'em. They're his favourite.'

Estelle selected a cake. 'Are they now? Thanks for the insider intel. Got any other secrets about him you can share?'

'Well—'

'No, she hasn't,' James interrupted, giving his mother a hard stare. Estelle was grinning at him as she chewed.

Beverley playfully slapped his arm. 'I'll only ever tell her the good stuff.'

'Humph,' he replied, putting the box behind his desk.

'What's that?' Estelle asked.

'It's a—' Beverley began.

'Nothing,' James said, beginning to regret the purchase he'd made whilst watching Estelle do yoga.

'Is it a present for me?' Estelle asked, getting to her feet.

Beverley laughed. 'It is if you like looking at muscles.'

'Thanks for the cakes, Mum,' he said, attempting to steer her out of the room. 'Don't you have to leave now?'

'No, babe.' She held the plate of cakes under his nose. 'Want one?'

His mouth watered. It was too late to pretend he didn't like them.

'Thank you.' He took one and went back to his desk.

Beverley perched on the edge. 'I've been thinking.'

Sirens went off in his head.

'Last night was a right laugh,' she continued. 'And it just shows how you two can get on. Yeah?'

Silence. James glanced over at Estelle, who was also gazing warily at his mother.

'I think it's important for you to get to know each other more.'

'That won't—' Estelle began.

'Find out how each other ticks,' Beverley continued. 'What you're interested in.'

Another silence. Last night, James had been forced to open the doors of his personal life and let Estelle in. He wasn't ready to give her the guided tour.

'Like horses,' his mum said to him. 'James, you should go and watch Estelle ride.'

His mind immediately, and inconveniently, provided an image of Estelle riding *him*.

'And you should show her how *you* like to exercise,' his mum continued.

There was a beat, then Estelle started choking on her cake.

'You alright, babe?' his mother said, going to her side and lightly tapping between her shoulder blades.

Estelle nodded and held up her hand as she coughed. 'I'm fine,' she eventually managed.

'And James should show you his lab, where—'

'Mum!'

'Yeah, babe?'

'Thank you for your suggestions. We'll give them due care and consideration.'

'I don't mind showing you the stables,' Estelle said. 'You've got a lot in common with them.'

His mum frowned. 'Huh?'

James rolled his eyes. 'It's because she thinks we're both full of shit.'

Beverley laughed. 'Oh, my Christ, that's funny! I'll have to tell your dad!'

Opening the door, James stood by it, hoping his mum would finally get the message.

She dabbed at the corners of her eyes and turned to Estelle. 'When can you show him around?'

'Saturday? If he's free. You're very welcome to come, too.'

'Nah, doll. Don't wanna be a third wheel.' She went to the door. 'If you ever need anything, just come through to the main house, okay? James will give you my number.' She turned to him. 'Won't you, babe?'

He didn't reply. The dam holding his personal life back from the rest of the world had been breached, and the hole was only getting bigger.

'And he bought a pull-up bar,' his mum said to Estelle. 'That's what's in the box.' She winked. 'So, if you want a front seat at the gun show, get him to whip it out and show you what he's got.'

Estelle snorted, then covered it up with another cough.

'Okay, kiddies. See you later!'

Beverley waved at them both, then left the room.

James shut the door behind her and went back to his desk. He opened up recruitment websites to start the new search for festival staff and waited to see if Estelle would reply to his last email.

She didn't.

❧ 17 ❧

'So, I'll see you tomorrow?' James asked Estelle.

He was standing by the office door, a messenger bag over his shoulder containing the apology letters to the councillors and save-the-date invitations.

'Yeah, sure,' she replied, her eyes on her two dogs. They were at his heels, tails wagging in hopeful excitement that he might take them with him.

James crouched. 'You two are staying right here.'

Joy, who got the gist of what he was saying, whined. Chester, who didn't, barked.

Estelle watched James as he stroked her dogs, soothing Joy and allowing Chester to lick and headbutt his other hand. It was very difficult to hate anyone who'd been ninety-eight per cent polite all day and was kind to animals.

'Good boy, good girl,' James continued. He straightened. 'Stay.'

'Chester! Joy! Come!' Estelle called to them.

They didn't move.

Fuck's sake.

She risked a glance at James.

He was grinning.

Pressing her lips tightly together, she went back to looking at her laptop, ignoring them all.

'You sure you don't want to come with me?' James asked.

'The dogs and me in your compensation car, or the dogs and you in the Defender?' she replied, pretending to type again. 'Your choice.'

'I'm going to go with option C.' He paused. 'See you tomorrow?'

She waved her hand as if to waft him away. 'Yeah, yeah. I'm contractually obliged to show up after I signed away my soul to the devil. Remember?'

He huffed out a short laugh, then left.

As the door closed behind him, Estelle leaned back in her chair and exhaled a long, slow breath. After the most stressful and strange dinner party, she'd spent the day reorganising her thoughts and feelings towards James and now found she had no proper place to put them.

On the one hand, he'd confounded her beliefs, then on the other he'd confirmed them. No matter how many nice things James did, he was still the man who'd bullied Henry at school and stolen his client at Conqueror.

She glanced over at the water bowls he'd painted for Chester and Joy. She would never have had the time, nor patience, to ensure every letter was the same size and perfection as the last. James had even decorated the insides. It must have taken him hours.

She shook her head. *A hot bloke being nice to your dogs does not mean you can fancy him!*

Pushing to her feet, she went to James's desk and sat behind it. She rested her head against the back of his chair, accidentally-on-purpose letting it loll to the side so she could breathe in the scent of him that clung faintly to the fabric.

A light bulb flashed on inside her. *Pheromones. That's all it is!* She knew there had to be a logical, rational and scientific explanation for the bizarre attraction she felt for James Hunter-Savage, and this was it! It was simply chemical warfare, designed to manipulate her into ripping his clothes off like a love Berserker, and sexing him to death.

A weight lifted from her shoulders. Now she knew what she was dealing with, she could plan accordingly. Striding back to her desk, she wrote an action plan.

Step one - Break out my BOB every morning before work. And again possibly after work? During the night as well??? USE AS NECESSARY!
Step two - Reactivate online dating profile. ASAP!!!
Step three - Throw myself at Isaac one last time and hope for the best? UNLIKELY TO WORK...
Step four - Remove sense of smell. How? Get a cold? Nasal plugs? GOOGLE LATER.
Step five - Tell JHS to stop using his witchcraft lust potion. DON'T MAKE IT OBVIOUS WHY!!!

ESTELLE'S CONVICTION IN THE EFFECTIVENESS OF HER action plan waned as she drove away from Shoscombe Manor towards the livery. Suddenly, all she could think of was impressing James by showing off her mounted archery skills that Saturday. She would show him what a sexy and badass woman she was, and he would...

Her mind immediately gave her an image of James pinning

her against a wall, his mouth on hers, his hand on her breast, his— 'Shut up!' she yelled out loud.

Joy and Chester barked.

'No, not you! Sorry!' she said to them as she pulled into the livery. Parking outside her cottage, she let them out of the car to run around, then went inside. It was clear that step one of her action plan needed to be activated immediately. Going to her bedroom, she closed the door, took her Battery-Operated-Boyfriend from the drawer of her bedside table, and flicked the switch on.

Dead.

A bit like my love life. Taking it with her, she went to the kitchen to rummage in an overstuffed drawer and find new batteries.

The doorbell went.

James? She rolled her eyes. *Why would it be him?* Chucking BOB in the nearest cupboard, she went to answer the door.

Standing on the other side, in tears and surrounded by suitcases, stood Elyse.

'He kicked me out,' she sobbed. 'I didn't have anywhere else to go!'

Stunned, Estelle stared at her.

'And yesterday you said I could stay with you.'

'Er...'

Elyse nodded and took a deep breath. 'It's okay, I can find a bed-and-breakfast somewhere.'

'No! It's fine! Of course you can stay here. Kick your shoes off over there and come in.'

Estelle helped Elyse bring her suitcases and bags in, then brought her through into the small kitchen.

'Take a seat. Cup of tea? Brandy?'

Elyse sat, looking like a pale and delicate flower whose petals were wilting.

'Do you have any chamomile?'

Estelle took a glass jar filled with yellow ochre buds from a cupboard. 'Biodynamic and hand-picked by my younger sister, Willow, so it's about as potently hippy as you can get.'

'Thank you.'

Cramming the dried flowers into a tea infuser, Estelle put the kettle on. She was dying to ask Elyse about her relationship with James, to try and iron out the discrepancies between Elyse's story and what she'd inferred from James and his mum. But Elyse seemed genuinely upset, so she kept her mouth shut.

'I won't stay long. I just need time to get back on my feet. I'll be at work during the day, so only here in the evenings and on weekends.'

Well, that buggers up James's visit to the stables on Saturday…

'Are things okay then with Kev—your boss?'

Elyse's eyes overflowed once more. 'Not really.'

'So, you need a new job as well?'

'No, I love working for Kev, and he's like a father to me. It's just…' She took a big breath. 'James made him choose between me and him. And…' She shrugged helplessly. 'Kev was always going to put his son first.'

Estelle ground her teeth.

'It'll be okay. I can be professional. And staying here means I don't have to see James.'

The kettle came to the boil. Estelle filled Elyse's mug and placed it on the table along with a tin of biscuits.

'Help yourself. I've got all the good ones—custard creams, Jaffa Cakes and chocolate chip cookies. I'm just going to clear out the spare bedroom for you.'

'Can I help?'

'No, it's fine. You just sit here and chill. I won't be long.'

. . .

Four hours later, after helping Elyse unpack, cooking for her, cleaning up afterwards, and allowing her to use the bathroom for an hour, Estelle went to bed, completely exhausted.

Is this what having children is like?

After long days interacting with people either at the livery or at Foxbrooke Manor, Estelle revelled in coming home to blissful silence. Her little cottage was her sanctuary, where she could decompress in peace and quiet. Now, however, she couldn't even use BOB without Elyse hearing. How long was she going to stay? Estelle wasn't going to turn her out, but she didn't know Elyse at all, and what she'd said about James didn't add up.

She took out her phone. *Time for step two.*

Estelle's dating app was so under-used it took a couple of minutes to install updates. When it finally opened, her inbox was full. On first signing up for the app, she'd been excited. Then she'd read the messages. It seemed the majority of men hadn't even bothered reading her profile and had no interest in anything more than a hook-up.

Message from: BeaverFarmer69

Profile picture: Shirtless man with his tongue out, holding an oversized chainsaw at crotch level.

Message: Hey...

Message from: Alf2008

Profile picture: Photo of shirtless man in his twenties with a baseball cap on back-to-front, standing in a gym and flexing.

Message: That body of yours is absurd. I may need to see the booty.

. . .

MESSAGE FROM: COBRA

Profile picture: Selfie of unsmiling man in his fifties with greasy hair, taken from a low angle.

Message: I am extremely well endowed. I do not want a woman who messes me around. Can I trust you?

MESSAGE FROM: SIMPLE TIEMAN

Profile picture: Out of focus photo of an unsmiling man in his forties wearing a loose grey t-shirt and holding a piece of rope in his hands.

Message: Hey Country Girl. I'm Si. I'm into ethical non-monogamy and pushing boundaries. Shibari switch. You let me tie you up and I'll be your slave. No cheating. Interested? Message me.

MESSAGE FROM: BAZ

Profile picture: Photo of shirtless man in his twenties, taken in the mirror of a public toilet.

Message: I bet your 50 times hotta in person. And so am i hahahahah

MESSAGE FROM: ANDREW54

Profile picture: Out of focus picture taken of a print photo, featuring a handsome man in nineteen-seventies clothes, standing next to a pristine sports car from the same era.

Message: Hello. My name is Andrew and I'm a solvent and mature man living in Bath. I would like to get to know you and explore what we have in common. I look forward to hearing from you at your earliest convenience.

Message from: Lightmyfire

Profile picture: Photo of shirtless man in his thirties, taken in the mirror of a public toilet.

Message: It is truly unreal how fucking hot you are. Like it blows my mind. DM me.

Estelle exited her inbox and scrolled mindlessly through the feed of men, hoping that someone would catch her eye. Two minutes later, her heart nearly stopped at the sight of James.

What the... Sitting up in bed, she opened his profile. *Why does he have to be so handsome?* If she hadn't known James, she would have assumed these were photos of a model that someone had substituted for ones of their actual face. *Maybe it isn't him?*

She looked at the profile name—*Lucifer*.

Hands trembling, she read what he'd written.

I'm a single city boy who likes complicated and challenging country girls. I like drinking double espressos and feasting on the trampled remains of my enemies whilst listening to the 'Imperial March' from Star Wars. My favourite colour is black, my favourite number is 666, and my favourite hobby is stargazing. I'm after a woman who is five foot eleven, with dark skin and curly black hair, who likes horses, dogs, and making my life interesting.

Estelle rang Eveline.

Jack picked up. 'Hey Stelle, Eveline's sleeping at the moment. You okay?'

'Is she alright?'

'I think so, yeah, just exhausted. Apparently, this is normal, at least for the first few weeks.'

'Will you give her my love when she wakes up?'

'Of course. Do you want me to pass on a message?'

'No, I just rang for a chat. Although... Now I've got you on the phone...'

'Should I be worried?'

She smiled. 'Not too worried.' She lowered her voice in case Elyse was listening outside the door. 'Yesterday, things went a bit Pete Tong. James and I had a massive bust-up in front of two council members from the licensing committee.'

Jack sighed on the other end of the phone.

'So, we're in damage limitation mode. We're inviting them all to a night of entertainment at the Manor a week on Saturday to showcase our plans and prove that James and I can get on.'

'And can you?'

'I think so. I just wanted to ask if you had any free time to help set it up.'

There was a pause. 'I'll do what I can, but only when Eveline is well enough to leave the rectory. As soon as she's back, I want to be there to help.'

'I understand.'

'Sorry, Stelle. I know it's not ideal. Why don't we chat about it now and I'll see what I can do over the next few days.'

BY THE TIME ESTELLE GOT OFF THE PHONE WITH JACK, SHE was too tired to do anything other than turn the light off and close her eyes.

There was a tentative knock on the door.

'Yes?'

Elyse appeared. 'I'm going to bed now.'

'Sleep well.'

'Thanks, you too.' She hovered in the doorway.

Estelle pushed up onto her elbows. 'Can I get you anything?'

She shook her head. 'I just wanted to ask a favour.'

'What is it?'

'Can you please not tell James or his family where I am?'

'Okay.'

'Thank you. And for everything else.' Elyse gave her a smile, then disappeared, closing the door behind her.

ESTELLE KNEW SHE WAS DREAMING, BUT WASN'T SURE IF IT was a fantasy or a nightmare. Darth Vader riding Duke, then taking off his helmet to reveal James. Tumbling off the balcony at the Winter Ball into the arms of BeaverFarmer69. James pressing her up against the office wall and calling her 'Star'. Isaac in a yoga class with a rope in his hand and a twinkle in his eye.

There was no clear narrative, just a series of images that morphed in and out of each other until she wasn't sure if she was going to have an orgasm or be sick. It was so exhausting that she forced her dreaming self to imagine she was going to sleep, to a place where her mind disappeared into blackness.

After what seemed like another lifetime of experiences, Estelle woke, disorientated. She stared at the light coming in under the bottom of the curtains.

Shit. What time is it?

Glancing at her bedside clock, she groaned. Nine-thirty. Hauling herself out of bed, she went to the bathroom, only remembering Elyse was now living there when she was confronted by an array of beauty products and wet towels left on the floor.

'Elyse?'

No answer.

Fuck's sake. Estelle had a quick wash, then took Elyse's towels to dry in the airing cupboard. The kitchen was another bombsite, with dirty dishes, crusts, and a used tea bag lying on the work surface. Estelle may have been messy, but not when it came to keeping herself or her house clean. She made sure Chester and Joy were fed, then bundled them into the Defender and set off for Shoscombe Manor. Breakfast could be French Fancies and a cappuccino.

AFTER PULLING UP OUTSIDE THE OFFICE'S FRONT DOOR, Estelle strode straight for the kitchen. She stopped in shock, her hand on the door, as through the glass panel she saw James embracing a woman.

He caught her eye, shook his head, and raised his finger as if to say for her to give him a minute.

Estelle dithered as confusion and hurt battled inside her. It was just like yesterday morning, all over again, when she'd heard James talking to his old colleague. Just when she was starting to think he was a decent human being who actually might *like* her, he ruined everything with his actions. Again.

She couldn't see the woman's face, but James was stroking up and down her back. How could he? The woman lifted her head from his chest and wiped her eyes.

He'd made her *cry*?

'Motherfucker!' Estelle yelled, pushing the door open. 'What have you done to *this* one?'

The woman spun around and screamed at the same time Chester and Joy started barking. The dogs leapt towards James, but the woman was in the way. James grabbed their collars and manhandled them out of the room.

'Don't worry,' Estelle said to the woman. 'I won't let him touch you again. Stay here and let me get rid of him.' She followed James into the hall, where he was crouched down, petting her dogs and shushing them.

'You just can't help yourself, can you?' she shouted.

'What? I told you to give me a minute!'

'Is that all you need to remove another broken-hearted woman from the premises? Or the length of time it takes for you to get your rocks off?'

'Excuse me?'

The woman came into the corridor. 'Er...'

Estelle held out her hand, her body firing with adrenaline. 'I'm Estelle. My car's just outside. I can take you where you need to go.'

The woman took it. 'Sophia. But—'

'Or if you don't have anywhere to go, you can stay at mine.' She huffed. 'I mean, why the fuck not? The more the merrier. We can turn the cottage into a refuge for women who've been screwed over by this arsehole,' she finished, flinging an accusatory finger at James.

He straightened and crossed his arms over his chest. 'And once again, you engage your mouth before your brain.'

'I'm trying to protect defenceless women from you!'

'Estelle,' the woman began.

James's eyes were flashing as he glared at her. 'You know nothing about how I treat women, and I'm sick and tired of your baseless accusations based on hearsay and conjecture.'

The door to the main house opened, and Beverley dashed down the corridor. 'Is everything alright, babes?' She took Sophia's hand. 'What's going on?'

Estelle stared at them. *Oh, god. Is she James's real girlfriend? Is this the one who kissed him? Or is she the replacement for Elyse? What's going on?*

Sophia put on the kind of smile that seemed designed to convince everyone around her that she hadn't just been crying. 'Nothing, Mum, I just got startled by the dogs, that's all.'

Mum? Estelle turned to look at James.

The anger in his eyes had been replaced with devilish delight and smug satisfaction that she'd once again put her size eights firmly in it.

'Allow me to introduce my sister, Sophia.'

'But you said your sister was called Char,' she blustered.

'It's a nickname.'

Estelle glanced at Sophia, as if needing confirmation.

'It's short for Chardonnay,' Sophia said. 'That's what my name was when I was born. I was two when Mum and Dad changed it.'

Oh, fuck. Oh fucking, fucking, fuck.

'I've had some, er, difficult stuff come up in my personal life recently,' she continued. 'So, I've moved home for a bit.'

Estelle took her in. She was almost as tall as she was, with thick, dark brown wavy hair and soulful eyes. Even though she seemed to have a completely different personality to her brother, Estelle could see the likeness.

'I'm sorry,' she stuttered. 'I didn't know.'

Sophia smiled shyly. 'And I'm sorry I screamed. I'm not great with dogs.'

'Do you want to meet mine or shall I get them out of your way?'

'As long as they don't jump up, I would love to meet them. James told me they're very sweet.'

'Just like their owner,' James drawled sarcastically behind her.

'Well then,' Beverley said. 'If there's no drama, I'm going back to watching "The Real Housewives of Chelsea". If anyone wants a French Fancy, I put a couple of boxes in the kitchen earlier for you.'

She gave them a wave and went back into the main house.

Estelle knelt by Chester and Joy, ignoring James standing next to them. She was too mortified to look at him. Holding their collars, she introduced them to Sophia.

'This is Joy, who is fairly clever and very gentle. And this is Chester, who is extremely stupid and excitable.'

Sophia cautiously extended her hand to stroke them. 'James said Chester keeps trying to hump him.'

'As I said,' Estelle replied. 'Stupid and excitable.'

'Just like his owner,' James growled behind her.

'James!' Sophia sounded shocked.

Estelle shrugged. 'I'll allow him that one. I'm so sorry about just now.'

'Me too. It's not the impression I was hoping to give you when we first met.' Sophia looked Chester and Joy deep in their eyes. 'And I'm sorry for scaring you two as well.'

Their tails wagged even faster, and they came forward as if to lick her.

Estelle dragged them away. 'You'll know they like you by the tail wagging and urge to give you a tongue bath.'

'What about humping?' James asked.

'That means they're just deeply confused.'

'James was making us a coffee before showing me your office,' Sophia said. 'He told me he'd been painting dog bowls, which I find extremely hard to believe.'

A wave of guilt rolled through Estelle's stomach at the words she'd just thrown at James. 'What he did was amazing. I wouldn't have had the patience. Why don't I show them to you?'

Sophia's smile was tentative, as if she'd just been befriended by the cool girl at school. 'Thank you, that would be lovely.'

'I'll make the coffee,' James said, going past them into the kitchen.

When the door shut behind him, Estelle turned to Sophia. 'I am so sorry I went mental,' she whispered.

'It's fine,' Sophia whispered back. 'My brother can elicit strong emotions.'

They went down the corridor together into the end office, and Estelle pointed to the dog bowls by the window.

'James painted them for Chester and Joy.'

Sophia knelt to look at them. 'Oh, they're so lovely!' She glanced at Estelle. 'I can't believe he did this!'

Estelle shrugged, feeling even more uncomfortable. 'He tried to pretend someone else did them.'

Getting to her feet, Sophia grinned. 'He's a big softy, really.'

'James? Soft?'

'Underneath the abs of steel he's mainly marshmallow.' She frowned. 'But I think only Mum and I get to see that side of him.'

Sophia looked so sad that Estelle expected tears to start flowing.

What to say? 'I, er...'

Sophia gestured to the mat rolled up behind Estelle's desk. 'Do you do yoga?'

'Yeah, kind of. I do it in the village.'

'I've always wanted to give it a go, but I'm not very bendy and feel uncomfortable wearing tight clothes.'

'Then you should definitely come to a class with me. Half the women there are over sixty and can't touch their toes. Plus, I swear to god that some of them come in their pyjamas.'

Sophia giggled. 'Is it suitable for beginners?'

'Definitely. Isaac gives variations for every level.'

'The teacher's a man?'

'Yeah, but he's not a sleaze or anything. He's painfully

professional. I've been trying to shag him for a couple of years now but haven't got anywhere.'

James entered with a tray of mugs and a box of French Fancies, placing it on his desk. He was acting as if he hadn't heard her, but Estelle knew full well he had. He passed her a cappuccino and his sister a latte. Both had patterns in the foam.

'He's just learned how to do that,' Estelle said to Sophia. 'He's getting quite good at them now.'

Sophia frowned. 'The leaf?'

She nodded.

'But he's been doing them for years.' Sophia sat on the chaise longue. 'He can do all sorts, even a swan.'

Narrowing her eyes, Estelle stared at James. He ignored her.

'I don't know if I told you,' he said to his sister, 'but Estelle does mounted archery.'

'Wow!'

'She's going to show me this Saturday.'

Shit. Elyse. She finally looked at him. 'Er, actually, we need to rearrange.'

He raised an eyebrow.

'Could we do it during the week and then work on the weekend to make up for it?'

Something that looked like relief flashed across his face, then he smiled. 'Tomorrow?'

She panicked. That seemed far too soon. 'Friday?'

'Friday.'

'Okay.' She turned to Sophia. 'And you can come too if you like?'

Sophia's gaze jumped between Estelle and her brother as if not sure what answer she should give.

'Thank you,' she replied. 'I'll see if I'm free.'

'Where's Sophia?' Estelle demanded as soon as James got out of his Ferrari in the livery car park.

He didn't immediately reply, turning his back and pretending to check that none of the rough stones from the driveway had jumped up and chipped any paint off his car. He knew he'd been slow enough to prevent that happening, but by averting his face, he could ensure he wasn't grinning with excitement at spending this time with Estelle.

'Well?'

And, he also had to concede, he was enjoying how unsettled she seemed at having him on her turf.

Driving in, he'd clocked there was something different about Estelle. And now, as he straightened and looked at her closely, his suspicions were confirmed.

She's wearing make-up.

Putting a hand to his jaw, he held it firmly in 'catalogue man pose number four - complex thought', the main purpose of which was to prevent a smile from spreading across his face.

'Some urgent work stuff came up.' He stretched, deliberately allowing his jacket to open, and his jumper and shirt to ride up, revealing his lower abs.

'She's an archaeologist!' Estelle replied indignantly, her eyes flicking to his happy trail.

Jackpot.

'How could anything archaeological be urgent?' she continued. 'Some bones about to go past their use-by date? Stonehenge about to fall down?'

James shrugged. Sophia was the only person in the world he'd told his deepest secret to—that he liked Estelle. *Really* liked her. So, she'd told him she wouldn't come today.

He knew nothing was going to happen between himself and Estelle. It wasn't just the situation they were in that meant they needed to keep their relationship professional. And it definitely wasn't the fact her twin hated him. The biggest obstacle was that Estelle still believed ninety-nine per cent of him was the devil incarnate.

However, that didn't stop him from wanting to spend time with her *out* of the office, or getting to know the most attractive and challenging woman he'd ever met.

Her hands were now on her hips. Her extremely *shapely* hips. Hips that were wearing tight-fitting jodhpurs. Hips that James wanted to hold onto for dear life as she rode him, her powerful thighs squeezing until—

'Well?'

He shrugged again to give him time to order his thoughts. 'I don't know. Something about a LiDAR machine?'

Estelle crossed her arms, pushing her breasts higher.

James's mouth watered.

'I like your sister. She's your antimatter.'

He raised an eyebrow.

'You're Satan in a sharp suit and she's an angel.'

'She *is* an angel, but I'm not the devil.'

Estelle didn't reply.

James saw that as progress. 'I can go home if you'd rather?'

Surprise flickered across her face, as if everything negative she'd just said was actually code for 'I really want you here, please don't leave'.

Throwing her hands in the air, she huffed as if to keep up appearances. 'You might as well stay. I'm all dressed up now.'

Her words were enough of an invitation for his gaze to rake unashamedly down and back up her body, taking in the tweed waistcoat over her white shirt, the top buttons of which were open to reveal her ample cleavage, the figure-hugging fawn jodhpurs and the fuck-me-now riding boots.

His dick twitched with appreciation and he quickly turned to the boot of his car, taking out a pair of wellies.

Behind him, Estelle giggled. 'They even match your poncy silk scarf. Are they brand new?'

Facing her, he nodded. 'I'm not much of a country boy.'

The use of those words, referencing Estelle's dating profile name of 'Country Girl', was entirely deliberate and completely effective. Her eyes widened and her plump lips parted with shock. James kept his features bland, but inside he was fist-pumping and yelling 'COME ON', like he'd just sunk a hole-in-one. She'd read his profile and now knew he liked her.

'I'm going to get Duke and find out where Chester and Joy have got to.' She walked off.

Play it cool. He took off his shoes and pulled the wellies on. *Just enjoy the moment.* His nose wrinkled. Easier said than done when surrounded by forty shades of shit. Much as James was attracted to Estelle, he didn't have the same admiration for the countryside. The natural world could be pleasant, but best experienced by a stroll through Kew Gardens or by buying a houseplant. James appreciated posh and expensive nature, not this bargain-basement mud-fest.

Chester and Joy ran at full pelt around the corner of the stable block towards him, tails wagging. James stroked them, whilst making sure neither of them tried to fornicate with his two-hundred-pound jeans.

The countryside may have been dirty and smelly, but all of that was forgotten when Estelle reappeared, leading her enormous horse, a bow slung over her shoulder and a quiver of arrows hanging at her hip. James already felt them hitting his heart *and* his crotch.

'You *sure* you don't want to ride with me?'

He resisted the urge to make a quip and shook his head. 'I've never ridden before, and today's not the day for me to start. I'm here for you.'

'Okay.' She swung herself up into the saddle.

Fuck me, she's hot.

'Did you say something?'

Was that out loud? He glanced up and shrugged. 'Don't think so?'

Her eyes narrowed.

'So, do I get a head start?'

She frowned. 'Huh?'

'Surely it's only fair, as I'm on foot. Or do you prefer to shoot at a standing target from close range?'

A snort of laughter escaped. 'Unfortunately, I need you.'

'You do?'

'For the festival!' Pulling on one side of Duke's reins, she walked him out of the yard. 'However, come July, I'm sending the Foxbrooke Hunt after you.'

He smirked. 'And where will you be? Leading the pack?'

She shrugged. 'Maybe. Or waiting at the end with a shotgun to finish you off.'

'Can't wait.'

Estelle led him around the back of the livery into the open countryside. The sleety rain that had battered Somerset over the last few days had moved on and cool sunlight shone through the barren trees, creating long, spindly shadows on the ground. It was still winter, but the solstice had passed and it seemed that spring was not far away.

James wanted to talk to Estelle, but she was riding a few feet ahead. So, he followed her up a hill, through a gate, to another large expanse of land. This area was flat, with targets attached to straw bales in a line covering the length of the field. Estelle whistled to the dogs, and they ran to a bale set up behind where she would be shooting from.

'You, too,' she said to him.

Doing as he was told, he watched as Duke trotted to the start of the course.

Dropping the reins, Estelle took the bow and notched an arrow into place.

His heart beat faster.

She let out a cry and Duke took off.

Holy shit. For some reason, James thought the horse would be trotting, but Duke was thundering across the ground at a gallop. Estelle's thighs were the only things keeping her upright, and they were also serving as shock absorbers to keep her upper body completely still.

He watched, transfixed, as Estelle let an arrow fly. It thudded straight into the first target. She took another arrow and shot again. And again. Because she couldn't see him, he allowed the joy he felt in his heart to spread out into a smile, whooping when she finished the run.

'Chester and Joy bounded forward at full tilt to retrieve the arrows on the ground, and James followed, pulling the ones from the bales.

Estelle trotted up to him, her face flushed and alive. 'Thanks.'

'That was amazing!'

The flush in her cheeks intensified.

'How many runs do you normally do in a session?'

'As many as I can. What takes up the most time is having to get on and off Duke to get my arrows back.'

'Well, you've got me to help you now.'

'Really?'

'Yes.' He gave her the arrows he was holding. 'I'll stand at one end, and the moment you've passed the first target, I'll begin collecting them.'

'Are you sure?'

'One hundred per cent.' He started towards the beginning of the course. 'Go on,' he called over his shoulder.

There was a whoop, then Duke shot past him.

Having spent so much time training to be an elite rower, James knew the number of hours it took to get to the top, and how little time Estelle had in comparison to practise her sport. He was used to being the centre of attention as the athlete, but watching her from the sidelines filled him with just as much satisfaction.

Estelle was a warrior princess. Genghis Khan would have wanted her on the frontline of any attack. And after the battle, in his bed.

Readjusting himself once more as his cock kept unsubtly reminding him of its presence, he pulled an arrow from the bullseye as Estelle finished another run.

'You're getting better,' he called out as she cantered towards him.

She smiled. 'I'm getting there.'

'Is this how competitions are configured?'

'Sometimes. They can also be on a circular track, and have

targets placed at different angles.'

'I can move some of them if you like?'

She hesitated, then swung herself to the ground. 'Let me help.'

'We could also put them at different heights?' he suggested as they walked together across the field, Chester and Joy at their heels. 'That would make it more difficult.'

She nodded. 'The bales are thick enough to stand on their end.'

James had already worked out that morning and the bales weren't particularly heavy in comparison, but after they'd finished resetting them, he was beginning to sweat.

'Who needs a gym, eh?' Estelle said with a grin.

'A gym is cleaner and has showers.'

'There's a drinking trough over by the hedge if you fancy a wash?'

He shuddered. 'No thanks.'

'Maybe in the summer you might be persuaded to take a dip in the Foxbrooke?'

'If you insist...'

In the pause that followed, he watched the double meaning of her words fall onto her like a ton of bricks.

'I meant the river!'

He grinned. 'Of course.'

She slapped his arm. 'You're such a pig.'

Her touch felt like foreplay.

'Is that all you've got?' He flexed under his jacket, hoping she might land an actual punch.

She did.

'Ow! Fucking hell!' she cried, rubbing her knuckles.

'You okay?' He reached for her hand.

She snatched it away. 'What have you got under there? Armour plating?'

'Want to see?'

'You're incorrigible.' She turned and strode towards Duke.

Well, that wasn't a no…

James went back to a position of safety and watched Estelle as she did another run. She only hit half of the targets.

'That was bollocks!' she shouted as she rode towards him.

'No, it means you're being challenged.' He handed her the arrows he'd collected. 'And that's good.'

She frowned. 'You *sure* you're not bored?'

He shook his head. This was the happiest he'd been since being forced out of London.

'Okay, then,' she said with a grin. 'I'm going again.'

Her improvement was quick over the next few runs, and he saw how happy it made her.

Cantering up, she leapt off Duke. 'I want to set up a jump. Make it even harder.'

'Do they do that in competition?'

'No. But if I can do that, then I can do anything.'

'It doesn't sound very safe.'

She rolled her eyes and pointed to the hedge bordering the field. 'I can clear that on Duke. A couple of straw bales are nothing.'

'But you're holding onto his reins whilst you do that, not a bow and arrow. Right?'

'Potato, tomato. Are you going to help me, or what?'

He followed her to the pile of bales that had been serving as a lookout station for Joy and Chester.

Estelle grabbed one. 'I'll only make it two high, okay? Duke could practically step over that.'

James was a risk taker, but never with anything that could endanger his life. Taking his phone from his pocket, he checked for signal strength.

'What are you doing?'

'Making sure I'm able to ring for the air ambulance if need-ed.' He glanced around. 'Good. This field is flat enough for them to land.'

'Seriously? I know what I'm doing. I could ride almost as soon as I could walk.'

James didn't want to get into an argument with Estelle when they were actually starting to get on, so instead helped her assemble the jump, then stood back.

'Why don't you have a go without the bow and arrow first? Just feel what it's like when you're more upright and not holding the reins.'

'Bollocks to that. I'm going for it.' She stuck her tongue out at him, then clicked Duke to a canter and made her way to the start of the run.

James's heart beat faster in his chest. He liked being in control, but right now, he was most definitely not. Memories of Estelle tumbling over the banister played on repeat, falling from his mind to hit the pit of his stomach with a sickening thud, over and over again.

Letting out another cry, she urged Duke to a gallop, her bow already raised and an arrow in place. She let it fly into the first target, then pulled another from the quiver and tried to notch it in place. But at that moment, Duke jumped. Suddenly her balance was gone, and she was tossed from the saddle.

Panic shot through James as he sprinted towards her, Chester and Joy barking loudly beside him. Estelle was lying face down on the ground, not moving.

'Estelle!' he shouted, reaching her side.

She stirred and pushed to a seated position. 'Fuck!'

'Are you okay? What's hurting? Can you move your legs?'

'I'm fine,' she muttered. 'But my clothes are ruined.'

Chester and Joy were trying to clean her with their

tongues. James pushed them back, his heart pounding as if attempting to exit through his ribs. 'Are you *sure* you're okay?'

He went to take her arm, but she batted his hand away and got to her feet. 'I told you, I'm fine!'

Part of him knew she was embarrassed, but most of him was still obsessed with needing to know she hadn't just sustained a serious spinal injury.

'Estelle, stop. Please. You don't know you're okay. You could—'

'I'm FINE!' She turned to the other end of the field where her horse had finally stopped. 'Duke! Come here!' Stomping forward, her attention was on Duke, not where she was walking. Her left foot caught on a clod of earth, her ankle turned, and she went down with a shriek of real pain.

Jesus Christ. James ran forward.

Estelle was clutching her boot, her eyes tightly closed.

He dropped to the muddy ground. 'I didn't hear a crack. Did you? Do you think it's broken?'

'Don't think so,' she hissed. 'But it really hurts.'

'We need to get your boot off before the swelling gets too much.'

She nodded.

He carefully unzipped it and took it off, followed by her sock. He couldn't see any obvious sign of a break, but her foot was beginning to swell.

Without a second thought, he pulled off his four-hundred-pound silk scarf.

'What on earth are you doing?'

'Getting the ankle strapped up before taking you to hospital.'

'I'm fine—'

He ignored her and took out his mobile phone. 'I don't have a splint, so this will have to do. Can you hold it in place?'

'This is ridiculous. I can walk.'

He moved away, standing and crossing his arms. 'Go on then.'

Estelle got onto her knees and tried to stand, but the pain must have been acute, as she flopped back to the ground, her eyes closed once more, her lashes damp with tears he knew she didn't want to shed.

Chester and Joy were whining, knowing something was wrong with their favourite human.

'Shh,' James said to them. 'It's okay. It's okay.' Crouching again by Estelle's side, he put his hand on her shoulder. 'Please, let me help you.'

She shook her head.

Fuck! Did she really think so little of him that she expected him to be a dick about this? To say 'I told you so'? *Would* he have done that in the past? Or to someone who wasn't her?

'Estelle,' he said quietly. 'The other night, when I told you the most frightening moment of my life was when you fell from the staircase, I wasn't lying. At the time, I think the adrenaline got me through it, but I keep getting flashbacks. And when you fell from Duke just now, I panicked.'

Her eyes opened, but she was still staring at the muddy ground.

'I know you think I'm an arsehole—'

'I don't,' she mumbled.

He let out a short laugh. 'You've called me that three times to my face, the last instance being two days ago.'

'I'm sorry.'

He was still touching her shoulder. Could he take her hand?

'I know I've been an arsehole in the past. But right now, I'm trying to be the opposite of that.'

She didn't reply.

Letting go of her shoulder, he held onto her little finger.

'Can this much of you give me a chance? Even if just for the time it takes to help you to the hospital?'

'I don't need to go,' she said petulantly.

'Well, back home then?'

She nodded.

James let out a breath. *Thank god.* 'Okay, I'm going to use my phone as a splint. Can you help by holding it?'

Taking it from him, she held it against the inside of her ankle and he began strapping her foot up with his scarf.

'You're ruining it,' she grumbled.

'It was cheap.'

'Bollocks was it. My Mom's a supermodel and my aunt's a fashion designer. That's made from silk and would have set you back three or four hundred quid.'

'I stole it.'

Her eyes shot up to meet his, as if needing to see if he was joking or not.

He grinned. 'It's just, what did you call it?' He revisited his 'catalogue man number four' pose, clasping his chin and furrowing his brow. 'Ah yes! A "poncy silk scarf".'

She looked away again.

'Estelle.' He squeezed her little finger. 'I don't give a shit about the scarf. But I do give a shit about you.'

'And all your nice clothes are ruined.'

He glanced down. 'People are going to think we've been mud wrestling.'

The corner of her mouth lifted.

'How about this?' he continued. 'I help you back home. But if we meet anyone on the way, I'll tell them you kicked my arse. Deal?'

She nodded.

'Good. Right, I'm going to help you up. Will Duke follow us or do I need to send someone back for him?'

'He'll follow.'

'Okay, I'll come back for your bow and arrows later. Take this now.' He gave her the riding boot he'd removed earlier. 'Hold on to it with one hand and put your other arm around my neck. Yep, that's it.'

Before she had a chance to work out what he was about to do, he'd lifted her into his arms.

'What are you doing?' she shrieked.

'This is quicker and will be less painful for you. And the sooner you ice your ankle, the better.'

'But I'm too heavy!'

'Estelle. Look at me.'

She stared at his lips, seeming unable to meet his gaze.

'Without meaning to sound like a dick, I can bench twice your weight. I'm really strong, so let me do this for you. Please?'

She nodded.

He gave an internal fist pump and set off down the hill.

$$\text{❧}\quad 19 \quad\text{❧}$$

stelle tensed as James carried her. This should have been romantic, but she was currently covering his designer clothes with mud, was terrified he was going to drop her, and her ankle was throbbing with pain.

You absolute twat. You were just trying to show off, weren't you?

The afternoon had been amazing, then she'd gone and ruined it.

'You *can* relax, you know.'

She didn't reply. He was being nice, which made everything more complicated. Living in a world of black and white, where she could lump James Hunter-Savage in the same category as mosquitos, dictators, and people who played music through their phone speakers on public transport, was far easier than having to deal with him being awful *and* wonderful.

Estelle liked to know where she stood with people, but with James, she was lost in a swirling fog of fifty shades of grey. Enjoying his company felt like she'd just snuck into the enemy's camp with the intention of betraying her brother and shagging the commander.

'When was the last time someone carried you like this?'

She shrugged. 'I can't remember. Must have been when I was a little kid.'

'Hmm.'

'Is that a good "hmm" or a bad one?'

She stared at his mouth as he smiled. In a body that seemed rock hard, James's lips appeared very soft. Hers tingled with the need to kiss them.

'Good, I think,' he replied. 'Because it will be memorable. And because it means I'm better than everyone else.'

'Excuse me?' Her voice went up along with her eyes, as they finally met his.

He was smirking at her, as if revelling in the fact he'd got her to look at him. 'Did I say better? Maybe I meant stronger.'

Estelle took a deep breath, filling her lungs with the incredible scent of him. It made her heart race faster and a pulse beat between her thighs.

'You're infuriating.'

His smile got bigger. 'As are you.'

Despite all her attempts not to, she smiled back at him and his face lit up. Even though he was carrying her down the hill, wearing clothes that were now covered in mud, James looked genuinely pleased to be there. Happiness expanded inside her, pushing the pain in her ankle to the background.

She breathed in deeply again. How could he smell so good? Then she remembered why. *Pheromones.*

'You okay?' he asked.

'What?'

'You frowned. How's the pain?'

'Oh...' For a moment, she'd forgotten all about it. 'Um...' *Think!* She faked a sneeze.

'Estelle?'

'Er... I've been meaning to say something to you for a while now, but didn't want to offend you.'

James's eyes widened with shock, then he burst out laughing.

Fuck's sake.

'*You* didn't want to offend *me*?' he finally managed.

'Yes. Because you might construe it as a personal criticism.'

'Heaven forbid you put a stop to the endless compliments. How will my cold, dead heart survive?'

She huffed.

'Will your words pierce my soul?' he continued. 'Oh, hang on, according to you, I don't have one.'

If James hadn't been laughing quite so much, Estelle would have felt dreadful remembering all the awful things she'd said to him.

'Go on then,' he said. 'Out with it. Do I smell bad? Am I too ugly to look at?'

Just tell him! If you don't, then the witchcraft will wear you down!

She let out another fake sneeze. 'I need you to stop wearing your cologne around me.'

'Why? You said you liked it.'

'When?'

'At the Winter Ball.'

Dammit. 'I was, er, in shock.' She sniffed. 'I'm actually really allergic to it.'

One eyebrow raised. 'In what way?'

'Achoo.'

James snorted with laughter.

'What? I am!'

'If you say so.'

He opened the gate behind the livery and carried her through.

'James! You have to stop wearing it! It's driving me nuts,' she hissed.

'That makes two of us,' he murmured under his breath, before calling out. 'Molly?'

'Oh, my god, Estelle! What happened?' Molly cried as she ran up to them.

'It's fine! I twisted my ankle, that's all.'

Molly took Duke's bridle. 'I'll put him away. Can I do anything?'

'Estelle's bow and arrows are still up there.' James inclined his head towards the slope. 'Do you have time to get them?'

'Yes. I'll do it as soon as Duke's sorted.'

'Thanks, and can you keep an eye on Chester and Joy?'

'Yeah, sure.'

'Sorry, Moll,' Estelle mumbled.

'Don't be daft. I'm more worried about you. Are you going to hospital?'

James said 'yes' at the same time that she said 'no'.

'Let's say it's up for discussion,' he said to Molly.

Molly's gaze darted between them, as if trying to work out what was going on underneath the obvious. 'Okay. If you need anything, just come and find me.' She grinned at Estelle, then led Duke away.

James strode towards Estelle's cottage. 'I presume the door's not locked?'

'Never.'

He came to an abrupt halt. 'Not even at night?'

She shrugged. 'I keep a shotgun by my bed.'

'Of course you do.' He shook his head and kept walking. 'That doesn't negate the need to lock your door.'

As they got closer, Estelle's nerves jangled inside her. She'd tidied away any evidence of Elyse just in case James came in for a cup of tea, but these were circumstances she never could have anticipated.

'Can you take off your boots and coat?' she asked. 'I don't want to bring mud into the house.'

'Of course.'

Outside the front door was a large covered porch. Estelle dropped the boot she was holding, unzipped the other one, and let it drop to the ground. James kicked off his wellies, then carefully carried her inside.

'Can I let you down now so I can take off my coat?' he asked.

She nodded, and he gently lowered her to the floor. Holding onto the wall for support, Estelle pulled off her muddy outer clothes, trying to keep her gaze averted from James as he did the same.

'We need to get your jodhpurs off.'

'*We?*'

He sighed. 'They're filthy and you need to be lying down with your foot elevated.'

The front door opened directly onto the living room and Estelle glanced around it, trying to figure out where she could sit without making everything dirty. Looking at her reflection in the hall mirror, she stared in horror at the mud in her hair and on her face.

'I need to get in a bath.'

'Stay there a sec.' James went through the living room towards the kitchen, returning with two wooden chairs. 'Sit on one and put your foot on the other.' He rolled his jacket up. 'Rest your ankle over this. I presume the bathroom is upstairs?'

She nodded and sat.

He helped position her foot on his coat. 'Got any Magnesium Sulphate?'

'What?'

'Epsom salts.'

'No.'

'Anything you want me to put in the bath?'

'Hot water.'

'Consider it done.' He made a move towards the stairs.

'Wait!'

'Yes?'

'Don't go into any other room.'

'I won't.'

'And don't look at anything.'

He paused. 'What *can* I look at?'

'Er... The stairs, the bathroom door, the floor, the bath.'

'Taps?'

'They're an integral part of the bath, so yes.'

'Any other instructions?'

'Not at the moment.'

Chuckling, he went up the stairs. A few moments later, Estelle heard the sound of running water.

Leaning forward, she carefully unwrapped her ankle and removed James's phone. As she did, the lock screen lit up, displaying a photo of Chester and Joy. The dogs were sitting on the floor of the office and looking up at the camera as if in love with the person behind it. Estelle's eyes prickled with conflicting emotion. Why did James have to be nice? It was far easier to hate him than change her mind about the person who'd been number one on her shit list since the age of thirteen.

Putting the phone down, she turned to her ankle. It was puffy, but she was still able to wiggle her toes. Glancing around the room, she noticed with horror the giant 'U' she'd made out of antique forks, then mounted on a piece of wood. She'd placed it in the middle of the coffee table, no longer hating James enough to give it to him. Where could she hide it?

Pushing onto her good foot, she hopped to the centre of the room and picked it up.

'Is that for me?'

Whipping around, she lost her balance and toppled towards a sofa. Not wanting to get it dirty, she pivoted and collapsed in a heap on the floor, the U clutched to her chest.

'Jesus!' James crouched by her side, gazing at her with concern. 'You okay?' He held out his hand.

She passed him the fork U.

'Thank you,' he said with a huge smile. 'My life is now complete.'

He held out his other hand, and she reluctantly took it, standing unsteadily.

'Your bath is ready. I didn't fill it all the way so you could adjust the temperature. Do you have any ice?'

'There are two bags of frozen peas in the freezer I can use.'

'Painkillers?'

'Paracetamol in the bathroom cabinet.'

'I'll get you a glass of water. Can I help you upstairs?'

Estelle shook her head even though her body was screaming *carry me!* at him.

'Can you put weight on it?' he asked sceptically.

'I can hop.'

'Upstairs?'

Bugger. 'I'll manage.'

He put the fork U down, frowned and moved closer, holding under her elbow as well as her hand. 'Use me as a crutch. Hold your breath if you must.'

'Huh?'

'So you don't have an anaphylactic reaction to my killer cologne.'

'Bugger off,' she grumbled. 'It's killing me.'

He laughed, then helped her hobble to the base of the stairs.

She stared up them. Her foot was throbbing now that gravity was sending blood straight to it.

'Come on,' he said. 'No-one can see me helping you, and I promise I won't tell.'

'You'd better not.'

He smirked and helped her onto the first step.

With James on one side, and the banister on the other, it was easy to get up without putting any weight on her bad foot. However, the enclosed space meant she was even more aware of James than normal—his size, strength, and how amazing he smelled.

'Your perfume suits you perfectly,' he said.

'What?'

'The one you're wearing.'

Shit. She was still using Elyse's perfume that she'd found in the toilets at work.

'It's not mine.'

'Yes, it is.'

She glanced at him. 'How would you know?'

He hesitated, and she stared at the changing emotions on his face, trying to mind read. James seemed to be working out whether or not he should say something. Then his expression became shuttered, and he indicated up the stairs.

'Come on, let's get you into the bath.'

In the bathroom, Estelle sat on the lid of the toilet. James had placed every single product that was hers around the edge of the bath so she could easily reach for them, and a pile of towels on the floor.

He glanced at her ankle. 'I'm not trying to be a sleaze, but can you get your jodhpurs off by yourself?'

'I don't know.'

'Well, have a think whilst I go and get the peas and a glass of water. Anything else?'

'My phone. It's in my coat pocket.'

He nodded and left.

Estelle pulled herself upright and undid her trousers, tugging them down to her knees, then sat again. Taking them off her good ankle, she was suddenly aware of how painful it was going to be getting them over her swollen one. But there was no way she was going to cut them.

There was a knock at the door.

Sod it. 'Come in.'

James entered, placing the peas on the corner of the bath, and passing her the glass of water. He made no comment on the fact she was half undressed in front of him.

'Which cabinet has the paracetamol?'

She pointed.

Her passed her the packet, then took her phone from his back pocket and put it on the floor by the bath.

'What do you want to change into when you're done?'

'I've got a towelling dressing gown hanging up behind my bedroom door.'

'Do you want to get it, or can I?'

She glanced down at the jodhpurs hanging off one leg and sighed. 'You do it. Room on the left.'

Estelle swallowed the painkillers and drained the glass. She desperately needed the loo and was still dithering about how to get her trousers off without James's help.

Coming back, he put the robe next to the towels. 'Can I do anything else to help?'

She gazed at him. There wasn't a whisper of snark to be seen on his face.

'Please, can you help get the jodhpurs off my foot?'

He nodded, then crouched down, running a finger along

the inside of the fabric, testing to see how much give there was in the material.

'I'm sorry I'm being such a wuss,' she said grumpily.

'You're not. You've hurt yourself and you're naturally worried about the potential of making it worse. Can you point your foot at all?'

She tried, and it sent a screaming shock of pain up her leg.

James frowned. 'Okay, don't do that.'

'It's fine. Just get them off.'

'Have you got any scissors?'

'No!'

'A sewing kit?'

'You going to fix them after you've cut them off?'

He smiled. 'I'm the best at most things, but I've never tried to sew. I was thinking I could unpick the stitching, then someone else could put them back together.'

'That's actually a good idea.'

'I know.'

She rolled her eyes. 'I don't have a sewing kit, but there's a pair of scissors in the cabinet where the paracetamol was.'

He got them, then returned to his position on the floor and began carefully unpicking the stitches around her ankle.

Many times, in the still and secret darkness of the night, Estelle had allowed herself to imagine being undressed by James. However, none of those fantasies had involved him doing so with a pair of nail scissors. His gaze was focused on his task, so she allowed hers to drift over him. His hair was dark and thick and usually artfully and perfectly tousled. Now, it looked as if he'd run his hands through it in frustration. Estelle wanted to tease it back into place. She watched the movements of his muscles underneath his cashmere jumper and shirt. What would he look like naked?

'You okay?' he asked, glancing up.

'Er, yes. Why?'

'You shivered.'

'Um...'

'I'm nearly done, then you can get in the bath.'

'Thank you.'

His smile was wide and open. It reminded Estelle of Leo, her youngest brother, who always seemed to get out of the right side of bed each morning.

James carefully worked the jodhpurs over her ankle. 'There we go.' He stood. 'I'll stay outside the door until you're in.'

'Are you going to leave?' *Seriously?* Her voice sounded so needy and plaintive.

'I'd like to stay, if that's okay? Just to help you out?'

'Of the bath?' she squeaked.

He held his hands up as if stopping her question from going any further. 'No! Just erm, around the house with anything you need.'

'Oh. Yes, of course.'

'Feed the dogs? And you, if you'll trust me?'

'That would be great. Thank you.'

He went to the door. 'I'll be right outside.'

'Could you go downstairs instead?'

'Why?'

'I need to pee and I don't want you listening.'

He grinned. 'Okay. I'll come and check on you in a few minutes.'

ESTELLE LET OUT A HAPPY SIGH. SHE WAS RELAXED AND warm, her hair and skin clean, and her bad ankle propped up out of the bath on a packet of peas with another one on top. The pain had faded into the background and the swelling had already gone down considerably. She wasn't sure what had happened to the *real* James Hunter-Savage, as his stupidly handsome body had been taken over by a maid-of-all-work. He'd prepared dinner for Chester and Joy, and by the sounds coming from downstairs, had also put clothes in the washing machine and vacuumed.

His footsteps sounded on the stairs.

'How are you doing?' he asked through the door.

'Amazing, thank you.' She yawned. 'I'm actually feeling really tired all of a sudden.'

'I found your first aid box, and it had bandages *and* witch hazel. As soon as you're out of the bath, I'll strap it up. There's also Arnica which you should take to help with the bruising.'

She blinked. 'You're recommending *Arnica*? I thought you'd have scoffed at homoeopathy.'

'Only when it doesn't work. But Arnica does, so...'

She shook her head, even though he couldn't see her. 'Can you please tell the body snatchers to keep the old James? This version is a big improvement.'

He laughed. 'Can I make you a cup of tea? Chamomile?'

She narrowed her eyes. 'Ye-es.'

'Don't sound so suspicious. You've got a glass jar of the stuff, a collection of tea infusers, and a pot of honey next to them. Working out you might like a cup doesn't make me Sherlock Holmes.'

'Okay, Miss Marple, that would be lovely, thanks.'

She heard him chuckle, then make his way back down the stairs.

❊ 20 ❊

Carefully getting out of the bath, Estelle put on her pyjamas and dressing gown. Her ankle started hurting again as soon as it was no longer elevated, so she bum-shuffled down the stairs and hopped to one of the sofas.

James came in from the kitchen. 'That was stealthy. I didn't hear you.'

'What can I say? I'm a veritable ninja.'

He grinned. 'Your tea's almost finished steeping. I'll get it for you, then we can get your foot strapped up.' He disappeared again.

This is all too comfortable and all too weird.

Estelle glanced at her watch. Still only four o'clock. At least an hour and a half before Elyse came home. Luckily, there was nothing to tell James his ex now lived here.

James re-appeared, pulled the coffee table nearer to her so she could reach the mug of tea, then sat on the arm of the sofa and began bandaging her ankle. His touch was careful but assured, and Estelle couldn't help but stare at his hands and wonder what they might feel like on different parts of her body...

'Before you go to bed tonight, drench it in witch hazel, then again in the morning. Use the peas and sleep with it elevated.'

'Yes, Miss Nightingale.'

He smirked. 'Can I cook you dinner?'

Her gaze flicked to her watch again. She wanted to spend more time with James when he was like this, but there was no way Elyse could come home and find him here, or James find out that Estelle was harbouring someone she wasn't even meant to know.

'I'm fine. You probably need to get back.'

'Not really. Apart from your injury, this has been the most enjoyable day I've had since arriving in Somerset.'

She fiddled with her watch strap, as if by doing so, she could somehow turn back time.

'Estelle...'

'You can go now. I'm fine.'

James sat on the sofa opposite her.

'Thank you for helping me,' she continued. 'I'll see you tomorrow.'

'I need to tell you something.'

Her head snapped up.

His expression was sombre. 'About Elyse.'

Huh? 'Who?'

His smile was sympathetic. 'I know she's staying here.'

'What? How?'

'I saw her beauty products in your bathroom.'

So *that* was why he'd only put Estelle's toiletries by the bath for her earlier. How had she not noticed he'd ignored Elyse's?

'I don't know how you know her, or what she's said to you,' James continued. 'But I want you to hear my version of events so you can make up your mind about who you choose to believe.'

Estelle stared numbly at him as he passed his hand over his face.

'I met Elyse in a bar three years ago. We dated for two weeks, then I ended it. She wasn't—' He broke off and sighed. 'She didn't agree with my decision, and for the next six months wouldn't stop calling. Then everything went quiet. Three months after that, Dad introduced me to his new PA.'

Estelle didn't know what to think.

'I only told my parents I'd dated her the morning after the dinner at Foxbrooke Manor. For the past couple of years, Mum and Dad have been trying to push the two of us together, and when they moved to Somerset, they moved Elyse in with them. I know what products she uses because she kept using my bathroom and leaving them there. Along with wet towels on the floor and her underwear on my bed.'

Elyse had never left any of her clothes on Estelle's bed, but she had left a messy trail of her stuff everywhere else.

James stood. 'I'm not asking you to take sides. I'm not asking you to do anything differently. It's just that there's a long list of reasons why you hate me, and some of them aren't true.'

'I don't hate you.'

He gave her a rueful smile. 'Despise then.' He ran a hand through his hair. 'I'm going to head back. Is there anything I can do for you before I go?'

'No, I'm all good. Thank you for helping me.'

'Thank you for showing me your archery. It was amazing.' He picked up the fork U. 'May I take this?'

Her cheeks burning, she nodded.

'Thank you. Will Elyse give you a lift to the manor tomorrow, or do you want me to come and pick you up? Or I can bring your laptop over and you can work from home?'

Estelle wasn't ready for Elyse to know she knew James's side of their dating story. After what Beverley had said about James's love life at the dinner, and what he'd just told her, she was fairly certain Elyse had lied about everything apart from being in love with James.

What would Eveline do? Whenever in a moral quandary, Estelle always asked herself what her saintly best friend's reaction would be. *Be kind to Elyse. If she's behaved like this, then it must come from a place of deep unhappiness.*

'Estelle?'

'Sorry, I was just having an imaginary conversation with God's representative on earth.'

'Eveline?'

She frowned. 'You reading my mind?'

'I'd rather not. I don't want to hear all the expletives levelled my way. No, I'm just clever and pay attention to things or people I'm interested in.'

Her heart sped up. 'You're interested in Eveline?'

He gave a half shrug. 'I'm more interested in you.'

Now her heart was racing.

'So, tomorrow?'

'I'll get Molly to drop me off,' she said quickly. 'I'm not going to tell Elyse we had this conversation.'

He nodded. 'Okay.'

She moved her leg off the arm of the sofa, meaning to get up and see him out.

'No, don't get up. Just rest. If you change your mind about coming in, just message me. Okay?'

'I will.'

He nodded again, then left.

Estelle let her head drop back to the sofa.

Well, today didn't pan out as intended.

She was simultaneously wired and exhausted, her brain needing to sleep in order to process all the information buzzing around inside it like a swarm of discombobulated bees. She took out her phone.

'Hello my lovely friend,' Eveline said when she picked up. 'How are you?'

'Having an existential crisis, but more to the point, how are *you?*'

'That doesn't sound good. I'm extremely tired, but currently on the sofa resting whilst my wonderful husband cooks dinner.'

'Good. Well, not about the tiredness, but about Jack looking after you.'

'I really couldn't do this without him. I'm so tired I can barely keep my eyes open most of the time.'

'I'm so sorry I haven't been able to see more of you recently.'

'Don't be a silly billy. Now tell me about your existential crisis. I want to use today's energy allocation on you.'

Estelle sighed. 'Promise you won't laugh at me?'

'I would never laugh *at* you, but if it's funny then I might laugh *with* you.'

'It's not funny. It's a disaster.'

'Oh, dear.'

'I can hear you smiling.'

'I'm just pleased to hear your voice.'

'Eveline! It *is* a disaster.'

'Do I need to organise a fundraiser?'

'Ha-de-ha. I'm not going to tell you now.'

Eveline giggled. 'I apologise. Do tell.'

'Okay.' Estelle took a fortifying breath. 'James Hunter-Savage might be a tiny bit nice.'

'And?'

'What do you mean "and"? He's the devil!'

'Estelle, he really isn't—'

'And he's been using black magic to make me like him.'

'Black magic?'

'Witchcraft. He's made a bloody potion.'

Eveline snorted down the phone.

'It's true!' Estelle huffed. 'His dad puts pheromones in the perfumes he sells, and James has been bathing in it.'

'And this makes him behave nicely?'

'Er, no, but it's part of his plan to—' Estelle broke off, fully aware she was sounding insane.

'Okay, so love potion aside. What has James done to make you think differently about him?'

Estelle didn't know how to reply. Whether it was hand-painting dog bowls for Chester and Joy, making her the perfect cup of coffee every morning, or spending his afternoon helping her train on Duke, the list of ways James showed his kindness was getting longer, and her reasons for disliking him were getting shorter.

'He carried me down from the top field after I sprained my ankle earlier.'

'Oh, my goodness! Are you okay?'

'Yeah, yeah, it's going to be fine. Annoying more than anything. I've been icing it and James strapped it up.'

'He strapped it up? At your house? I'm terribly confused, Estelle. What were you doing with James in the top field?'

'Nothing! Oh, my god, Eveline! I wasn't shagging him!'

In the silence that followed, Estelle closed her eyes and prayed for the ground to swallow her up.

'I, er, wasn't imagining that you were,' Eveline eventually replied. 'It's still winter and rather cold and muddy for that sort of thing.'

Estelle took a deep breath. 'James wanted to see my archery, so I was showing him. I tripped over a clod of earth when we were up there and fell over.'

'Oh.'

'And he wasn't a dick about it.'

'I wouldn't have expected him to be one.'

'But...' Estelle trailed off. She'd run out of ways to embarrass herself.

'Estelle, what would happen if you were friends with James?'

'I don't want to be friends with him,' she muttered petulantly.

'Lovers then.'

'What?' Estelle screeched. 'What are you talking about?'

'Well, there is a strong attraction between you.'

'No, there isn't!'

'My lovely friend,' Eveline replied with an irritatingly calm and patient tone. 'It's perfectly clear James is drawn to you as a person *and* as a woman. There's nothing wrong with finding him attractive. In whatever way that might manifest.'

'But all the things he did to Henry! He stole his bloody client!'

'Everyone makes mistakes, and everyone has the capacity to change. I understand your loyalty to Henry, but don't you think you should try and judge James on how he is now, not how he was in the past?'

Estelle was silent, a wave of confused exhaustion rolling through her. She didn't *want* to like James. It wasn't as if any relationship between them could even go anywhere. He'd made it clear he wanted to get back to London as soon as he could, and she couldn't betray her twin by copping off with his worst enemy.

'Estelle, Jack's just come in and wants a word. Can I pass the phone to him?'

'Yeah, sure.'

There was a pause, then Jack was on the line. 'Hey Stelle, you got a sec to chat about the do at the manor a week Saturday?'

'Yeah, sure, go for it.'

Estelle was relieved to be talking business with Jack. The event was vital. If they couldn't change the councillors' minds about approving the festival application, then all their hard work and money would be down the drain. Not only that, but Estelle would then have to see what other assets she could sell to keep the Foxbrooke estate from being sold off. Over the years, she'd already sold the most valuable paintings in the house and replaced them with reproductions. Soon the only thing left of value would be the manor itself.

Estelle spoke to Jack until a car pulled up outside.

'Can we carry this on tomorrow, Jack? I can get Molly to drop me off tomorrow morning at the rectory once I've picked my laptop up from the office.'

'No worries, I've gotta go anyway and see how the shepherd's pie is doing.'

She said her goodbyes and hung up as Elyse entered the house.

'What happened to you?' Elyse asked.

'I tripped and went over onto my ankle.'

'Oh.' Elyse hovered, one hand twisting around the strap of her bag, as if she wasn't sure what to do. 'Does it hurt?'

'Not when it's elevated and I've taken painkillers. I'll see how it is tomorrow. If I can't put any weight on it, I might need to pick up a pair of crutches to get about.'

Elyse nodded.

'Can we have a quick chat?'

Elyse's face went white, her eyes darting around the room as if looking for the nearest exit. She perched on the sofa opposite Estelle, her back straight and her hands clasped on her lap.

'You can stay here as long as you need,' Estelle began, 'but you've got to tidy up after yourself. Hang your towel up to dry and clean the kitchen after you've used it, okay?'

Elyse let out a breath as if she'd been steeling herself for much worse, then nodded.

'Yes, I will. I know I'm not very good at things like that.'

'Didn't your parents make you tidy your room when you were growing up?'

She shook her head. 'The maids did it.'

'Bloody hell. I'm apparently an aristocrat and even I didn't have that. Where did you grow up?'

'Kenya until I was six, then my parents split up and I came to London with my mum.'

'Did you go back to Africa during the holidays?'

'No, I've only seen my dad once since we left.'

'What? Why? Sorry, Elyse, you don't have to tell me.'

She shrugged. 'He started a new family and was too busy.'

'Shit. I'm so sorry.'

Elyse smiled. 'It's fine. You can't miss what you don't have. Right?'

Estelle nodded, even though she didn't believe it. 'Is your mum still in London?'

'No. She rented out her house to go travelling with her boyfriend a few years ago.'

'They've been travelling for years?'

'They're in Mongolia now.'

Estelle didn't know what to believe. She was sure Elyse had lied about her relationship with James, but was this true?

Elyse brought out her phone, tapped on the screen, then handed it to Estelle.

It was an Instagram account entitled 'wanderlustluvers' and showed a blonde woman who looked remarkably like Elyse, in the arms of a tall, dark and handsome man. The feed showed the two of them travelling with a Mongolian family, putting their yurt up and helping with chores.

Estelle handed the phone back. 'Wow, that's pretty full-on.'

Elyse nodded. 'Yeah. I could never do it, but at least she's happy.'

Estelle's heart tugged. If this was all true, then her dad had abandoned her, and now her mum was off as well. Elyse may not have lived in Shoscombe Manor as James's girlfriend, but from what James had told her, his parents liked her enough to have wanted them to get together. Had Kev 'n' Bev been surrogate parents for Elyse? If they had been, it must have been heartbreaking to have been asked to leave.

Why does life have to be so messy and complicated?

'Can I get you anything?' Elyse asked.

'Yeah, can you pass me the takeaway menus on the fridge door? I'm going to get a curry if you fancy joining me?'

❧ 21 ❧

James threw another tie onto the bed and growled at his reflection. Why was it so hard to choose an outfit?

There was a quiet knock at the door, and his mood softened slightly.

'Come in,' he called out. 'You can give me a hand.'

Sophia entered the room and gave him two thumbs up. 'You look very dashing.'

He frowned. 'Really? I don't know whether to wear a tie or not. I need to look like I'm making an effort, but not like I'm a corporate twat.'

His sister sat cross-legged on the flowery bedspread and picked through his discarded ties. 'Are these all made of silk?'

'Of course.' He picked up another pair of trousers. 'Should I go with Zegna instead?'

'I can't tell the difference. They both look fine to me.'

'I can't look "fine", Char, I've got to look perfect.'

'You always do. And anyway, a suit isn't going to make the difference.'

James was silent. He knew that was true, but tonight was

the one chance to change the councillors' minds, and if his suit was on point, then hopefully his mood would follow.

'Is Estelle's ankle better yet?'

He went to the wardrobe. 'Yeah, I think so.'

'You still haven't seen her since she hurt it?'

'No.'

The day after his visit to the livery, Molly had arrived to pick up Estelle's laptop. Estelle had worked from home and the rectory the next week, and their communication had been via email and the occasional text message. She'd even turned down his offer to help set the manor up for the event, saying that her family and Jack had it handled. James felt sidelined and irritated. But most of all, he missed seeing Estelle every day.

'Have you upset her?'

'Huh?' He paused. 'Why would you think that?'

She shrugged. 'Because you've been super grumpy and I know how much she means to you.'

'Shush!' He glanced at the closed bedroom door.

'They're both downstairs. We're good.' Sophia patted the bed. 'Sit down. You've got plenty of time.'

He sat next to her and let out a sigh. 'There's a laundry list of reasons why I've upset her, but right now I think she's ignoring me because she can't cope with the fact I might actually be a human being.'

'You could just tell her why you did what you did at Conqueror?'

'No way.'

'She might understand?'

'I don't want to test your theory. Right now, we just need to get through tonight without yelling at each other.'

'You can do it.'

'You sure you don't want to come?'

Her head shook so fast, her hair whipped around her face.

'I'll take that as a maybe?'

'It's a "definitely not". You know I'm only good with people if they've been buried for five hundred years.' She shuddered. 'And by the sound of it, the Foxbrookes are all so posh and loud and confident and—just no.'

'Mum and Dad are loud and confident.'

'Yes, but I'm used to them.' She picked up a dark navy suit. 'Wear this one.'

'Okay.' He stood. 'Tie?'

'Probably, yes. Councillors are usually pretty traditional.'

He changed, then frowned at himself in the mirror again.

'I think she really likes you.'

James didn't reply.

'Estelle.'

He ran a hand through his hair. 'As long as you qualify that with "against her will", then you might be right.'

'What are you talking about? You're not forcing her to like you, you're just showing her the *real* you.'

He turned to face her. 'She's so desperate to dislike me, she asked me to stop wearing my aftershave because she claims she's allergic to it.'

'Maybe she is?'

'One hundred per cent not. She breathes in deeper when I'm close.'

Sophia squealed with delight and clapped her hands. 'This is wonderful!'

James rolled his eyes. 'She acts like I've laced it with pheromones to con her into liking me.'

'Did you?'

'Course I didn't. Anyway, you know pheromones are a load of bollocks.'

'Hamster bollocks?'

He grinned. 'Probably.'

JAMES TUCKED HIS CAR IN THE FAR CORNER OF THE CAR PARK outside Saint Saviour's church and the gates of Foxbrooke Manor. The black Ferrari suddenly felt too ostentatious, the kind of car that would make the councillors think he was a flash git.

Glancing down at his designer suit and handmade shoes, he sighed. Should he have nipped into Bath to grab something made from polyester that didn't fit and worn that instead?

Fuck it. It's not like they're going to be looking at the label.

He turned for the manor, hoping the short walk would clear his head. The councillors were due at seven and Estelle had told him to arrive at six forty-five, so he was doing exactly as instructed.

Despite the cold weather the front doors were already open, but he knocked anyway, then poked his head inside the entrance hall. Clothes rails stood to one side awaiting coats, and fairy lights wound up the banisters of the enormous staircase in front of him.

James's gaze travelled up to the landing where Estelle had tumbled, his muscles tensing as if preparing to act again. There was a flash of gold at the edge of his vision, then she appeared, stopping at the point she fell, staring at her hand on the banister.

'Estelle?'

Her head snapped up and her mouth opened. She raised a hand in greeting, but didn't move.

'How's the ankle?'

'Fine.'

She started along the landing and he went to the bottom of the stairs to wait for her.

As she rounded the corner, she paused, then squared her shoulders and stepped down towards him.

James held his breath. He'd seen the hint of gold through the ornate carving of the banister, but now there was nothing between him and Estelle. Wearing a bandage dress, the iridescent strips of material coiled around her curves. She was like a Christmas present he wanted to unwrap immediately.

Shimmering gold eyeshadow highlighted her eyes, and jewelled clips pinned back her hair. Gazing at her was like staring into the sun. Her beauty was blinding.

Uncertainty flickered behind her outwardly confident expression as she descended, her feet stopping a step from the floor so they were the same height.

'Star.' The word was out before he could stop it.

Her full lips parted and she sucked in a breath.

'You're beautiful,' he continued, as all the filters between his brain and mouth continued to malfunction.

'It's just the clothes. I borrowed this from Mom,' she said in a rush. 'And Willow did my make-up.'

'No, it's you.' *Stop talking!* 'The dress only highlights what's already there.'

Estelle's breath came quicker, her chest rising and falling, flooding his body with need.

James's arm, in solidarity with his mouth, was also refusing to listen to reason, and he held out his hand.

She hesitated, then took it. A lightning bolt of desire shot from where their fingers touched, straight to his dick.

'Ah! There you are!'

Estelle snatched her hand away and James turned.

Arthur Foxbrooke was crossing the entrance hall towards them, wearing a black-tie suit that looked a size too small, and a purple silk cummerbund stretched around his middle.

'Look! I dressed up!' He pointed proudly at himself.

'Haven't worn this since the last century!' He grabbed James's hand and pumped it up and down. 'Glad you're here. Bev still coming?'

'She's arriving shortly from Bath.'

'Kev's business trip to China going well?'

'Yes, I believe so.'

'Jolly good, jolly good. Has Estelle shown you what we've set up?'

'Not yet. I just arrived.'

Arthur turned to his daughter. 'Come along, darling! Chop-chop! The buggers'll be here in a jiffy.'

Estelle's face tightened. 'Dad, everything's in hand.' She stepped down the rest of the stairs, her body wobbling as her foot reached the floor.

James's hand shot out towards her. 'Your ankle?'

'It's fine,' she ground out. 'I'm wearing ballet pumps tonight.'

He extended his elbow. 'Indulge me?'

Without meeting his gaze, she looped her arm through his and led him into the main body of the manor.

James matched her pace, revelling in the feeling of her body next to his, the intoxicating scent of her, the sense of victory that she was choosing to touch him rather than punch him.

'We'll meet the councillors out front and bring them into the largest drawing room,' she began. 'I'll give a short speech about what we want to achieve with the festival and you can add whatever you want. We've set up a map and other presentations for them to see how it's going to work. I've also printed out a proposal for each of them to take away with them, the one I emailed you a couple of days ago.'

'It was great.'

She led him into a room full of immaculately laid round

tables, with a buffet at one end and a baby grand piano at the other.

'Most people have RSVP'd, but not all, so we've got a buffet and people can sit where they like. You and I will split up and move between the tables, answering any questions. Willow and Connor are providing music whilst they eat. When Perry brings out the coffee and chocolates, Mom's going to read some Shakespeare sonnets and Leo's begged to do Hamlet's soliloquy.'

'Isn't that a bit dark?'

She finally met his eyes. 'It'll stir their souls. He's actually a very good actor even though he knows it.'

He smiled, and a rush of warmth filled his chest as she smiled back. The heat very quickly made its way south, and his gaze flicked to her mouth.

She turned, pulling him out of the room.

'Then Libby's going to run a short Regency dancing workshop in the ballroom. After that, we'll have some more music and maybe some people will stay a bit longer.'

'Sounds perfect,' he said, his voice low.

Estelle pushed open the door to the ballroom, and they entered. The space was empty and quiet, and they stood together in silence. Once again, Estelle's scent drifted towards his nostrils like a siren call.

'I love that perfume on you,' he said without thinking.

She stiffened. 'I, er, have a confession to make.'

'You do?'

Her focus was firmly on the parquet floor beneath their feet. 'It doesn't belong to me. I stole it from Elyse.'

Huh? 'No, you didn't.'

'I did. She'd left it in the office toilets. I tried it, loved it, and started wearing it.'

Pride and happiness filled his chest. 'Estelle...'

'I'm sorry,' she mumbled. 'It must be weird smelling it and thinking of her.'

'It's not Elyse's perfume. It's yours.'

Her head jerked up. 'What are you talking about? It's in a bottle with the letter "E" on it.'

He smiled. 'The "E" is for Estelle.'

She stared blankly at him.

'I made it for you.'

'Made it?'

'I read chemistry at Oxford and always liked playing around with scents. I have a small lab upstairs in the manor and I made that one for you.'

Estelle blinked a couple of times, as if she didn't believe him.

'I made the one I wear as well. The one you're allergic to.'

Her cheeks darkened. 'But I can smell it on you now.'

He raised an eyebrow. 'I'm trying to work out exactly *how* allergic you are.' *Stop flirting!*

Her nostrils flared slightly as she took a breath in. She was so close, all he could see was the liquid warmth of her eyes, drawing him in, deeper and deeper.

'You made that perfume for *me*?' she whispered.

He nodded.

'But it's gorgeous. It's perfect.'

Dropping her arm, he took her hand in his, all rational thoughts leaving the building to be replaced with wild and untamed longing. 'Like you,' he murmured.

She gasped.

'They've started to arrive!' Arthur yelled, barging into the room.

James felt Estelle's hand leaving his.

'Chop-chop! Shake a leg!' Arthur herded the two of them through the door.

James kept an eye on Estelle in case she needed any support. Her ankle didn't look swollen, but she still had a tubigrip bandage around it.

Vivienne and Dervla were already in the entrance hall greeting arrivals, as were Henry and Libby. James tensed when he saw Henry, but switched on the charm that always sealed the deal at work and with women, and went forward to welcome the guests.

Estelle was all smiles, but didn't look at him. Had he ruined things between them?

Connor, Leo and Willow arrived to help take people's coats and lead them into the drawing room.

Estelle checked a clipboard hidden behind the front door when there was no-one left outside. 'I think that's everyone.'

'Bally marvellous!' Arthur exclaimed. 'That's more than expected!'

James held his elbow out again to Estelle. 'Shall we go through?'

She hesitated for a second, then took it.

'I'm nervous,' she whispered as they followed Arthur down the corridor.

He squeezed the hand she was resting on his arm. 'Don't be. You're amazing. You've got this.'

As they entered the room she led him over to the fireplace to stand next to her.

Arthur clinked his wedding rings against a glass and the room fell silent.

'Thank you all so much for coming tonight,' Estelle began. 'For those of you I haven't yet met, I'm Estelle Foxbrooke representing the Foxbrooke estate, and this is James Hunter-Savage, the CEO of BDE Entertainment. As you can see, we've got lots of information for you about the festival, and we've also created copies for you to take home and read at your leisure.'

Despite the beautiful surroundings, and Perry and her daughter, Leia, circling the room with trays of drinks, most of the councillors didn't seem impressed. Arms were crossed, faces were pinched, and noses twitched as if itching to sneer.

'We'll be in here for the next twenty or so minutes, then we'll go through for dinner,' Estelle continued. 'Both James and I will circulate throughout the evening and welcome the opportunity to answer any questions you may have.'

James kept smiling, trying to project positivity he suddenly didn't feel.

'During dinner, you'll be entertained by my family. Afterwards there will be more music and a Regency dancing workshop with Libby Fletcher, who runs our living history tours.'

There was silence when Estelle finished speaking, but it wasn't a comfortable one. It was cold, flat and empty.

'I, er...' she continued. 'I understand many of you have reservations about my family and the partnership between the Foxbrooke estate and BDE Entertainment. I hope tonight you'll allow us the opportunity to share our passion for this project and the many ways it will positively benefit the local economy and community.'

Mark and Sarah, the two councillors who'd witnessed his blow-up with Estelle, were standing right at the front of the crowd, with faces like stone.

Estelle's gaze flicked to them and she swallowed. James saw how nervous she was getting. He moved closer to her, his hand brushing her side.

She grabbed it. 'I also want to take this opportunity to apologise publicly to Councillor Pensford and Councillor Hughes who witnessed an argument between myself and Mr Hunter—*James*, a couple of weeks ago. I'm the most hot-headed woman in our family, and that morning I'd been told some things about him that weren't true.'

She squeezed his hand tightly and his nerve endings prickled with fear.

What's she doing?

'What is true is that I'd fallen in love.'

With who?

'With James.'

Oh, fuck.

'We're in a relationship.'

In front of him was a sea of shocked faces.

'He's my boyfriend and I'm his girlfriend, and the music and arts festival is our baby.'

James's gaze snagged on Henry, who was moving from the back of the room towards them, a look of murder on his face and his hands bunched into fists.

'So, none of you need to worry about whether or not James and I can get on,' Estelle continued, her voice getting louder as if she was getting to the end of a toast at a wedding, 'because we're in love!'

She tugged sharply on his hand, pulling him towards her, then kissed his cheek.

'Aren't we, darling?'

❧ 22 ❧

Estelle's heart was racing, a cold sweat shivering across her skin as James stared at her, his face rigid with shock.

What have I done?

He smiled, but there was panic behind his eyes.

'Yes, we are,' he said to her, before turning to the rest of the room to continue the lie. 'We're deeply in love. From the moment I met Estelle last year, she bewitched me, and this year, she's almost driven me out of my mind.'

Oh, god. I'm a witch who's made him crazy.

'Hurrah and Huzzah!' cried Arthur.

Estelle's head jerked from James to her father, who was clapping loudly, his hands in the air as if trying to encourage others to join in.

'And aren't they an attractive pairing?' Arthur pointed at them as he pushed his way to the front of the crowd. 'Think of how beautiful their babies will be!'

'Ladies and gentlemen,' Vivienne said loudly from the back

of the room. 'If you'd all like to follow me into the dining room, dinner is served.'

Estelle kept her smile in place as her mom and mammy shepherded everyone out of the room, leaving Arthur, James, his mum, Henry, and Libby behind.

When the door shut, she dropped James's hand.

'Ho ho ho!' her father chortled. 'You took my advice! Jolly good!' He paused, looking hopeful. 'Unless this is real?'

'No,' Henry said forcefully. 'It's not.'

James tensed beside her.

'Do you think they believed it?' Bev asked, her face pinched with worry.

Arthur frowned. 'I don't know. That kiss was a bit lacklustre.' He eyeballed Estelle and James, his gaze flicking between them like a sergeant major giving orders. 'Next time, give it a bit more oomph!'

'No,' Henry repeated. 'Dad, this is madness.'

'Whatcha talking about? It's just like you and Libby! Had us all fooled. Even me!'

'But I had a contract to protect her. What does Estelle have?'

'Your sister doesn't need protecting!' Arthur turned to her. 'Do you, darling?'

'Of course not.' Her nails pressed into her palms. She looked at James. 'I'm sorry for putting you on the spot like that. They were all looking so bloody hostile and I panicked.'

'It's okay.' His expression was unreadable. 'We can do this.'

'No, you can't,' Henry said, his face thunderous. 'From now on, you need to remain at least eight inches away from my sister at all times.'

'Only eight inches?' James replied blandly. 'I don't think that's going to be enough.'

Henry took a breath, but his reply was curtailed by Libby dragging him away, and Arthur's booming laugh.

'Ha, ha, ha!' Arthur clapped James on the back. 'That's BDE right there!' He turned to Beverley and extended his arm. 'Shall we get some nosh, Bev? I don't know about you, but I could eat a bally horse!'

They went towards the door after Henry and Libby, leaving Estelle standing next to James. She didn't know whether to step closer to him or further away.

'I'm sorry,' she muttered.

'Don't be. We don't have to act any differently.'

Oh.

Disappointed, are we?

Shut up.

'Estelle?'

'Okay, come on then, let's get this evening over with.'

Striding to the door, she followed her dad and Bev down the corridor, upset and anger swirling inside her. Why did things always work out for Henry and not for her? Why could her brother fake-date and it turn into something wonderful, but when she tried it, it was an abject failure? She knew these feelings of insecurity went back to their childhood, but their roots seemed unshakably deep. And despite how much her feelings were changing towards James, it was clear his feelings for her hadn't altered one iota.

But he made the perfume for you. He said you were beautiful!

Shut up! Shut up, shut up, shut up!

James reached her side. 'You alright?'

'I'm fine.'

He huffed. 'When a woman tells you she's "fine", she's most definitely not.'

A hubbub of voices drifted towards them from the dining

room up ahead. Estelle didn't know what to do or how to act anymore.

James took her hand and pulled her to a stop. Suddenly she was facing a hard wall of heat that smelled so irresistible she wanted to plaster herself against it.

'Are you mad at me or yourself right now?'

Both? She couldn't say that word out loud without having to explain herself, so she just shrugged and stared at the centre of his chest, watching it rise and fall as he breathed.

'Estelle,' he began, his voice a dark rumble. 'If I'm the one you're mad at, then once the last guest leaves, you can say or do whatever you like to me.'

Oh, god. A whoosh of sensation scorched up through her body. Her mind knew exactly what she wanted to do to him, starting with getting him naked.

'But right now,' he continued, 'I need you to act as if you like me. Can you do that?'

She nodded, focusing on the silky darkness of his tie.

'Good.'

Pushing open the door, he led her to the table where Mark Pensford was sitting, a large plate of food in front of him.

'Is this seat taken?' James asked him.

Mark looked up. 'No.'

James pulled a chair out, sat Estelle down, then leaned in. 'Star, you stay here and chat to Mark. I'll get you your favourites from the buffet.'

He raised his head to smile at the councillor. 'Estelle was doing mounted archery training last week and took a tumble. Her ankle is still a bit sore so I want to make sure she doesn't spend too much time on her feet tonight.'

'Mounted archery?'

'Yes. She's going to compete for the first time soon.' James stroked the side of her face and gazed at her with such love in his eyes that Estelle felt hers welling up. 'Why don't you tell him about it? I'll be back in a bit.' He dropped a kiss on her forehead and strode off.

She stared after him. James was the tallest and most handsome man in the room, cutting through the crowds like a charismatic billionaire moonlighting as a supermodel.

'So, how does a mounted archery competition work?' Mark asked.

Estelle blinked, suddenly remembering her purpose here was to charm the councillors and get them back on side. Turning to give Mark her full attention, she smiled and began telling him about the roots of the sport and how she was training.

A few minutes later, James returned and placed a plate of food in front of her.

'I'm going to speak to Sarah,' he said. 'If you need anything else, just give me a wave.' Leaning down, he grazed her cheek with his lips. 'See you in a bit, Star.'

Estelle shivered at his words, her heart racing. She desperately wanted him to kiss her again, but this time his lips to touch hers.

'If you don't mind me saying...' Mark interrupted her fantasies. 'I would never have put you two together, especially after hearing you argue.'

Shit. Did he know this was all a lie?

'Well, they do say opposites attract.'

'Hmmm. I wouldn't say you were opposites. I think you're both cut from the same cloth.'

That doesn't sound like a good thing... Change the subject!

She smiled. 'I so appreciate you taking the time to come here this evening so we can share our ideas for the festival. Even though we've got acts from further afield than

Foxbrooke, I want to make this an event that celebrates home-grown talent and uses local businesses.'

'In what way?'

'Everything from food to fencing. For example, we're working with the owners of The Colour Palate on the high street to make the outside catering not only local, but affordable, the Shakespeare performances in the garden will be staged by The Foxbrooke Players, and we're aiming for at least sixty per cent of the musicians at the festival to be from the local area.'

As if on cue, Willow started playing the piano, and Connor began singing. Mark glanced up to watch them, chewing his food more slowly.

Knowing she had a captive and well-fed audience, Estelle kept talking about her plans, hoping at least some of the passion and enthusiasm she had for it filtered into Mark's ears and down to his heart. When his attention was on his plate or her brother and sister, her eyes sought out James. He was working the room like a seasoned pro, his smile broad, his expression engaged, his body language relaxed and confident.

As if someone like that would ever truly want someone like me...

Meaning? Shut up with the trash talk. You're a badass motherfucker!

Men don't want a woman like that. They want someone like Eveline or Summer. Willow or Libby.

Says who?

Remind me the last time I had sex? Or the last time a man wanted an actual relationship with me?

James might want one?

Yeah, right. And anyway, he's off-limits. Remember what he did to Henry?

Despite her smiles, Estelle was miserable. There was no guarantee the evening would be a success, and without a licence, the event couldn't go ahead. If it didn't, the estate would incur more losses and would never be able to repay the money they'd already spent securing acts. But despite those huge and very real worries, her main concern seemed to be that James Hunter-Savage didn't fancy her, and this made her furious.

You're not a stupid, love-struck teenager. Get a grip!

But even if he does like me, he's not going to make a move.

Hello? Are you even listening to me?

It's like he starts flirting then draws back. He might fancy me, but he doesn't want to take it any further.

Oi! Cut it out!

I mean, why would he? He hates Somerset, despises my brother, and god knows what he thinks of Dad. He wants someone like Elyse, not me.

Blah, blah, blah...

He's coming back over. Be cool!

'How's it going?' James asked Mark as he sat next to Estelle and took her hand.

'Interesting,' Mark replied in a tone that gave nothing away.

'Vivienne and Leo are going to give a short Shakespeare performance now,' James said. 'It'll give you a taste of the standard of the acts we've booked for the festival.'

'Hmmm.'

James leaned back in his chair, facing the side of the room where Leo and Vivienne were standing.

Her mom began reciting sonnet eighteen. "'Shall I compare thee to a summer's day? Thou art more lovely and more temperate...'"

The poem was one Estelle knew by heart, but even though she'd studied the meaning of the words, its message hadn't hit. But now, as James's thumb drew leisurely circles across the back of her hand, the words travelled straight to her heart and made it weep.

"'But thy eternal summer shall not fade... When in eternal lines to time thou grow'st...'"

Was her own summer already fading? She was thirty-one in five months and no man had ever wanted to take her on. She could blame her eccentric family or her long working hours, but ultimately, none of that should have mattered. The truth was that she was too much for anyone to handle.

Feeling James's eyes on her, she clenched her jaw to stop tears from spilling out. It was her idea for them to fake a relationship for the evening, but having his attention turn from professional to personal made her yearn even more for what she couldn't have.

She pulled her hand from his. 'I need to circulate,' she whispered, then left the table and made her way to one on the other side of the room. She needed distance in order to keep her emotions in check. She'd already jeopardised the festival once. She couldn't do it again.

ESTELLE KEPT AWAY FROM JAMES AS THE EVENING progressed, trying to speak to every guest in turn, even if it was to just thank them for coming. Libby's Regency dancing workshop went down a storm, and when it was over, Willow sat back at the piano to play easy-listening music and people coupled up to dance.

Estelle glanced nervously around the room. Had the night worked? She caught Sarah Hughes' eye, the other councillor who'd witnessed her bust-up with James. Sarah's gaze flicked between her and James, who was standing at the other end of the room.

Shit! Had she messed everything up by avoiding him since

dinner?

Before she could second guess herself, she strode over. 'We need to dance,' she said under her breath.

He nodded and extended his hand.

Taking it, her heart fluttering, she let herself be drawn into the centre of the room and into his arms.

Next to him, in her ballet flats, Estelle suddenly felt smaller than normal. She was taller than the average man, however nothing was average about James Hunter-Savage, and he now had over five inches on her.

Willow was playing 'Moon River', and Estelle let James pull her closer, until she was against his hard chest. One of his hands grazed her shoulder, the other rested at the base of her spine.

She shivered, her body craving more of his touch.

He dipped his head. 'Are you cold?' he murmured in her ear.

'Do you think they bought it?' she whispered back.

'The festival?'

'No, *us.*'

He paused before replying. 'I don't know.'

Estelle looked around. Henry stood at the side of the room, his arms folded across his chest as he glared at them. Several people glanced from his grim expression to the two of them dancing.

Where's Libby got to?

Vivienne glided to her son's side and walked him away. Was it too late? Did everyone know they were faking it?

'We need to kiss,' she hissed.

James's head snapped back. 'What?'

'You have to kiss me. To make this look real.'

His gaze flicked to her lips, becoming heated and intense.

'Are you sure?' he asked, his voice a low rumble.

Unable to summon words, she nodded.

His face lowered, then stopped, his features tight with tension. 'How do you want me to kiss you?'

'What do you mean?' she stammered.

'How should I kiss you?' he repeated, his tone rough and demanding.

'Er, the normal way?'

'Closed or open lips?'

A flush rippled through her. 'I don't know! Just get on with it!'

'Estelle,' he growled. 'If I'm going to kiss you in front of everyone, and make it look like we've done it a thousand times before, then I need to know what you like.'

'It doesn't matter.'

'Yes, it does.'

He suddenly stepped away, took her hand, and marched her across the dance floor to the exit.

'Where are we going?' she whispered.

He didn't reply, leading her along the empty corridor and around the first corner. No-one was about.

Stopping, James dropped her hand. 'Show me how you want to be kissed.'

She licked her lips. 'Um...'

He moved closer. 'Estelle...'

Stepping back, her heels hit the skirting board.

Placing his hands on the wall, James lowered his head, stopping with his mouth just inches from hers.

His presence was intoxicating and overwhelming, his scent making her knees wobble, the inky blackness of his eyes drawing her in, his ragged breaths caressing her skin like a flame.

'Show me.' His voice was a command and a plea.

Just kiss him! It doesn't matter if it doesn't mean anything!

His gaze travelled over her face, as if wanting to drink in every part of her.

'Star,' he murmured.

The word was her undoing, unravelling any resolve and letting it drop to the floor. Trembling, she brought her hands to the sides of his face, then lifted her mouth to his.

His lips were warm and soft, but the thrill that darted through her the moment her skin touched his was one of sharp, breath-taking pleasure.

James was still, his body tense and strained.

Estelle kissed him lightly again, as if tentatively asking for entry, and ran her fingers into his hair.

Letting out a low groan, his hands left the wall, one threading through her curls to hold the back of her head, the other cupping her bottom to tug her body flush with his.

Desire cracked through her like a whip and she gasped, her lips opening. His tongue slicked into her mouth and met hers with a jolt, the sensation so powerful she felt she was falling.

Dizzy, she gripped handfuls of his hair, clinging to him, giving herself over to the lust that had been simmering for months.

He growled, then without breaking their frenzied kiss, lifted her off the floor. She spread her legs, the miniskirt of her gold dress riding up her thighs, and locked her ankles behind his back.

Estelle had never been kissed like this before, felt like this before, wanted someone so much before. There was no room for thought or logic. She ground against the rock-hard ridge of his cock, begging with her body for everything he had to give.

James was power, heat and sex, imprisoning her in his arms and unleashing a storm of passion. As her tongue clashed with his, her body shook with the need to come. It was a desperate, intense, physical ache only he could satisfy.

He pushed his pelvis forward, holding her up as she rubbed her swollen clit against him. Her pants were soaked through and the swells of her orgasm were beginning to build. Her heart was pounding faster and faster, her lungs dragging air in and out. She wanted, she needed, she—

James froze, then his lips lifted from hers, his breath ragged.

What?

'Don't stop on my account,' came a voice.

Brain befuddled and gaze unfocused, Estelle's attention left the orbit of planet James and landed on the figure of Councillor Sarah Hughes as she strolled past them with a grin.

'We should plug you two into the National Grid,' she continued. 'Could power the whole of Bath and North-East Somerset.'

Estelle blinked, her chest still heaving as she tried to draw in enough air to stay conscious.

'Thank you both for this evening,' Sarah said over her shoulder. 'It was very informative.' She continued towards the front door of the manor.

Reality crashed into Estelle like a racing car hitting the tyre wall at over a hundred miles an hour. James Hunter-Savage was holding her up against a wall. Her legs were clasped around his back as if they were wrestling, her dress was at the top of her thighs, and her pussy was up close and very personal with a bit of his body she'd never seen, yet had fantasised about frequently.

Hearing voices coming from around the corner, she pushed him away, unable to meet his gaze.

He let her down to the floor and she tugged the hem of her dress back to her knees, just as Henry, Libby, Arthur, and several of the councillors appeared.

'Ah! There you are!' Arthur boomed. 'Having a bit of nookie were we?'

Estelle could hardly breathe. She looked from her father to her twin. Henry's eyes narrowed as he stared past her at James.

'Oh, Arthur,' Libby said. 'Leave them be.' She smiled brightly at Estelle. 'Everyone's heading off now, so we're just saying our goodbyes.'

Estelle nodded and summoned a smile, even though adrenaline was still rushing through her veins and sending her heart tripping over itself. 'We'll come with you. Sarah's just gone.'

She carried on up the corridor with them, making sure she was as far away from James as possible. What the hell had she just done?

'You okay?' Henry whispered.

'Of course I am. Why wouldn't I be?'

'Let's talk when they've gone.'

In the entrance hall, they helped the guests with their coats, then stood as more people came from the dining room, escorted by Vivienne, Dervla, Connor, Leo and Willow.

As Arthur closed the front door behind the last one, Jack arrived with Beverley.

'Well, unless anyone's hiding in the toilets, I think that's the last of them gone,' he said.

'Well done all of you!' Arthur cried. 'Fingers crossed it did the trick. And top marks go to Estelle and James for their very convincing little charade.' He turned to her. 'Although next time, darling, give him a smacker on the lips, not the bally cheek. He's not Gram-Gram.'

'There isn't going to *be* a next time,' Henry said curtly.

In her peripheral vision, Estelle saw James freeze.

'You never know...' Arthur continued, a hopeful look on his face, as if the thought of Estelle and James getting together suddenly doubled his chances of becoming a grandfather.

'I'm willing to continue a relationship with Estelle,' James said. 'If it helps the festival.'

'A *relationship?*' Henry growled. 'That's the opposite of what she wants.'

'Henry...' Libby began.

'Really?' James said. 'Then why did she suggest it?'

'And it wasn't even remotely a relationship,' Henry continued. 'It was a few hours of fakery for my sister to endure for the greater good.'

'Henry!' Libby hissed. 'Why don't we go and help clear up?'

'Wasn't it, Estelle?' Henry asked.

The spotlight was suddenly on her. Her father looked hopeful, her twin worried, her family interested, and James? She glanced at him. His face was expressionless as he gazed at her. This felt like a test she was destined to fail no matter what response she gave.

'I, er...' she began, panic rising. Staring at James, she willed him to say something to deflect the attention away from her.

He raised an eyebrow. Was he mocking her? Calling her a coward? Had he been faking when he'd kissed her? His body may have been into it, but was his heart and mind?

She smiled. 'We just did what we needed to do to make this evening work.' She shrugged. 'And if they all fell for it, then it means I must have inherited Mom's acting genes.'

Silence.

James's chin lifted slightly and he let out a little huff, as if she'd done exactly what he'd expected.

Estelle's stomach clenched with shame.

'See, Dad?' Henry said. 'Fake.'

'James, babe,' his mother said. 'Can we go now? I want to ring your dad before it gets too late.'

'Sure.' He crossed the room and took her arm. 'Is it alright

If we leave you to handle the clear up?' he asked everyone except for Estelle and Henry.

'Of course,' Jack replied. 'You go. We've got it in hand.'

'Thank you,' James said. 'And thank you to everyone for all your amazing work tonight.'

'It was our pleasure.' Vivienne came forward to kiss him. 'You both must come for dinner again this week. Promise?'

James nodded.

'Thanks, babe,' Bev said to Vivienne. 'That would be nice. Maybe we could watch *The Real Housewives of Chelsea* together?'

'Ooh, yes!' Dervla said. 'I'd love that!'

As her parents saw James and his mother towards the door, Estelle crept away. She wanted to leave without further interrogation from anyone, process what the hell had just happened, and figure out how on earth she was going to act the next time she saw James.

$$\text{❋}\quad 23\quad\text{❋}$$

Duke trotted along the archery track and Estelle let arrow after arrow fly. Her ankle wasn't fully healed, but it was good enough to get back in the saddle, even if at one third of the normal speed. At the end of the run she brought Duke to a stop and pulled out her phone.

Still nothing from James.

Her gaze went to the fence at the far edge of the field and the direction of Shoscombe Manor. Could she ride over there? She checked the time. *Ten a.m.* Surely even on a Sunday they were up by now?

We kissed. Her eyelids fluttered closed and heat flared through her, every cell in her body reliving the experience. Those super-charged minutes had been replayed for hours, even in her fitful dreams. Sure, she'd initiated the kiss, but James had responded with such passion that she'd lost her mind.

Since that moment, she couldn't get him out of her head, and her body had hummed at a higher frequency. James had activated something inside her that was impossible to turn off, and now, no matter how hard she tried, her sexual sonar was locked onto his torpedo.

Get a grip!

Turning Duke for home, she made a mental list of chores for the day that would take her attention away from James.

You're delaying the inevitable. You still have to see him tomorrow.

I could work from home? Say my ankle's worse?

You'll have to see him at some point.

But I don't know what to say!

What would Eveline do if she were you?

Pray? Be honest with James about how I feel?

And are you going to do either of those things?

Yeah, right.

Coward.

Shut up.

ESTELLE SANG SPICE GIRLS SONGS ALL THE WAY BACK TO THE livery, through brushing Duke down, and up to the point she got back into her house to find Elyse awake and in the living room watching television.

Elyse muted the volume. 'How did it go last night?'

Estelle's mind instantly replayed James holding her up against the wall, her legs locked around his waist. Had he been like that with Elyse?

'Um, well, I think. But that doesn't mean anything. We have to wait for the committee to meet and vote.'

'Okay.' Elyse lapsed into silence, her eyes unfocused.

Estelle braced herself for what might be coming next.

'How was James?'

'Same old, same old,' she replied with breezy enthusiasm. 'I'm going to make coffee. Want one?'

Elyse got up. 'Yes, please. I'll help.'

She followed Estelle through into the kitchen, then leaned against the countertop, staring once more into the middle distance.

'Could you grab a couple of mugs?'

'Oh! Yeah.' Elyse opened a cupboard and took two out. 'Did James say anything about me last night?'

Estelle shook her head. *No, he was too busy calling me 'Star' and tongue-fucking my mouth.*

'Oh.'

Estelle's phone buzzed, and she grabbed it from her back pocket.

'Is it him?'

'No... It's my mate, Finn. He's—' *Single and alright looking if you like grumpy men with beards...* Estelle smiled. 'He's asking if I want to go to the pub later. It's quiz night.'

'Are you going?'

'Do you want to come too?'

Elyse's cheeks coloured. 'Me?'

'Yeah. I think you need to get out more. And Finn's single.'

The colour in Elyse's face intensified. 'I couldn't. It's too soon.'

Come on. Be brave. 'Elyse... Beverley told me she's never known James to be in a relationship.'

Elyse abruptly turned away.

'I don't care when you and James broke up. But whatever you had is over and you need to try and move on.'

'You want him for yourself,' Elyse muttered.

I'm not going to admit that, even to myself. Estelle took a big breath. 'My relationship with James is purely professional.'

'He likes you.'

He does? Tell me more! Tell me everything!

Elyse faced her with a resigned expression. 'He tries not to let it show. But he talks about you. A lot.'

'That doesn't mean anything. This is about you moving on.'

'I still think I've got a chance. I just need to spend more time with him.'

Seriously? Just take no for an answer!

'Haven't you ever been so in love that you don't want to give up hope of it all working out?' Elyse asked.

'Of course not,' Estelle retorted, then her mind summoned an image of Isaac, the hottest yoga teacher in the world. He clearly wasn't interested in her, but she'd still pursued him relentlessly.

'Look,' she continued, 'Finn's nice, and apparently good-looking. I'm not saying anything will happen with him, but at least come with me tonight. You're stunning and new in town. That combination is kryptonite in somewhere as small as Foxbrooke.'

Elyse was silent. When they'd first met, she'd seemed even more confident and self-assured than Estelle's youngest sister, Summer. But now the shell had cracked and an unsure and broken version of Elyse had emerged.

'Do you have a photo of him?'

Estelle resisted the urge to fist pump. 'Whenever I take a picture of Finn, he pulls a face, so you're not seeing any of them. He's taller than me, broad, and has a beard. That's all you're getting.'

Elyse's pert nose wrinkled. 'He's got a *beard?*'

Fuck's sake! 'It's very short,' she replied quickly. 'And, er, sexy.'

'If it's sexy, then why do you look like you might be sick?'

Estelle rolled her eyes. 'Because he's like a brother to me. I literally cannot think sexy thoughts about him or I'll throw up then arrest myself for incest.'

Elyse gave a small smile. 'Okay, I'll come. Thank you.'

Estelle: Yes, coming tonight, but you have to shave off your beard

Finn: What?

Estelle: And wear a suit

Finn: I don't have a suit

Estelle: Borrow one from Henry. And dye your hair black

Finn: It's quiz night, not fucking Halloween

Finn: Who do you want me to be? Head of the Sicilian Mafia?

Estelle: Kind of. You've got to look like James Hunter-Savage

Finn: PMSL. Why the fuck would I want to do that?

Estelle: I'm bringing James's ex with me tonight

Finn: His ex?

Estelle: Her name's Elyse and she's really pretty

Finn: And...

Estelle: She needs to move on

Finn: And I'm the sexual sacrifice? You want me to dress up like some city wanker, dye my hair and shave off my fucking beard so I can con some woman into bed, just so she'll lie there with her eyes shut, wishing I was someone else?

Estelle: Yeah, that's about the size of it

Finn: You're fucking tapped, Stelle

Estelle: Awww, come on! Will you do it?

Finn: Yeah, why not! Anything for a friend

Estelle: Really?

Finn: Are you for real? Of course I'm not going to do it

Estelle: Fuck's sake

Finn: Why do you care so much anyway about her 'moving on'?

Finn: Is that to leave the way clear for you?

Estelle: Shut up

Finn: Jack said last night you told everyone James was your boyfriend

Estelle: It was fake!

Finn: Stelle and Savage, sitting in a tree…

Estelle: I'm going to kill Jack for telling you

Finn: Henry and Connor told me too

Estelle: Bastards. Nothing happened!

Finn: Stelle, people only say 'nothing happened' to cover up the fact that something did

Estelle. Look, are you going to shave off your manky beard or not?

Finn: Nope. You going to admit you boned Hunter-Savage?

Estelle: I DID NOT!

Finn: But you want to

Estelle: I don't!

Finn: If you admit you like him, I'll trim my beard and wear my best shirt tonight

Finn: Stelle?

Estelle: Promise?

Finn: Scout's honour

Estelle: And this conversation is CONFIDENTIAL?

Finn: YES

Estelle: Okay, I like him a little bit. But only a tiny bit! And nothing is going to happen. And I don't want anything to happen, okay? It's just he hand-painted dog bowls for Chester and Joy and he was nice when I did my ankle in, and he makes the best cappuccino

Finn: Wow. You really like him

Estelle: Fuck off! No, I don't. Now go and sort your beard out and make an effort when you meet Elyse. Okay?

Finn: Yes, Ms Hunter-Foxbrooke

Estelle: Not funny

Finn: I think it's got a nice ring to it

Estelle: Shut up

Finn: Henry's going to be thrilled. Do you think James will ask him to be the best man at your wedding?

Estelle: Do not say a fucking word, Finn, or I will end you

Finn: See you later, Stelle...

'YOU SURE YOU WON'T LEAVE ME ALONE?' ELYSE ASKED AS she drove her and Estelle slowly down the winding country lane, the headlights illuminating the barren hedgerows on either side of the road.

'I promise I won't unless my bladder is bursting and you have someone nice to talk to.'

'Does Finn know I'm coming?'

'He hasn't got a clue.'

'Okay, good.'

Estelle's phone buzzed with a message. She pulled it out and stared at the screen.

James: Thank you for last night

Oh, my god!
'Is that him?'
'What?'
'Finn.'
'Er, no, it's my brother.'
'Which one?'
'Connor. He might be coming later. Let me message him back.'

Angling the phone screen away from Elyse, she typed out a message.

Estelle: Do you think it went well?

James: Yes. Do you?

Estelle: Yes

Shit! How could she get more information out of him without revealing her own hand?

James: Are you free now?

Her heart skipped a beat.

Estelle: Why?

James: Would you like to go for a drink?
There's a pub on the high street we could meet at

Estelle: I'm on my way there now. With Elyse

James: Ah. Girls night?

Estelle: Quiz night. Plus, my friend Finn is single

James: The grumpy one with the beard?

Estelle: How do you know him?

James: I saw him at the Winter Ball in a suit two sizes too small. He glared at me as if it were my fault he was there

Estelle: It was

James: Explain?

Estelle: He was roped in at the last minute to protect Summer from you

James: I didn't know I was that dangerous

Oh, yes you are, James. So fucking dangerous.
'Is he coming?' Elyse asked.
'Who?'
'Connor.'
'Erm, not sure yet. We're just chatting about our youngest sister.'
'The influencer?'
'If that's what you want to call her.'
'I follow her. She's so hot right now.'
Estelle's phone buzzed.

James: Do you still think I prefer blondes?

Her pulse quickened and her skin prickled with heat.

Estelle: I don't know what you like

James: Really? And there was me thinking I
made it pretty clear last night...

'Can I park anywhere around here?' Elyse asked.
'Oh, er, yeah.'

Estelle: Pulling up outside the pub. Two secs

Heart racing, she pocketed her phone. She needed to get Elyse settled with Finn, then dash to the loo to reply.

Why? Just leave it at that! Don't message him back!

Her phone buzzed again and her fingers itched to take it out.

I mean, where do you think this is going?

The ride of my life?

Are you insane? It's James Hunter-Savage!

'Is everything okay?' Elyse was now chewing on her lower lip.

'Yes! I've just got a lot on my plate right now.' She grabbed Elyse's arm. 'Come on. Let's find Finn.'

The Horse and Hounds was warm and homely, having welcomed people through its doors for hundreds of years. Past the bar, at the far end of the main room, was a mic on a stand connected to a speaker. Finn and two of his friends sat at one of the small tables dotted about.

Estelle pulled Elyse forward. 'Hi! I'd like you to meet Elyse. She's new to the area. Elyse, these are three quarters of the Beardy Boys: Finn, Tommy and Ryan.'

The men stood. Estelle felt Elyse try to take a step backward, so held even tighter to her arm.

All three men were well over six feet, and Tommy and Ryan were even broader than Finn, thanks to the powerlifting training they did together. They all had beards—Finn's brown, Tommy's a dirty blond, and Ryan's as black as night.

Finn held out his hand. 'Nice to meet you.'

Elyse took it. 'And you.'

'Finn is normally clean-shaven and only wears suits,' Estelle said to Elyse. 'But he's let things slide a bit recently.'

Finn glared at her and his friends bit back grins. They'd obviously been briefed about Elyse, and Estelle knew they would have taken the piss out of Finn the moment they'd clocked his neatly trimmed beard and ironed shirt.

Tommy and Ryan introduced themselves to Elyse. Her smile was still in place, but her eyes were wide as she stared at them.

'Where's Scott?' Estelle asked.

'Can't come,' Ryan said. 'So, we're a man down.'

Finn cleared his throat and his friends tensed as if they knew what was coming.

'I was wondering if you and Stelle would be interested in joining our team tonight?' Finn asked Elyse. 'We can have up to five, so...'

'Yes! We'd love to,' Estelle said, pushing Elyse into the spare chair between Finn and Ryan. 'Grab me a seat, would you? I've just got to pop to the loo.'

She rushed off, making her way through the pub and around the side of the bar so no one at Finn's table could see her. Taking out her phone, her heart raced at the prospect of another oxytocin fix courtesy of James.

James: Are you on a team?

Estelle: Nope. Nobody wants me

James: Why not?

Estelle: I'm too competitive

James: Not a bad thing

Estelle: I get shouty and argumentative

James: Strange. You're normally so quiet and reserved

Estelle grinned, her tummy flip-flopping.

Estelle: But tonight, Finn has let Elyse and me join the Beardy Boys

James: How well you must fit in

Estelle paused, her thumbs over the screen, then tapped out a message before she could stop herself.

Estelle: Did you want to go out for a drink with me for professional reasons?

James: No

'Stelle! What are you doing?' Finn hissed behind her.

She jumped, her hand flying to her chest. 'Jesus Christ, Finn! You scared the crap out of me! I was just going for a wee.'

'Bollocks were you. You can't just fuck off and leave me with Elyse. You know I'm shit at small talk.'

'Do you like her?'

Finn ran his hands through his hair, leaving it sticking up in all directions. 'Stelle, I don't *know* her.'

'But do you fancy her?'

He shrugged. 'I dunno.'

'Finn! She's really pretty!'

'So what? You're stunning, but I don't fancy you.'

She growled at him. 'I thought this was a sure thing.'

'What about Tommy? Ryan? They're single.'

'Are you nuts? Elyse likes slick city boys, not lumberbears.'

Finn snorted. 'Lumberbears?'

'You know what I mean. Stick a couple of grizzlies in plaid shirts, cover them in tattoos and you've got Yogi and Boo-Boo over there. I thought she was going to shit herself when they stood up.'

'So why did you run off?'

'Because I was giving you room to make your move!'

'Not messaging lover-boy?'

She hesitated, and Finn raised an eyebrow.

'He asked me out for a drink.'

'And...'

'He wanted to come here. Tonight.'

'With Henry in the same room? You know I find it hilarious your brother's turned into a beta version of Travis Bickle, but you can't jeopardise the festival by having him kick off at James in public.'

'I know.'

Finn drew her in for a hug. 'It'll sort itself out, Stelle. These things generally do.'

She rested her head on his shoulder. 'I don't know how. It's like the deck is stacked against us before the game has even started.'

'Well, you could always play a couple of rounds of "poke-her" then call it quits?'

'Finn!' She pushed him away, trying not to laugh.

He grinned. 'Now come back to the table and save me from Elyse, or Elyse from having to talk to people with facial hair.'

'Okay, give me a minute and I'll be there.'

Finn glanced at his watch. 'Be quick. It's starting soon.'

He went back across the pub and Estelle took out her phone.

> James: I want to spend time with you outside of the office

> James: Last night didn't feel like faking to me

Her heart pitter-pattered inside her chest, the vibrations fluttering down into her belly. Hands trembling, she typed out a reply.

> Estelle: What did it feel like?

> James: The hottest experience of my life

Estelle's feet stumbled as a wave of desire rolled through her. Holding onto the bar to steady herself, she glanced around the pub, positive that everyone knew the words she'd just read and how they made her feel.

'Stelle!' Finn yelled across the room. 'They're starting!'

He was sat next to Elyse, then there was an empty chair next to Ryan. As Estelle approached, Elyse moved into the spare chair next to Ryan, leaving Estelle to sit between Elyse and Finn.

'Sorry everyone, I'm here now,' Estelle said. 'Elyse, have you got a drink?'

Elyse nodded. 'Ryan got me one and you a rum and coke.'

'Cheers Ryan. Next one's on me.'

Leaning back in her seat, Estelle sent a message to James. He'd been honest, so she could be, too.

> Estelle: It was for me too

'Stelle! Switch it off,' Finn grumbled.

'Why?'

He gave her a look. 'Because it's cheating, you muppet. You have to have it on airplane mode or else it sits over there.'

She glanced at a table next to the mic stand. A clear plastic box sat on top containing a pile of mobile phones.

'Okay, two secs.'

> Estelle: They're making me turn off my phone

Flicking airplane mode on, she put it back in her pocket, still feeling horny, but now disconnected from the source. Her rational mind objected to James and any possible relationship with him, but her libido played whack-a-mole with each thought that popped up, gleefully bashing it back down.

She tried to engage with the quiz as it started, but had nothing to offer. Thankfully, Finn and his friends were making Elyse feel welcome, so Estelle didn't have to make an effort. Her brain was now entirely focused on a man she was supposed to hate and how he'd made her feel the opposite of that emotion.

The final round of questions was underway, and Estelle was still replaying James kissing her. Staring off into the middle distance, the faces in the bar blurring, she relived the memories as if they were happening again, sensations barrelling through her until her body ached and her head spun.

Her heart jolted, and she blinked to bring her vision back into focus.

James was here.

Striding across the bar towards their table, his expression was determined, his gaze fixed on... *Elyse?*

Estelle stood.

Elyse turned. 'James?'

Ryan immediately got to his feet, followed by Finn.

James's eyes flicked to Estelle's, then he crouched so his face was level with Elyse's.

'I need to speak to you. Urgently,' he said to her.

'Hold your horses,' the quiz master called out. 'No interruptions during questions or the Beardy Boys will be disqualified.'

Elyse's hand was pressed to her chest. 'I, er...'

'It's Dad. It can't wait.'

Elyse's eyes widened, and she got to her feet. 'I'm so sorry,' she said to her teammates.

James stood, his gaze flicking to Estelle. He looked as if he was using every ounce of strength to hold in a scream of anger and pain. What was going on?

'I'm so sorry,' Elyse repeated to the room, then followed James as he wove through the bar to the front door.

For a second, Estelle dithered, then she hurried after them, Henry joining her from his seat at another table.

'Who's that with Hunter-Savage?' he asked.

'Elyse. His ex. She's now living with me.'

'What? When did this happen?' Henry rubbed a hand across his forehead. 'Jesus Christ. That man just leaves a trail of devastation in his wake.'

'You don't know that,' she hissed as she pushed open the door.

Outside, James was facing Elyse. His Ferrari was at an angle in front of the pub, as if he'd had no time to park properly.

'What's going on?' Estelle asked.

James's eyes flicked from Henry to her. 'Dad's been arrested.'

She gasped. 'Why?'

'I don't know all the details, but it's really serious. Elyse and I have got to get on the next available flight to China to try and help him.'

Elyse started crying.

Moving forward, Estelle hugged her and rubbed her back. 'Everything's going to be okay. I promise.'

'Is there anything I can do to help?' Henry asked James.

James looked shocked. 'Er, I don't know at the moment, but thanks.' He ran a hand through his hair. 'Right now, I just need to get back. Mum's losing it and I need to book flights and find out more information.' He turned to Estelle. 'Can you make sure Elyse is okay?'

Estelle nodded, her heart cracking.

'And can you come into work any earlier tomorrow?' he continued.

Drawing on all her reserves, she stood a little straighter. 'Yes, of course.'

'Thank you. I'll see you then.'

James nodded at Henry, glanced at Elyse, who was still crying into Estelle's chest, then got in his car and screeched away.

Elyse lifted her head and wiped her eyes. 'I'm so sorry.'

'No need. Shall we go now? I can drive if you want? I've only had one drink.'

'No, I can do it. Just give me a second to get my bag.' She dashed back into the pub.

'Well, she's certainly his type,' Henry said as he watched her go.

'What's that supposed to mean?'

He frowned. 'She's just like Elizabeth and Summer. Blonde, slim and pretty.' He let out a sigh. 'I don't know how long he'll be away, or what this is going to mean for the festival, but I'm here for you, Estelle. We all are. Okay?'

She nodded. 'I'll speak to you tomorrow as soon as I know more.'

❧ 24 ❧

'We're so proud of you, honey.'

'Promise to write, darling?'

'Don't do anything I wouldn't do. Ha!'

In her dream, Estelle was thirteen again, standing with her parents outside the manor as they waved Henry off to Eton. The cord that had bound her and her brother so tightly since the womb was stretching until she feared it would snap.

Heart aching, she reached for her twin.

Henry's gaze passed over her as if she wasn't there, then he walked away.

She turned to her parents. 'Don't let him go!'

They ignored her. Her mom had her arms around her mammy, who was dabbing the corners of her eyes. Her father had his arm aloft as he waved goodbye.

Estelle ran towards Henry, but no matter how fast she pumped her legs, she couldn't catch up with him. His uniform was archaic but pristine, the white collar starched, his black shoes shiny. Glancing down, she saw the dinosaur-patterned pyjamas she'd loved as a child. One year she'd asked for them for Christmas, but they'd been gifted to Henry instead, and she was given pink Minnie Mouse ones. She'd eventually got her brother's cast-offs, but by that time they had holes in them and the pattern had faded.

'Henry! Wait!'

He turned, but now it wasn't Henry anymore in the smart clothes, it was James.

Stopping, he glanced at what she was wearing and frowned.

'Please,' she began. 'Don't go.'

He looked at her with a mixture of sympathy and condescension. 'It isn't your place. You have to stay here.'

'But I can't keep doing this on my own!'

His expression hardened. 'Stop being so selfish. Learn to put others before yourself. Who's going to look after them if you don't?'

Suddenly she was surrounded by her siblings as their younger selves. Willow was a baby, lying on the ground and screaming. Leo was four, crying, with wee running down his stubby little legs. Henry was frozen, petrified and unable to speak, and Connor, only seven, was fighting a police officer trying to take them from their parents.

'Mom! Mammy! Daddy!' she screamed.

They were in the distance, dancing together around a fire, her father with antlers on his head.

'Estelle...'

She turned back to James. He was now wearing a pilot's uniform. Elyse and Summer were standing on either side of him, dressed as cabin crew. They had their hands on each of his shoulders, one leg raised behind them. Giggling, they leant forward and kissed his cheek, leaving lipstick marks behind.

James smirked at Estelle. 'You belong here. In bumfuck nowhere.'

Turning to Elyse, he cradled the back of her head, then brought his lips towards hers.

'Noooooo!'

Estelle's scream wrenched her from the nightmare and she pushed herself up to sit, her chest heaving as she breathed.

'It's just a dream,' she whispered. 'It's not true.'

But the feelings ran down to her bones. She'd grown up in Henry's shadow, her father allowing him to go to private school, but forcing her to stay at the local secondary, which she'd hated. Henry and James were very different, but they were both successful. They'd had the natural advantage of coming from privileged backgrounds and having been born men. And if that wasn't enough of a head start, they'd gone to the most elite school in the world, then to Oxford University. Whereas she had...

Stop playing the 'woe is me' game. Look at your life and what you've got!

Dragging herself out of bed, she went to the bathroom.

It *was* selfish of her to expect James to stay. She just needed to carry on doing what she'd done her whole adult life; sucking it up and saving the day.

'Hı,' Estelle called out into the main body of Shoscombe Manor from the office wing. 'Can I come in?'

The door was wide open, but she still waited. It was eight a.m. but she knew at least some people must be up as Elyse had left the livery earlier than her, and the lights were on in the corridor.

Footsteps sounded, then James appeared, striding towards her. His clothes looked fresh, but his face was crumpled with stress.

'Thank you for being here. I...' he trailed off.

Reaching out, Estelle touched his arm. 'It's okay.'

He shook his head. 'It's really not.'

She dropped her hand from his arm, but he caught it before it reached her side, his thumb rubbing her palm as if it was a worry stone. She took his other hand in hers. After all the hatred she'd harboured towards James over the years, suddenly holding his hands seemed the most natural thing in the world.

'What do you know?' she asked.

'There's been a problem with the factory manufacturing Dad's line of perfumes. He's been accused of using banned chemicals in them, which is bullshit, because I created the recipes. So, if it's true, then it's the manufacturer at fault. Dad went to sort it out but tried to bribe the wrong person. He's in jail. That's all I know.'

She squeezed his hands. 'When do you leave?'

'Later today. The plane takes off first thing tomorrow, so we're staying at a hotel in Heathrow tonight. Elyse has to go because she knows who Dad's been dealing with and what they've discussed. I have to go because I know the chemistry and what to look for at the factory.'

'Plus, you're an equal mix of charming and intimidating, which should come in handy when you're trying to sort everything out.'

His gaze softened. 'You're so fucking incredible.'

Pulling on her hands, he drew her closer, wrapping her arms around his waist, then holding her tightly to him.

James's body was hard, yet Estelle felt herself melting into the warmth of it.

'I don't know how long I'm going to be,' he murmured. 'But every moment I'm not trying to get Dad home, I'll be working on the festival. I promise.'

Estelle didn't reply. James didn't know what he was heading

into, and she didn't want to accept a promise he couldn't keep. No matter what he said, she couldn't help her abandonment issues clawing at her guts. She'd wanted to run the festival on her own, but after making the decision last year to partner with an external company, the event had grown into a beast that needed a team to handle, not one person on their own. And she was tired of being the one who the buck stopped with. Estelle wanted to do this with James by her side.

But he was leaving. And just as the really hard work was about to start. How long would it take to get his dad out of jail? A week? A month? Till the festival itself? And what would happen when it was over? James had made no secret of his desire to leave Somerset behind as soon as it was done. It had taken months for Estelle to admit she liked him, and now nothing was ever going to happen between them. The loss of what might have been felt more painful than the loss of any actual relationship from her past.

As he held her tighter, Estelle became aware of the only soft part of James now becoming hard enough to hammer in nails. Glancing up, she raised an eyebrow.

'I'm stressed out of my mind,' he said. 'Not dead.'

His gaze became heated, and her pulse quickened. Now she was giving herself permission to find James attractive, her body was purring like a sports car, just waiting for his touch to accelerate her from nought to sexty in under two seconds.

Her lips parted in an unconscious invitation, her tongue darting out to lick them.

James made a low sound in the base of his throat and brought his head towards hers.

Yes! Yes! Yes!

Estelle knew exactly what his kisses felt like, and her body flushed with anticipation of what was to come.

'Babe! There you are! And Estelle!'

She jerked away from him as his mother hurried down the corridor towards them, her face make-up free and her eyes red and puffy.

'How are you holding up?' Estelle asked.

Beverley grabbed her hands and squeezed tightly, the rings on her fingers digging into Estelle's skin. 'Oh, doll, I'm a mess!'

'How can I help?'

'I dunno, babe. Just be here? Soph can't stay all the time and if I'm rattling about here on my own, I'm gonna lose it.'

'Absolutely.' Estelle's heart sank. Did this mean she'd have to move in? What about the livery? Duke? Chester and Joy?

Beverley glanced around. 'Where are your doggies?'

'I didn't know how today would pan out, so thought it best they stayed at home.'

'I could do with the distraction, if I'm honest.'

'Shall I bring them tomorrow then?'

'You're coming back?' Beverley's chin wobbled. 'Even though our James isn't here?'

'Of course. Hopefully, we'll have staff soon, so I'll need to be on site, anyway.'

Still clasping Estelle's hands so hard the blood supply was being cut off, Beverley turned to her son, her eyes liquid. 'Isn't she the best, babe?'

'She is,' James replied, his voice a dark rumble that vibrated through Estelle.

'Have you had any brekkie?' Beverley asked.

'Not yet, I—'

'Well, come with me then.' She pulled Estelle down the corridor towards the manor's kitchen. 'James will make your coffee unless you want a cup of instant?'

Estelle glanced back over her shoulder at James and pulled a face.

'I'll make Estelle a cappuccino now.'

'Thanks, babe. That machine of yours scares the shit out of me.'

FIVE MINUTES LATER, ESTELLE WAS HALFWAY THROUGH HER second pain au chocolat when James re-appeared and placed a cup on the table in front of her.

She stared at the perfect unicorn drawn in the foam, then up at him. '*This* is what you've been trying to do?'

He nodded. 'It was more challenging than I expected.'

Emotion filled her throat. Why was this happening? Life was so unfair.

'Ooh, take a look at that.' Beverley turned the cup around to see. 'You're so clever, babe.'

'What's he done?' Elyse asked from the doorway.

James moved to the side as she entered the room and came to the table. Elyse was immaculately dressed as always, but her face was pale and pinched under the make-up.

'Oh,' she said as she gazed at the unicorn. 'James once...' Her hand reached out as if to touch it, then withdrew. 'That's... nice,' she finally managed.

Repressing a territorial growl, Estelle lifted the cup and took a sip. It was painfully hot, but she still swallowed.

Elyse turned to James. 'I've had an email come in just now that I think you should see. Shall we go to your dad's office to discuss?'

James's expression hardened, and he nodded. He extended his arm towards the door and followed Elyse out.

CLOSING HER EYES, ESTELLE RUBBED HER TEMPLES, AS IF THE massage would make the two paracetamol she'd taken hurry up and get rid of her headache. It was five o'clock, and she'd barely left her desk. James had promised to work on the festival when he was in China, but if today was representative of the attention he could give it, Estelle didn't know what he hoped to achieve. Within ten minutes of him returning to their office, either his mother or Elyse would appear, and he'd leave. It was a nightmare.

There was a knock at the door and Elyse poked her head into the room.

'How's it going?' Estelle asked.

Elyse's smile was wobbly. 'It's midnight in China, so we can't do any more today. We've got an hour and a half before we leave, so I'm going to go back to yours, pack and make dinner.'

Estelle stood. 'I'll do it.'

Elyse was about as competent in the kitchen as Summer, and Estelle didn't want to add 'house burning down' to the current crisis. Closing her laptop, she grabbed her bag and followed Elyse out.

Standing by the open door that marked the boundary between the office and the main body of the manor, Estelle called through, 'We're leaving.'

There was no response.

'You can say goodbye to James later when he comes to pick me up,' Elyse said.

Clenching her jaw, Estelle nodded. Reality was starting to bite. James and Elyse were going to be living in each other's pockets for god knows how long. The scenario was Elyse's dream, and Estelle's nightmare.

Would James cave and rekindle what they'd had in the past?

Shut up! He kissed you, remember?

But he's slept with Elyse!

Three years ago! You need to trust him.

I don't know him! He's just a man!

So are Connor, Leo, Jack, Finn, Henry. And they wouldn't do that!

The thought of Henry stopped her in her tracks. No matter what she'd discovered about James, he'd never once tried to excuse or explain the fact he'd stolen Henry's client and deal in London.

'Shall we go?' Elyse said behind her.

Estelle pushed open the door, seeing her dirty and battered Defender sitting on the gravel next to Elyse's clean and pretty car. 'Yeah, come on. Let's get back to mine and I'll put dinner on.'

JUST AFTER SIX, JAMES'S FERRARI PULLED UP OUTSIDE Estelle's house with a throaty roar.

'He's here!' Elyse called through from the living room.

Leaving the washing-up, Estelle dashed out of the kitchen, shaking water off her hands and drying them on her jeans.

Elyse was already wheeling her suitcase through the front door.

Outside, Chester and Joy were sitting obediently, their tails brushing the ground, their tongues lolling, and their eyes following James as he manhandled Elyse's suitcase into the small boot.

'You ready?' he said to her.

She nodded, glancing between James and Estelle as if waiting to see how they would say goodbye.

A muscle twitched in James's jaw.

Staying where she was in the doorway, Estelle raised a hand. 'Safe travels.'

'I'll message you when we get there,' James said. 'We'll head off now.'

He didn't move. Estelle yearned to close the gap between them and let him know just how much she wanted him to stay.

The silence was becoming uncomfortable.

'Okay!' she said brightly. 'You two go. I'll get back to the dishes.'

Before either of them could reply, she closed the door and strode back to the kitchen.

You can still message him.

She picked up her phone.

> Estelle: I'm going to miss you more than I want to admit

> Estelle: And think of you even more

TWO AND A HALF HOURS LATER, ESTELLE SAW THAT JAMES had seen the messages.

He didn't reply.

Putting on the Spice Girls, she channelled her hurt into cleaning the mess that was Elyse's room. After throwing the bedclothes in the washing machine, Estelle got in a bath to soak, periodically checking her phone in case James had replied. What was he doing now?

Probably shagging Elyse.

Get over yourself!

Her heart was thumping painfully in her chest, full of emotion she didn't want to express. No-one would know if she cried now. But if she took the lid off her tears, she could no longer deny how much of her heart she'd given to James.

Go to sleep.

Putting Chester and Joy to bed in the kitchen, she turned off the lights and went upstairs.

Lying in the darkness, she stared at the shadowy ceiling,

the corners of her eyes liquid. She was exhausted, alone, and the prospect of the festival now filled her with dread.

I can't do it.

You can. You've been fighting fires for the last ten years on your own. Different circus, same clowns.

I don't think I've got the strength for it anymore.

You need to see Eveline.

I know, but she's so tired making a baby.

She's your best friend!

And that's why I don't want to load more of my shit onto her.

Chester and Joy barked from the kitchen. Their tone was different; frantic and urgent. Estelle's nervous system sprinted off the blocks. They'd only ever barked like this once before, when the livery had been broken into.

Throwing back the covers, she grabbed the shotgun from under her bed, pulled on her dressing gown, filled the pockets with more shells, then dashed out of the room.

Joy was now making a noise like a Wookie being strangled and Chester sounded as if he was wrestling a honey badger. Estelle didn't want to let them out. She knew they would attack to protect her, but she didn't want to risk them getting hurt in case whoever was out there was armed.

Half way down the stairs, there was a sound at the front door. A knock? Someone trying to break in?

Heart racing, she opened the living room window at the back of the house and climbed through. The grass was cold and wet on her feet, but she didn't stop. Raising the shotgun, she crept around the side, giving her a clear sight line to the front door.

It was dark, but she could make out a shadowy figure under the porch.

Bracing the butt of the gun against her shoulder, she let off a shot—an inch to the left of their head.

The sound screamed in her ears, then ricocheted around the nearby buildings.

'It's double-barrelled, motherfucker!' she snarled. 'Get off my land or the next one's going to take out your dick.'

She stalked forward, eye trained down the barrel.

The person stepped slowly away from the door, their arms raised.

'I'd rather you didn't,' James said. 'I'm quite attached to it.'

＊ 25 ＊

'Jesus Christ!' Estelle screamed, dropping the end of the barrel. 'What are you doing? I nearly shot your dick off!'

Despite the adrenaline racing around his body, the corners of James's mouth twitched up.

'For the second time, no less,' he replied. 'Although I see you've upgraded from a bow and arrow to a shotgun. What should I expect next? A grenade launcher?'

Letting his hands fall to his sides, he strolled across the driveway towards her. Her hair was in a bun with a silk wrap tied around it, and the pockets of her fluffy dressing gown were bulging with ammunition. A cartridge fell out and dropped to the ground.

'You're packing a lot of heat, Estelle.'

'What the fuck, James!' she yelled.

'I apologise. I should have told you I was coming back.'

Silence.

'Back?' she asked, hope in her voice.

Shit. 'Only for three hours. I dropped Elyse at the hotel, then drove straight here.'

'Why?' Her voice was a whisper.

He crossed the distance between them. The moonlight reflected in her eyes.

'Because I need you to know that I don't want to go. I want to be here. With you.'

She swallowed. 'We should go inside. I need to calm the dogs and wash my feet.'

He glanced down, then swept her into his arms.

'What are you doing?' she gasped.

'It's always been a fantasy of mine to carry a heavily armed, barefoot woman.'

She giggled. 'What other fantasies do you have?'

'Can I show you?'

'Will I like them?'

'That's the whole point,' he rumbled, his voice dropping an octave. 'Getting you off is at the core of all of them.'

Her lips parted and she sucked in a breath.

Despite the desire raging through him, urging him to lower his mouth to hers, he carried her into the house then lowered her to the floor. 'I'll calm the dogs.'

'I'll sort my feet and put the gun away,' she replied breathlessly.

He nodded, then turned towards the kitchen before he hauled her into his arms.

CHESTER AND JOY WERE DELIRIOUS WITH EXCITEMENT AT the sight of him, jumping up and down in their cage. James quietened them, had a glass of water and washed his hands.

Butterflies fluttered in his stomach. He'd closed the most high profile of deals, rowed Oxford to victory in the boat race, and successfully kept his parents out of his public life since he was seven. Yet none of these situations generated the same kind of nerves as the prospect of sleeping with Estelle Foxbrooke. The feelings were deeper, the stakes higher. He had to prove himself worthy of her.

Turning off the kitchen light, he made his way through the night-silent house and up the stairs.

He paused outside her room. 'Estelle?'

She opened the door. Her hair was down, her robe gone to reveal a silky nightdress that ended just above her knees.

He unashamedly took her in, her endless dark eyes, her flushed face, the creamy lace of the nightgown that framed her cleavage. His gaze snagged on her nipples, poking through the fabric as if begging to be sucked, and his cock throbbed inside his jeans.

'Star,' he murmured.

She swallowed. 'Take off your clothes.'

Unbuttoning his shirt, he pulled it off and dropped it to the floor.

She stared at his chest, her breath quickening.

Pride surged through him at all the work he'd put into his physique.

Undoing his jeans, he tugged them off, taking his boxers and socks with them, then stood naked in front of her, feet apart, arms slightly away from his sides, his palms facing forward, his cock pointing straight at her.

It's all yours.

Her hand flew to her heart and she ran her tongue across her lips. 'You are...'

He clenched, and his dick slapped loudly against his belly.

She swallowed again. 'One arrogant bastard.'

He raised an eyebrow. 'How about you put me in my place?'

Crooking a finger, she beckoned him forward. 'It will be my pleasure.'

Game on.

Taking a step forward, James caught her outstretched hand and brought it to his mouth. Starting with her index finger he was going to pleasure the fuck out of Estelle Foxbrooke until she couldn't remember the amount of times she'd come, let alone her own name. He dragged the tip of her finger over his lower lip and she stared as if mesmerised, her breathing shallow. Before she could anticipate his next move, he lightly bit the end.

A full-body shiver ran through her.

Circling his thumb into her palm, he kissed, nipped and sucked at each of her fingers until her eyes were glassy.

Then, before she could get used to the sensations, he tugged her forward and lifted her, wrapping her legs around his waist. She grabbed the sides of his face, crushing her mouth to his, and every cell in his body exploded with light. Estelle was the hottest woman he'd ever known, and she was turning him supernova. Sharp shocks of sensation flashed through him, piercing his skin and heading straight for the base of his throbbing cock.

She pushed on his shoulders, breaking the kiss, then tugged her nightdress up and off. James gazed at her full breasts in the half light, then down to the dark thatch of hair between her legs, pressed up against his abs. For a brief moment his mind tripped its circuits and went blank, then desire roared inside him like a wild animal hurling itself at the bars of a cage, raging to be free.

Grabbing her bare backside with one hand, the other buried itself in her luscious hair and pulled her mouth back to his. His tongue clashed with hers, but it wasn't a fight for dominance, it was for survival against an onslaught of pleasure. James was trying to stay in control, but when Estelle ground her wet pussy against him, he knew he was about to be sexed to death.

A growl rumbled from the base of his throat and he walked them forward to the bed, laying her down, their bodies still pressed together. She was writhing against him, as if desperate to find the perfect friction and angle that would make her come.

Through the chaotic cacophony of lust, the faint tick-tick-tick of the clock counted down the seconds until he had to leave. James didn't have the luxury of all night, the pleasure of kissing Estelle for hours and building her orgasm incrementally. He had only a short amount of time to leave her breathless and boneless, and it was time to step it up a gear.

At least that was what he told himself. But as he lifted his lips from hers and scooted down the bed, he also felt like a kid heading straight for the dessert table at a buffet, his mouth watering.

'Wha—oh—aah!'

Holding her legs apart, he covered the whole of her pussy with his mouth, his tongue diving inside her. She was so hot, so swollen, so sweet. His hips unconsciously pistoned into the bed, grinding his cock against the sheets as urgent pleasure shot through him. Growling, he sucked the hard nub of her clit.

'Oh fuck, oh fuck, oh fuck!' she cried, the words coming faster as if she was running towards the edge of a cliff.

Her fingers tangled in his hair, clutching the strands as she held him tightly to her. The pain should have been a welcome distraction, but it only amplified the sensations sparking across his skin. His balls drew up, and he forced his hips to stay still, staving off his climax. There was no way he was going to lose it unless her hand, mouth, or pussy was wrapped around his cock.

He thrummed his tongue over her clit, feeling her muscles tightening at the top of every breath. Her words were now incoherent cries, and it was music to his ears. He followed her breathing, slowing the pace of his licks as she exhaled, then speeding up as she gulped in air and held it. He felt like a surfer, riding the swells as they got bigger, waiting for the one to carry him to shore.

Her legs were trembling beneath his hands, the gap between her breaths getting shorter and shorter. Suddenly she stiffened beneath him, gripping his hair as if holding on for dear life. Sucking her clit hard into his mouth, he vibrated the tip of his tongue against the end.

She screamed then convulsed, her body jerking beneath him.

Holding her firmly, he kept up the pace, drawing out every sensation in her body until she collapsed back on the bed, panting.

Releasing her grip on his hair, she smoothed it back down with fluttering fingers, then pulled the nape of his neck as if to encourage him upward.

You think that's it? He smiled, then dragged his tongue up the length of her. As he flicked it over her clit, she gasped again, her hips twitching. Circling it lazily, he wrote her name, then his, hearing the pattern of her breathing changing, feeling the trembles in her muscles building to shudders as everything inside her drew up for another climax.

Inching his middle finger into her, his cock twitched with jealousy, and his head spun as she tightened around it.

'More,' she cried, pushing down until she'd taken it up to the base.

Easing another inside, he curled them, rubbing against the rough front wall.

'Oh, my god!'

James licked faster, finding the exact speed and pressure that made Estelle cry out, relentlessly pushing her orgasm forward. Each time she clenched around him, heat pulsed through him, down to his needy cock. With his fingers in her, his tongue on her, his consciousness seemed to interweave with hers until her pleasure became his own.

As he felt her reach the point of no return, he pushed his fingers hard against her G spot. Her thighs clamped around his ears, muffling her keening cry as her climax hit. She shook as if rocked by an earthquake and a rush of liquid hit his tongue.

Yes.

Eventually, her thighs relaxed, flopping back to the bed, but she was trembling all the way to her toes. She pulled on his hair and he slowly withdrew his fingers, moving up to lie beside her and pressing soft kisses to her face.

She stared at him. 'What the fuck just happened?' she whispered.

His smile was unstoppable. '*I* happened.'

A laugh burst out of her. 'You're so full of yourself!'

James was too happy to give a shit about modesty. He'd made Estelle come twice *and* ejaculate, so right now he was king of the world.

'Have you ever squirted before?'

She shook her head.

He brought his lips to her ear. 'Big dick energy, Star...'

Snorting with laughter, she rolled him onto his back, then straddled him. 'You are unbelievable.'

He grinned. 'Thank you.'

She rolled her eyes in return.

James didn't know if he'd ever been happier. His body buzzed with contentment and the sense of being exactly in the right place and with the right person.

Her expression changed as if she could read his thoughts and she lowered her lips to his. As her tongue swept into his mouth, he lost himself in the feelings of her. Estelle was hot and wet, fire and earth, energy and light. From her sparking mind to her soft skin, from her strong muscles to her full breasts, she was perfect. And now he'd made her come, he wanted to kiss every part of her he'd missed, starting with her tits.

Flipping her onto her back, he kissed and sucked down her neck.

She grabbed a handful of his hair and yanked his head up. 'What are you doing?'

He palmed her breast. 'Would you like me to stop?'

As she hesitated, he rubbed the pad of his thumb across her nipple.

She gasped, her stomach muscles contracting.

'I'll do anything you want,' he murmured, moving lower and circling his tongue over the other one.

As if she couldn't help herself, her chest arched off the bed and she moaned.

That was his invitation to step it up, licking, sucking, tweaking, until she was panting and writhing beneath him. He'd never felt more powerful. No sporting or business victory had felt sweeter than pleasuring this warrior of a woman.

She pulled on his hair again.

'Hmmmm?'

She blinked as if needing to focus. 'This isn't all about me.'

'I know.' He rolled a nipple between his thumb and middle finger. 'So far, it's been all about me.'

'What?'

'I'm well aware how selfish I am.' He pressed a kiss to her other breast. 'And so far, all I've done is take what I want.'

'You're insane!' She pushed him off and rolled him onto his back. 'Are you going to do what you're told?'

He gazed at her spectacular body. 'Probably not.'

She raised an eyebrow.

'Maybe?' he continued. 'If you say please...'

'I've got a loaded shotgun within arm's reach.'

He grinned. 'That's close enough. What do you want me to do?'

'Don't move and keep your eyes open.'

'That won't be difficult. I don't want to look anywhere else. And besides, I couldn't even close them if I tried. Ever since you shot an arrow at my balls last year, I've even been sleeping with one eye open.'

She smirked, then straddled him so his dick was in front of her, rock hard and swollen, the end touching his belly button. Raising her thighs a fraction, she dragged her wet pussy along the length of it.

Gritting his teeth, he hissed out a long breath. He'd thought he could handle whatever Estelle was about to do, but his confidence in his ability to resist shooting his load prematurely was already beginning to erode.

She rubbed herself from base to tip. 'Keep your eyes open.'

Clenching his jaw, he gazed at her. The sight was agonisingly erotic. She licked her fingers, then brought them to her nipples.

'Fuck!' he growled, raising his hands to take over.

She batted them away. 'I thought I told you not to move?'

'Are you trying to kill me?'

'You've only just worked that out?'

He let out a strangled laugh and thumped his head against the pillows. 'I need to touch you. Please?'

'Wow.' Her voice was breathless as she rubbed her clit up and down the length of his cock. 'You said *please*.'

'I'm just a man,' he grunted. 'And I'm about to start begging.'

'But you're not just *any* man,' she murmured, her hips moving quicker. 'You're James Hunter-Savage.'

Grabbing the sheet beneath him, he held on for dear life as

her taunt hit the spot. Estelle would break a lesser man, but she wasn't going to break him. He would orgasm on his terms, and only after she'd had a few more of her own.

But... *Fuck my life, just look at her...*

She was rocking faster, her lips parted as she breathed, her fingers pulling her nipples, her dark eyes fixed on his.

She's close. Just hold on. You can do this.

Every gasp she made was a lightning bolt, shooting from her and electrocuting him in the balls. The pleasure was excruciating, and he knew he was teetering at the edge of the precipice, holding on by his fingernails.

As her gasps became cries, her eyes started to flutter closed.

Thank god.

James squeezed his own tightly shut, his mind focused on pushing his climax down. Every muscle he had was screaming, refusing to give in. He couldn't look at Estelle, couldn't think about her. If he did, then he was a goner.

Don't come, don't come, don't come.

He kept the mantra up, trying to ignore her ecstatic cry as she orgasmed, her thighs clenching and shuddering, her wet pussy slipping and sliding along his cock.

Even when she collapsed onto him, he didn't move. It wasn't just lust that overwhelmed him, but feelings he didn't want to name, filling his heart until it overflowed. So he kept his eyes closed, trying to disassociate from the moment. And from Estelle.

She sat back up. 'Open your eyes.'

He did, then immediately shut them again. She was too beautiful.

'James...'

He grunted in response.

'Look at me.'

Feeling his climax taking a few steps away from the edge of no return, he did. Now back on safer ground, he wanted to return to driving the sex bus.

He took a steadying breath. 'Can I touch you now?'

'No.'

'Why not?'

'I haven't finished with you yet...'

'You do know this is torture?'

She shrugged. 'If you say so.' Her eyes glinted. 'And I haven't even brought out my crop.'

His dick twitched again at the thought of her riding him. 'So, when *can* I touch you?'

She shifted further down his legs. 'When I say so.'

'But—Fuuuuck!' he yelled as Estelle sucked his cock into her mouth.

She released it with a pop. 'Yes?'

Bashing his head back against the pillow, he let out a strangled laugh.

'Is the mighty James Hunter-Savage about to lose control?' she purred.

He stared her down, even as stars spun behind his eyes. 'If you do that, then yes, I will. Happy?'

'Ecstatic.' She brought one hand to cup his balls, the other running lightly up and down his shaft.

Goosebumps broke out across his skin, rippling up his body. His frequent and detailed fantasies of sex with Estelle had not adequately prepared him for the reality. The scent of her skin, the sweetness of her pussy, her power and sexual energy that heated his blood to boiling point.

She licked up his length, then swiped her tongue through his slit.

I'm dying. I'm dead. I'm fucking dead.

He was helpless. If he closed his eyes, the loss of sight only magnified the sensations rushing through him. But if he opened them, he saw exactly what she was doing, and that was even more intense.

Clutching the bedsheets and grinding his teeth to dust, he oscillated between watching his cock disappearing into her mouth, and squeezing his eyes closed so tightly, all he could see was white light.

His orgasm was like flood water, building up against a dam, the weight of it pushing with so much force that the wall was already cracked. Every lick and suck increased the pressure until there was nothing he could do to hold it in.

Then she stopped.

His chest heaved as he clawed back control. *Keep it together. You can do this.*

He risked a glance down. Estelle gave him a devilish smile, then parted her plump lips and sucked him deep.

'Fuck! Fuck! Fuck!'

She laughed around his cock, the vibrations only heightening the mind-blowing things she was doing with her mouth.

Chemistry. Maths. Science. Rowing.

She stopped again and he let out a groan—half frustration and half relief. This *was* torture. Estelle was edging him until his mind had no choice but to go into meltdown and his body dissolve.

She moved off him and he opened his eyes. 'Where are you going?' he asked, his voice pathetic and desperate.

Opening a drawer, she took out a condom.

James didn't know if this was the greatest moment of his life or the most terrifying. If he didn't last, then he'd never be able to look at himself in a mirror again.

Straddling him, Estelle tore the packet open.

'Wait.' He placed his hand on her thigh.

She gave him a questioning look. 'You don't want this?'

'Oh, I want it, but I need you to do something first or this isn't going to happen at all.'

'What do you need me to do?'

'Sit on my face.'

She inhaled sharply.

'Please?'

Pulling the condom out, she rolled it down over his cock.

'Star?'

She smiled. 'Forward planning.'

God, I lo— He stopped the thought in its tracks. 'Come here,' he growled.

Scooting forwards, she carefully sat on his upper chest.

Grasping behind her thighs, he tugged her forward, his tongue diving into her pussy.

'Oh!'

He sucked, then flicked her clit, single-minded in his dedication to bring her off as quickly as possible. He could feel her glutes tensing as she rocked herself onto his face, hear her voice change in pitch. Pleasure surged through him as he sighted the victory line.

Then she pulled away, scooting down and positioning herself at the head of his shaft.

Holding his breath, James watched her inch down. This was it. The pinnacle of his life so far—Estelle Foxbrooke taking his cock.

She moved slowly, lifting then squirming to take him a little deeper. Her eyes were drowsy, her cheeks darker, her nipples rock hard. She was breathtaking, and it was taking every ounce of his control not to pull her onto him and rut her till his balls emptied.

'Much as it pains me to say,' she murmured, taking another inch. 'You have a massive dick.'

Despite the desire rushing through him, he managed a grin. 'So, I'm no longer a massive dick, I just have one?'

'You're growing on me.'

'Right now, I think I'm growing *in* you.'

She squeezed around him, and he groaned. He'd slept with a lot of women in the past, but no sexual encounter had been as all-encompassing as this. Every cell was vibrating at the same frequency, pulsing with pleasure. The sensations were so powerful they shimmered out of him until his skin no longer felt like the boundary of his body. He was an ever-expanding being of energy, joining with Estelle.

Sinking down to take all of him, she let out a sigh and reached forward. Interlacing his fingers with hers, he anchored his elbows by his sides so she could brace herself on him. As she held his gaze in a perfect moment of connection, his heart rushed out of his body towards her. She was so beautiful, so incredible, so fucking awe-inspiring. And she was here. With him.

Straightening her arms, she put her weight through them and squeezed his hands.

'You okay?' she whispered.

He nodded, his throat so tight he could hardly speak. 'Star...'

She circled her hips, and he shut his eyes. He needed to stay in control, and the sight of her only increased the physical and emotional sensations overwhelming every part of him.

'James?'

The sound of his name on her lips was an arrow straight to his heart. He was coming undone. He needed her to fuck him. To break his body apart, not his soul.

'James?'

Summoning every last bit of mental strength, he opened his eyes. Her expression was uncertain.

'I don't think you're capable of making me lose control, Estelle Foxbrooke. You don't have it in you.'

'Really?'

He nodded. 'No matter how hard you ride me, I'm not going to break.' *You are so full of shit.*

'Really now... I think you'll lose it before I get to a canter.'

'Try me.'

'Oh, I will.' She circled her hips again, then rose up and immediately dropped back down.

Pleasure shot through his body and he let out a grunt.

She squeezed his hands. 'Hold on tight...'

Leaning her weight forward, she raised, then dropped her hips.

He stifled a groan as he stared at her working his cock, his climax building at the base of his spine. There was no way he could go the distance. Estelle was a goddess, with a body more perfect than heaven and a pussy hotter than hell.

The only hope he had was that she fell before he did.

Letting go of her hands and moving them to lean on his chest, he brought his fingers to her clit and rubbed her slickness over it.

Her lips parted, and she shivered.

With his other hand, he palmed her breast, tweaking the nipple.

Her eyes fluttered as if to close, then she held his gaze. 'Giddy-up, Jamesy-boy. We're on the home straight.'

She changed her movement, rocking now, faster and faster. James's heart was thumping in his chest, sensation flashing through his body, seizing every muscle and shocking it with pleasure so intense it stole his breath.

He'd never fainted before, but a fleeting thought came to him that he was about to; that or die. His head was dizzy, his vision narrowing to a circle with Estelle at the centre. He was aware of his fingers on her breast and clit, but every other part of him was detonating like a firework.

Estelle was crying out now, her pussy grinding into his hand and onto his cock. He sensed she was close, but his own orgasm was bearing down on him, too unstoppable to avoid. The only thing he could do was pray she went supernova first and took him with her.

He roared her name, but the sound was distant, lost under the rushing of blood in his ears and her scream as she fell forward, contracting around his cock. He clutched her to him, hips jerking as his own orgasm hit, so powerful that every sensation collided and magnified into a unity of light and noise and pleasure, then shattered into darkness.

Time was passing, but he was floating, disorientated and lost. Sleep's siren song called to him, her tendrils wrapping themselves around his heavy limbs, tangling around any thread of conscious thought, dragging him down to the depths. He tried to stay on the surface, but it was too late. He slipped into an endless void of nothing.

'James?'

He knew that voice, even if he didn't know who or where he was.

'You've got to wake up now.'

The cloud of sleep he was drifting in disappeared in an instant, plummeting him to the hard ground of reality.

His eyes snapped open. 'I was asleep?'

Estelle smiled and nodded. She was perched on the side of the bed, back in her dressing gown.

Panic sliced through him. 'What's the time?' He threw back the covers she must have laid over him and sat up.

She put her hand on his arm. 'It's okay. You've got twenty minutes at least before you need to leave.'

Sinking his head in relief, he pinched the bridge of his nose. 'I can't believe I fell asleep.'

She put her arms around him and brought her mouth to his ear. 'Did I break you?'

He huffed. Estelle had broken, schooled and tethered him, but he wasn't going to let her know that. He'd already given up more of himself than he'd intended, and falling asleep was a level of vulnerability he'd never stooped to before.

'Sleep was a physiological response to a near death experience.'

'I'll take that as a "yes" then. Do you want me to make you a coffee? I don't have a poncy set-up like you, but I have a cafetiere, a milk frother, and a pod machine. And I can lend you a travel mug.'

He raised his head. 'Thank you. Could you please make me a cappuccino with a double shot? I hear all the best people drink them.'

She grinned and hopped off the bed. 'That they do. I'll see you downstairs. You know where the bathroom is if you need it.'

James watched her go, then let out a breath. He didn't want to leave. The thought of what lay ahead of him in China sat like a lead weight in his stomach. Swinging his legs out of bed, he went to the bathroom, then redressed and went to find Estelle.

As soon as he opened the kitchen door, Chester and Joy raced to him with excited yelps. James couldn't help but smile.

Estelle rolled her eyes and crossed her arms with a huff. 'They're never this excited to see *me*.'

He crouched down, stroking Joy with one hand, the other

rolling Chester onto his back as the little dog wrestled with him. 'It's just because I'm new.'

'That's bollocks and you know it. They go this mental because you're a great big slab of testosterone that's been dosed in dognip cologne.'

'Ah yes, the pheromone magic potion you think I bathe in.'

She poured milk foam into a large travel mug. 'I stand by my accusation of witchcraft. If Eveline wasn't so bloody nice, I'd get her to goad her acolytes into coming after you with pitchforks.'

As if to reinforce her theory, Chester began pistoning his hips against his knee, and Joy, his arm. He stood and pointed at the crate. 'Go to bed.'

They trotted inside.

He shut the door behind them. 'Lie down.'

They did.

'Go to sleep.'

Joy lay her head on her paws and closed her eyes. Chester was still gazing at him in hopeful excitement, tail thumping on the blankets behind him.

'See?' Estelle passed him the travel mug. 'Witchcraft.'

'Their behaviour is entirely your fault.'

'Excuse me?' she spluttered.

'Unless, of course, you want to blame Eveline?'

She frowned at him in confusion.

'Does she often give you lost property from the church?'

She froze as the penny dropped.

He laughed. 'Were you using my jumper to train them to hate me or hump me?'

A sheepish grin spread across her face. 'Do you want it back?'

He glanced at the crate. Chester was rearranging it with his teeth and front paws. The little dog finally seemed happy, spun in two circles, then flopped down with a contented sigh.

'I think he should keep it. He's clearly got a taste for Ralph Lauren.'

'Alongside all the rats.'

He faced her. 'Well, they do live at your stables, so they must be classy.'

Silence fell upon the room. It was full of possibilities, uncertainty, and questions that didn't yet have an answer.

'I'll be seven hours ahead of you, so depending on what's happening on the ground, I'll be able to work on the festival during your day and my evening,' he began. 'I don't know how long it'll take to get Dad back, but I'll do everything I can.'

She nodded, as all the happiness that had animated her for the past few hours drained from her expression.

Holding the travel mug tighter, he glanced at the clock on the wall. 'I have to go.'

She nodded and led the way to the front door.

Outside, it was dark and still. Estelle crossed her arms across her chest as if she was cold. James wanted to reach out and hold her, to reassure her everything would be okay, but he could already feel her withdrawing.

He bit back a sigh. 'I'll message you when we get there.'

A flash of something painful passed across her features at the word 'we'. Until that moment, he'd forgotten he would be living with Elyse for god knew how long. The thought made him nauseous.

Estelle took a step back. All their earlier intimacy had disappeared as if it had been a dream.

I'll miss you. I need you. I lo— 'Please lock the door behind you when you go in.'

She nodded.

He strode to his car and got in. Switching on the engine, he turned his head to wave goodbye.

She'd already gone and the front door was shut.

Setting his jaw, James eased out of the yard. He just needed to get his dad home. Then he could make everything he and Estelle had begun that night, unbreakable.

❃ 26 ❃

From: James Hunter-Savage
To: Estelle Foxbrooke
Subject: Arrived

We've finally got to the town where Dad is meant to be. I've got a VPN, but it's patchy and I'm not sure if all my messages will get through. I've left my login details on my desk so you can access my email if you need to. Let me know your thoughts on the new batch of CVs I sent through for the key positions when you get a chance.

Got to go. More later.

Yours, James

From: Estelle Foxbrooke
To: James Hunter-Savage
Subject: Re: Arrived

So glad you got there okay. Things are in hand here, so just focus on getting your dad back. I've gone through the CVs and emailed the best candidates to come in for interview. We'll know the week after next how the licensing committee voted, so if we get a thumbs up, hopefully whoever we choose can start straight away.

Estelle x

FROM: JAMES HUNTER-SAVAGE

To: Estelle Foxbrooke

Subject: Update

It's a shitshow here. Elyse and I are doing our best, but this isn't going to be quick or straightforward. I've got no idea how long it's going to take to sort out. How's Mum doing? And Sophia? They keep telling me they're fine, but I don't believe it.

Thanks, James x

FROM: ESTELLE FOXBROOKE

To: James Hunter-Savage

Subject: Re: Update.

I'm not going to lie, your mum is in bits. Sophia is better, but can't be there the whole time because of work. I'm staying over every other night to make sure your mum has company. Can you give me access to the bank account? I need to make payments when you're not around.

Hope things are starting to happen,

Estelle x

FROM: ESTELLE FOXBROOKE

To: James Hunter-Savage

Subject: WE GOT OUR APPLICATION APPROVED!!!!

It was a narrow margin, but the vote went our way! The

new hires are starting on Monday and I need access to the bank account so I can set up payroll. Things are going to step up now and I need the ability to authorise payments.

Thinking of you,

Estelle x

FROM: JAMES HUNTER-SAVAGE

To: Estelle Foxbrooke

Subject: Re: WE GOT OUR APPLICATION APPROVED!!!!

Great news about the vote. I can't give you access to the bank account without being there. Just keep sending invoices to me and I'll deal with them.

Got to go,

James x

March

FROM: ESTELLE FOXBROOKE

To: James Hunter-Savage

Subject: Any clue when you might be back?

It's been six weeks now. Can anyone give you an idea as to when you might be able to get your dad out? I know you're doing two jobs at once, but we really need you here so we don't have to wait sometimes forty-eight hours for payments to be made.

Thanks,

Estelle x

FROM: JAMES HUNTER-SAVAGE

To: Estelle Foxbrooke
Subject: Re: Any idea of when you might be back?
No. We're working as hard as we can and I'm not going to promise anything I can't deliver.
I'm sorry. I don't want to be here, but I have to.
James x

FROM: ESTELLE FOXBROOKE
To: James Hunter-Savage
Subject: Re: Any idea of when you might be back?
I know you don't want to be there. I just wish you were here.

FROM: JAMES HUNTER-SAVAGE
To: Estelle Foxbrooke
Subject: Re: Any idea of when you might be back?
Me too.

April

FROM: ESTELLE FOXBROOKE
To: James Hunter-Savage
Subject: Why are you changing things again???

1. I've just spoken to the fencing company and you've changed the order to a lower spec. Why?????
2. And Jed, who's in charge of the main stage, says we need to spend more money on it, not less, or it might collapse. You need to put the order back to what he's specified. NOW.

. . .

FROM: JAMES HUNTER-SAVAGE
To: Estelle Foxbrooke
Subject: Re: Why are you changing things again???

1. We don't need the fence you want.
2. The stage won't collapse. It's well within tolerance.
   The order stays as amended.

FROM: ESTELLE FOXBROOKE
To: James Hunter-Savage
Subject: Re: Why are you changing things again???

1. You don't know that. You've never run a festival
   before! What if we're overrun by UberGraft fans?
2. Again, how do you know? You're a chemist, not a
   structural engineer! We've got the budget for this.
   We can't cut corners!

FROM: JAMES HUNTER-SAVAGE
To: Estelle Foxbrooke
Subject: Re: Why are you changing things again???
We're not cutting corners, we're staying within budget.

FROM: ESTELLE FOXBROOKE
To: James Hunter-Savage
Subject: Re: Why are you changing things again???

We ARE within budget! Is there any way we can chat on the phone about this?

FROM: JAMES HUNTER-SAVAGE

To: Estelle Foxbrooke

Subject: Re: Why are you changing things again???

Not at the moment. I've got a meeting with the lawyers, then I'm going back to the factory.

May

FROM: ESTELLE FOXBROOKE

To: James Hunter-Savage

Subject: Now the fucking food???

I thought we'd agreed to use local suppliers? It's all crappy burgers and soggy chips. This is NOT what the festival is meant to be about! I spoke to Leia, and she told me you said you didn't need their help. WHY THE FUCK NOT????

FROM: JAMES HUNTER-SAVAGE

To: Estelle Foxbrooke

Subject: Re: Now the fucking food???

As a gesture of goodwill as per your original verbal agreement with The Colour Palette, their business has been allocated a free pitch. All other concessions have to pay in order to cover their extortionate electricity requirements and for the privilege of making money from the festival. Local businesses were approached first.

James

FROM: ESTELLE FOXBROOKE

To: James Hunter-Savage

Subject: Re: Now the fucking food???

But apart from Leia and Ben, it's now bargain-basement dross! You're changing everything that makes this festival special!

FROM: JAMES HUNTER-SAVAGE

To: Estelle Foxbrooke

Subject: Re: Now the fucking food???

No, I'm not. None of the acts are changing. I'm trying to bring us in on or under budget. Not everyone has the same expectations when it comes to the catering as you.

James

FROM: ESTELLE FOXBROOKE

To: James Hunter-Savage

Subject: Re: Now the fucking food???

We need to get on a call. I can't keep doing this over email.

FROM: ESTELLE FOXBROOKE

To: James Hunter-Savage

Subject: CALL ME!

I know things are hectic there, but please find a way for us to thrash this out over the phone.

FROM: ESTELLE FOXBROOKE

To: James Hunter-Savage

Subject: Re: CALL ME!

James???????

'MOTHERFUCKER!' ESTELLE YELLED, THEN THREW HER moody cow stress ball at James's empty desk. It crashed into the fur Q, knocking it over.

There was a knock at the office door.

'It had better be important because I'm in a foul mood!' Estelle shouted.

The door opened and a smiling head appeared. 'Am I important enough?' Eveline asked.

'Oh, my god, yes!' Estelle pushed her chair back and ran to greet her best friend. 'What are you doing here? Are you alright? The baby? Come and sit down.'

Eveline laughed as Estelle dragged her to the chaise longue. 'I'm absolutely fine. I'm pregnant, not ill.'

Estelle's heart rate returned to normal as she inspected her friend. 'You do look even more gorgeous than normal. And your hair! It's glossier than Duke's mane.'

'I consider it the highest compliment to be likened to him,' Eveline replied with a huge smile. 'Apparently my hair follicles are now stuck in their anagen phase.'

'Their what?'

'It means they don't stop growing. Jack read it in one of the books he's bought. And the diameter of each hair is increasing as well. That's why it's so thick.'

'Oh.' Estelle was once again struck into silence by the living proof that life never stood still. She'd only ever known Eveline as single and Jack living permanently abroad. Now her past and present friends had met, fallen in love, got married, and were having a baby. It was surreal.

She shook herself. 'So, why are you here?'

'Because if Mohammed won't come to the mountain, the mountain must come to Mohammed.'

'So, if I'm Mohammed, then you're a mountain? I thought pregnant women were more like hippos. Or elephants?'

Eveline rolled her eyes. 'It's an idiom and you know it. The point is that you've been so busy I haven't seen you in what feels like weeks. So, I thought I'd pop over and visit you here, then see how Beverley is holding up. Jack and I are off to Monaco in a few days and I didn't want to go without seeing you.'

'That's come around so soon.'

'Well, time does fly when you're working every hour of the day and every day of the week.'

Estelle was silent. The weight of it all went down to her bones. She knew James hadn't abandoned her, but it was like all the years she'd spent trying to keep the Foxbrooke estate afloat whilst Henry hid in London. Again, she felt very alone. Only this time, it was more and more difficult to drag herself out of bed each morning.

Eveline reached across and took her hand. 'I'm concerned about you.'

Estelle bristled. 'I'm fine.'

'I know you are. I just wonder when you're going to take any time out. Since meeting Jack, I've learnt to give myself the same care as others and I want you to do the same. When did you last ride Duke? Practice your archery?'

Estelle shrugged. She'd ridden her beloved horse only a handful of times in the last few months. 'I'll take a break when the festival's over.'

'And what about your birthday? Do you have any plans for that?'

'None. My thirtieth last year with Henry was enough celebrating for one decade. I don't have any time and I don't want any fuss.'

Eveline was quiet. Estelle could almost see the workings of her mind as she calculated how far she could push it.

'Well,' she began brightly, 'if you're at a loose end, I want you to come to the rectory, even if just for a bacon sandwich.'

Estelle smiled, but her heart was heavy. The festival was her chance to do something wonderful, but it was sucking the life out of her and not turning out how she'd envisaged.

'Is everything on track?'

She puffed out her cheeks. 'It doesn't feel like it is. And...' She lowered her voice even though there was no-one else in the room. 'I know I should feel empathy for James, but right now I want to kill him.'

'Oh, dear. Why?'

'He won't give me access to the bank account and makes every payment go through him. He's cutting corners even though there's the budget to cover the costs.'

'Is there?'

'What?'

'Enough money?'

'Of course there is. How much BDE Entertainment is providing is in the contract I signed.'

Eveline gave her a look and lowered her own voice. 'Do you think that maybe James is having to divert some of the cash flow into, er, *helping* get Kevin out of prison?'

'Don't you mean bribe?'

Eveline gave a half shrug.

'I don't know. Maybe that's part of it? But it started at the beginning of the year.'

'Have you spoken to him about it?'

'Yes, but he just fobs me off and says he wants us to come in under budget.'

'Surely that's a good thing?'

'Not if it's going to make the festival crap.'

'Has he changed any of the acts?'

Estelle shook her head.

'Well then, that's the main bit. Isn't it?'

'But if the fence doesn't hold, then we'll break our licensing agreement.'

'Have you sold out of tickets?'

'No.'

'Then it's unlikely there'll be gatecrashers.'

Estelle knew Eveline was being pragmatic, but it didn't make her feel any better. On the issue of the budget, James was being a cheapskate, a quality she abhorred. After nearly a lifetime of hating him, she'd almost performed a complete one-eighty. But this nagged at her, making her question her revised opinion of him.

'Apart from this,' Eveline asked, 'how are you getting on with James?'

Estelle's body flushed with heat. Had she really had sex with him? The memories seemed like a fever dream. She didn't know how to answer without giving a blatant lie or confessing everything. She knew Eveline wouldn't judge, but the fact remained that James was leaving Foxbrooke the moment the festival was over. That was, if he ever returned from China.

'Just remember, it's not long to go now,' Eveline continued in a cheery voice. 'Then you never have to see him again.'

Estelle's silence continued.

'Unless you want to?' The question hung in the air.

The sound of running footsteps in the corridor outside was a blessed relief. Estelle could avoid answering and get back to fire-fighting.

But it wasn't one of the new hires that burst into the room. It was Beverley.

'They're on their way home, babes! Kev's coming back!'

Adrenaline shot Estelle to her feet. 'What happened?'

'I don't know!' Beverley crossed the room, smoothing her hair with shaking hands as if Kevin was about to arrive. She glanced at Eveline. 'Maybe it was all your praying?' Biting her lip, she cast her eye around the office as if checking it was clean and tidy enough for the return of the king.

Estelle's heart thumped in her chest. 'When are they arriving?'

'Tonight.' Beverley's fingers were now brushing invisible lint off her skirt. 'Can you stay until they get here?'

'Yes, of course,' she replied, suddenly desperate for a change of clothes, a hair wash and a full face of make-up.

'Thanks, babe. That way you can give Elyse a lift back to yours.'

Elyse. A sudden pang of frustration and sadness stabbed at Estelle's heart. Nothing was simple. James couldn't sneak out of his parent's house to visit her when Elyse was in the room next door, and she couldn't visit him here either. And anyway, what was she hoping for? They'd had a one-night-stand months ago, followed by emails and the occasional terse call, all about the festival. Once James was back, there was no time for anything other than work.

Beverley's eyes darted from side-to-side as if tracking a hyperactive fly. 'I've gotta go. I need to get the manor cleaned up. Eveline, lovely to see you, babes. Pop by next week?'

Eveline took a breath, but Beverley didn't wait for a reply, scuttling from the room and closing the door behind her.

'What a wonderful turn of events,' Eveline said. 'I'm so pleased Kevin's on his way home.'

James is coming back.

'And James and Elyse as well. You must be so relieved.'

The butterflies in Estelle's stomach didn't feel particularly relieved. They were flapping about and colliding with each other like teenagers at a house party after the unexpected arrival of the host's parents.

Eveline sighed happily. 'I bet James is looking forward to leaping back in the saddle and getting his hands all over things in person again.'

Estelle bit her tongue, remembering the last time James had his hands over *her* in person.

'He'll be able to get stuck right back in,' Eveline continued, then caught sight of Estelle's face and frowned. 'Oh, I didn't think. You must have got used to your own space again. Will you be gentle with him? He's been through an awful lot.'

'Gentle?'

'Yes. I can't imagine the stress he's been under. He may be big and strong, but inside, all men are little boys who want to be loved.'

Estelle blinked.

'Oh, I didn't mean you should *love* him. That's a silly thing for me to say. What I meant was—'

'Why is it silly?'

Eveline's mouth opened and closed a few times before she spoke. 'Well,' she began carefully, 'because you've made it very clear you find James objectionable on almost every level.'

Estelle didn't know how to reply. Even if she'd changed her mind about James in private, in public he was still enemy number one and her twin brother's nemesis. And could she ever forgive him for how he'd treated Henry? As a child, yes. But as an adult?

'Please forgive me for running my mouth off,' Eveline said. 'I just hope James coming back makes your life better. Now, why don't we have a cup of tea and you can tell me all about your exciting life running Foxbrooke's first festival!'

• • •

EVELINE DIDN'T STAY LONG. ESTELLE CRAVED TIME WITH HER friend, but every few minutes there was a knock at the door and another question which broke the flow of their conversation. The rest of the day flew by, and Estelle threw herself into work to stop thoughts of James. For brief snatches of time he was gone from her mind, but then he would reappear, lounging at the edge of her consciousness and smouldering at her.

After the festival staff had left for the day, and Estelle was so tired she accidentally signed off an email to a Portaloo company with four kisses, she shut her laptop and went to find Beverley and Sophia.

She found them in the kitchen. Beverley was dressed in her cleaning tabard and rubber gloves and attempting to remove a layer of stainless steel from the cooker through the use of elbow grease and microfibre cloths alone.

'There you are, babe,' she called over her shoulder. 'I'll be with you in a sec.'

'Mum!' Sophia said. 'All bacteria surrendered and left the manor hours ago. Please stop.' She threw Estelle a pleading look.

'Sophia's correct. And there are currently so many chemicals in the air I think my nasal hairs are melting.'

Beverley stopped and held the back of her hand to her forehead. 'You're right. I've been through three bottles of cleaner already since this morning.' She tugged off her gloves. 'You want some food? I'm too nervous to eat but I can get you something? Do the doggies need dinner?'

Estelle shook her head. 'They ate earlier.' She turned to them. 'Go to bed.' They dutifully padded over to two temporary dog beds she'd brought when she started sleeping the odd night at the manor.

'I suppose you'll be taking the beds back with you tonight now you're not staying here anymore?'

Estelle couldn't tell if Beverley was happy or sad at the prospect of her going back to living permanently at the livery. She was happy to be heading home, but it was tinged with sadness at her role changing back to being James's business partner only. She needed to woman-up and get over herself.

'Yes. I've cleared my things from the spare room already, so I can take these when I go later.'

Beverley took off her rubber gloves. 'It'll be a shame not having them around all the time. But now the men are here to take care of us, I suppose we don't need them.'

Silence settled on the room. Once more things were changing and Estelle was on the outside looking in.

'Can I make you something to eat?' Sophia asked her.

'Are you having anything?'

'Only cake. My stomach's too knotted for anything else.'

'Sounds good to me.'

The three women sat at the kitchen table with mugs of tea and French Fancies whilst the ticking of the clock filled the silence. The anticipation was unbearable. It wrapped itself around Estelle, tighter and tighter, whilst painful flashes of adrenaline stabbed at her skin.

A little after eight, the throaty roar of James's Ferrari outside had all three of them leaping to their feet.

Beverley ran from the room, Sophia following.

Estelle hung back, then picked up Chester and carried him to the front of the manor, the fingers of her free hand tight on Joy's collar.

Heart thumping, she stood inside the house, looking out the open door as James exited the car. He immediately turned to move his seat forward to let Elyse out of the back. Almost midsummer, it was still light and Estelle's breath quickened as she took him in. Had he lost weight?

Chester and Joy barked frantically and James's head turned

to the house, his eyes catching Estelle's. He looked... pleased? Relieved? She couldn't make out his expression as his attention was dragged to his sister, who was hugging him and crying.

Beverley was at the passenger side, her arms around—*holy shit*. Kevin's hair had gone from coal black to snow white and he seemed shrunken and exhausted.

Elyse, still as perfectly put together as ever, gave Estelle a wave, then called to James to open the boot. He unlocked it, then was grabbed by his mother.

Collecting a small bag, Elyse came to Estelle's side. 'Can we go now? I'm so tired.'

'Er, yes. Where is your suitcase?'

'James is having the rest of the luggage sent here tomorrow. We had too much to bring in the Ferrari.'

'Okay, let me just get my bag.' Putting Chester down and letting go of Joy's collar, she dashed back inside the house, a sudden punch of emotion to her throat making her want to cry.

Did you honestly think he would come to you first? Take you in his arms and tell you how much he'd missed you?

Shut up.

After the arsey emails you've been sending him? And anyway, you're not family or his girlfriend.

I know!

Then suck it up and go home.

Slinging her bag over her shoulder, she tucked the fleece dog beds under her arm and went back outside, loading them into the back of the Defender as Beverley and Sophia were all over Kevin, and James was petting Chester and Joy.

'Are we off now?' Elyse asked, then climbed into the car.

'Yes, let me just call the hounds.' She whistled for them, but they ignored her.

'Heel!'

James stood, holding an overly-excited Chester, as Joy frantically humped his leg.

'Oi,' he growled at them. 'Knock it off.'

He strode to Estelle's side. 'I believe these are yours?'

She nodded, struggling to find words. James was even better looking than she'd remembered, even though he appeared wiped out and had clearly lost weight.

'They missed you,' she eventually replied.

James gently passed her Chester. 'And I missed them. More than they'll ever know.'

'Can we go?' Elyse called from inside the car.

The spell was broken.

Estelle turned away from James, opening the boot for Chester and Joy.

James followed her to the driver's side as she got in. 'I'll see you tomorrow?'

She gave him a brief nod.

'James!' Beverley called over. 'Let's get inside!'

He took a step back.

Estelle fired up the car and drove away. In the rear-view mirror, James had already turned and was entering the house.

✻ 27 ✻

ames woke, panicked and disorientated, arms flailing across the counterpane.

His eyes flicked around the room, then closed with relief. He was back in the UK and his dad was home too.

Lying on his back, his bones leaden, the sun shone golden through his eyelids.

What was the time? He glanced at the clock on his bedside table. Ten o'clock.

Shit. He'd slept for thirteen hours.

He grabbed his phone from where it was lying on the bed next to him. What had he been doing before he passed out?

Estelle. He'd been trying to formulate the right message to send her.

But what could he say? Over the last few months, every correspondence had been about the festival, with Estelle getting more and more irate at his refusal to allow her to make any payments. If BDE Entertainment's financial situation had been dire *before* his dad was arrested, now it was way worse.

Just tell her the truth.

What, that I've been lying to her since the start of the year? That we don't even have the funds for the staff wage bill next month?

Pushing out of bed, he went to the shower. He needed to get downstairs and meet the new hires in person. Smile at them even though he knew he couldn't afford their next pay packet.

Running the water hot, he ran his hands over the lean planes of his body. He hadn't done enough exercise or eaten enough protein when he was away and had lost at least a stone of muscle mass.

Think. You can do this.

As well as the day-to-day work that Estelle knew about, he'd also been looking for sponsors to help make up the shortfall. But without being able to make his case in person, every lead had come to nothing. They needed an influencer to get on board.

Someone like Summer Foxbrooke...

He turned the water ice cold and shook his head. No way was he reaching out to Estelle's youngest sister. He'd only met Summer once, and five minutes later his nose had been broken by Henry. If Estelle still believed he preferred blondes, or had once flirted with her sister, then sliding into Summer's DMs would kill off any chance of him and Estelle ever being together.

His cock swelled as he remembered Estelle's body on his, the feeling of being buried so deeply inside her it was as if she'd swallowed his soul as well. Arriving back last night, all he'd wanted to do was take her in his arms. But she'd hung back, and then Elyse had called her away.

Ignoring his cock, he turned the shower off and dried himself. At least Elyse hadn't tried it on in China. When they weren't in meetings or discussing his dad, she'd kept herself to herself, which had been a blessed relief. But now she was back with Estelle and he was living—

'Babe? You up? I heard the shower,' his mum called through the bedroom door. 'You want some brekkie?'

'Thanks, but I'll get something later,' he called back, pulling on clean clothes.

'You sure? You've got all skinny.'

As if to emphasise her point, his jeans now needed a belt to hold them up.

He went to the door and opened it. 'I'm fine. I'll grab something once I've met the staff. How's Dad?'

His mother frowned as she took him in. 'He's like you, babe. I could play the piano on his ribs. I'm gonna take him to Maccy D's once he's done his hair. Want me to bring you something back?'

'Any steaks in the fridge?'

She shook her head. 'I didn't have time to shop yesterday. Shall I get you some from Waitrose in town?'

'Thanks. And eggs, and a couple of tubs of their Number One Madagascan vanilla ice cream.'

'The posh stuff?'

'That's the one.'

'Any French Fancies?'

'What do you think?'

She smiled at him, then her eyes filled with tears. She hugged him tightly. 'I'm so glad you're home, babe,' she said into his chest. 'Thank you for bringing your dad back to me.'

PAUSING OUTSIDE THE DOOR BETWEEN THE MANOR AND THE office wing, James stood straighter and put on a smile. He was calm, confident, and in control.

The entry hall was filled with jackets and shoes. So much

had changed since he'd left. Even though he knew the names of the new staff and had been in touch with them daily, he'd never met them in person.

The door at the end of the corridor was ajar. Chester's fluffy head poked itself through the gap, then the whole of him barrelled forward, yapping loudly.

James picked him up. 'Hey, little buddy. Pleased to see me?'

A second later, Joy was by his side, her front paws on his waist.

Doors opened and heads poked out to stare at them.

Estelle exited their office. 'James, meet everyone. Everyone, meet James. Why don't we all go into the conference room for some proper introductions?'

James followed Estelle into the largest of the rooms, which was already a hive of activity. He kept his stance relaxed, but all eyes were on him. Extending his hand to the person nearest him, he turned on the charm, clocking which of the staff fancied him and which ones wanted to be his new best friend. It wasn't arrogance. Ever since he was seven, he'd trained himself to be highly attuned to how people viewed him, and, thank fuck, none of the new hires had the same attitude as Max.

'Right, I think that's done it,' Estelle said brightly as he'd finished greeting the last person. 'James now has to crack on, starting by making me a cappuccino with a unicorn drawn in the foam.'

There were a few giggles.

'It's true,' he said. 'Although I'm a little out of practice, so it might be more of a sea monster.'

More giggles.

Estelle rolled her eyes and went to the door. 'I'll be in my office if anyone needs me.'

'And I'll be in Estelle's office too,' James added. 'If the cappuccino is up to scratch.'

'Do you need help?' Carly, one of the new hires asked. 'The machine's in Italian.'

'Grazie mille, ma so come lavorarci,' James replied. 'I know how to work it.'

Carly took a sharp intake of breath. 'Parli Italiano?'

He smiled and tilted his head. 'Sì, un po. Capisco abbastanza per far funzionare la mia macchina da cafe. Enough to work my coffee machine.'

'Mio Dio,' Carly murmured, her hand flying to her chest.

'Fuck my life,' Estelle muttered, then clapped her hands. 'Right, back to work, everyone.' She eyeballed James. 'A cappuccino please, Casanova. And make it a double shot.'

He grinned at her. 'Il tuo desiderio è il mio comando, Stella.'

She scowled. 'What does that mean?'

He lifted a shoulder in a nonchalant Italian-style shrug.

Estelle turned to Carly. 'What did he just say?'

Carly blushed. 'Er, he said "your wish is my command", and called you "Star".'

The silence in the room was electric.

What's wrong with you? You're flirting with her in front of the staff!

Estelle cleared her throat. 'Well, er, let's hope—er, marvellous. Carry on.' She strode out of the room.

James followed, but by the time he entered the corridor, Estelle had disappeared.

Get a hold of yourself, dickhead.

As if to emphasise his internal thoughts, his cock twitched in his pants.

Idiot.

Going to the kitchen to make Estelle her coffee, he tried to talk some sense into himself. Her life was in Somerset and he wanted his back in London. They'd had sex, but that didn't mean she actually liked him. From her emails over the last few weeks, it was clear how pissed off he'd made her.

By the time he walked the perfect cappuccino along the corridor, he'd got everything straight again. He would be professional all the way and wait for Estelle to make a move.

'What was all that?' she hissed as he entered the office.

He rifled through the mess on her desk until he found the coaster he was looking for, one which had the words 'make me wet' on it.

Placing the coffee down, he met her gaze. 'All what?'

'The Italian stallion act. Were you trying to make Carly spontaneously orgasm?'

Going to his desk, he adjusted the position of the fur Q and fork U. 'No, solo tu.' *Shut up, shut up, shut up!*

Estelle may not have spoken Italian, but by the change in her expression, he knew she'd worked out he'd just said 'no, only you'.

She stalked towards him. 'You've lost weight,' she said crossly, her chest rising as she breathed. 'You need to eat more. Get your stamina back. You're going to need it.'

A traitorous eyebrow raised.

She swallowed. 'For the festival.'

James's resolve was crumbling. When he was apart from Estelle, he could almost convince himself to do the right thing. But then, when he was with her, his mouth ceded operational control to his dick.

'It's going to be hard,' she said, her voice cracking.

'It already is,' he murmured.

Sense memories assaulted him; the taste of her skin, her tongue slicking against his, the sight of her as she orgasmed, the feel of her pussy squeezing his cock.

Her eyes widened and she nervously licked her lips.

A bolt of lust hit him in the balls.

Somehow, the space between them had narrowed. Her scent travelled up his nostrils and straight into his bloodstream.

'James,' she whispered. 'We—'

He wasn't sure who moved first, but suddenly their bodies collided. He enveloped her in his arms and she dug her nails through his shirt into his back. Blinding sensation seared through him as his tongue clashed with hers. Grabbing her backside, he tugged her onto his cock and she ground against him, moaning low in her throat. The sound was fuel to the fire inside him. It had been smouldering every moment they'd been apart, and now it was raging.

Over the roaring of blood in his ears, he heard a loud knocking, then barking.

Estelle leapt away, running back to her side of the room, and he dashed behind his desk and sat, hiding his obvious arousal.

'Yes?' Estelle asked, then lifted her cappuccino and tried to bury her face in it.

James ran his hands through his hair as the door opened and Zeke, another new staff member, came in.

'Sorry to bother you,' he began, looking at Estelle. 'I've got the numbers you wanted for ticket sales.' He held a piece of paper out. 'Should I...'

'Thanks,' Estelle said. 'Just leave it with me. I'll go over it now with James, so he knows where we're at.'

Zeke placed it on her desk and left the room.

In the silence that followed, James held Estelle's gaze, the corners of his mouth lifting at her struggle to keep a straight face. Eventually, she burst out laughing. The sound made his soul sing.

'You're still on my shit list,' she said.

'I know.'

'And I'm blaming the hamster-bollock pheromones for my inability to control myself around you.'

'I'm not complaining.'

'It's chemical warfare. That's all.'

'So, underneath the animal attraction you don't like me?'

She hesitated. 'I don't *not* like you.'

'I'll take that as a win.'

Another silence. A frown appeared between Estelle's eyebrows. She took a breath as if to speak, then stopped.

Just do it. 'I used funds from the BDE account to pay people off to get Dad back.'

She gave him a brief nod, as if she'd already guessed as such.

'I didn't tell you because all calls and messages are monitored. I couldn't take the risk of anyone finding out.'

'So—'

'But that's not all.'

There was a knock at the door.

'Come in,' Estelle called out.

Carly poked her head in. 'Just a quick one. UberGraft management has got in touch. They do want to stay at the cottage in the woods.'

'Ah, okay. I'll let Henry know and we won't give it to anyone else.'

Carly gave her a nod and left.

Estelle turned back to him. 'The Foxbrooke estate is giving all their holiday rental properties to festival acts, as well as any free rooms in the manor. They aren't charging the performers, or us.'

Her statement was a challenge. She was showing how much she and her family were doing to save money. It made what he was about to tell her next even harder.

'Last year,' he began. 'Dad moved the offices here because he couldn't afford the ones in Bath. He overextended by buying this place and didn't have enough money left.'

Estelle's face froze, her hands clasped tightly around the coffee mug.

'There wasn't enough to honour the contract you signed and therefore zero contingency. This year, prices have gone up across the board and I had to find even more savings.'

'You should have told me.'

'You already hated me. That would have just made things even worse. I had to make it work. If the festival doesn't turn a profit, then my parents lose their home.'

Her eyes widened.

'And now the situation is even more dire.'

'How?'

He glanced at the door, making sure it was shut, but still kept his voice low. 'We don't have enough money to pay the wage bill next month.'

There was a stunned silence.

Then she exploded. 'What the fuck? So, you've just glad-handed them, made them fall in love with you, whilst knowing that you're—*we're*—about to stab—'

'Keep your voice down!' He strode to the door, checking the corridor was empty. Closing it, he turned to Estelle. 'I'm trying to find a solution.'

'Why didn't you trust me with this?'

'At the start of the year, you hated me enough to walk away from the festival. If you'd have known, you would have bailed.'

She shook her head.

'Yes, you would. Before Christmas, at the church, I saw it in your eyes. You had an out and were prepared to take it. And in China, I couldn't tell you about bribing people, or the whole thing could have collapsed. I wasn't going to risk that. I wasn't going to leave Dad there.'

Memories stabbed at his stomach. He'd pushed down his emotions when he'd been abroad, not allowing the fear of failure to impede his actions. But now, with his father home, the 'what-ifs' pounded through him like surf from a storm.

Estelle sat on the chaise longue, her head in her hands. 'So, we can't pay our staff, but you're still taking a nice fat paycheck at the end of every month?'

'No, I'm not.'

She glanced up, the frown back in place.

'I haven't ever drawn a wage. If I was, then I wouldn't be living with my parents.'

'But—'

'I've told you. I'm trying to find a solution. One that involves the festival going ahead, people getting paid, and my parents having a home.' He let out a bitter laugh. 'But you wouldn't know about worries like that.'

'*Excuse* me?'

'You're Lady Estelle Foxbrooke, born with a silver spoon up your arse. You've never had to deal with the kind of shit commoners like me have had to.'

She sprung to her feet. 'You know *nothing* about me *or* my family.'

'Really? The festival's just a hobby for you. There's no actual risk.'

Shut up! Now!

Her eyes were liquid but still blazed with fury. She advanced on him, her index finger pointing like a weapon.

'You. Know. Nothing.' Each word was punctuated by a stab to his chest. 'I've given my *life* to the estate. If it hadn't been for me, it would have been sold off to property developers or the National Trust a decade ago. Did you see the Holbeins on the wall last time you were there? The Vermeers? They're all fake. Over the years, I've sold off every asset I can and paid for reproductions to go in their place. The festival is *not* a hobby. If *it* fails, then the Foxbrooke estate fails. And you think *I'm* privileged? Take a look at yourself. Eton, Oxford, the City. Want to know where I went to school? Huh?' She didn't let him reply. 'Foxbrooke Primary, then Foxbrooke Secondary School. *State* education. I didn't fit in and hated every fucking second.'

'But Henry—'

'Dad let Mom pay for him to go to Eton, but he wouldn't let her pay for me, or Connor, or Leo, or Willow. The only reason Summer went to private school was because Henry paid every penny of the fees from his Conqueror wages.'

James's mind was reeling.

'Yes, I've got a title and my family live in a fancy house, but it means jack shit. You've met my dad. Does he look like the kind of man who makes sensible business decisions? Someone had to be the adult in our family, and for the last twelve years that job has fallen to me. Oh, and don't forget the livery I saved from going under. So, whilst you went to the best school and university on the planet, then swanned around London living the high life, I was enduring the local comp, then ankle deep in horse shit and family bullshit.'

'I'm—'

'Out of the two of us, *you're* the privileged one. And the wages I've been paid by BDE? They've gone straight back into the festival.' She shook her head, the fight seeming to leave her body, her expression desolate. 'Why do you have to be such an arsehole?'

Going to the window, she stared out at the rose garden.

James ran his hands through his hair. What had he done?

'I'm sorry,' he began. 'I didn't know any of that.'

'Does it matter? You still judged me.'

'That goes both ways.'

She shrugged. 'So, we're now in an even worse position than before. We hate each other and the festival's about to fail, taking both our families with it.'

'I don't hate you. I've never hated you.'

There was a pause before she replied. 'Please don't tell anyone about the paintings being reproductions. Only me, Henry, and our parents know.'

'I won't.' Going to her side, he gazed at the set of her jaw. 'I'm sorry for what I said. I wish I'd taken my frustration out on the rowing machine and not you.'

She gave an almost imperceptible nod. 'It must have been a nightmare for you in China.'

'It was the most stressful period of my life. Even worse than—' He broke off and sighed. 'Are you up for brainstorming how to turn the festival around? I want to do this with you.'

Turning away from the window, she took the printout from Zeke, then sat on the chaise longue. He joined her, making sure there were a few inches between them. She may have hated him, but every part of him still wanted her.

'See for yourself.' She handed him the piece of paper. 'We're not sold out yet and we should have been months ago.'

He ran his eyes over the figures. Ticket sales had started strong then petered out. He pointed at the week they started to fall. 'This was when I cut the advertising budget.'

She nodded. 'And now I know we can't resurrect it, whatever we do for promotion has to be free.'

'I've been speaking to more companies about sponsorship, but without being able to meet them face-to-face, so far it's come to nothing. Can you talk to the acts and ask them to promote it more?'

'I already have, and most of them have done something. I'm just hoping all the UberGraft fans that couldn't get tickets for Glastonbury will come to our festival to see them.'

James was silent. Even though he knew getting Summer Foxbrooke on board to help with promotion would help, he didn't want to suggest the idea and risk the fragile peace between him and Estelle.

There was another knock at the door.

'Come in,' Estelle called out.

Zeke entered the room. 'Your luggage has arrived from Heathrow,' he said to James. 'It's in the entry hall. Do you want me to do anything with it?'

'No thanks,' he replied. 'I'll deal with it in a minute.'

Zeke left and James let out a sigh. 'Are the interruptions this constant?'

Estelle nodded. 'You get used to it. But they're good people. We can't let them down.'

James hung his head, pushing the heels of his hands into his eye sockets. *What a mess.*

Feeling a hand on his knee, he glanced up.

'We'll find a way,' she said. 'We can do this. We're awesome.'

He huffed. 'I don't feel particularly awesome right now. More like a total arsehole.'

A faint smile ghosted across her lips. 'Is this finally a chink in the Hunter-Savage armour? A small glimpse of humanity lurking inside?'

'Inside my cold, dead heart?'

She cringed. 'How many times have I said that to you?'

'To my face? Twice. Behind my back? Probably too many to count.'

'Sorry. I don't think you're cold.'

Heat coursed through him and his heart beat faster. Estelle swallowed, and his gaze unconsciously flicked to her mouth.

She moved a little closer.

There was yet another knock at the door, and Estelle sprang to her feet. 'Come in!'

Jed entered the room. 'Have you got time now to run through a few things?'

'Yeah, sure.' Hurrying to her desk, she grabbed her laptop, then turned to glance back at James. 'You okay?'

Yeah, peachy. My dick's hard enough to hammer nails and currently diverting all the blood from my brain. He cleared his throat. 'Yeah, all good.' His phone rang. 'I'm going to get this. You do what you need to do.'

She nodded, then left.

As the door closed behind her, James pulled out his phone.

Sebastian Mayfield. A former colleague and one of the best-connected men in London.

'Mate,' James began, slipping back into an assured drawl. 'Long time. What's up?'

'You back from China then?'

'Yeah.'

'Brought back a wife?'

'Fuck, no. Too much paperwork.'

Sebastian laughed. 'You try organising a wedding.'

'Shit! You're engaged?'

'Popped the question on her birthday.'

'Congrats, man.' James rubbed his chest. He was happy for Seb, but somehow the news made his heart hurt.

'So, she's officially off-limits now. Okay?'

'Fair do's. When you getting hitched?'

'Next year. We need that long to plan the bloody thing. I'm in charge of the ushers and turning up. That's all I've been trusted with.'

James laughed. 'Sounds like my kind of deal.'

'Yeah.' Sebastian paused. 'So, I wanted to ask. You up for being a groomsman?'

James was floored. He'd never thought of Seb being more than a colleague and casual drinking buddy. 'Mate, it would be an honour.'

'And organise the stag do?'

'You sure about that?'

Seb laughed. 'As long as there are no strippers. Don't take the piss, but I'd really like a long weekend playing golf in Scotland.'

'So you can practise finding the right hole on your wedding night?'

'Fuck off.'

James smiled. He'd take a weekend playing golf over enduring a visit to a strip club every time. 'Yeah, I'll sort it for you. Email me a list of names and I can take it from there.'

'Cheers, mate, you're a legend. You still looking for work in London?'

James's heart jumped. 'One hundred per cent. What have you got?'

❧ 28 ❧

Estelle: Hey, little sister. I can never get through to you when I call, so I'm sending you this message. The festival's in deep shit and we need to sell more tickets. You're coming back for it, right? Apparently, you're fairly popular online. Can you help? Xxx

Summer: 'Fairly' popular?

Summer: I've got three million followers on Tiktok, and one-point-two million on Insta

Estelle: Fuck me. Did you buy them?

Summer: Rude! When are you going to follow me?

Estelle: I don't do social media

Summer: YOLO. Who told you I was popular? Anyone I know?

Estelle. You

Summer: Ha-dee-ha

Estelle: Look, we're really up against it here.
Is there anything you can do?

Summer: If you'd been following me, then
you'd have seen I'm already all over it

Estelle: Thanks, but I don't think it's working

Summer: That's because I've only done
stage one...

Estelle: And what's that?

Summer: Getting my followers to come to the
festival

Estelle: Oh, do you need tickets?

Summer: It's been sorted already

Estelle: Okay, so what's stage two?

Summer: I'm going to advertise a talk in the
acoustic tent on the Sunday

Estelle: With who?

Summer: Me! Who else?

Estelle: You think that will work?

Summer: Watch ticket sales over the next
forty-eight hours. Summer Foxbrooke is going
to save the day

Estelle: Thank you, your majesty

Estelle flipped down the sun visor and gave herself another once-over in the mirror.

Chester barked his approval.

'You know what?' she said to him, 'I think I look at myself in a mirror more than Summer these days, and that's saying something.'

Easing the Defender away from the cottage, she frowned at the sight of Elyse's car.

'I don't know if I'm going mad, doggos, but I'm positive it wasn't parked like that last night.'

Even though they were living under the same roof and both working at Shoscombe Manor, they hardly ever saw each other. When Estelle got back each evening, Elyse was either about to go to bed or already in it, and when she got up the next morning, Elyse had already left or was still asleep. But this was the fifth time that Elyse's car appeared to have changed position from where it had been left the previous evening.

Is she creeping out at night somewhere?

To see James?

Oh, get over yourself. You don't honestly believe that?

Well then, where is she going?

Finn?

We can but hope. I want my house back.

So you can shag James…

Turning the car onto the main road, Estelle growled with frustration. She hated not being in control. Trying to keep the festival on track with just under two weeks to go was bad enough. But being around James she was dick-drunk on a cocktail of hormones that made every cell of hers want to reproduce with every cell of his. The situation had become so bad she'd even dreamt about how beautiful their children would be.

'Get a grip!'

Chester barked again.

Estelle was never alone with James for more than five minutes before someone interrupted them. There was no time to sneak off anywhere, and even if they did, where could they go? He'd emailed her a list of local hotels with the subject header 'Want to check any of these out?' but every day there was a new crisis to swallow up any second of free time.

The only thing that made the situation even half bearable was that James was often out of the office, trying to pin down last-minute sponsorship, and when he *was* around, he appeared even more frustrated than she was. Estelle grinned. It only took one look from her to cause a bulge in his trousers.

Pulling up outside Shoscombe Manor, her thudding heart slowed as she saw his car had already gone.

This is a good thing! No distractions!

Whatever. I need my cappuccino.

That's not all you need from him.

Shuddup.

Letting herself in, Estelle went straight to her office and flipped open her laptop. Over sixty emails had come in overnight. She took a deep breath and got to work, not moving from her seat until half past ten, when there was a knock at the door.

'Come in.'

It was Carly. 'Could you come to the conference room for a second? I need to show you something.'

'Please tell me it's a good something?'

Carly grinned. 'It is.'

'Thank god.' Estelle stretched, then followed her out of the room and along the corridor.

'After you,' Carly said, indicating the door.

Frowning, Estelle pushed it open and entered.

'Happy birthday!'

She blinked. The room was filled with people and balloons. James stood in the centre of the crowd, a big smile on his face. He raised his hands and led everyone in singing 'Happy Birthday'.

How did he know? Estelle hadn't told anyone and had wanted the day to go by without any fuss. She'd even told her family she was too busy to see them.

On the table was a huge cake, decorated with a picture of a unicorn leaping over a shooting star and the words 'Happy Birthday Estelle'. She glanced from the cake to James and his smile got even bigger.

When the singing finished, James started a round of applause, then handed her a knife. 'It's time to make a wish.'

She took it from him. 'I wish I knew how you found out it was my birthday.'

'The wish has to be secret. And you have to make it as you stick the knife in.'

Narrowing her eyes, she pointed the blade at his chest. 'Does it matter where I stick it?'

Everyone laughed.

'I would prefer you cut the cake,' he replied. 'And anyway, I'm not suitable for vegetarians.'

Estelle had a sudden vision of licking James. She'd take him over cake, any day. As if reading her mind, his expression grew hungry.

'Okay!' She wrenched her gaze away. 'Here we go.' She'd decided to wish for the festival to be a success, but as the knife hit the board, different words came to her.

I wish I could have James.

Heat rose up her neck. Keeping her focus on the cake, she cut it into pieces, placing each portion on a napkin and handing them out.

James waited for everyone else to go first.

Estelle took the piece of cake containing the star and gave it to him.

'Thank you,' he murmured. 'That's the one I wished for.'

She swallowed. 'Does the wish count if you say it out loud?'

'We'll have to see.'

'Estelle! You need a piece!' Carly said.

Estelle cut out the bit that contained her name. Biting into it, she let out a low moan. 'Oh, eye 'od! Ih 'ummy!'

'James got it from the restaurant in the village,' Carly said. 'The Colour Palette. Apparently, one of the owners won loads of awards when he worked in Australia.'

There was a pop, and Estelle turned to see James opening a bottle of Prosecco. Her eyes widened. There was no way they could afford it, *or* the time to drink it.

'We sold out of tickets two weeks ago,' he said. 'You're allowed to take five minutes off.' He poured the drink into paper cups, then opened a second bottle. 'And anyway, this is a present from my parents. No festival funds were harmed in its purchase.' With a roguish grin, he held out a cup. 'Happy birthday.'

She took it. 'I'll thank them later. And thank you for the cake. It's a wonderful present.'

'That's not your present.'

Her tummy flipped over. 'What?'

'I've got something else for you.' He continued passing out cups of Prosecco.

'You have?' She glanced around the room. 'Where is it? When can I have it?'

He hesitated. 'Another time. Not here.'

Oh, hello... 'Is it big?' she asked innocently.

'It is, actually.'

'I want it now.'

'No can do.'

She pouted. 'But I'm the birthday girl.'

James grinned at her and she smiled back. Alcohol was fizzing through her blood and making her skin tingle.

'I like it when you smile,' she said, then clapped a hand over her mouth.

He burst out laughing. 'Have you eaten anything besides cake so far today?'

She shook her head, her cheeks on fire.

'I'll go make you a birthday sandwich and a cappuccino. And if we get a chance later, I'll go get your gift. Okay?'

'Deal.' She didn't trust herself to say anything more without announcing to the whole room how much she wanted James to be her birthday strippergram.

BY SIX O'CLOCK, THERE HAD BEEN NO OPPORTUNITY FOR Estelle to be alone with James. They'd worked straight through, eating at their desks.

'Did you have any plans for this evening?' he asked.

'I was going to work here until I went cross-eyed, then go home. Elyse said something about cooking tonight.'

'Do you have time now for a quick meeting up at the site? The main-stage manager wanted to chat about disabled access.'

She frowned. 'But we've got disabled access. Please don't tell me he's taking it out?'

'I don't think so. But...' He shrugged as if it were a possibility.

'Okay, let's go.' Closing her laptop, she put it in her bag. 'After we're done, I'll work from home.'

Estelle was hungry and irritated. This time last year she'd turned thirty, and it seemed like the past twelve months had gone by in the blink of an eye. Her twin was coupled up with Libby and her best friend was married and pregnant. Everything was changing for the people around her, but her life seemed stuck in the mud. She'd planned her birthday to be a non-event, but couldn't help feeling sad.

Get over yourself! You had cake and prosecco earlier. And everyone knew you weren't celebrating but still messaged to say happy birthday!

Estelle followed James's Ferrari out onto the country roads towards Foxbrooke Manor, Chester and Joy on the back seat of the Defender. As soon as they turned into the open area in front of the gates to the manor, it was clear just how much the festival was taking shape. Construction was everywhere, with gates already in place and hard standing on the grass verges on either side of the long drive.

She parked outside the house and got out. 'Are we meeting him at the main stage?'

James checked his watch, then his phone. 'Yep. We'll go around the back and see what the issue is.'

Estelle led the way, her annoyance growing with every step. She didn't have time for this. There was too much else to do. She let her hunger and frustration mask the deeper feelings of loneliness inside that she didn't want to dwell on.

James frowned. 'I should have got us food this afternoon. Time just ran away from me.'

'It's not your job to tame the hangry beast,' she muttered.

His frown turned into a sexy smile. 'That sounds exactly like the kind of job I'd enjoy.'

Estelle's heart flip-flopped in her chest. 'I need my present. Can we go back and get it after we've dealt with this?'

'I think it's going to have to wait.'

They'd reached the backstage area, but it was empty.

Estelle glanced around. 'Where is he?'

'Maybe on the stage itself?'

She strode ahead. 'I don't know what he's on about. Look, the disabled access is here exactly as we planned it. I really can't see what the issue is.'

James shrugged. 'He told me he was here.'

'For god's sake.' She stomped up the ramp that led to the back of the stage. 'I don't have time for this. I'm hungry and—' She stopped abruptly when she rounded the corner.

In the centre of the stage, picnic tables and chairs had been set up, with pretty gingham tablecloths. Around them stood her three parents, Henry and Libby, Connor, Leo, Willow and Summer, as well as Jack, Eveline and Finn.

'Happy birthday!' her father roared. 'Think you could get away without celebrating? Fat bally chance!'

Estelle glanced back at James. He inclined his head towards her friends and family.

Arthur came forward and enveloped her in an enormous hug. 'My first child,' he said proudly. 'Just think, thirty-one years ago I watched your cranium squeezing out of your mom's vagina. Happiest day of my life.'

'Dad!'

Arthur disengaged, wiped the corners of his eyes, then turned to Henry. 'And twenty minutes later, you forged your own path through her love canal. What a day that was!'

Henry dropped his chin to his chest and let out a sigh.

Vivienne came forward to hug Estelle. 'Happy birthday, honey.'

'Thanks, Mom. You shouldn't have gone to all this trouble.'

'Nonsense. You can take a time out, just for tonight. I—where do you think you're going, young man?'

Estelle's head snapped in the direction of her mom's question. James was stepping away from the group.

'I was going to leave you to it.'

'I think not,' Vivienne said firmly.

Dervla bustled up to James and took his hand. 'When was the last time you ate?'

His eyes flicked to Estelle's as if asking for her permission to stay.

'He hasn't eaten anything since a slice of cake and a sandwich this morning,' she said.

Dervla looked stricken. 'Well, that won't do, will it now? You can have the first stab at the buffet.' She dragged him to the back of the stage, where four long tables were groaning with food.

Vivienne led Estelle forward. 'You too. You've lost weight.'

'And that's a bad thing? You've been trying to get me to shed a stone since I was a teenager.'

Vivienne sniffed. 'Well, I prefer you the way you were.'

Estelle rolled her eyes but allowed her mom to fuss over her, piling her plate high with all her favourite foods, then leading her to sit down.

Her father was off to the side, feeding Chester and Joy, who ate their dinner in a few gulps, then ran around investigating the space and people.

Eveline sat next to Estelle, her large baby bump touching the table. 'Happy birthday, my lovely.'

'Whose idea was this?' Estelle asked. 'And you look incredible, by the way.'

'Thank you, I still feel great, although the next couple of months should be a little more challenging.' She gazed out from the stage at the parkland. 'Look at what you've achieved, Estelle. You should be so proud of yourself.'

'We're not out of the woods yet. Far from it. We're having to defer paying our staff until it's over because we don't have the cash and can't take out any more loans.'

'Oh, dear. Are they understanding?'

'Yes, thank god. They've been amazing. So, go on, who set this up?'

Eveline's smile was a ray of sunshine. 'James did. He suggested it to me.'

'What? When?'

'A couple of weeks ago. He wondered if you were going to take any time out to celebrate your birthday, and if not, could we put on a little surprise for you?'

Estelle glanced over to the next table, where James was sitting next to Dervla and making her laugh. Henry was at another table, looking warily at him.

'He'll come around,' Eveline said.

'What?'

'Henry. He'll fall in love with James just as much as the rest of us.'

'Excuse me?'

Eveline glanced up as Jack arrived at the table. He sat and gave her a kiss.

'Jack!' Estelle cried. 'Did you hear what your wife just said?'

He smiled. 'She loves everyone, even if they don't deserve it.'

'That's true,' she replied, even though her heart was pounding at the word 'love' in the same sentence as 'James'.

'But, as ever, she's right.'

'Huh?'

'I've spent enough time with James now to know I really like him,' Jack continued. 'He's a good person.'

Estelle stared over at James's table as Summer sat next to him. Uncomfortable feelings of anger, jealousy and inadequacy crawled like spiders over her skin. Her gaze flicked to Henry. He was also eyeballing James and their youngest sister.

Finn bashed his plate of food on the table next to Estelle and sat down with a thump. 'Should I step in?' he growled.

'Ye—' Estelle began.

'No,' both Eveline and Jack replied as one.

'Finley, Estelle,' Eveline said in her sternest voice. 'Stop staring at them and eat your food. James can take care of himself.'

'What?' Estelle hissed.

'It's not James we're looking out for,' Finn added.

'Well, it should be,' Eveline said firmly. 'Be honest with yourselves. Who seems more uncomfortable over there, Summer or James?'

Estelle glanced over again. James had moved his chair closer to Dervla and his legs were crossed away from Summer. He was smiling at her youngest sister, but it looked forced.

'See what I mean?' Eveline asked.

Estelle and Finn grunted.

'If you make any more noises like that, my wife will turn you into sausages,' Jack said with a grin. 'The pair of you are worse than Ham Solo and Chewbaccon.'

Estelle snorted with laughter.

'Do you see it now?' Jack asked Eveline. 'It's like we're back in the pigpen.'

'Rude!' Estelle said, still laughing. She turned to Finn. 'Speaking of porking, are you and Elyse playing hide the chipolata?'

Finn's jaw dropped. 'What? No! Why would you think that?'

'Because I'm convinced she's sneaking out at night.'

'And a *chipolata*? Fuck off. I'm packing a jumbo.'

Jack cleared his throat.

Finn glanced at Eveline. 'Sorry. It's Stelle's fault. She started it.'

Eveline's eyes were sparkling. 'Don't mind me. This is wonderful entertainment.'

Finn turned back to Estelle. 'I haven't seen Elyse since quiz night. Okay?'

She nodded. Where was Elyse going?

James?

Shut up! Just shut up!

Pulling her phone from her pocket, she checked her messages.

Elyse: What time are you coming home? Do you need dinner?

Estelle glanced across the stage. If she decided to have a drink, then she could always stay the night here.

Estelle: I'm at Foxbrooke Manor with my family. I'll probably sleep here

Elyse: Okay, have fun x

Estelle pocketed her phone. She needed to let worries about Elyse *and* James go for one evening and enjoy spending time with the people closest to her.

JUST BEFORE HALF-PAST NINE, THE SUN SET, BUT IT WAS STILL light enough to see. Estelle was warm and happy, but also utterly exhausted. The time out had made her pause, and her body was now screaming at her for sleep.

James had sloped off earlier, but only a very tiny part of her was worried about him being with Elyse. Estelle was tired of her mind projecting images that made her unhappy. She wanted to drift into a dreamless sleep where she could let everything go.

Calling Chester and Joy, she said her thanks and goodbyes, got in the Defender and drove back to the livery.

Elyse's car wasn't there.

Entering the house, she put the dogs in their crate and checked Elyse's room. Empty. In the bathroom, her wash bag and toothbrush were also nowhere to be seen.

Let it go!

Estelle brushed her teeth, had a quick shower, and got into bed. For the first time in weeks she had the house to herself, and despite being shattered, her mind and body were wired. Throwing back the covers, she went to find her vibrator. Maybe that would take the edge off.

Taking it out, she compared it to James. BOB may have had multiple speeds, but he was not attached to the hottest man she'd ever known, and certainly didn't have his wicked tongue.

Before she could second guess herself, she grabbed her phone, ran down the stairs and took her car keys off the hook by the front door.

I want my birthday present.

29

James stepped out of the shower and towelled himself dry. He'd skipped out of Estelle's surprise birthday dinner early after Summer's attention and Henry's glares had become too much, then gone home and punished himself in the gym.

Assessing his body in the mirror, he frowned. Since returning from China, he'd regained some of his lost muscle, but he wasn't in the shape he was the night before he left. The night he'd spent with Estelle.

As if acknowledging the memory, his dick twitched.

Ignoring it, he wrapped the towel around his waist and exited the bathroom. Summer Foxbrooke may have flirted with him, but he knew it was an act. For whose benefit, though? Summer had kept glancing over to the table where Estelle was to see if any of them were looking her way. Was she trying to piss her sister off? Make Finn, the beardy grump, jealous?

Going to the window, James stared out at the darkening sky. An owl hooted somewhere in the distance.

I'm going to miss this.

Huh?

The peace and quiet. It's not as bad as I thought.

You're joking, right?

I don't know anymore. I—

What was that?

There was a noise outside his window.

Bird? Squirrel?

The rustling was getting louder. James pulled the sash up and leaned out.

What the—

'Er, hello,' Estelle said from her position on the trellis.

James tried to process the sight of her dressed in her pyjamas, halfway up the side of the wall. 'What are you doing?'

'Sleep-climbing?'

He blinked. 'I don't think it was built to support a person. Go back down before it fails.'

'Bollocks to that, I'm nearly there.' She hauled herself higher, and James held out his hand to help her through the window.

Inside his bedroom, she pulled off her boots then went towards the bathroom. 'I'm just going to wash my hands.'

'You seem to know your way around.'

'Of course I do,' she called out over the sound of running water. 'I practically lived here when you were away.' He heard the taps shut off, then she came back into the room, wiping her hands on her pyjamas. 'And, in the interests of full disclosure, I once gave myself multiple orgasms whilst lying on your bed.'

His cock swelled.

'Although I had to close my eyes. All this chintz reminds me of Gram-Gram.'

'I didn't choose it.'

'Didn't think you did.' She faced him. Her breathing was fast, pushing her hardened nipples against the fabric of her top with every inhale. 'I want my present now, please.'

He stepped away.

'Where are you going?'

'To get it.'

'But *you're* my present.'

He grinned at her over his shoulder. 'No, I'm not.'

She stamped her foot. 'I knew I should have brought the shotgun.'

Retrieving a large box from the corner of the room, he placed it on the bed. '*This* is your present.'

Her eyes widened. 'You actually got me something.'

'Uh-huh.'

She seemed floored. 'Oh.'

'Want to open it?'

'I don't know. I'm really nervous.'

So am I. His heart was thumping faster and faster in his chest. *What if she doesn't like it?*

'But what if I don't like it?'

He huffed. 'Okay, how about this? If you don't, then you can do whatever you want to me.'

Her eyes flicked to where his cock was tenting the towel. 'And if I *do* like it?'

He held her gaze. 'Then I can do whatever *I* want to *you*.'

She swallowed. 'Deal.'

Estelle moved towards the box slowly, as if it were a bomb she had to defuse. It was plain black, with Chinese symbols in red on the top. Flicking the catches on the side open, she lifted the lid.

'Oh!' She glanced at him, then back to what he'd bought her. 'Oh, my god, James!'

His soul sang. He'd made the right choice.

Taking the unstrung bow from the case, she ran her fingers over the laminated wood. 'I've never come across anything quite like this before,' she whispered. 'I think it's the most beautiful one I've ever seen.'

'It's called the "Nökhör". The word is Mongolian for comrade, companion or friend. Genghis Khan gave the title to soldiers who devoted themselves exclusively to their leader—the ones who were the most valiant and loyal warriors.'

She gave him a look. 'And who am I devoting myself to?'

'Everyone. It's what you've been doing all your life. But I hope in the future you'll give a little more of that devotion to yourself. Using the bow should be a reminder to put yourself first.'

She didn't answer—her gaze falling to the mother-of-pearl stars he'd requested be inlaid into the bow.

'There are thirty-one of them. For each year of your life so far.'

Running her finger across them, her lower lip wobbled. She clamped it between her teeth as if to keep it still.

'There's also a specialist quiver for horse archery, arrows, and a few other bits and bobs. I told the makers your height and showed them a video I took of you practising, so it should all be suitable.'

She still didn't speak.

'Do you like it?'

She nodded. 'It's the most perfect gift I've ever received.' She placed the bow carefully back in the box. 'Thank you.'

Emotion gripped his throat. Moving forward, he took the box from the bed, put it by the window, then turned and faced her. 'Ready?'

Her nostrils flared. 'For what?'

His heart sped up, but he kept his posture relaxed. 'To hold up your end of our deal. You liked my present. So now I get to do whatever I want to you.'

She took a sharp breath, her hands twisting in the cotton of her pyjama bottoms. 'Your parents are two rooms away.'

'Can you be quiet?'

'Yes.'

'Good... Now, take off your clothes.'

She ran her gaze down his body. 'Ditch the towel.'

He raised an eyebrow. 'And there was me thinking *I* was in charge. Are you going to say please?'

'Now.'

He smirked. 'That'll do.' Tugging the towel away, he dropped it to the floor, then gripped his cock and ran his hand from base to tip. Pleasure shivered across his skin, but he kept his breathing steady. He'd had months to prepare himself mentally for this moment. The second time he had sex with Estelle, he was determined to keep his body *and* his emotions under control.

She, on the other hand, he wanted to pleasure so completely that when she thought of her ideal man, all she saw was him.

She was trying to be cool, but goosebumps were spreading across her lower arms as she stared at him stroking his shaft. Widening his stance, he clenched his abs.

'Star?'

Her eyes darted to meet his, as if shocked to find his cock had a person attached to it.

'You want this?'

She nodded.

He took a step forward. 'Then take off your clothes.'

Tearing them off, she stood before him, one hand straying to her inner thigh as if wanting to touch herself.

James held his breath as he took her in. Everything about Estelle seemed designed to drive him out of his mind. From her wild curly hair, her velvet dark eyes and voluptuous curves, to her strong thighs that he wanted clamped around his head. She licked her lips, and he stifled a groan. Whether verbally slicing and dicing him, or sucking his soul out through his cock, he couldn't get enough of Estelle's sharp and sinful mouth.

'Sit,' he commanded.

She perched on the edge of the bed.

He stepped closer. 'Spread your legs.'

She hesitated, her cheeks darkening.

'I want to see all of you.'

Slowly, her knees parted until she was completely open to him.

Gritting his teeth, he forced the rush of desire back down, then went forward until they were almost touching.

She leaned in as if to suck his cock, and he shook his head. 'Lie back.'

She did, one hand moving to her pussy.

'I don't think so,' he murmured, lifting it away. 'Tonight, that's mine.'

Her breath was rapid, her teeth biting into her lower lip.

Placing her arms above her, he caught her wrists lightly in one hand, holding them to the mattress. She arched her chest, as if begging to be touched.

Even though he wanted nothing more than to press his body to hers, he kept an inch of space between them, ghosting kisses across the skin of her neck until she was squirming, her legs locking behind his, trying to pull him onto her. Leaning his hips forward, he rubbed the length of his cock against her pussy and she let out a little cry.

'I thought you were going to be quiet,' he whispered. 'Should I stop?'

'No, no, no, no, no,' she panted. 'I'll be quiet. Don't stop.'

Leaning his weight onto her, his hips kept up a rhythm against her clit, and his lips found hers. His tongue teased her, sweeping into her mouth, then withdrawing. She whimpered, and he kissed her again, his free hand cupping her breast. As his fingers captured her nipple, he swallowed her cry, his kiss now possessive, ravaging.

She writhed beneath him, but he wasn't forcing her wrists to the bed above her head. She'd completely surrendered, her back arching higher with every breath, her legs tightening around his.

James tried to divorce his mind from the sensations shooting through his body, keeping focused with clinical precision on the task of making Estelle come apart. He wasn't inside her, but his cock was slick with her juices, and the friction between it, her pussy and his abs, was almost enough to send him over the edge.

Her tongue tangled with his, her body trembling, frantic, as if she was lost in a collapsing maze, desperately trying to find the way out.

Stay with me, Star. I'll get you there.

As he felt her hurtling towards her own release, he pinned her to the bed with his mouth and his cock, grinding into her pussy as she stiffened then jerked beneath him. He kept circling his hips, slowing as she softened, then went limp beneath him.

Releasing her hands, he moved down her body, kneeling on the floor and hooking her legs over his shoulders.

She made a small sound of confusion, shifting as if to get up, but he lay her back, his hands coming to her breasts as he buried his face in her pussy.

'Oh, my god,' she whispered as he sucked her clit. 'Ohhhhh...'

He glanced up and tweaked her nipples. 'Quiet,' he rumbled. 'Or I'm going to stop.'

Her expression was dazed, but she nodded, flopping back, her hand covering her mouth.

James lowered his head, using all the tricks he knew to get a woman off. Every one of his senses was attuned to each small and subtle movement Estelle made: every sound, every breath. There was no compromise, no room for laziness in his performance. He was James Hunter-Savage, and he was going to be the fuck of Estelle Foxbrooke's life.

Power rushed through him as her thighs shook and shuddered. Every flick of his tongue seemed to send an electric shock through her. Rolling her hardened nipples, he held her to the bed, licking faster and faster until she went stratospheric, her body twisting into his touch, a strangled cry escaping.

He eased her gently down, but as soon as she went boneless, he inched two fingers inside her, his other hand pressing on her lower abdomen, pulling her clit higher. She didn't resist, angling her hips to his mouth, squeezing around his fingers as he curled the tips, rubbing them against her G-spot.

His cock throbbed painfully, but he ignored it. Nothing mattered more than proving himself to her. Estelle had disdained and dismissed him, but now he wanted to leave no doubt in her mind that he was the man for her, both in bed and out of it. His life had been a car crash for over a year, but now he was on the up. He could get his life back in London *and* he could win Estelle.

Her moans were getting louder, and he prayed his parents were fast asleep in their room down the hall. As Estelle's breath became a gasp and her pussy clenched around his fingers, he pressed firmly on her G-spot and sucked hard on her clit. She detonated with a cut-off scream, thrashing on the bed, her pussy gushing as she came.

He rode out the waves of her orgasm, then stood, going to the bathroom for a condom. Returning, he stared at her sprawled out on his bed, her legs still hanging off the end. She was a goddess. A warrior. *Mine*.

Crooking a finger, she beckoned him forward. 'Gimme.'

Lifting her onto the bed, he settled between her legs and gazed at her, his heart tripping over itself.

Keep it together.

Lowering his lips to her ear, he bit the lobe.

She squeaked.

'How do you want it?' he rumbled.

'Dealer's choice,' she murmured. 'You won. So you get to do whatever you want to me.'

He dropped his forehead to the bed with a thump as desire pounded through him, urging him to take her hard and fast. Taking a breath, he forced himself to move slowly, pressing in an inch. She moaned, and he clenched his jaw. The sound was like being shot in the dick with Viagra.

Keep. It. Together.

She angled her hips up and he pushed in a little further. She was so tight, so hot, so perfect he didn't know what was going to blow first—his cock or his mind.

'More,' she whispered.

He kept his face buried in the mattress as electricity shot through every nerve. He couldn't raise his head and look at her. His imagination was enough to bring him to the brink. If he gazed at her flushed features, her perfect body beneath him, he would be completely undone.

Eye on the prize.

He couldn't fail. This was the ultimate job interview, and he couldn't fuck it up.

Nudging deeper, he tried to put his focus elsewhere—anywhere. But every thought, every feeling, sprang back to the sensation of his cock easing inside her.

'Oh, god, yes, yes, more,' she murmured.

Her voice poured yet more fuel on his internal fires, making his hips jerk forward, burying himself deep.

'Oh!' she gasped. 'Yes!'

She circled her hips and he clenched every muscle, white light flashing behind his eyes.

Control!

Raising his chest, he braced his weight through his arms.

'You ready?' he growled.

She lifted her chin. 'Bring it.'

Withdrawing, he suddenly thrust forward with a grunt.

Estelle shivered beneath him, letting out a breathy sigh.

He did it again and again, grinding into her clit and sending goosebumps rippling across her skin.

Each time he pistoned his hips, she raised hers to meet him, sending a crashing wave of desire through his pelvis to the base of his cock. His heart was pounding, his skin on fire, but he kept up the rhythm, watching her face flush, her eyelids fluttering, her breath coming faster.

'More,' she panted.

He didn't react, too focused on pushing his climax back down.

Reaching forward, she slapped his arse, sending a shockwave down to his balls.

Raising an eyebrow, he slowed his pace.

She slapped him again. 'You're walking. I need you to gallop.'

'Do you now? And what's the magic word?'

'Now!'

Despite the lust coursing through him, he managed a cocky grin. 'Try again.'

'Giddy-up, Jamesy-boy?'

'Giddy-up, Jamesy-boy *what?*'

'Please?'

Lowering himself, he braced his forearms on either side of her head and sucked the flesh beneath her ear.

'Pretty please!'

'Well... As you asked so nicely...'

She took a breath as he withdrew an inch, then exhaled it in a rush as he snapped his hips forward. He didn't wait for her to take another breath, thrusting again and again, moving faster and faster.

'Ohmygodyes!'

Blood pounded in his temples, sweat prickling across his brow, but he didn't stop, drilling Estelle into the bed as her cries dissolved into incoherence.

'Fuckyesyesyesshitohmygod!'

She'd lost all ability to keep quiet, her words spilling into each other, then morphing into a keening cry.

Then it cut off in a silent scream and she stiffened, her pussy squeezing his cock till he thought he'd go blind. He kept pounding as she convulsed beneath him, digging her nails into his skin, her head thrown back in bliss.

His heart squeezed as he watched her, emotion flooding into his blood. He was overwhelmed with desire, but now intense vulnerability poured in. His feelings for Estelle went beyond anything he'd ever experienced before, and he felt exposed and defenceless.

Withdrawing, he flipped her over, then hauled her onto her hands and knees. She spread her legs, angling her bottom up, and he filled her to the hilt with one thrust. Holding onto her hip with one hand, he reached around to find her clit with the other.

'Yes,' she gasped. 'Yes, yes, yes!'

With each affirmation she gave, he pounded into her, closing his eyes to try and hold back the onrushing climax. Pleasure pummelled him like shooting stars, light searing through his skin. Every cell of his body was drawing together, tightening to the point where he had no choice but to let go.

Come for me, baby, one last time. Please.

Gritting his jaw, he snapped his hips faster, feeling Estelle shake, her pussy contracting again around his cock. He let himself fall, his climax hurtling him off the cliff into an oblivion where his body imploded, turning itself inside out. Blinded by pleasure, the waves of his orgasm kept coming, pulling out every last drop of sensation, milking him dry until he collapsed onto the bed, Estelle curled in his arms.

His chest heaved, his fingers tingled and spots still danced behind his eyes. He blinked, hardly believing he'd survived the experience. Did this make him superhuman?

'Wow,' Estelle slurred. 'That was intense.'

He nuzzled the back of her head, letting the softness of her curls tickle his face.

'Did I just have *five* orgasms?'

He smiled. 'My pleasure.'

Shuffling out of his hold, she turned so she was facing him. 'Can we do that again?'

Now? Jesus... 'Can you give me ten minutes?'

She giggled. 'Not now, I'm barely conscious. When the festival's over.'

'If you want to wait that long? Tomorrow I'm moving my bedroom to the ground floor and sleeping with the window open. Just in case you feel like sleepwalking again.'

Her smile was soft and relaxed. 'I was rocket-fuelled by

birthday wishes and adrenaline. Tomorrow I'll be so tired I don't know if I'll be able to get out of bed.'

'You could always stay here?'

She hesitated, as if running the scenario through her mind, then shook her head. 'I need to let the dogs out in the morning. Plus, I don't feel like going to work in my PJs.'

He stroked her cheek. 'I could go to yours now, get you some clothes and bring the dogs back?'

Her eyes widened. 'Are you serious? Chester and Joy in your penis extension?'

A chuckle escaped. 'Do you think I *need* a penis extension?'

She pulled a face. 'God no. If you were any bigger, you'd permanently re-home my cervix.'

He grinned at her and she grinned back. Warmth filled his chest. Estelle was the most incredible person he'd ever met, and she was here, now, with him.

'We should go on holiday after the festival,' she said suddenly.

'Holiday?'

'Yes! Just you and me.'

The happiness inside him froze.

Her expression glitched, and she moved away a fraction. 'If you want to?'

'Yes, of course I do.'

She sat up. 'Then what is it? I'm not talking about Saint Barts. A week in Bognor would do me. We could find the money for that?'

He pushed himself up. 'Definitely. I just need to see what I'm doing.'

She frowned. 'What do you mean?'

His stomach tensed, but he forced the words out. 'I've got a job interview in London.'

Silence.

Dread crawled inside him. Had he completely fucked this up before it had even started? Emotions scudded across Estelle's face. None of them looked positive.

'It doesn't mean anything for us,' he continued quickly. 'I want to be with you. We can make it work.'

'How?'

He didn't know. He'd fantasised about having his London life back *and* being with Estelle, but none of his dreams had included any details.

Getting off the bed, she pulled on her pyjamas. 'When's the interview?'

'Thursday. I'm taking the train so I can work when I'm travelling, and I'm trying to fit in a meeting with a last-minute sponsor on the same day.'

'Okay, cool.'

Going to the window, she slung a leg out.

He leapt off the bed. 'Stop! It's dangerous!'

But she'd already turned and was disappearing. 'It's fine,' she called up. 'I'll see you in the morning.'

He leaned out of the window. 'Can we talk about this?'

She smiled up at him. 'Nothing to talk about. Everything's hunky dory.'

Her attention went back to the trellis. When she reached the ground, she gave him a wave and ran off.

James hung his head. What could he do? He had to get a job because he had no money. Even if the last-minute sponsorship deal with the vodka company panned out, it wouldn't be enough to give him the wages he was owed from the last eight months. The priority was paying the staff, not him. He'd never seen himself living in the countryside. But then, he'd never known Estelle Foxbrooke. He found his phone.

> James: Please can we talk? I promise this won't change anything X

Twenty minutes later, she replied.

> Estelle: No need. All good. No drama. See you tomorrow

James lay back on the bed, staring blankly at the ceiling. Had he blown it?

30

Balancing the weight of the wheelbarrow, Estelle ran it across the yard, the pile of manure steaming in the early morning air. It had been two days since she'd had sex with James and she'd spent most of her time avoiding him.

When in doubt, muck the horses out.

She'd been with her family at the riverbank the previous evening celebrating Midsummer's Eve. It should have been a reprieve from thoughts about love and relationships, but then Henry had proposed to Libby...

Estelle was happy for the two of them, especially for her reserved and often far too uptight brother, but a tiny part of her was wailing 'what about me?'

So she'd come back to the livery and done what she always did when she didn't want to lie awake in bed, thoughts churning through her mind like a washing machine with no off-switch. She'd started mucking out the stables.

A car pulled into the yard and Molly got out. 'Things that bad, boss?'

Putting the wheelbarrow down, Estelle straightened with a

grimace as her muscles protested. 'I don't know what you mean.'

Molly looked from Estelle's sweaty figure to the dung heap. 'Have you been at this all night?'

She shrugged. 'It needed doing.'

'By us, not you. What happened?'

Where to begin? 'Henry and Libby got engaged a few hours ago.'

Molly's face lit up. 'That's amazing news!'

Estelle smiled. 'Yeah, it is. It means I don't need to worry about him anymore.'

'He *is* thirty-one.'

'He'll always be my younger brother.'

'And never as badass as you.'

They stood in silence. Estelle's back was beginning to scream at her and she was feeling nauseous from lack of sleep.

'So, what else is going on?'

Estelle dropped her gaze to the dirty concrete of the yard. 'He's going to London today for a job interview.'

'Oh.' There was no need for Molly to clarify who 'he' was. The saga between Estelle and James had been playing out for nearly a year now.

'What about the festival?' Molly continued. 'It starts at the end of next week. He's not going to ditch you at the last minute, is he?'

Estelle internally winced at the word 'ditched'. James may have fancied *her*, but he certainly didn't fancy staying in Somerset any longer than he had to. She was an idiot to have hoped he'd go back on what he'd always said and stick around.

'I don't think so, but as soon as he can, he'll be off.'

'But what about next year's festival?'

Estelle's laugh was hollow. 'I love your optimism, but we don't even know if we can pull off this one. If a miracle happens and we do it again next year, I'll just have to work with James's dad.'

'Is he taking over BDE Entertainment then?'

She shrugged. 'I suppose so. It was his money that bought the company. Or he'll bring in someone new. Who knows?' She stretched and glanced at her watch. 'Anyway, I've got to get cleaned up and back over there to start the day.'

'No way. You've got to get a few hours' sleep. I'm taking the keys to the Defender if you even think about leaving now.'

'I could ride over?'

'As manager of this livery, I'm saying no.'

Estelle opened her mouth to argue, but a yawn escaped instead.

'Please go to bed for a bit. I promise I'll wake you up before lunchtime.'

Giving up the fight, Estelle nodded. 'Okay, you win. I'll see you later.'

She trudged back to her cottage, forcing herself to have a quick shower before getting into bed.

Lying under the covers, she stared at the ceiling, her eyes refusing to shut. Her body had gone beyond the point of exhaustion. Every cell was crying for sleep, but her mind was stuck on the same thought loop like a hamster on a wheel, hyped up on amphetamines.

Why did I suggest we go on holiday?

She cringed at the memories from two nights ago. She'd been caught up in a post-orgasmic, oxytocin rush of optimism where she and James skipped off, hand-in-hand, into the sunset together.

His reality check was a needle scratch to all her fantasies.

He's said multiple times that he's leaving for London as soon as the festival's over, and he's only doing the job to help his dad out. And anyway, he doesn't want to live in Somerset, hates Henry, and Henry hates him. Plus, we've only had casual sex twice. It's not like it's a 'thing'.

Estelle bit the inside of her mouth. Sex with James had not felt casual at all. It had been life-altering, earth-shattering and paradigm-shifting. But there was no way in hell she was going to be that open around him again and ask for more than his cock. Being vulnerable around James was only setting herself up for the ultimate fall.

But he said he wanted to be with you! What if you showed him enough of Somerset to make him stick around?

Are you going to give him a guided tour like you did for Libby? Take him to the Little Knob cheese festival? The Big Knob sausage festival? The Frome Young Farmers ploughing competition? Wow. How will London ever compare after any of that?

Shuddup.

But Foxbrooke *could* provide the same level of sophistication that London did. Even if just in one place. Before she could argue herself out of it, she grabbed her phone.

> Estelle: Good luck with your job interview today. Fancy meeting me for an early dinner at The Colour Palette when you get back?

Her phone dinged with a reply almost immediately.

> James: Yes, please. What time?

> Estelle: Half-six?

> James: I'll see you there

As the the train sped west, James stretched out in first class, letting the greens of the countryside glide by as he replayed the day.

Slipping back into the role of James Hunter-Savage, apex alpha had been effortless. He was taller, better looking and better dressed than anyone he'd met that day and knew how to work a room. He hadn't yet been introduced to the biggest players at the American software company, but by the time the meeting was over, the underlings that had interviewed him were almost salivating at the prospect of him working there.

Buoyed by that success, he'd taken a taxi across town and sealed the deal with a luxury vodka brand for last-minute sponsorship of the festival. With their money, the staff could be paid, and they'd actually turn a profit. Life was finally on the up.

Spreading his legs, testosterone-fuelled confidence pumping through his veins, he thought of Estelle. They'd hardly seen each other since they'd had sex again. A tiny part of him wondered if she was avoiding him after he'd told her about the London job. But now she was inviting him on a date.

Is it a date, though?
What else is it? If it's work, then she could just email or phone.
She wasn't happy when she left the other night.
She will be when I tell her about the sponsorship deal.

Collecting his Ferrari from the station car park, James drove to Foxbrooke, parking at the other end of the high street from the manor, next to Estelle's Defender. Why hadn't she parked at her family's home? Was she avoiding any questions about what she was up to? Shrugging off the insecurity, he glanced at his watch and strode towards the restaurant. Tonight he was going to prove to Estelle he could come through for her *and* convince her to make their fledgling relationship official.

Outside The Colour Palette, he stopped. Through the window was Estelle, her back to him as she chatted to Leia. Memories of his body on hers, in hers, slammed into him with visceral intensity.

She was wearing a pair of tight jeans that made him want to bite into her peachy arse, a form-fitting top that he wanted to see the front of, and—*heels?* His cock twitched in his boxers and his heart swelled. Was she doing this for him?

Leia caught his eye and gave a wave.

Dick down, shoulders back, winning smile on. You can do this. He entered the restaurant as Estelle turned. *Oh, fuck.* She was wearing make-up. It wasn't a lot, but it accentuated her natural beauty to blinding levels and turned the situation in his trousers critical.

Crossing the room, he greeted Leia then gave every ounce of his attention to Estelle, kissing her cheek.

'You're so beautiful,' he murmured in her ear.

She swallowed, her body coming closer for a second, then pulling away.

'Shall we sit?' she asked, her voice breathless.

He nodded and Leia led them to a table in the corner.

James pulled out Estelle's chair and her eyes widened as if surprised. As she sat, he snagged his finger on her bra strap and gave it a tug.

She jumped.

'Tonight's menus are on the placemats,' Leia said as James took his seat. She indicated pieces of A2 size paper covering the table and also serving as tablecloths. 'There's so much incredible local produce at the moment that they change every day.' She laid a card menu down. 'But the drinks list remains the same.'

As well as the food menu printed on the paper, there were also swirling line drawings of flowers, birds and butterflies, and a tin pot next to the salt and pepper containing crayons.

'You can colour them in, or there's space for you to draw your own pictures,' Leia said. 'This week's artist is Ella Chamberlain.'

'She's my brother Leo's best friend,' Estelle said. 'So you can't say anything bad about them.'

He gazed across at her. 'I wasn't going to.' His voice sounded lower than he'd intended.

'Right, I'll leave you to it,' Leia said. 'If you have any questions, just give me a wave. There's an allergen list next to each dish and we can substitute pretty much anything if you need.' She smiled then went off to greet new customers.

Estelle looked at the menu, but James's eyes were on her. He wanted her with a hunger that felt as if it could never be satiated. Had the day's successes shot his testosterone levels higher than normal? Or perhaps sex with her a few days ago had flooded his body with enough hormones to repopulate the world after an asteroid strike. Biting back a groan, he took in the cross wrap top she was wearing. It hugged the curves of her breasts as if it didn't want to let go. James had never wanted to be an item of women's clothing as much as he did right now.

Focus! 'The vodka company signed off on the sponsorship deal today.'

Her head shot up. 'The full amount?'

He nodded. 'It means we can pay the staff.'

'Thank you, god.'

'My pleasure.'

She fixed him with a look. 'You're not god.'

He shrugged. 'And there was me thinking I showed you heaven the other night.'

Estelle snorted with laughter, then clapped a hand over her mouth. James grinned, his heart lifting at her sparkling face.

Then her light dimmed slightly and her hand lowered to the table. 'How did your job interview go?'

I nailed it, but that's probably not what you want to hear. He lifted a shoulder. 'I think it went okay.'

'When will you know if you've got it?'

'Maybe next week?'

'And when would you start?'

Immediately... 'I'm not sure.' An uncomfortable sensation scratched at his stomach. He'd been so convinced he could have the job *and* Estelle, but the thought of the two of them coexisting set off a jarring dissonance in his brain, like a preschooler with a recorder attempting to harmonise with a werewolf scraping its claws down a blackboard.

'Have you looked at the menu?' she asked. 'The food is incredible.'

He stared blankly at the lines of text, his appetite suddenly gone.

'They're going for their first Michelin star.'

Really? His head jerked up.

'Don't look like that,' she said crossly. 'The countryside isn't just turnips and village idiot competitions.'

'Foxbrooke has a village idiot competition?'

'Yes, and you've received more nominations for this year's award than anyone else.'

He smirked. 'Nice to know I'm the most popular.'

Estelle rolled her eyes and waved Leia over.

'You ready to order?' she asked.

'Yes. I'd like the cured meat plate with fennel, then the osso bucco with seasonal greens on the side. James?'

He hadn't taken any of the menu in. 'I'll have the same. And whatever alcohol-free beer you'd recommend.'

Leia nodded, then turned to Estelle. 'Any drinks for you?'

'Lime and soda, please. And a jug of tap water.'

'Coming right up.' Leia took the drinks menu and left.

Silence.

James was used to being in control, knowing what to say, and when, to make the most impact. But now, on his first semi-official date with Estelle, he was tongue tied.

Is this a date? An assessment? An ending?

She appeared on edge as well, her hands fidgeting in her lap. He wanted to reach across the table to her but wasn't sure how such a gesture, especially one made in public, would be received.

Estelle reached for a crayon and began colouring in one of the flowers. 'Thank you for coming.'

'Thank you for inviting me. On this date.'

Her hand stilled. Was she about to contradict him?

'It's not...' The crayon moved back and forth over the same area. 'I'm just trying to...'

'Would you rather be here with someone else?'

Her gaze shot up. 'Like who?'

He shrugged. 'Isaac?'

She frowned as if trying to place the name with someone she knew, then her cheeks darkened and she shook her head.

James internally fist-pumped. Foxbrooke's hottest yoga instructor was no longer doing a downward dog rent-free in Estelle's mind.

'Or one of the Spice Girls?'

'I don't know them.'

'It doesn't matter. Who would you rather be having dinner with right now, out of anyone who's ever lived or been imagined? Boudicca? Joan of Arc? Xena: Warrior Princess?'

Estelle hesitated and something resembling sadness passed across her face.

'It's not that I would *rather* be with this person...'

James's hackles rose. There was someone else in her life?

'But I would do anything to sit down with them again.'

He forced his tone to remain level. 'Who?'

'Alexis.'

James thought about all the people he'd met or heard about since moving to Somerset. Alexis was not someone he'd come across.

'She ran the livery before I took it over. She died eleven years ago.'

Before he could stop himself, he breathed a sigh of relief that his rival was not only a platonic friend but also dead.

Estelle frowned. 'Does that make you happy?'

Fuck. He held up his hands in a gesture of surrender. 'No. I'm sorry. I thought...' He let out a breath. 'I was jealous.'

Both her eyebrows raised. 'You? The mighty Hunter Savage? Jealous?'

Embarrassment prickled the back of his neck. 'It has happened once or twice.'

Estelle smiled. 'Well, there's no need. And if Alexis were still alive, she would have adored you.'

'She was obviously a woman of good taste.'

'Alexis was an absolute dragon. If I had even half of her fire, I wouldn't have missed when I shot that arrow at you.'

He shifted in his chair as his dick, which up until that moment had been extremely happy, shrivelled a little.

'What happened to it, by the way?' she asked. 'The arrow?'

'It's in one of the drawers in my bedroom.'

'You kept it?'

He nodded. 'It's part of the holy trinity of gifts.'

'Huh?'

'A fur Q, a fork U, and an arrow that missed my balls by a

couple of inches. Three different ways you've expressed your feelings for me. I'm truly blessed.'

She giggled. 'I'm sorry.'

He grinned. 'No, you're not.'

She pulled a face that told him he was right and that she didn't regret any of them.

Leia arrived with their drinks and starters. James allowed his gaze to move from Estelle to the food in front of them, and his stomach rumbled.

'Go on,' Estelle said. 'Try it.'

He speared a slice of salami and put it in his mouth. It was full of robust flavour, zinging with black pepper and the sweetness of fennel seeds.

'See? It's amazing.'

He nodded. 'It is. So, tell me about Alexis. Did she hand the livery over to you before...'

Estelle's nose scrunched up, and she took a sip of her drink. 'Kind of. I don't remember the first time I got on a horse, but Alexis would have been the one to put me on it and lead me around the manège. Growing up, if I wasn't at home then I was at the livery, especially after I went to secondary school.'

She picked up a chunk of chorizo and ate it before continuing.

'I wanted to do a degree in equine studies, but Dad said I knew so much about horses already it would be a waste of time and money, and Mom wanted me to be an actress and model instead.'

Stabbing her fork into the food in front of her, she speared capers, pickled carrot slices and salami, then shoved them into her mouth.

'So, what did you do?'

Estelle shrugged as she chewed then swallowed. 'I tried to

fulfil my destiny as a member of the British aristocracy and please my father at the same time.'

'Doing?'

'History of Art, of course. It's one of Dad's passions and I know a fair bit about the subject. But I was as out of place with the poshos as I was with the hoi polloi at Foxbrooke secondary. Officially, I was "one of them", but with my family background, I most certainly wasn't.'

James was silent. Estelle could have been talking about how he felt growing up. But whereas she'd had the confidence to stick out, he'd spent most of his life trying to fit in.

'I first knew Alexis was ill in the summer after my first year,' she continued. 'She'd kept it from me for at least twelve months, and when I saw her again that Christmas, I knew she wasn't going to make it.'

'I'm sorry.'

She didn't meet his gaze, seeming lost in her memories.

'When she died, Dad wanted to sell the stables. Because of her illness, the business had been struggling, and he wanted to get shot of it. I persuaded him to let me take it on and left uni for good. I threw myself into saving the livery, and once it was on an even keel, I started working more and more for the wider estate. Trying to stop Dad and his crazy ideas running the entire place into the ground.'

'What happened when you were seven?' he asked softly.

She glanced up, a look of shock on her face. 'You remembered?'

He nodded.

'What happened when *you* were seven?' she countered.

'You remembered.'

'You said it was the last time you ever cried.'

James shifted in his seat. *Did* he want to tell her? No, of course he didn't. But she'd just shared something with him he doubted many people knew.

Just rip the plaster off.

'I was seven when Dad decided to upgrade our family and change my name. It was weird, but he made it sound like an exciting game our family were destined to win. As well as the new name, we had a new house, and I was enrolled in the nearest prep school. The uniform felt like some kind of super-hero costume.'

Estelle had stopped eating and was listening intently.

'A lot of boys started with me at seven, so I wasn't the odd one out. I made a friend, Jeremy, that week, and invited him to my house on Saturday afternoon for a game of football. He came, I thought we had a good time, then he left.'

James was silent as the childhood pain flashed back with such intensity it felt as if he couldn't breathe.

'But on Monday?'

'You can imagine,' he said bitterly. 'He told everyone that Mum and Dad were "chavs", and gleefully tore apart every-thing about them and our home. I remember being so shocked at the vitriol and scorn. It was the first experience I'd ever had of how the upper classes could be, and I couldn't believe someone I thought was my friend could be so mean.'

Estelle nodded, her expression telling him that she knew exactly what he was talking about.

'So, what did you do?'

He huffed. 'I became meaner. I cornered him in the toilet, punched him as hard as a seven-year-old could, and told him my dad was an East End gangster. I told the little shit if he ever breathed a word to anyone again about my family, then my dad would burn his house down with his whole family in it. At the end of the day, I told my folks I needed to go to a new school, and was never inviting anyone home again.'

'I'm sorry. That sounds a lot like our experiences growing up. Me, Connor, and Henry in particular.'

The uncomfortable feeling in James's stomach intensified as he remembered how much of a casual bully he'd been to Henry when they were at Eton. He'd been trying to protect the persona he'd created so fiercely, it never crossed his mind that Henry was living with similar pain.

'I presume other kids gave you shit as well?' he asked.

'Yup. Every day.' Estelle paused as Leia cleared the table, then she continued. 'Dad wouldn't let me or Connor go to another school, but at least we had each other, as well as Finn and Jack. But it was still brutal.'

She took a crayon, fiddling with it as she continued. 'Your origin story started when you were seven and so did mine.'

His whole body was wired as he listened, as if readying to leave the restaurant to hunt down and slay whichever monster had harmed her in the past.

'Mom, Dad and Mammy were even more outrageous when we were younger than they are now, and Dad in particular used to love pissing people off. But it wasn't so much locals, as the kind of folks who enjoy being offended and read the Daily Mail. You know, so they know who to blame the rise in house prices on. Anyway, the newspaper organised this letter-writing campaign against my folks, and my dad decided it would be a fantastic idea to dress up, take us all into the centre of Foxbrooke one Saturday afternoon and burn them all.'

Fucking hell. James could only imagine the spectacle that had been. He waited for her to continue.

'A reporter had infiltrated one of the sex parties a couple of weeks before this and reported that not only were there tons of drugs, but that we were also in the house at the time.'

What the—

Estelle held up her hands. 'We were in a separate wing with

Mammy and never heard or saw anything. I didn't even know what the word "sex" was until after everything kicked off.'

'What happened?'

The crayon in Estelle's fingers snapped. She stared at it, as if surprised it had broken.

She put the pieces to one side. 'The police were called and took all us kids into emergency care for a week.'

'Jesus.'

She nodded. 'It was terrifying. Willow was a baby at the time and was screaming like she was being murdered. Leo wet himself, Henry froze, and Connor and I copied our parents and kicked off like rabid dogs. After that, everything changed.'

Leia arrived with their mains. The smell was incredible, and also comforting, as if an Italian nonna had made it, not a strapping bloke with a *Star Wars* obsession. James was silent as they ate, picturing Estelle at seven being taken from her parents. He'd always thought Henry and his siblings had led the most privileged of lives, but he now knew just how wrong he'd been. James's coping strategy had been to be brash and aggressively alpha, but Henry had gone the other way. Memories of how he'd treated him filtered into James's stomach like bile.

'We can't choose our parents,' Estelle said, 'but we can learn to deal with, or modify our reaction to them. And the most important thing of all is that they love us. They might drive us up the wall, but their hearts are in the right place.'

Even if their brains aren't... James finished his mouthful and steeled himself. One of the reasons he'd never had a long-term girlfriend before was that the thought of introducing them to his parents had brought on the same anxiety that had riddled his childhood. But Estelle had met his family and hadn't ever passed judgement. Now he needed to take out his last locked box, show her what was inside, and hope she still gave him, and his dad, the time of day.

'I want to tell you why I stole Henry's client and the deal he'd been working on.'

Her knife and fork clattered to the plate. 'You don't deny it?'

'I've never denied it. I've just never told anyone why.'

'Go on then. Why did you do it?' Her features were hard, but he could see the vulnerability behind them. Estelle loved her twin and was loyal to him, so liking James, even being with him now, must have felt like a betrayal.

'I was with my parents one weekend and it was late on Saturday night,' he began. 'Mum had gone to bed and Dad and I were drunk and having a macho pissing contest about how successful we were.' He shook his head. 'Looking back, I think both of us felt insecure compared to the other, so kept upping the ante until we must have sounded like a couple of absolute twats.'

James took a drink, his mouth suddenly dry, then leaned forward. There was no-one around them but he didn't want to risk anyone overhearing.

'I was showing off about deals I was making, name-dropping companies, and sharing information that was completely confidential.'

He took a deep breath. *Here goes...*

'Dad took what I'd told him and used it to make a killing on the stock market. But he didn't keep his mouth shut about it and the shit hit the fan. I was accused of insider trading, which of course it was, even though I had no idea it was happening.'

Estelle was staring at him, her lips parted.

'So I panicked. I thought if I proved myself indispensable to Conqueror, there was no way they would let me go. So I pushed harder on my own projects and stole Henry's in the hope it would save my arse.'

'And did it?' she whispered.

'No, I had to leave. I can't work in the City anymore and have spent every penny I have on lawyers' fees. Dad bought Excelsior for me to run as a way of saying sorry, but I never wanted it. And when his investments went south, I felt I had no choice but to stay on here and try and make the festival work for the sake of Mum.'

'But the job you went for today?'

'It's a sales gig for an American software company. They want a "charming attack dog", and a friend of mine thought I fitted the bill.'

'Oh.'

He rubbed a hand over his face. 'I've done a lot in my life that I regret, and doing that to Henry was one of the biggest mistakes I've ever made.'

'You need to tell him.'

'No.'

'But—'

'What's the point? It's not going to change anything. He'll still hate me, and now he'll hate Dad as well. Dad's been through enough and I don't want to risk him losing the friendship with your family. He thinks the world of your father, and Mum thinks she's died and gone to heaven hanging out with your mom and mammy.'

Estelle was silent. What was she thinking?

He reached across the table, his palm facing up in invitation. 'I meant what I said to you the other night. I want to be with you. If you'll have me?'

Her hand inched towards his, then she took it. An electric shock ran up his arm and he reflexively squeezed his fingers around hers, as if never wanting to let go.

Her deep brown eyes held his, her expression guarded. He knew it was a far bigger step for her to enter a relationship with him than it was for him to begin one with her. She'd publicly hated him for years and her closest sibling still did. He thought about how he'd feel if Sophia announced she was dating Jeremy, the twat who'd trashed his family when they were seven, and an involuntary shudder ran through him.

'Is everything okay?'

He nodded. 'We can make this work, I promise. I—'

Snatching her hand away, she stood, staring at the front of the restaurant.

James turned to see Henry and Libby coming through the door.

Henry's love-struck eyes were on his girlfriend, but Libby's were on them. Her gaze flicked from him to Estelle's outfit, then back to him again. The shock on her face was quickly masked by a huge smile.

'Henry! Look who it is!' she said enthusiastically. 'It's Estelle and James!'

James stood as they approached. Henry's forehead furrowed as he took the two of them in. But whereas his girlfriend could at least fake pleasure at the sight, Henry most definitely could not.

'What are you doing here?' Henry and Estelle asked at the same time.

'Business meeting,' Estelle snapped.

'We're celebrating our engagement!' Libby held out her hand, showing off a ring.

'Congratulations,' James said. 'When's the wedding?'

'No idea,' Libby replied, still overflowing with smiles. 'Probably next summer. We just have to see what's in the diary at the manor.'

Like if the festival's going to happen a second time…

Henry cleared his throat and stood a little taller as he faced James. 'What are your plans for after the festival?'

James straightened his spine, making sure the extra two inches he had on Henry were used to full effect. 'I'm not sure yet. I have—'

'He went for a job interview in London today,' Estelle interrupted.

Henry looked surprised. 'With whom?'

'Global Tech,' James said.

'I thought they were a US company?'

'They are, but—'

'So, you'll be relocating to Seattle? Isn't that where they're based?'

James ground his teeth. 'Yes, they're in Seattle, but no, I won't be relocating. There'll be plenty of—*some* travel State-side, but they're looking to open a London office to acquire more business in Europe.'

Even though James's attention was on Henry, out of the corner of his eye, he saw Estelle stiffen. *Fuck*.

'What role did you interview for?' Henry continued.

'European Director of Sales.'

'So, you'd be travelling some of the time to the States and the rest of the time within the EU?'

Shut up! Henry's questions were perfectly reasonable, but James didn't want this to be the way that Estelle found out what his new job might entail.

Her phone rang and she stepped back to answer it.

'I don't know any of the details yet,' James replied. 'I'm sure I can make the job my own.'

He knew that statement was eighty per cent a lie, and by Henry's raised eyebrows, he knew it, too.

Estelle was now striding to the back of the restaurant to talk to Leia.

'Is everything okay?' Henry and James called out at the same time, then glared at each other.

Estelle handed her bank card to Leia, then turned and looked at James. 'We've got to go.'

'What? Why?'

'The main stage is collapsing.'

'I TOLD YOU THIS WOULD HAPPEN,' JED WHINED AS JAMES and Estelle looked under the staging to see the support poles sinking into the ground.

'No, you said it *could* happen,' James retorted. 'There's a semantic difference.'

'It doesn't matter!' Estelle exploded. 'This is what happens when you cut corners.'

James clamped his mouth shut. He didn't want to get into an argument in front of the staff, nor remind Estelle of all the reasons why he'd gone for the cheapest option, and therefore let Jed know how dire their financial position really was.

'It's because of the rain,' Jed said. 'The ground under the stage is lower than the rest of the park, so the water's drained here.'

'How can we fix it?' Estelle asked.

'We need to take it up and put steel plating underneath to spread the load.'

'Can we get that in time?'

Jed scratched his chin. 'I dunno. I'll call in all the favours I can, but it's going to cost.'

James hung his head. No doubt this would swallow up the sponsorship money he'd just acquired, leaving them right back at square one.

'Okay,' Estelle said. 'Whatever you need, you'll get it. Liaise with James to make any payments, but keep me informed.'

Jed nodded.

'And make sure all site crew know this is out of bounds until it's been secured. Can you tape the area off?'

'Will do,' Jed said to her. 'I'll get on it now.'

Estelle strode up the high street towards her car in silence, James keeping pace beside her. She seemed to be vibrating with fury and he wasn't going to make it any worse by speaking. The festival was just over a week away. How many other things might go wrong before then?

He wanted to run away. But he also wanted Estelle. Right now, he couldn't do the first and wasn't sure if he'd ever get the second. He just had to pray this was the last disaster they'd have to deal with and when everything was over, Estelle was still willing to give him a chance.

31

'Fucking cockwomble of a coffee machine!' Estelle yelled as an error message appeared in Italian for the third time in a row.

Bracing her arms on the edge of the countertop in the office kitchen, she focused on taking long, slow breaths.

Just hold it together. You can do this.

Biting into her lower lip, she squeezed her eyes shut, pushing down a swell of tears. She hadn't cried since the happy news of Eveline's pregnancy, and she wasn't planning on crying again until the baby arrived. But right now, she wanted to weep. Despite being surrounded by people, she felt utterly alone.

Both she, James, and most of the festival admin team had worked through the weekend, not only rebuilding the main stage, but preparing for the start of the festival on the following Friday. Each time Estelle thought they had a handle on things, another crisis reared its head, demanding attention, money, or both.

And now it was Monday morning and James was on his way

to London for two days to meet the CEO of Global Tech, who'd flown in from Seattle. Estelle knew there wasn't much he could do now the festival was so close, but she wanted him there. It felt like he'd already moved on and she was left carrying the can.

There was a knock at the kitchen door, and Carly entered.

'Do you want me to make you a cappuccino?'

Estelle nodded. 'I didn't want to bother you, but I can't work the bloody thing.'

Carly grinned. 'I speak Italian and it still took me a while to get to grips with it.'

'I didn't realise I was such an addict until my supply ran out.'

'Don't worry, I'll get your fix sorted,' Carly said, pushing buttons on the machine.

'Thanks.' Estelle opened a drawer and pulled out a box of French Fancies. 'Want one?'

'Yes, please. I love the fact the drawer is always full of them. Do you think Bev will keep stocking them after James leaves?'

Estelle shrugged. The core admin team were still employed beyond the end of the festival to oversee the dismantling of everything and settlement of bills, but Estelle didn't know where James was going to be.

Carly poured milk into a jug, then stuck the steam wand inside to froth it. 'Do you have any idea who Kev is going to sell BDE Entertainment to?' she asked over the noise of the machine.

Shock cut into Estelle's chest. Kevin was selling the company? 'Er, what have you heard?'

Carly poured the frothed milk into Estelle's mug. 'He told me over the weekend that he's offloading the company now James is going back to London.'

Estelle's blood pressure rose. She couldn't believe she was finding this out second-hand. James was obviously too busy starting his new life and couldn't be bothered to tell her. She still hoped to run another festival next year. But with whom?

Carly passed her the coffee. 'Estelle, I'm sure whoever buys BDE will want to work with you again. You've done an amazing job.'

'I can't even pay your wages on time.'

'We all understand about cash flow. We can wait until it's over to be paid.'

'I'm so sorry it's come to this.'

'Don't be. It's not my first rodeo and you need to know what you've created is special. There'll always be teething issues, but we'll get through them. I promise.'

'I'm sorry James isn't here.'

Carly waved her hand dismissively. 'It's all good. He's on the other end of the phone if we need anything. Honestly, Estelle, you've got this.'

The door opened, and Zeke poked his head in. 'I've got the management for UberGraft on the line,' he said to Estelle. 'The band want to arrive today rather than Thursday and are asking for you to show their PA the accommodation.'

'Me?' Estelle exclaimed. 'Why?'

Zeke pulled an apologetic face. 'It's a privacy thing. They want you or James to meet their PA this afternoon at the cottage with the keys.'

'But I can't! I'm already triple booked!' *And James has buggered off to London...*

'Can you send your brother?'

'Which one?'

Zeke shrugged. 'Any of them?'

Estelle nodded. 'I'll get on it. What time did they want to meet there?'

'Three.'

'Okay, leave it with me.' She turned to Carly and lifted her cappuccino. 'Thank you for this.'

'Anytime, boss,' Carly replied with a grin. 'Now go and find a handsome Foxbrooke man to placate UberGraft.'

Estelle rolled her eyes. 'They're my brothers, so as far as I'm concerned, they're all gross. Let's just hope their PA likes a British accent...'

⚜

James ducked into the toilet stall and pulled out his phone. It had been buzzing repeatedly since he left for London that morning, but he could only deal with the messages when he wasn't schmoozing Garrett Ross, the owner of Global Tech.

Fingers tapping and swiping, he answered as many emails as he could.

'Dude, you in here?' an American voice drawled from outside.

Fuck. 'Yeah, hang on.' James pocketed his phone, flushed the toilet for effect, then exited the stall and went to the sinks.

Garrett was at the urinal and glanced at James over his shoulder. 'We've got a table at Soho House. You ready?'

'Sure.' James ran his hands under the taps, wishing he could wash Garrett off his skin as easily as the soap.

Garrett shook his hips, then zipped up his fly. 'Let's do this.' He gave James's shoulder a slap and headed for the door.

James followed with a sigh. His new boss was exactly as he'd dreaded. Rich and entitled, Garrett Ross was a geek with old money backing. His father had bankrolled Global Tech from the start and helped him find clients. The company was now a big player in the software industry, and Garrett truly believed he was a self-made man.

And you think you're so different? Who paid for your education? Bought you BDE to run? Your fairy godfather?

The voice in his head sounded exactly like Estelle, and it stung because she was right. James may have accused her and Henry of being privileged, but in his own way, so was he.

So, I'm just like this little prick then?

Garrett was James's age, five-foot-ten and wiry. Dressed in Converse trainers, low-slung jeans and a t-shirt advertising the Burning Man festival, at first glance Garrett didn't look like a multi-millionaire. But he'd made sure James noticed his limited edition Patek Philippe watch and knew about his garage of all-white supercars.

'In the fall, we should take a road trip to the Nürburgring,' Garrett said as they exited the hotel where they'd had their meeting. 'See whose Ferrari is the fastest.'

'It's all about who's in the driving seat.'

Garrett laughed. 'I'm gonna smoke your ass.'

James smiled. 'We'll see.' His tone was confident and relaxed, but inside he was tired of the performance. He'd had over a year away from London life and whilst he could still walk the walk and talk the talk, Garrett grated on him. The man oscillated between admiring James's looks, strength and charisma, and reminding him who was the boss.

Entering the nondescript front door of Soho House behind Garrett, James's phone vibrated in his pocket. Letting Garrett go up the stairs in front of him, he took it out to see who was calling.

Theo Knight, his lawyer for the insider trading case. Did he have news? Shoving the phone away, James thought about how he could escape to ring him back.

On the first floor, Garrett led the way to the bar, his gaze travelling around the open-plan space, openly eyeing up the women. He was either an unsubtle horndog or hadn't got laid in a while.

'Drink?' Garrett asked.

'Vodka Martini on the rocks.'

'See those chicks?' Garrett said under his breath. 'They're checking us out.'

James repressed an eye roll and the urge to point out that they were checking *him* out and not Garrett. 'I think I know one of them,' he lied. 'Want me to invite them over?'

'Fuck man, you've got balls. You gonna do it? Really?'

James nodded. 'Order a bottle of vintage Dom Perignon.' Peeling away from the bar, he approached the two women. They were trying to play it cool, but he knew the colour in their faces was not entirely due to the alcohol they were drinking.

'Hi, I'm James,' he said, channelling as much charm as he could muster. 'I wondered if you could help me?'

The women's eyes widened and the one who looked the most nervous, glanced at her friend.

'How may we be of assistance?' the friend asked in a sultry voice, her fingers stroking the stem of her wine glass.

James rubbed his chin, making sure to flex his arm muscles as he did. 'Well, I'm in the middle of a job interview and it's not going well...'

'What's the job?'

'European CEO of Global Tech. The gentleman at the bar is the owner, Garrett Ross.' James took out his phone and googled his new boss, making sure he showed the women the online article showing exactly how rich and single Garrett was.

'Oh, my god,' the first woman muttered under her breath.

Her more confident friend handed James his phone back. 'And what do you want us to do for you?'

Back in the day, James would have charmed either or both

of them into bed, but right now, all he wanted to do was get Garrett off his back and check in with his lawyer and the festival team back in Foxbrooke. Plus, he needed to see if the ad he placed a few days ago had got any traction.

'Well...' He lowered his voice so the two women leaned in a little closer. 'Here's the thing. I'm boring him.'

The friend raised an eyebrow as if she couldn't believe it.

James gave her a sexy half-shrug. 'There's only so much I can say about the benefits I bring to the table or what kind of package I want.'

He was choosing his words carefully, and the double entendres were working as both women giggled.

'I'd love it if you would join us for a drink and take some of the heat off me. We've got a bottle of vintage Dom Perignon on ice.'

The shyer woman shot a glance at her friend, as if begging her to say 'yes'.

The friend extended a hand. 'I'm Iris, and this is Kristen.'

James took it. 'Thank you. I appreciate your kindness.'

Iris smirked. 'Okay, James, introduce us to your potential new boss.'

He led them over to Garrett and made the introductions, getting the conversation and the drink flowing. Iris was a film producer and her friend, Kristen, was a production accountant. Garrett wanted to know the inside gossip on every famous actress they'd worked with.

When the second bottle of champagne had been opened, James excused himself and dashed out into the stairwell.

Taking out his phone, he saw another missed call from his lawyer. He rang him straight back.

'Mate?' Theo asked as the call connected.

'What have you got for me?'

'Good news. In fact, it's fantastic news.'

James slumped against the wall. 'Tell me.'

'They're dropping the case against you due to lack of evidence. You can go back to financial services now with a clean slate.'

'Thank fuck.'

'You're welcome. And that's not all, my fine friend.'

'Let me guess. I owe you a pound of flesh or my first-born child?'

Theo laughed. 'Actually, mate, you're due a refund. After our final bill's been settled, there's about twenty big ones left on your account.'

James closed his eyes, letting the relief wash through him. It was over. He could take this job with Garrett, or he could find something else with less foreign travel. He had choices. And he had freedom.

'Thank you.'

'No worries. I've emailed everything over to you and sent the refund details to accounts. Go celebrate.'

'Will do. Thanks, Theo, and speak soon.'

Getting off the call, James checked his email. He'd had two responses to his ad, and one in particular looked promising. There was nothing from Estelle.

What do you expect? A poem about how much she misses you?

His thumb hovered over the message app.

> James: I haven't seen anything big come through on email so presume everything's in hand?

He sent the message, not knowing what else to say. Estelle didn't need charm, she needed him back in Foxbrooke.

But still, his heart ached for her. Before he could stop himself, he sent another message.

James: I miss you

Pocketing the phone, he went back into the bar.

'Dude!' Garrett called out. 'The girls are joining us for dinner.'

James didn't know whether to be pleased or not. Their presence was a buffer against his new boss, but he was all out of small talk.

He forced a smile. 'Great. Are we going through now?'

AN HOUR AND A HALF LATER, JAMES WAS BACK IN THE MEN'S bathroom with his phone. There were only a few emails to deal with, and still radio silence from Estelle.

Why hasn't she replied?

Because she's up to her eyeballs in organising the festival, you tool.

He called her. The phone seemed to ring forever before she picked up.

'Hello?' she answered, as if she didn't know who it was, but was already irritated.

'It's me. I wanted to see how you were?'

She sighed. 'It's late, and I've just got in. I was about to go to bed.'

'How's it going?'

'Fucking marvellous.'

'I'm sorry I'm not there. This was the only time Garrett's visiting the UK for the next few months.'

'He works in computers, right? Has he ever come across Zoom?'

'He wanted to meet me in person.'

'Of course he did. Everyone wants James Hunter-Savage in the flesh.' Estelle sighed in his ear. 'Look, I need to go to sleep. I'm ratty and exhausted.'

'I'm sorry.'

She huffed. 'Me too.' There was a short silence. 'I presume you're still out?'

'Yeah, just finished dinner.'

'Somewhere nice?'

'Yes.'

'As good as the Colour Palette?'

Had it been? He remembered the meal as being outstanding, but then everything had gone to shit, starting with the arrival of Henry.

'Different.'

The door to the bathroom opened and Garrett entered, his body swaying slightly and his eyes bloodshot. 'Dude! The girls are up for the club. Come on!'

Shit. Had Estelle heard that?

Garrett moved closer. 'Who you talking to?'

'My girlfriend.'

Garrett lurched forward to shout into James's phone. 'Hey girlfriend!' He glanced up. 'What's her name?'

'Estelle.'

'Don't worry, Estelle. He's being a good boy.' Garrett sniggered, his breath feeling like an assault. 'Just don't google the Pentangle.'

Jesus! He wanted to go *there*?

James stepped away from Garrett towards the door. 'Let me just finish my call.' He strode out, a finger stuck in his other ear. 'Estelle? You there?'

She wasn't.

He rang her back. It cut off after two rings.

Trying again, it went straight to voicemail.

Fuck.

❧ 32 ❧

From: James Hunter-Savage
To: Garrett Ross
Subject: Apologies

Garrett,

I'm afraid I'm going to have to cancel our meetings today and leave directly for Somerset. Yesterday gave me a good handle on the product and your vision for it. I'm confident I can deliver the growth you want.

If you'd like a couple of VIP tickets for this weekend, I can arrange them for you. Just let me know.

Kind regards and thank you for your time yesterday,
James

SUNSHINE RADIATED THROUGH THE WINDOW ONTO JAMES'S hands as the train tore past Reading. After the torrential rain that had sunk the stage, the British summer had done an about-face and was delivering the kind of heat that broke air conditioning units and shop fridges.

Pulling the collar of his shirt away from the back of his neck, James continued hacking his way through the perpetual forest of emails that clogged his inbox. Next year, he needed a PA.

Next year? He shook his head. Was there going to *be* a next year? They were currently struggling to pull off a this year, let alone think about the future.

And anyway, he'd be working for Garrett, or another company like Conqueror, not running the festival with Estelle. Where would he be living? Now he was finally off the hook with the insider trading charges, he could move back into his flat when his tenant's lease was up. But the thought of living there without Estelle was jarring.

He hadn't heard back from her, despite leaving a voice message letting her know he didn't go to the club and was cutting his trip short.

Pentangle... James knew it well. It was extremely exclusive and high end, with stage shows that mixed burlesque with the kind of interactive performances you'd expect from a Bangkok sex club. When he'd been at Conqueror, James's clients had lapped it up. Literally.

James couldn't stand the place. It was titillation for the monied classes. It didn't matter that as many women as men went there, it still felt tawdry.

But that didn't stop you taking clients there, did it?

They wanted to go.

So what?

Dropping his phone to the table, he bowed his head. The last few months in China had been hell, and now, in the run-up to the festival opening, it was like being in the middle of a hurricane. He just had to ride it out until the end, then hope Estelle was still with him.

Girlfriend. It was what he wanted her to be, however

uttering the word to Garrett first had been every level of wrong. If James had thought Henry was the biggest obstacle to him and Estelle being together, then he'd just pushed Henry to second place with one word.

When he'd been accused of insider trading and sacked from Conqueror, it seemed like his life was falling apart. But inside his skin, he was still James Hunter-Savage, confident and self-assured. He knew he would find a way back to his old life.

But now? Estelle had pulled on one thread of his being and then another, unravelling him until he didn't know who he really was anymore or where he was meant to be.

He knew he could live in Somerset, commute when he needed to by train, fly abroad from Bristol airport, work remotely as much as he could. But did she want him as much as he wanted her? Or would everything in their past always come between them?

DRIVING OUT OF THE STATION CAR PARK, JAMES'S FERRARI purred as if delighted to see him again. Running his hand over the soft leather of the steering wheel, James's heart tugged with a sense of loss. The car had symbolised his success, but time never stood still, and now he had to make a change.

Heading away from Bath towards Swindon, he drove for forty minutes, then pulled into the dealership he'd been communicating with.

An older man in a shiny suit came out to greet him, his beady eyes entirely on James's car.

'Nice,' he said in a thick Essex accent. 'I'm Tony.'

James stood a little taller. The man looked and sounded like his father's old East End cronies, one foot in the business world, the other in the underworld.

'Tony finally brought his attention to James, his gaze shrewd and assessing. 'Why d'you want such a quick sale?'

James gave a nonchalant half-shrug in return.

'You got all the papers?'

'Full-service history and not a ding on it.'

'And you don't want the plates?'

James shook his head, then leaned into the car to get the particulars. He most definitely *did* want to keep the personalised number plate, but that would mean a wait before he could sell the Ferrari and he didn't have that luxury. Both 'JHS 1' and the beloved car it was attached to would have to drive into the sunset together, and James would have to let go of that chapter of his life.

Tony inspected the papers, then spent half an hour going over every bit of the Ferrari he could reach. James stood back, his stomach nauseous, as if he were his car and Tony was performing a rigorous prostate exam minus the lube.

He then took the car for a test drive. James's hands and right foot twitched in the passenger seat as the older man put the Ferrari through its paces.

'I handle her more carefully than this,' he finally gritted out.

'No need. She's a feisty little bitch.'

James ground his teeth. Even though Tony wouldn't be the final owner, he hated the thought of the Ferrari spending any more time in his company.

Get a grip. It's just a car. Again, the voice sounded exactly like Estelle's.

Unclenching his fists, James let out a long, slow breath. *Don't forget why you're doing this.*

BACK AT THE DEALERSHIP, THE BARGAINING COMMENCED.

'Two hundred and fifty grand,' James said.

'Fuck off,' Tony scoffed. 'One hundred.'

'No, *you* fuck off. Start with a better number or I walk.'

'You want a quick sale?'

'I want a sale, not an arse-fuck.'

'One hundred and twenty.'

'No.'

'One hundred and twenty-five.'

James crossed his arms. 'Cut the shit. I've got other options. You were just the closest.'

Tony mirrored his stance and puffed out his chest.

James lifted his chin and flexed his crossed arms. He'd been up against bigger and uglier bastards than Tony and wasn't going to settle until he got what he wanted.

Tony was the first to cave. 'One fifty.'

'Two thirty.'

'Fuck off.'

James held his hands up, ticking off each point as he made it. 'One extremely careful owner, immaculate interior and not a mark on the body. Full-service history, MOT and a full tank of petrol. I know how much you can get for her, and so do you. It just depends how much profit you want to make.'

'One seventy. And that's my final—Hey!'

But James was striding off.

Tony trotted after him. 'Wait! Two hundred on the nose.'

James turned, waiting a beat before he replied. 'Two hundred and one of the cars you've got here.'

'What?'

'Your choice and between five and ten grand asking price. But it has to have low mileage, full-service history, MOT, not a scratch on the body, and only one previous owner.'

'What second-hand car has only had one owner?' Tony spluttered.

James shrugged. If he was giving up his Ferrari, then he had to replace it with something that wouldn't break down the moment he drove it off the forecourt.

Something flared in Tony's eyes, and the corner of his mouth twitched. 'I've actually got exactly what you want.'

That doesn't sound good. 'I want to see the full papers.'

'Not a problem.' Tony extended an arm. 'Do we have a deal?'

'Two hundred for the Ferrari, and I drive away in the next hour with a reliable car?'

'Yep. You can't get a better condition ride than the one you're getting.'

'Apart from my Ferrari.'

Tony shrugged. 'They're on a par.'

Reaching out, James shook his hand. 'Deal.'

J AMES PULLED TO A STOP AT THE TRAFFIC LIGHTS, KEEPING his gaze dead ahead.

'Awright Barb!' a man called from the window of a white van.

'Twat!' his friend added.

James ignored them, repressing the urge to do a U-turn and go back to rip Tony's head off.

On the journey from the dealership to Foxbrooke, James had been beeped every couple of minutes. Men hurled abuse as soon as they clocked him behind the wheel, and women laughed. Used to admiring glances from both sexes when he was in the Ferrari, this driving experience had ripped him from heaven and dropped him into the seventh circle of hell.

From the age of seven, James's image had been carefully cultivated. There was no room for embarrassment or vulnerability, and no-one *ever* laughed at him. Was his new car some kind of cosmic karma for everything he'd ever done wrong? If so, his list of transgressions must have been really bloody long to justify this level of humiliation. He couldn't even use the money Theo's company owed him. It was needed to pay the credit card bills he'd accumulated. And anyway, the money wouldn't have come through fast enough for what he needed.

Parking at the far end of Foxbrooke high street, James strode toward the manor, getting as much distance from his new car as possible. It was blisteringly hot and he kept to the shady side of the street, going into BDE's bank account to authorise payments as he walked, then ringing Estelle.

She didn't pick up.

He rang Carly, who answered immediately. 'Hey James, you still in London?'

'No, I cut the trip short. I'm just entering the main gates. How's it going?'

'Right now? It's a shitshow in the formal gardens.'

His heart sank. 'I'm on my way.'

He cut through the main house to the formal gardens behind. This was where the acoustic tent was situated and the open-air Shakespeare production. Glancing around, he tried to see what had happened. Then the smell hit him. Had the vicar's pigs got out?

Following his nose, he found a bank of portaloos. Four were lying face down, the backs ripped off, and their contents now coating everything within a forty-yard radius.

In the middle of a crowd of people with buckets and hoses, was Estelle, shouting orders. Noticing him, she stomped over.

'Ah, the prodigal son. How kind of you to grace us with your presence.'

Despite the frustration firing through him, he forced himself to remain calm. 'How can I help?'

'Maybe find some toilets that don't explode when placed in full sunshine? Like the ones I specified in the first place?'

He lowered his voice. 'Come on, you know why I had to do that.'

She hesitated, then nodded.

'Can we have a quick chat?' he continued. 'I need to talk to you about something.'

'Seriously? Now? We open in three days!'

'I know. Please?'

Estelle stalked away from the toilets, stopping behind a yew hedge where there was more privacy. Turning to face him, she crossed her arms. Behind her obvious fury, she looked shattered.

'How was Pentangle with "the girls"?'

'I told you, I didn't go.'

She shrugged as if she didn't believe him. 'And the meet and greet with the great Garrett Ross?'

'It went well. I also got a call from my lawyer. The insider-trading charges are being dropped due to insufficient evidence. It means I can return to working in financial services.'

She frowned as if she didn't get where he was going with this.

'It means I don't have to take the job with Global Tech and spend so much time abroad. I can go back to working in the City.'

'As in London?'

'Yes.'

'And why are you telling me this?'

The ground suddenly felt unsteady beneath his feet. *Focus!*

'It'll make it easier for us to be together. I can commute every day, or stay at my flat and come back on weekends.'

'And where are you going to live? Shoscombe Manor?'

'No. In a few months I could afford to rent locally, or...'

'Move in with me?'

'Um—'

'And Elyse? Won't that be cosy? Maybe you can also bring "the girls" back with you on weekends.'

Fuck. This was a total disaster. 'We can make it work.'

'Can *we*? Because from where I'm standing, this is all about what *you* want. You haven't thought at all about what *I* might want.' She huffed out a short laugh. 'You even decided I was your girlfriend without asking me.'

'That was just to get Garrett off my back.'

'Was it now? I'm so glad to have been useful.'

'No! That's not what I meant. I want a relationship with you. I want you to be my girlfriend. Tell me what you want and I'll do my best to make it happen.'

She shook her head. 'It's never going to work. Let's just draw a line under this—' she gestured between them, '—and quit while we're ahead. We want completely different things, and I don't want what you're offering. Let's just get through the festival, then you can go back—'

'What *do* you want? Come on Estelle, tell me.'

She held his gaze. 'I want what Henry has with Libby and what Eveline has with Jack. I want to share my life with someone who gets me. I want to be loved.'

James's heart stopped. Estelle had filled his waking consciousness and fevered dreams for nearly a year now, but he'd never allowed himself to label the thoughts and feelings. Now they threatened to overwhelm him.

'You once told me you've always dreamed of falling in love,' she continued. 'Well, I have too. But my version doesn't involve a life split between the city and the countryside.'

'I... I—' *Just tell her! Tell her you love her!* But the enormity of the words stuck in his throat. He'd never uttered them out loud to anyone before, not even to his parents or sister.

Estelle laid a hand on his arm, her eyes full of compassion. 'Don't say anything you don't mean, just to get me to go along with what you want. You're better than that.' She sighed. 'Look, I really like you, James. You're a good person. You're just not *my* person.' She gave his arm a squeeze. 'I've got to go and deal with the portaloos. Are there any funds left to get the compost toilets I specified? At least for this location?'

He nodded, utterly lost.

'Good. Can I leave that with you?'

He nodded again.

She dropped her hand. 'Okay, let's keep in touch via email. And congratulations on getting the legal issue sorted.' She gave him a brief smile, then walked away.

James watched her go, his mind blank and his body a wasteland. He was always so sure about everything, but now the only certainty in his life was that he'd mucked everything up with the only woman he'd ever loved.

But what could he do?

His phone rang and he took the call.

'Hi, Elyse, everything okay?'

'No. Your dad's been admitted to hospital with chest pains. He didn't want you to know, but I disagree. Can you come?'

James started running. 'I'm on my way.'

❧ 33 ❧

'What happened?' James asked Elyse as she met him at the main entrance to the Royal United Hospital.

Her face was pinched and pale, her eyes red-rimmed as if she'd been crying.

'He hasn't been the same since coming back from China.' Elyse led him through a set of doors and down a corridor. 'And I kept catching him rubbing his chest and flexing his fingers as if they were stiff or he had pins and needles.' She glanced at him. 'I'm sorry. I thought it was because of all the fidget toys.'

'Did you talk to Mum?'

She nodded. 'She'd had her own suspicions, so we spoke to him together this morning. He... He wasn't very...'

'Receptive?'

Elyse pulled a face. 'He started shouting. And then he had to stop because he was out of breath and in pain. Your mum called an ambulance.'

'What have the doctors said?'

'Not a lot yet. They're running tests.'

'How is he now?'

'One hundred and ten per cent alive.' Entering the ward, Elyse turned left into the first room.

Five of the beds contained older men who were dozing. The sixth contained Kevin Hunter-Savage.

'Babe! What the fuck did you tell Jamesy-boy for?'

Kevin was sitting up in bed, his white-haired chest covered in sticky patches with wires coming off them, connected to a machine.

'I told you. Don't tell 'im. He's meant to be in London.'

James went to the side of the bed. 'How are you feeling?'

'Fine,' his dad replied testily. 'Sit down. You're giving me a neck crick.'

Pulling out a chair, James sat. 'Where's Mum?'

'Getting a cup of tea. Look, son, there's nothing wrong with me.' He glanced over James's shoulder to eyeball Elyse. 'You didn't tell Sophia as well, did you, babe?'

'She's on her way now.'

Kevin thumped his head back against the pillows. 'Fuck!'

'I'll leave you with him for a bit,' Elyse said to James. She held up her phone. 'I'm going to check my messages. I'll be in the corridor outside.'

'You shouldn't be here,' Kevin said to him as she rounded the corner.

'Why not?'

His dad indicated the pads covering his chest. 'This is all a fuss about nothing. You should be in London with that Global Tech bloke.'

'I came back early.'

'Why?'

'The festival.'

'You've done your bit. Now you need to get back to what you're meant to be doing.'

'And what's that?'

'Being the big man. In London.'

Silence hung between them. James didn't need to point out that living in Somerset, running the festival, then spending months in China, had all been thanks to the man in the bed beside him.

His dad sighed and rubbed his hands over his face as if trying to erase the memories, then gave James his full attention.

'I'm proud of you, son,' he said, his voice scratchy and low. 'You know that. Right?'

James nodded.

'Me and your mum came from nothing. And it didn't matter how much moolah I made, it weren't ever gonna make us talk all la-di-da and fit in proper. But you and Soph? We bought you a step up the ladder. And then, Jamesey-boy, you legged it right to the top.'

Kevin rested his head on the pillow, staring up at the ceiling. 'What you had in London, what you'll get back with Global Tech, it's what I always wanted for you.'

James knew his dad was proud of his achievements, but he'd never considered the possibility that the career decisions he'd made were more about his father's expectations than what he actually wanted. But how could he unpick who he really was? Was he the football-obsessed Kevin Skinner, or the rugby-playing, rowing champion, James Hunter-Savage?

He saw himself as a mannequin in a sharp suit, with a perfect physique and winning smile. Cracks appeared on its face, running into each other, faster and faster until the whole thing shattered and fell to the floor, revealing the emptiness inside.

What made him genuinely happy? *Estelle*. She made every part of him sing in harmony. There was no dissonance, no tone missing. She was the first and last note, the intro, verse and chorus of a song that resonated in his every cell. Painting the dog bowls had made him happy. Perfecting a unicorn for her cappuccino, smelling the perfume he'd made on her skin, helping her train on Duke, bandaging her ankle, making her come... In those moments he'd been truly content. The happiness had seeped down to his bones. There was nothing superficial about it. It was just right.

'Anyway, I've been thinking...' Kevin interrupted James's thoughts. 'I'm gonna cut my losses. I know your mum ain't gonna like it, but I'm selling up. We'll downsize and go back east.'

'What?'

'I'm offloading the house and BDE.'

'But... What about next year?'

'What *about* next year?'

'The festival.'

Kevin laughed. 'I don't give two shits about that. Estelle can partner with the new owners of BDE.'

'But who would buy it off you when it's hundreds of thousands of pounds in debt?'

His father shrugged. 'Then I'll file for bankruptcy and the creditors will have to suck it up.'

'Dad!'

'What? It's business, Jamesey-boy, not personal. You know that.'

'The principal creditor is *me*, Dad,' he ground out. '*I'm* the one who's owed money.'

'Eh? But I thought you were on the skids?'

'I sold the car to prop the company up and make sure the staff were paid.'

'Not the Ferrari!'

'It's just a car.'

'No, it's not!' his dad whined like a little boy. 'It's the dog's bollocks!'

'And what about Mum? She's made friends here. Isn't this her dream?'

His father glanced away and shrugged. 'That business in China added ten years to me. I don't feel as strong as I was. I don't know if I can hustle hard enough to keep the place.'

James sank his head. Everything was going down the toilet. He'd lost Estelle, he'd never get his money back, and now his parents were leaving Foxbrooke.

Elyse came back into the room. 'I'm sorry to interrupt.'

Kevin waved his hand. 'No worries, babe. What's up?'

Elyse glanced at James. 'It's to do with the festival.'

'Eh?' Kevin sat up straighter.

'What's happened?' James asked.

Her gaze flicked between them.

'Spit it out,' Kevin said.

'I've kept in touch with Max,' she began.

Kevin turned to James. 'The little gobshite who landed you in it with the licensing committee?'

He nodded in reply.

'Max has been in various Facebook groups for festival goers,' Elyse continued. 'Telling people that the fence for the Foxbrooke festival is weak, and where the best places are to get through.'

James's chin dropped to his chest. First the stage, then the toilets, and now this. The festival was screwed.

'Can you strengthen the fence?' his dad asked. 'Get more security?'

'No, Dad,' James replied wearily. 'There's no money left.'

'Maybe we could find some volunteers to help?' Elyse asked.

'From where?' James asked. 'We need big scary men, not spotty students or a bunch of oldies.'

Elyse's cheeks turned pink. 'I think I can find a few men who fit the bill.'

'And I can find you more than a few who'd love the chance to terrify a bunch of long-haired, tent-carrying twats,' Kevin added. 'I think it's time to call in a few favours. Elyse, babe, you got my phone?'

She took it from her bag and passed it over.

James stood. 'I'm going to brief the security we do have and reply to the Facebook posts. Elyse, can you screenshot the messages and send them to me?'

She nodded.

'And can you keep this from Estelle? She's got enough on her plate right now.'

'Okay.'

James turned to his dad. 'I'll be back later. We need to finish our conversation.'

'I'll be back home by tonight.'

'Wait and see what the doctor says first.' He hesitated. Was this the moment he told his dad he loved him?

'You alright, Jamesey-boy? You got gas?'

Even Elyse was frowning at him.

Fuck's sake. Who knew showing basic human emotion could be so challenging?

He shook his head. 'I'm good. I'll see you later.' He strode from the room. If he couldn't even manage to be emotionally open with his own father, then it was time to practise on one of his least favourite people.

JAMES KNOCKED ON THE DOOR, THE SOUND LOUD IN THE quiet corridor, and prayed that Perry had been wrong, and that no-one was currently in the room.

'Come in,' came a male voice from inside.

Taking a deep breath, James entered, closing the door behind him.

Henry stood, his expression guarded. 'Can I help you?'

'I wondered if I could have a word.'

Henry nodded, moving out from behind his desk towards a coffee machine and kettle on a small table near the window. 'Can I make you a drink?'

'Double espresso, please.'

Henry flipped the appliance on, then weighed out the correct amount of beans. The machine was not as high end as the one James had, but James was impressed with the care Henry was taking.

When it was made, Henry passed the cup to James and indicated a round table by the window. 'Please, take a seat.'

James sat, and Henry joined him, holding a glass of water between his hands.

Not knowing how to start the conversation, James took a sip of his coffee and gazed out of the window. A couple of metres away was a lightweight mesh fence, designed to keep festival punters from trampling on the flower beds and sticking their noses through the windows. Beyond the fence, the grounds were a hive of activity. His chest filled with a rush of pride. He couldn't believe they'd got this far.

Sensing Henry waiting for him to speak, James put his cup down and focused on the man he'd behaved so badly towards for so long. Guilt and remorse choked him. The fault had never been Henry's. It had arisen from James's own insecurities and jealousy.

'I want to apologise.' His voice sounded like he'd been gargling gravel.

Henry's eyes widened slightly, as if shocked to hear those words coming from his mouth.

James cleared his throat. 'I have a lot to be sorry for, and I know one conversation won't be enough to repair the damage, but I wanted to make a start.'

Henry inclined his head slightly, as if encouraging him to go on.

'I was envious of you when we were at school,' James said. 'I thought you had it all. I expected you to be brash, loud and confident—characteristics I believed held the most value, and was irritated when you weren't.'

He took another sip of his espresso, letting the bitter flavour coat his tongue, then swallowed.

'Since the age of seven, I'd created the persona of James Hunter-Savage. On the one hand, it was a house of cards that could fall at any time, and on the other, it became a role I embodied so completely, I didn't think I could be anyone else, or act in a different way.'

Henry didn't move a muscle, as if the slightest movement might break the spell.

'So, it became easy and instinctive to act like a twat towards you and never question why I behaved that way. I made it your fault when it was entirely my own.'

He stared at the coffee cup. 'About a year and a half ago, I got drunk with Dad and bragged about the deals I was brokering. Without my knowledge, he took that information and used it to make a mint on the stock market. I was then accused of insider trading.'

James sighed. 'I believed if I proved my value to Conqueror, they wouldn't let me go. So, I stole your deal.' He brought his gaze to meet Henry's. 'I'm sorry.'

'Is that why you left?'

He nodded. 'Dad bought BDE as an apology gift, but he cocked that up as well, not holding the owners to a non-compete clause, and changing the name. When I took it over, the bank account was empty and there was only one client, the Foxbrooke estate. On top of that, Dad's business deals had gone south, so he needed me to make the festival work or he and Mum would lose their home. But I was left with only two-thirds of the original budget. Then Dad got arrested in China...'

'Does Estelle know any of this?'

'Yes. But my budget cutting has had consequences. I've just found out that Max, the guy I fired at the start of the year, has been posting in Facebook groups that the fence isn't strong enough, and where's best to breach it.'

Henry rubbed his head. 'What options do you have?'

'None, financially. The only personal asset I have left to strip is my London flat, but I can't sell that or re-mortgage within the next forty-eight hours.'

'How can I be of assistance?'

Henry's words pricked at James's heart. James had been an arsehole to Henry for nearly twenty years, and yet now he was offering to help.

He swallowed his emotion. 'I need extra bodies to beef up the security. Preferably big men with faces only a mother could love.'

A smile tugged at the corner of Henry's mouth. 'I know at least one man that fits that description.'

'Your mate Finn?'

'You know him?'

'I've met him a couple of times. He'd be perfect.'

Henry nodded. 'Well, if he's free, then that's one. I'll get calling and see what I can do.'

'Please don't tell Estelle.'

'Why not?'

'She's at the end of her tether. As long as we can handle it, she doesn't need to know.'

'Okay.' Henry paused, his expression searching. 'What's going on between you and my sister?'

James's stomach lurched. 'Nothing.' He failed to keep the bitterness from his voice.

Henry opened his mouth to speak, but was interrupted by a knocking at the door.

'My liege!' a female voice called out as the door opened. 'Are you—oh!'

Both James and Henry stood as Libby entered the room.

'Sorry!' she continued. 'Should I come back later?'

'No,' James said. 'I was just heading out.' He drained his coffee and held Henry's gaze. 'Thank you.'

Henry nodded. 'I'll see what I can do.'

James crossed the room to Libby. 'I want to apologise to you for the way I behaved at the workshop you ran at Conqueror last year. I was in a very bad place and felt too exposed by what you were asking us to do.'

Libby beamed at him as if he'd just figured out how to turn piss into champagne. 'That's alright. I know people think improv is just a bit of fun, but it's powerful stuff.'

James thought he'd feel worse after saying sorry to Henry and Libby, as if it would mean he'd lose part of himself. But he felt bigger, lighter, stronger. Apologising hadn't taken anything away from him. It had only given him more.

'Thank you.' He nodded at Libby and Henry, then left, quietly closing the door behind him.

The fog filling his mind was beginning to lift. Now he was starting to see clearly, he could make a plan and try and find a way to persuade Estelle to give him a second chance.

❧ 34 ❧

Static burst from Estelle's radio, then a voice.

'Calling Estelle or James. It's Gate One. We've got an issue and need either or both of you here immediately. Over.'

Estelle took a deep breath and raised the radio to her mouth.

'Roger that,' James's deep voice crackled through the speaker. 'On my way. Over.'

Estelle depressed the call button. 'You don't need to. I'll do it. Over.'

No-one replied.

She set off across the parkland towards the manor. It would take at least ten minutes to get from the far end of the temporary car park to the main entrance. Day one had only officially started a few hours ago and already there was a problem so big it required either her or James to sort it out.

Pulling her Day-Glo vest away from her body, Estelle flapped it in an attempt to cool down. The weather gods had shone on the event and removed every trace of a cloud from

441

the sky. However, it was blisteringly hot and there was no breeze. Ideal weather for a day by the river, but a perfect storm for dehydration, sunburn and heatstroke.

Passing through into the spectators' field behind the manor, she immediately saw sunstroke waiting to happen. Five young lads had positioned themselves on a small incline facing the main stage and were settling in for the day. Each one was sitting in a garden chair they'd brought and had a twelve pack of beer by their feet. They may have had something to drink and somewhere to sit, but they'd forgotten half their clothes. They were shirtless, their lily-white chests shining so brightly that Estelle had to squint when she looked at them, and their only sun protection appeared to be shades.

Making a mental note to speak to the nearest Saint John's Ambulance crew about them as soon as she'd sorted the issue at the main gate, Estelle continued on, registering all the free water stations they'd installed to cut down on single use plastic bottles and help people stay hydrated.

'Darling!'

The booming voice stopped Estelle in her tracks. She turned, blinking rapidly as her father strode towards her, one arm outstretched.

What the—

She pushed her sunglasses into her hair, as if that would change the sight in front of her.

Good grief.

Arthur Foxbrooke had taken his love of nature, dressing-up, and spectacle to a whole new level. The colour palette he'd chosen was green and the inspiration for his outfit, Estelle guessed, was 'The Green Man goes to Mardi Gras'. Antlers adorned his head, coated with trailing strands of cleavers and bindweed. His face and various sections of skin were painted in swirls of mossy green, while the rest of his costume consisted of battered pieces of fur and leather, leaves and small branches. It looked as if he'd coated himself in glue, wrestled a warren of rabbits, run through a hedge, then fallen into a swamp.

'Dad! What on earth are you wearing?'

'Ho, ho, ho! Aren't I simply marvellous?' He flung his arms wide and gave her a twirl.

Estelle ducked to avoid a branch taking her eye out.

'Willow and Summer helped. Haven't they done a splendid job?'

'Dad, you've got to lose the branches. They're dangerous.'

'Poppycock. I've got excellent spatial awareness and have an early warning system in place in case I have to walk through crowds.' He lifted a hunting horn to his lips and blew loudly through it.

'But the Morris dancing workshop?'

Her father's face fell. 'Yes, I will have to change for that. But right now I'm taking the opportunity to show off.'

Reaching forward, Estelle snapped the ends off the widest branches.

'What are you doing?'

'Dad, this costume is lethal. People are going to be drunk and their attention will be on the performers, not a sentient hedge. We can't afford to be sued again.'

'I promise I'll behave.'

'Just stick to open spaces, okay? Or why don't you stand somewhere and people can take pictures with you?'

'Ooh! I like the sound of that. I can put a hat out and make a bit of money.'

'Dad!'

'For the festival, darling.'

Estelle threw her hands in the air and let out an exasperated sigh. 'Why the hell not? We need every bloody penny.'

'Jolly good. Can you grab my fedora?'

'I can't. There's an issue at the main gate that needs sorting.'

'Isn't James over there now? I think I saw him.'

'I don't know, but I've got to go. Please don't get into trouble.'

'Hang on, hang on. There's a reason why I stopped you.'

'What?'

Arthur rummaged in a small leather bag and brought out a sheet of stickers. 'We need to get you in the festival mood.'

'I'm working.'

'You can still enjoy yourself,' he replied, pressing silver stars onto her face.

'Dad!'

He stepped back. 'Perfect. Now, off you trot, Superstar, and I'll see you later.'

Estelle nodded at her father and dashed towards the front of the house, swiping the stickers off. At the start of the long drive towards the main gate, she saw James in the distance and her tummy turned over. Contradictory thoughts and emotions battled for her attention. She wanted to be the one to solve the problem, but if he hadn't stepped up, she would have been just as mad. She was desperate to see him, but each time she did, it hurt her heart.

Why can't he just leave already?

Had she made the right decision in telling him they were over before they'd even started? Could a long-distance relationship with him work?

Up ahead, she noticed Summer and Henry were with him and her jaw instinctively clenched. One sibling hated him and the other fancied him. Two more nails in the 'Estelle and James' coffin. The men were wearing the same fugly high-vis vests as she was, but Summer was in a boho-chic floral minidress with glittering butterflies painted across her cheekbones.

Estelle walked a little faster. *Please, Henry. Don't hit him again.*

'What's going on?' she asked as she reached them.

'There's been a small issue but we've resolved it,' James replied, his gaze inscrutable.

'What issue?'

'Why don't we do this away from the entrance?' Henry said, moving towards a quiet corner behind the gates.

Estelle followed him. 'Well?'

Henry glanced at James.

'It appears that Max has been in contact with Summer,' James said. 'Using his BDE email address, which hadn't been deactivated.'

Estelle's head swivelled to look at her youngest sister. 'What did he do? Are you okay?'

Summer rolled her eyes. 'Chill, I'm fine. I've never even met the guy.'

'Max gave Summer fake passes she could give to her followers,' James continued. 'And the first person just tried to use one to get in.'

'How many?' The public relations disaster was unfolding in her mind's eye.

There was a brief hesitation before James replied. 'Two thousand.'

'Two *thousand*?'

He nodded. 'But it's been handled.'

'How?'

'Anyone who shows up with one of the fake tickets will be told they're worthless and that Summer's account was hacked—'

'But they'll go straight to the press! That—'

'Is why we're giving them a choice,' James continued. 'They can either walk away, or they can enter the festival with a financial contribution that gets them an exclusive audience with Summer.'

'What? How much?'

'I just persuaded the first person to cough up one hundred pounds.'

'A hundred quid? Just to meet *Summer*?'

'Oi!' Summer replied. 'That's cheap. I'm used to charging thousands for appearances. And anyway, the money's not going to me, it's going to the festival.' She dropped a curtsey. 'You can thank me later for saving the day.'

'But if they all show up, we'll be over capacity,' Estelle hissed. 'The council could shut us down.'

'Yes, we have sold out,' James said placidly, 'but that doesn't mean everyone with a ticket will come. Nor will everyone Summer gave free passes to. The site can accommodate the extra numbers and won't feel crowded. There's no way the councillors will be able to count who's here, and I believe the rewards vastly outweigh any risk.'

Estelle's throat squeezed with emotion, but she still managed to spit her words out. 'So you just made that decision, did you?'

'Estelle——' Henry began.

'It doesn't matter to you, does it?' she continued, addressing James. 'Because as soon as it's over, you're out of here. You don't care if the Foxbrooke festival falls on its arse and never gets up again. You only care about you.'

James shook his head. 'That's not true.'

'You might as well leave right now.'

'Estelle!' Henry shouted.

'What?' she yelled.

James took a step back, his hands raised as if trying to

defuse the situation. 'I'm going to do a walk through. I'll be on my radio.' He nodded at Henry, then turned and left.

'Why do you have to be such a bitch?' Summer whispered. 'He's actually really nice once you get to know him.'

'Summer—' Henry began.

'And how well *have* you been getting to know him?' Estelle spat.

'Oh, puh-*lease*. You're just—'

'Summer! Shut it!' Henry barked. 'Please, can you go and social-media something? Anything. Just make the festival look good.'

Summer tossed her hair. 'Easy peasy, I'll throw a few more selfies out there.' She glanced at Estelle. 'You need to let this go. James isn't my type and I'm certainly not his.' She gave her a wink, then flounced off.

Estelle hung her head. 'Dammit,' she muttered.

Henry took her hand and pulled her in for a hug. 'It's going to be okay. I promise.'

'How?' she murmured against his shoulder. 'He's going to ruin everything.'

'No, he's not.' Henry rubbed her back. 'He discussed what to do about the fake tickets with me and Summer and I think his solution is excellent.'

Estelle pulled away. 'But he didn't discuss it with *me*, did he?'

Henry sighed. 'Time was of the essence and he didn't want you to have to worry about it.'

'So now I've got to worry instead about the council shutting us down?'

'It'll be fine. James is right. It won't feel crowded and they'll never be able to count everyone.'

Estelle stared in shock at her brother. 'Are you feeling okay?

Since when did you have a single nice thing to say about James Hunter-Savage?'

He gave her a rueful smile. 'My feelings towards him have changed.'

'Say *what* now?'

'I like him. Underneath the swagger, he's genuinely nice.'

'*Nice?*' Estelle blinked rapidly, then scanned the sky.

'What is it?'

'I'm looking for Ham Solo and Chewbaccon. They must be flying by now.'

Henry chuckled.

'Are you being serious? You don't hate him anymore?'

He shook his head. 'Our parents love him, as does Eveline—'

'She loves everyone.'

'Jack thinks he's a good person, as do all the staff at BDE. Connor, Leo and Willow like him, and you just heard what Summer thinks. The only people I know who were still holding out against James were me... and you.'

Estelle didn't know what to say.

'Libby's always said his arrogance was a mask for insecurity and she was correct. It's far easier to hang onto a belief than to change it. But I've changed my mind about James.'

'Since when?'

'It's been happening slowly for months. I saw how supportive he was of you when we had to put on that event for the councillors, and how great he is with our folks, no matter what they throw at him. It's little things, and it's big things. He shows up, and not just because he's in l—'

'In what?'

Henry let out a long breath. 'Last year, Eveline was right. James never wanted Summer. He's only ever wanted you.'

Estelle's mouth fell open.

'It's only been my own bloody-minded belligerence that's stopped me from seeing it sooner. Once I'd stopped hating him, it was blindingly obvious.'

'But he's leaving,' she said in a small voice.

'Have you asked him to stay?'

'He doesn't want to.'

'Yes, but have you given him a reason not to go? Have you actually *asked* him if he would stay?'

She gave a half-shrug. 'It doesn't matter. It's too late now.'

'It's never too late. Look at me and Libby.'

Estelle huffed. 'Yeah, but you're perfect for each other.'

'Don't you think you and James might be perfect for each other, too?'

Estelle looked down, scuffing at the grass with her shoe.

'You're a force of nature. And James is... Well, he's James Hunter-Savage. The two of you together are likely to be fierier than one of Dad's curries.'

The corners of Estelle's mouth twitched up as she stared at the ground. 'I really like him, Henry,' she mumbled. 'But I think I've messed it all up.'

'Nonsense. Wait till the chaos of the festival is over, then talk to him. Or go and find him now.'

Estelle brought her gaze to meet her brother's. 'I don't know if it would work or make a difference. I don't want a relationship where he's away all the time, and I sure as shit don't want to move to London.'

'Just talk to him. Open your heart.'

Huh? 'Open my heart? What the hell, Henry. Have you been drinking one of Mammy's weird teas?'

He grinned. 'Nope, I'm just hopelessly in love with my fiancée and want everyone else to be as happy as I am.'

Estelle hugged him tightly. 'You're the best, little brother. Thank you.'

He hugged her back. 'It's going to be alright. I promise.'

ESTELLE SWUNG THE DEFENDER INTO THE LIVERY JUST AFTER midnight. The lights of her house were on, the front door wide open, and an unfamiliar pickup truck was parked outside. Climbing out of her car, she went forward cautiously, wishing that Chester and Joy were there and not enjoying a three-day holiday with Molly.

Where was Elyse? And who the fuck was in her home?

There was the sound of heavy footfall, then a wall of muscle and tattoos came out the front door carrying two suitcases.

'Ryan?' she spluttered.

'Oh, hey Stelle. First day of the festival go okay?'

She stood with her mouth open as Ryan opened the tailgate of his truck and put the suitcases inside.

'What are you doing?'

'Moving Elyse out, then going back to fence duty.'

'Elyse?'

There was a broad smile on his bearded face. 'Yeah, I persuaded her to move in. Didn't she tell you?'

'Er...?'

Ryan may have been six foot six and an amateur power-lifting champion, but his smile suddenly turned sheepish. 'I gave her my number at that quiz night you brought her to. Then we got to know each other when she was away in China. We've been, er...' He rubbed the back of his neck. 'And now she's moving in.'

'Oh.'

Ryan lowered his voice. 'She didn't know how to tell you. She's embarrassed.'

'By you?'

'Me?' He chuckled. 'Nah, she said she hadn't told you the truth about James and felt really bad because you'd been so nice.'

'Yeah, "nice" is always the word that springs to mind when people think of me,' she replied sarcastically.

Ryan let out a belly laugh. 'You're solid, Stelle. Nothing wrong with you.'

'Is she inside?'

'Yep, just packing up the rest of her stuff. I've cleaned her room and vacuumed, so it's not left in a mess.'

'You vacuumed?'

'Yeah. And you should see my place now. It's spotless. I've even got flowers and shit for her.'

'Rose petals on the bed?'

Ryan lowered his head, but Estelle could still see him blush.

'Holy shit, Ryan! You're in love.'

He nodded, then brought his gaze back up to meet hers. 'She's the one for me.'

'Wow.' Estelle was side-swiped. 'You do know she's not the most domesticated?'

'Don't care. Anyway, I love cooking and I'm a tidy bloke. It's going to be great.'

'Well, congratulations. Does anyone else know?'

'I told Finn and Tommy tonight when I left them at the fence.'

'The fence? What are you talking about?'

He puffed out his chest. 'We're your new security guards. Along with a load of blokes from our gym, Connor, Leo, a bunch of their mates, and some right scary old fuckers from London.'

'Explain.'

'Didn't you know?'

'Know *what*?'

'Elyse found out some dude called Max you used to work with was in Facebook groups telling people the fence was weak and where they could get in. She called me to get some volunteer muscle, James spoke to Henry to see who he could rope in, and James's dad called in the Kray's kids. We're taking shifts over the next three days to make sure no-one gets through.'

'Has anyone tried?'

'Yeah!' Ryan's smile was huge. 'Me and Tommy growled at them and they shat themselves and legged it. It was brilliant.'

Estelle turned as Elyse appeared, a large bag slung over her shoulder.

'Sorry,' Elyse said. 'I didn't know how to tell you.'

'About you moving out or Max and the fence?'

'Me moving out. James told Henry not to tell you about the fence as he didn't want you to have another thing to worry about.'

'Oh.'

'Is that everything, babe?' Ryan asked Elyse.

She nodded, and he took the bag from her. 'I'll take this. You say your goodbyes.' Ryan gave Estelle a salute, got in the truck, and started the engine.

Elyse took a step closer to Estelle, her slim fingers twisting in front of her.

'I'm sorry,' she began. 'You've been so lovely. I should have told you sooner.'

Estelle closed the gap between them and pulled her in for a hug. 'Don't be daft. I'm happy for you.' She disengaged. 'Ryan's a good bloke.'

Elyse's cheeks were pink. 'I know.' She looked towards the truck. 'He's so manly.'

'That he is. I bet he can bench press you over his head.'

Elyse's whole face now turned red.

'Oh, my god, has he done that?'

'Not yet.'

'Hey, Ryan!'

The truck window lowered. 'Yeah?'

'Do you think you're strong enough to bench press Elyse over your head?'

He leant an arm out of the window and flexed. 'Easy.'

Elyse made a tiny squeaking sound, like a mouse with a chew toy.

'She doesn't believe you can.'

Ryan's gaze slid to Elyse and became incendiary. 'Babe, shall we get going? I think I've got a point to prove.'

'Oh, er, yes,' Elyse replied, stepping quickly around the truck.

Ryan leaned across the seats and opened the door for her.

Estelle waved as they drove off, then went into the silent house, up the stairs and lay on her bed.

What was going on? Elyse had moved out to be with Ryan, and Henry had decided he liked James. Estelle hadn't managed to see James since shouting at him to leave, and right now she was too tired to even formulate a sentence.

She closed her eyes. Tomorrow she would find him and see if Henry was right. Could he really be persuaded to ditch his life in London for her?

35

'Calling Estelle or James. It's Carly. Over.'

'James here. Over.'

Estelle grabbed her radio. 'What's up? Over.'

'Can you switch to channel two?' Carly replied. 'Over.'

'Roger that. Over,' James said.

'Yes, yes, me too,' Estelle added, switching channels and stepping through the canvas doors of the medical tent to stand in the blazing heat outside.

'Are either of you free to collect the Spice Cadets from Bath?' Carly asked. 'Their van blew up and I can't find anyone who can leave their post to go and get them. Over.'

'But they're on in a couple of hours!' Estelle cried. 'Where's their manager?'

'Already here and too drunk to drive. Over.'

'Can't you find a taxi?'

'It's Sunday, so there's less capacity and I've been given a two-hour waiting time. Over.'

'I'll go,' James's voice rumbled through the speaker. 'They're a four-piece, right? Over.'

'Yes,' Carly replied. 'But they've also got six guitars and lord knows what else. The drum kit and keyboard are already here, thank god. Over.'

'Roger that. I can fit them in my car. Over.'

'How?' Estelle asked. 'You've got a two-and-a-half-seater! I could go in the Defender, but I'd have to clear all my shit out first and then it'll need a clean. And I'm at the medical tent right now with a few cases of sunstroke and a woman in labour. I don't want to leave until I know the ambulance is on the way. Er... Over.'

'My car can fit five and has a large boot,' James said. 'Carly, can you message me the address? I can leave in the next ten minutes. Over.'

'Roger that,' she replied. 'Will do. Can you let me know when you're five minutes away with them? I'll get the front gates opened and you can drive straight to the main stage. It'll be quicker than using the back route. Over.'

'Roger that,' James said. 'Over and out.'

The radio went silent in Estelle's hand. How on earth was he going to fit the Spice Cadets in his Ferrari?

Ducking back inside the medical tent, she went to the far end where a pregnant woman was on a bed, gripping her partner's hand.

'How's she doing?' Estelle whispered to him. 'Any news on the ambulance?'

He nodded. 'Nearly here. We're going to wheelchair her out to them in a sec.'

'Can I do anything?'

'Could you grab our bags? I don't think I'm going to get my hand back anytime soon.'

As if in agreement, the woman on the bed moaned.

'I'm not going anywhere, love,' he said to her. 'I'm right here.'

Estelle stepped back, a lump in her throat. She wanted someone to look at her the same way, as if her pain was their pain, and nothing mattered more than her comfort and happiness.

A thought suddenly struck her. Was this what Eveline was going to go through in a couple of months' time?

I doubt she'll be in a medical tent at a festival, dumbass.

Shut-up. You know what I mean—all the pain.

God's on her side. She'll probably orgasm with every contraction.

True.

One of the nurses arrived with a wheelchair and they helped the woman into it. Estelle took the couple's bags and led the way to the car park in front of the main gates where the ambulance met them.

She waved the couple off, then took the wheelchair back to the medical tent, taking a moment to look around with eyes truly open.

It's a success.

Everyone she could see was smiling. From the caterers sweating in their food trucks to the punters queuing for burgers, beer or ice cream. From the paid and voluntary staff, to the acts, most of whom were staying for the whole festival once they'd performed.

Despite all the drama, they'd managed to pull it off. At least on one level... Financially, it was a completely different matter. She only hoped that over the next week, when all the money was accounted for, they had enough to pay their staff. Guilt sat in her stomach like a corroding battery, slowly dripping acid. Estelle had wondered if there was anything she owned that could be sold, but nothing would have raised enough money.

She radioed Carly, then went to the front of the manor to wait for her. She didn't need to be there to greet the Spice Cadets, but she hadn't seen James since the start of the festival and was desperate to know he was actually still in Somerset, and not just a voice crackling through her radio.

Since her conversation with Henry, she'd tried to find time to speak to James, but the moment one crisis had been averted another popped up demanding her immediate attention. James was also spending a lot of time at the festival perimeter and had apparently paid for Leia and Ben to feed all the volunteers who were guarding the fence. Although Estelle had no idea where he'd found the money to pay for that.

'Hey, boss!'

'I don't want to jinx anything,' Estelle said as Carly came to her side, 'but I think we've nearly pulled it off.'

'Yep. And UberGraft are already on site so we've got our headliners.'

'Thank god for that. Is running a festival always this stressful?'

Carly grinned. 'That's what makes it fun. It's a rollercoaster running on adrenaline, luck and the right kind of weather.'

Estelle glanced at the cloudless sky. 'My best mate's the local vicar. She must have been praying for us twenty-four-seven.'

'Well, something's obviously worked. Shall we wander to the main gate? James should be here soon.'

Estelle's heart sped up at the thought of seeing him again.

'I haven't had a chance to say thank you,' Carly said as they strolled down the main drive.

'For what?'

'This job, the experience, being so cool. Everything really. I know it's been a nightmare for you, especially with James in China for so long, but you've been amazing throughout all of it.'

'Oh. Er, thank you.' Estelle didn't know what else to say. She'd tried her best, but wasn't sure if she'd always succeeded.

'And I couldn't believe it when this month's wages popped into my account. We all thought we'd have to wait weeks to be paid.'

'Huh?'

'You paid all the BDE staff yesterday.'

'What? *All* of you?'

'Yeah. Didn't you know?'

Estelle shook her head. How had James found that kind of money? Surely not from fleecing Summer's superfans?

'Well, we appreciate it. I don't know who's going to buy BDE from Kevin, or if the new owners will want to partner with you, but I really hope you do this again next year.'

Estelle wasn't sure how to reply. The thought of doing it all again without James to help, or his mother bringing her French Fancies, made her feel flat and deflated rather than energised. She'd started the year doing everything in her power to get James to leave, and now she was desperate for him to stay.

Carly's phone rang and she took the call. 'Hi, you nearly here?' she said, before mouthing '*it's James*' at Estelle. 'Yup, we're at the gates... Who? I'm with Estelle.' Carly glanced at her and frowned. 'Why?' she said into the phone. 'And where?'

'What's he saying?' Estelle hissed.

Carly pulled another face. 'Okay, I'll see what I can do. See you in a bit.' She ended the call and looked apologetically at Estelle. 'He said he doesn't want you here when he arrives.'

What? 'Oh.' Her words to James on Friday must have been the last straw for him. It wasn't just the workload of the festival and securing the fence that had kept him busy. He'd been actively avoiding her.

'I've no idea why. It's not like he's collecting a cake for your second birthday.'

'It's okay,' Estelle replied, the pain of rejection stinging her eyes. 'I've got plenty to be getting on with, anyway. I'll leave you to it.' Without waiting for a response, she strode back up the drive.

See, you fucked it up with him.

There could be another reason!

Like...

I don't know, but he's been trying to shield me from things that are going wrong. Maybe something's happened to the Spice Cadets? Go back and see.

You can't.

Why not? There's plenty of people at the gate. I'll be stealthy. He won't have a clue I'm there.

Pivoting, Estelle jogged back to the gate, veering onto the verge to hide behind the corner of a temporary kiosk.

Carly and one of the security guards opened the main gates, and a car drove slowly in.

Estelle blinked.

James was in the driver's seat, and all four band members of the Spice Cadets were passengers, but that information was rapidly processed and filed so her brain had space to compute the car that they were in.

It was a lurid pink Renault Kangoo, the same eye-watering shade as one of Bev's cleaning tabards, with huge plastic eyelashes above the headlights. By the fuel cap was a sticker of Tinkerbell and the words 'runs on fairy dust', and emblazoned across the body were the words 'Barb's Beauty Boutique' in black glitter.

As the car moved through the gates, Estelle noticed the personalised number plate reading 'BARB13'.

What on earth was this and where was the Ferrari?

Carly was leaning down to talk to James through the window. Estelle's feet moved unconsciously towards them.

Then her mouth moved of its own accord, too. 'Who does this monstrosity belong to?'

Carly moved to the side, so there was nothing between Estelle and James. A look of utter mortification flashed across his face, then he composed his features.

'Me,' he replied.

'What happened to the Ferrari?'

He cleared his throat. 'I traded it in.'

'For *this*?'

'Yes.'

'I'm Barb, and I'm gonna make you beautiful,' came a farcically high-pitched voice from the back seat followed by giggles from the other men in the car.

'They've been inhaling nitrous oxide ever since I picked them up,' James said, his jaw tight.

'I need a touch-up, Barb,' came another squeaky voice. 'Touch me up and make me feel gooood.'

The Spice Cadets now sounded like a pack of hyenas at a comedy club.

Estelle bit the inside of her mouth to stop her smile. 'Why did you trade the Ferrari in?'

James's eyes flicked to Carly, then back to her, his gaze intent as if trying to communicate a message without words.

Holy shit. Is that how he paid the staff wages?

'Carly,' James said. 'Would you be able to take it from here?'

'Sure, I'm going to clear a path and lead you to the stage.'

'No, I need you to drive.'

'But I'm not insured.'

'You'll be doing less than four miles per hour on a private road,' he replied tersely.

'Why can't *you* drive?' Estelle asked him.

'Drive me hard, Barb!' one of the men squealed. 'I've been a bad boy!'

James briefly closed his eyes, then gave Estelle a hard stare.

The snort was too big to hold back, but Estelle still clapped a hand to her mouth.

'Please?' he asked.

She passed her hand over her face to try and remove the grin. 'I'm glad to see you've been getting in touch with your feminine side. This new look suits you.'

He raised an eyebrow.

'You should enjoy the moment,' she continued. 'What do you think, Carly?'

Carly had turned away, but her shoulders were shaking with laughter.

James sighed. 'Alright, let's get this over with.'

'Be gentle, Barb! It's my first time!' squeaked a voice from the back seat.

Estelle stepped away from the car, put her fingers in her mouth, and whistled loudly. 'Ladies, gentlemen, boys and girls, can I have your full attention please?' she shouted. 'We have a moving motor vehicle in transit. For your safety, please stand well clear!'

'Fuck's sake,' James growled behind her.

'This car contains one of the acts who will shortly be performing on the main stage,' she continued. 'Get a good look, ladies and gents and feel free to take as many pictures as you like!'

Stepping in front of the car, she walked backwards, gesturing for James to follow.

He revved the engine.

She winked at him. 'Car with celebrities coming through! Stand back but shout out if you recognise who they are!'

Carly joined her. 'I think he's going to kill you,' she said out of the corner of her mouth.

Estelle flashed her a grin. 'Yeah, but totally worth it.'

Every person around them seemed to be holding up a

phone, and there were excited cries of 'It's the Spice Cadets!' as people clocked who James was driving.

Carly giggled. 'I think this is one of the funniest things I've ever seen. Did he really sell the Ferrari for that? And if so, why?'

'I'm not sure. I'll ask him later,' Estelle replied, then broke off to yell to the crowds once more. 'Incoming pop stars! Stand clear of the moving motor vehicle!'

'Do you think you could possibly go a little faster?' James called from behind them.

Estelle ground to a halt. 'What was that? I couldn't quite hear you.'

James growled again, then head-butted the centre of the steering wheel, sounding the horn.

'You're wicked,' Carly hissed.

Estelle carried on walking. 'What can I say? I'm an evil genius.'

Carly glanced over her shoulder. 'As soon as we get to the main stage, I'd leg it if I were you. I think he's either going to strangle or spank you.'

A rush of heat shot through Estelle's body. It didn't matter that James was leaving Foxbrooke, or that she'd told him nothing would ever happen between them. She still wanted him with a visceral intensity that knocked out her breath. But she wanted to talk to him when the festival was over. When there was nothing to distract them or drag one of them away.

'Good idea. I'll peel off just before we get there. UberGraft finish their set at ten-thirty, right?'

'Yep, and that allows for encores. We should have the site clear within an hour and a half, and anyone camping back in their field.'

'How many of the staff do you think could get to the main stage at midnight? I'd like to make a speech to say thank you.'

'Pretty much everyone except for a skeleton security detail on the main entry and exit points.'

'And I suppose by that time we won't need so many extra bodies patrolling the fence, either.'

Carly shook her head. 'We've only had a handful of people try and get through today. I think word's got out about the unofficial guards and that's put people off trying.'

'How many people got in using Summer's fake passes?'

'Last count was nearly a thousand, but their average spend's been eighty quid, so we've actually made a ton of money off them. Plus, they've been posting so much positive content to social media that #FoxbrookeFestival has been trending for the past twenty-four hours.'

'Holy shit! That's amazing!'

'It really is. I haven't had a chance to fill you in on it all, but you'll get a full breakdown by the end of next week with all the stats.'

'And how's Summer getting on? I haven't seen her at all.'

'She's been meeting and greeting groups in the manor every hour since Friday lunchtime. I put Zeke in charge of coordinating everyone to make sure no-one got missed. Honestly, Estelle, she's been incredible. Zeke says she hasn't stopped smiling and making everyone feel special.'

'Shit. She must be exhausted. I can't imagine anything worse than having to be nice to strangers all day.'

Carly laughed. 'What do you think you've been doing for the last few months?'

Estelle shrugged. 'Yeah, but you're my friends now. It's easy.'

Carly put her arm around Estelle's shoulder and gave her a squeeze. 'You've been the best boss ever. I'm going to miss you.'

'You too,' Estelle managed, even though her throat was

tightening. They were nearly at the main stage. 'Can you put the call out to get everyone together at midnight? I'm going to take your advice and do a runner.'

'Will do.'

Estelle threw her arms around Carly, gave her a quick hug, then dashed away without looking back.

❧ 36 ❧

'*Please baby, won't you stay? Love is the only way. I need you night and day. Yeah, love is the only way.*'

Estelle listened to the crowd as they sang along to the chorus of UberGrafts's most famous song. Even though the sun had set an hour ago, the edge of the sky was still pale behind the main stage. It framed the riot of coloured lights and pyrotechnics and the bobbing sea of glowing mobile phones from the audience dancing and filming the band.

Standing at the very back of the field, Estelle took in the enormity of what had been achieved. Despite all the cock-ups and compromises, the festival had exceeded all her expectations and everyone seemed to have enjoyed themselves. She was currently running on empty, but adrenaline was going to take her over the line.

Now all she had to do was speak to James before he left for London.

She hung back as UberGraft finished and the crowds began to filter towards the exits. Roadies were removing instruments and equipment from the stage with speedy efficiency, and

Estelle felt a pang of sadness that it was all over. The clear-up and final admin would take a few weeks, but the peak high had passed. Now was the comedown.

Raising her head, she stared at the stars and breathed in the warm night air. Even if she couldn't have James, even if this was the first and last festival ever to take place at the manor, she could give herself this moment to appreciate how hard she'd worked to make it happen.

'Estelle?'

She turned at the sound of Connor's voice. A group of shadowy figures were walking across the park from the direction of the fence, one with their hand raised in greeting.

She waved back. 'Yeah, it's me. Who's with you?'

'Leo, Ella, Finn, Scott and Tommy.'

They were close enough now to make out their faces.

'Hey!' Estelle called out. 'Did you manage to hear the show at all?'

Finn snorted.

'Rude!' Ella cried.

'We couldn't hear much,' Connor said. 'But Ella and Leo knew all the words, so they performed it for us.'

'And we nailed it.' Leo lifted a hand for his best friend to high five him.

Tommy huffed. 'I had no idea he could make all those high notes.'

'It's because I kicked him in the nuts before they started,' Finn said.

'Love is the only way,' Leo sang. 'My bollocks saved the day.'

'Stelle, make him stop,' Finn grumbled.

'Do you need us for anything else?' Connor asked.

She shook her head. 'I can't thank you enough for what

you've done. The festival could have been shut down without you.'

'My bollocks saved the day,' Leo sang again.

Finn punched him on the arm. 'Shut it.'

'Ow!' Leo cried. 'Ella! Hit him for me.'

Ella rolled her eyes. 'You're on your own.'

'That's the title of his sex tape,' Finn said, and everyone apart from Leo, laughed.

'Mom, Dad and Mammy are bringing a load of champagne to the main stage now,' Estelle said. 'I'm trying to get as many of the staff there as we can at midnight for a small celebration. So, if you're not too tired, I'd love you to stay for that.'

'Thanks, Stelle,' Scott said. 'Sounds great.'

The group strolled across the field, then Estelle led them around the back and up onto the stage itself.

'So this is the rockstar view,' Connor murmured as he gazed out over the parkland.

Estelle stood by his side. 'You don't fancy it then?'

'Never. I'm quite happy with my little life, thank you very much.'

As midnight approached, more people arrived. Eveline and Jack were tucked up asleep, but Estelle's other close friends and family were there, as well as all the key staff from BDE Entertainment.

James was nowhere to be seen.

Just as she was about to start without him, he arrived with his mum and dad. Kevin seemed different, slower in his movements and less vital. Bev had a frown etched into her features as she watched him.

Estelle went to their side. 'Are you okay?' she asked Kevin.

'I'm fine, babe.'

Estelle glanced at James.

'Dad was diagnosed with angina on Tuesday and had a stent fitted.'

Estelle's hand flew to her chest. 'Oh, my god!'

Kevin took her hand and squeezed it. 'Babe, I'm fighting fit. Don't you worry about me.'

'I'm so sorry.'

'No need. I'll be right as rain by next week.'

'Let me get you a chair.'

'I don't need—' Kev began, but Estelle ignored him and dashed backstage, returning with two folding ones.

'Sit down,' Bev said to her husband. 'Or we're going straight home.'

Kevin made a series of grumbling noises, but allowed James to seat him and Bev at the side of the stage.

'Are you going to make a speech now?' James asked Estelle.

She nodded, words temporarily deserting her as she revelled in being so near to him again. His scent, his warmth, his strength, all drew her in until all she wanted to do was close the gap between them.

'I see your parents have brought champagne. Do you want me to help pass it out?'

She nodded. 'Thank you.'

They handed out paper cups and bottles, then James stood to one side behind her and she took centre stage.

'Thank you all so much for coming to this small celebration for what has been a very big event,' she began, meeting every-one's gaze. 'We couldn't have done this without each and every one of you. Whether you handled contract and rider negotia-tions with artists, wrote endless risk assessments, scared wannabe fence-jumpers off, or sat for hours entertaining total strangers, all of you made this happen.'

Even though she couldn't see James, she sensed his pres-ence and it electrified her.

'I want to recite to you the only poem I ever learnt at school. I think the reason I liked it was because it was about horses... "For want of a nail the shoe was lost. For want of a shoe the horse was lost. For want of a horse the rider was lost. For want of a rider the battle was lost. For want of a battle the kingdom was lost. And all for the want of a horseshoe nail".'

She held up her cup of champagne.

'I expect this will be the first time in your life you've ever been likened to a nail, a shoe, or even a horse. But in this analogy, the battle was the festival, and the kingdom is my family's home. We won't know the final figures until next week, but thanks to you we've at least broken even, and showed the council and community just what kind of event we're capable of putting on here.'

Estelle wasn't sure whether it was tiredness or overwhelm, but tears pushed their way up to the back of her throat.

'Each one of you, no matter what you did, made the festival not only happen, but succeed. So...' Starting to her left, Estelle proceeded to name every person on the stage, until the last one left was James. Facing him, her back to everyone else, she held his searing gaze and mouthed the words *'thank you'*, before turning back to the group. 'So, to all of you, and everyone else who isn't here with us now, thank you.'

Estelle held up her cup, and everyone followed suit. As she downed the champagne, the stage broke out into cheers and whistles.

She turned to James. 'Would you like to say something?'

He nodded and came to her side. Normally so self-assured, he seemed a little nervous, and her hand itched to hold his and let him know she was there.

'When I took over BDE Entertainment,' he began, 'I knew nothing about running events and had never been to a festival before. For over a decade, my work and life had been in

London, and, to my shame, I once told Estelle I'd rather spend six months in a Siberian salt mine than in Somerset.'

'That can still be arranged,' Finn called out, and everyone laughed.

James smiled. 'But sometimes it's a good thing to be forced out of your comfort zone. Challenge brings growth, and this year I've had to reevaluate how I lived my life and what was important to me.'

He glanced at Estelle and her heart thumped faster in her chest.

'I thought that after the festival, everything would, or should, go back to how it was. But I was wrong.' He gave a rueful smile. 'Those words don't often come out of my mouth, so enjoy the moment.'

'Go James! Go James!' Libby whooped.

'Sometimes it's difficult to acknowledge that stepping onto a different road will be the start of an incredible journey. One that's going to bring so much more than what you'd get just treading the same comfortable path over and over again. London may appear to offer the world...' He glanced from the stage into the darkness of the night. 'But here you can see the stars, and they shine brighter than anywhere else.'

Estelle's skin tingled, and she dug her nails into her palms. Was James going to stay in Somerset after all?

'And to me...' His gaze passed over everyone, not meeting hers. 'The brightest star of all is Estelle.'

She held her breath as James let the words hang in the air.

'Estelle is my North Star, guiding me to make the right decisions and be the best version of myself. This festival was *her* vision, *her* dream, and she's led from the front every step of the way. It's Estelle's determination and hard work that's brought us together and made all of this happen.'

The silence was electric.

'I know some of you have heard that my father is selling BDE Entertainment. And it's true.'

No!

James cleared his throat. 'He's sold it to me.'

Oh my god, oh my god, oh my god.

'I want to secure investment, build the company, and continue working with you all here in Somerset. My dream is to partner with the Foxbrooke estate again and put on another festival next year.' He finally brought his eyes to meet hers. 'If Estelle will still have me?'

Yes! Yes, yes, yes, yes, yes! She nodded, and his face flooded with relief.

He lifted his paper cup. 'To Estelle!'

'To Estelle!' people chorused, then stamped their feet and cheered.

James's smile was so big she thought her heart would burst. Then he turned his head towards the dark field.

'Henry?' he bellowed. 'Arthur?'

Estelle's gaze flicked across the stage. Where had her dad and brother gone?

'You ready?' Henry's voice called out from somewhere in the darkness.

'Yes!' James yelled back.

'Roger, roger, jammy dodger!' Arthur roared.

Estelle squinted out into the night at two bobbing lights. What were they doing?

Suddenly there was a whoosh, and a firework took off into the air. Followed by another, then another.

She laughed with delight, then turned to find James by her side. Reaching out her hand, he caught it, pulling her body flush with his.

'You're staying,' she whispered, heat flooding through her.

He nodded. 'I thought I still wanted a life in London, but I don't. I want to be with you. Wherever you are.'

'Did you sell the Ferrari to pay the staff?'

'Yes.'

'Oh, James...'

'It's just a car.'

'But you loved it.'

He smiled, his face illuminated by the fireworks. 'I loved it, but I wasn't *in* love with it. I'm in love with you.'

She sucked in a breath.

'I've always wanted to fall in love, and now I have. And just like you, love is awe-inspiring, incredible, and slightly terrifying. But when it comes to the job of being your boyfriend, I'm going to nail it.'

Her eyebrow raised with her heartbeat. 'Fancy nailing anything else?'

His gaze darkened and he shifted his hips, pressing his hard length against her.

'I'll take that as a yes, then...' Estelle glanced around. They were at the back of the stage. Everyone else was facing away, watching the fireworks. 'Could we just leave?'

James took her hand and led her backstage. 'Where's your car?'

'Blocked in by Finn's truck. Should I go back and get him?'

'No, we'll take mine. It's in the car park in front of the gates.'

Jogging down the steps behind the stage, they strode towards the manor.

'You replaced the Ferrari with a Kangoo?'

James's grip on her hand tightened. 'It was a high-pressure bargaining situation and I got played at the last minute.'

Estelle snorted with laughter.

'But the joke's going to be on Tony. Because I'm going to reclaim pink as a masculine colour, just like in the late nineteenth century, and use my extensive knowledge of chemistry to create a clean and renewable source of energy from fairy dust.'

'And change your name to Barb?'

He pulled a face. 'I'm not going that far. One name change in a lifetime is enough. Although... I'm up for amending my surname again.'

Butterflies fluttered in her tummy. 'Oh? What to?'

'I'm not sure,' he replied casually. 'But I think Hunter-Foxbrooke has a nice ring to it. What do you think?'

'Oh, my god, did you talk to Finn?'

He frowned. 'Finn? No... Why?'

Heat rose in her cheeks. 'He was taking the piss a few months ago, and said the exact same thing.'

James looked delighted. 'Good man.'

They reached the main gates and the security guard let them through. Ahead of them, the roof of the bright pink Kangoo was taller than any other car and glowed in the darkness.

'Well, at least you'll never have to remember where you've parked it.'

'Another bonus I need to thank Tony for.' James went to the passenger side and opened the door for her. 'Your chariot awaits.'

She hesitated. 'Where are we going?'

'Wherever you want.'

'Elyse has moved out of my place.'

'I know.'

'Er...'

'I met Ryan at the fence yesterday.'

'And how did that go?'

'He challenged me to an arm-wrestling competition and I let him win.'

'What? Hang on... You "let" him win? Ryan's built like a brick shit house!'

James grinned. 'That made it more believable. But I would have let him win even if he was five-foot-five and couldn't punch his way out of a paper bag.'

'Why?'

He paused. 'Because it was the right thing to do. Ryan needed to prove to Elyse that she'd made the right decision by choosing him over me. And Elyse needed to see I'm not who or what she really wants.'

Estelle cupped his face. 'You're a good man.'

He rested his forehead on hers. 'I'm trying.'

'You don't need to try. You do it naturally.' She pressed a soft kiss to his lips. 'I love you.'

He started, as if shocked. 'You...?'

She smiled. 'I love you. Now please take me home so I can show you just how much.'

The car was filled with an expectant silence as James drove along the night-drenched country lanes towards the livery. Estelle snuck glances at him in the darkness, her awareness of him expanding as the inside of the car seemed to shrink.

With each yard they travelled, the pulse between her legs beat faster until she was swollen with pleasure to the point of painful frustration. She shifted in her seat and James's eyes briefly flicked from the road to hers. His expression was so powerful, so hot, so intent, that she gulped in a breath as if to keep her afloat.

'How wet are you?' he rumbled.

'Very.'

'Show me.'

'How?'

'Undo your trousers and put your finger in your pussy. Then let me taste you.'

Her heart was pounding so fast, she wasn't sure if she could stay conscious.

'Star?'

Hands trembling, she flicked the button on her jeans and tugged the zip down. Sliding her finger under the waistband of her pants, she ran it over her clit, sending a shiver through her.

'Yes,' James growled.

Angling her hips, she inched her middle finger inside herself. Everything was hot, tight and wet. Her eyes fluttered closed and she let out a shaky breath.

The car jerked forward, moving faster.

Pulling her hand out, she reached across the console and ran her middle finger along his lower lip.

His tongue darted out to capture it, then he sucked it into his mouth.

Memories of his mouth on her pussy slammed into her with such force her legs began to shake. She withdrew her hand, letting it drop to his cock.

'I need you,' she whispered.

'And you're going to get me. For as long as you want. I'm yours.'

Turning into the livery, he screeched to a stop outside her house. 'The dogs?'

'With Molly.'

'Good. I'm not in a sharing mood.'

Leaping out of the car, Estelle dashed to the front door, her key already in hand.

'You locked it?' James sounded surprised.

'I've been taking your advice.'

He nuzzled the back of her neck. 'First time for everything.'

She giggled, then managed to unlock the door and push it open.

James closed it behind her, slamming the top bolt across. 'Upstairs or right here?'

She made for the stairs. 'My bed.'

The sensation of him right behind her sent her heart tripping over itself. And when he slapped her backside, a flare of desire whooshed up her body. All she could think of was his body on hers, his cock pounding deep inside her, relieving the itch that nothing else could scratch.

Inside her room, James made short work of getting her naked. There were no kisses, no endearments, no touching or appreciation of her underwear. He stripped off her clothes as if they were on fire.

Then he stilled, his breath ragged as he took her in. His gaze raked across her with such intensity that goosebumps followed in its wake and her nipples hardened till they ached.

'God, I love you.' His voice was low, as if the words were a thought that had escaped.

'I—I love you too,' she stuttered.

For a moment, his expression was disbelieving and vulnerable, as if he couldn't quite believe her feelings met his own. Then he blinked, and the fire returned.

'Sit.'

Her legs gave way before her brain could protest, and she sat on the edge of the bed with a thump.

James dropped to his knees, hitched her legs over his shoulders, and buried his face in her pussy.

Estelle let out an incoherent cry as pleasure shot through her. It was as if her clit had been building a charge for days, and the touch of his tongue released it with a sudden crack of lightning.

Shaking, she grabbed handfuls of his hair, holding on for dear life as he licked, sucked and flicked her clit. His tongue was so fast she couldn't keep pace with the sensations. Feelings spun and splintered, her body twisting and tumbling, turning itself inside out as it hurtled towards the point of no return.

There was nothing she could do to stop it. She was at the crest of a wave as it thundered towards shore, and all she could do was wait for it to break.

James groaned into her pussy and the vibrations were the tipping point for an orgasm so sudden and so powerful, the breath was knocked from her lungs. Throwing back her head with a silent scream, the climax crashed through her, pummelling every cell with pleasure until she was drowning in it.

She clung to James's hair as he held her fast to the bed, anchoring herself to some form of reality as every muscle shuddered with sensation. Just as she felt she might pass out, the intensity began to ebb, and her breath returned in gasps.

'Oh my god, oh my god, oh my god.'

She thought James might let her catch her breath, but the flat of his tongue swept up her length, then he flicked the tip over her clit.

'Ah!' Her toes curled at the shock of pleasure.

He did it again. Then again, the time between each pass and flick getting shorter and shorter, until his tongue was vibrating faster than she could process and another orgasm coiled inside her. Lifting her hands from James's head, she rolled her hardened nipples between her fingers and thumbs. Electricity arced down to her core, lighting the touch paper of her climax.

'I'm gonna come,' she cried. 'I'm gonna come!'

His response was to thrust two fingers inside her, rubbing the tips against her G-spot as he sucked her clit hard into his mouth.

She screamed as blinding pleasure tore up her body. Convulsing on the bed, her pussy gushed as if to put out the fires scorching through every cell.

The aftershocks kept coming, but underneath them all, a

deeper seismic shift was occurring, cracking her open. The love she had for James was an ocean, vast and fathomless. Emotion swelled through her and she grabbed his hair, pulling him up so he was lying on her, then wrapped her arms and legs around him, never wanting to let go.

'I love you, and it's terrifying,' she whispered in his ear.

He huffed, then his head raised.

Estelle's heart skipped several beats, then restarted at double time. James looked like a fallen angel with fire in his eyes, gazing at her as if she were the beginning and end of his world.

He stroked a curl from her forehead. 'We can be terrified together.'

'But no-one else can know.'

He smiled. 'Most definitely not. Estelle Foxbrooke and James Hunter-Savage don't know the meaning of the word "fear". You eat horseshoes for breakfast, and I chow down on —what did you say last year? "The trampled remains of my enemies"?'

She grinned. 'Only when you've exhausted your supply of babies.'

'Ah yes, I remember now.'

'I'm so sorry I was such a dick to you.'

He kissed her brow. 'Don't be. It was fucking hot. I never thought being metaphorically kicked in the balls was such a turn on.'

'I promise I'll be nicer to you in the future.'

He shook his head. 'Don't make an effort to be anyone other than yourself. You're perfect just the way you are.'

Insecurity suddenly stabbed her stomach. 'Are you *sure* you're happy to live here?'

A smile lit up his face. 'Is that an invitation? I can bring my things over later today.'

'I mean, in Somerset!'

He raised an eyebrow.

'Oh, what the hell. In for a penny, in for a pound. Would you like to move in with me?'

'One hundred per cent. And am I allowed to loudly and obnoxiously tell everyone that you're my girlfriend?'

She frowned. '*How* obnoxiously?'

'Is that a challenge?'

A giggle burst out of her.

'After all,' he continued, 'I'm James Hunter-Savage. No other man at Conqueror has been nominated for "most objectionable colleague" more times than me.'

'Did all the nominations come from Henry?'

He grinned. 'Pretty much.'

'Thank you for speaking to him.'

'I'm glad I did. He's a really decent man, and I'll always regret not seeing that sooner.'

She shook her head. 'What's in the past is done now, and he's a very forgiving sort.'

'Well, if James two-point-zero can't win him over, then I do have an ace up my sleeve.'

Huh? 'What?'

He shrugged. 'Easy. I'll ask him to be the best man at our wedding.'

Estelle let out a shriek of laughter. 'Oh, my god! You *did* talk to Finn!'

James laughed. 'Did he suggest that? What a legend. I swear I haven't talked to him about us, but now I feel I owe him a beer for being on my side.'

She snorted. 'Finn's on *my* side.'

'And as I'm also on your side, I think that means he's on *our* side?'

'You're impossible.'

'And imperfect, but also improving?'

'Like a fine wine.'

'And don't forget, I'm also impressive.' He pressed the hard bulge of his cock against her.

'Hmmm…' She circled her hips onto it. 'You know you told me you hadn't had sex for over a year before me?'

'Ye-es?'

'Did you test afterwards?'

He nodded, light flaring in his eyes.

An excited thrill ran through her. 'I've never had sex without a condom before.'

He swallowed. 'Me neither.'

'I mean, I'm not going to get pregnant, so don't worry about that.'

'I'm not. But if you're ever up for it, I'd quite like to help produce the world's most beautiful children.'

Her chest tightened. 'Do you mean that?' she whispered.

He nodded. 'At the dinner party, I told you I'd always wanted to fall in love. That was true, but I've also always wanted kids. But only if that works for you. I want you more than anything else.'

Her eyes stung with tears. 'I really want children.'

His gaze was searching. 'Have you ever told anyone that before?'

'Not even Eveline,' she said quietly. 'I've always pretended I didn't even *like* kids, and that dogs were better. But I only said that because I didn't think I'd ever meet anyone.'

With his thumbs, he wiped the corners of her eyes. 'My Star. Whatever you want, I'm going to give it to you.'

Her heart squeezed. How had she got so lucky? Pulling his head to hers, she kissed him, her lips parting to allow his tongue to tangle with hers. Love and lust looped around each other, weaving into an unbreakable rope, binding her to him.

James shifted position, one hand finding her nipple. Desire shot down to her clit, and she moaned into his mouth.

His response was to kiss her harder, his tongue sweeping against hers with licks of fire that left her breathless. Her legs spread wider, her hips moving unconsciously, as if trying to find his cock.

She tore her mouth from his. 'Get naked and get in me.'

He leapt away, pulling off his clothes.

Estelle sat up, staring with unashamed admiration at the solid planes of his body, his rock-hard abs, and even harder cock. Reaching forward, she cupped his balls with one hand, tugging slightly, then ran her other up the length of his shaft.

A shiver ran through him, and he exhaled roughly. 'Fuck...'

Eyes locked on his, she licked his slit.

He inhaled a sharp breath, his hands in tight fists by his sides.

Still holding his gaze, she sucked the head into her mouth. The tension thrummed from his muscles against her skin.

She took him deeper, working his cock and rolling and tugging his balls.

'Estelle...' His expression was desperate, his lips parted, his eyes hooded and dark.

Holding her breath, she sank onto him.

'Jesus!' Jerking away, he leaned forward, hands tensed on his muscled thighs, then let out a tortured laugh. 'Are you *sure* you're not still trying to kill me?'

Scooting back on the bed, she spread her legs and opened her pussy to him. 'Want a ride up to heaven?'

He let out another laugh, then moved forward, pinning her to the bed and sucking down her neck.

'I think I'm already there,' he rumbled in between kisses, one hand moving between her legs and stroking her clit.

Desire pulsed through her, and she arched her body into his hand.

Then his mouth was on her breast, his tongue roughing over the sensitive tip till she thought she might pass out with pleasure. Running her hands into his hair, her fingers flexed as tingles danced across her skin. Another climax was building deep inside her, but she ached to come around his cock.

'James,' she panted, 'get inside me.'

He didn't seem to hear, continuing to lavish her with his tongue and fingers as if she was a goddess, and by showing her his utter devotion, he could save his soul.

Reaching down, she landed a stinging slap across his perfect backside.

He released her nipple with a pop and gave her a wolfish grin. 'I'm waiting for the magic word.'

'Now,' she hissed.

'That'll do.' Positioning himself between her legs, without any preamble, he pushed slowly and completely inside her.

'Oh! Oh! Oh my god!' she gasped as everything stretched and sparkled.

Bracing his forearms on either side of her head, he took a ragged breath, then lowered his mouth to her ear. 'Isn't that what you wanted?'

She struggled to form words as she adjusted to his size.

'I can always pull out,' he said, starting to withdraw.

She slapped his arse again. 'Don't you dare. I want you to fuck me within an inch of my life.'

He chuckled. 'Maybe later.'

'What?'

'Right now, I want to do something that might break both of us.'

'And that is...?'

He raised his head. 'I want to make love to you.'

She blinked rapidly, her throat tightening.

'And gaze into your eyes until I drown in them.'

Her heart was going to burst. *This man...*

'When I'm inside you, it feels like I might die with how much I love you.'

There was no flippant comment to make in reply. His raw emotion matched her own.

His body and gaze pinned her to the bed. 'I need you to know how much you mean to me. I'm yours, Estelle. Completely.'

'Why does this feel like the scariest thing I've ever done?' she whispered.

'Because we're leaping into the unknown and hoping the other person will be there to catch us.'

Memories of tumbling over the banister at the Winter Ball crashed through her mind.

Leaning down, James brushed a kiss over her lips. 'I've got you,' he murmured. 'I'll never let you fall.'

Estelle wrapped her legs around the back of his and her arms around his broad back, clinging to him like a limpet.

'I've got you.' He withdrew an inch then slowly buried himself deep inside her again.

The sensations were otherworldly, his cock filling her body and touching her soul. Nothing had ever felt so raw, so intimate, so right.

Raising himself onto his hands, James's eyes locked on hers as he undulated his hips, slowly thrusting, over and over again. Each time he filled her, pleasure shivered across her skin and her heart beat faster. As he held her gaze, she saw his love, his passion, and the knife edge he was on as he tried to hold back the tide of his climax.

Everything else fell away apart from an awareness of him,

the heat of his body, his thick cock, the love for her pouring off him in waves.

Her orgasm was spiralling up inside her, but it didn't feel like the bright sparks and colours of a firework. It felt like she was watching the sun go supernova, filling the sky, expanding until she knew it would utterly obliterate her.

Gulping in a breath, she shook with emotion. It was too much. She couldn't do it.

'Stay with me, Star,' James said, the tendons in his neck taut, his hips thrusting faster.

She forced her eyes to stay open, her breath turning into cries as she began dissolving into light.

'I love you,' he murmured. 'I love you, I love you, I love you.'

The orgasm hit with a blinding flash so powerful, yet so painfully sweet, that she sobbed, her body trembling.

His arms tightened, holding her to him as his cock continued to move, pushing more pleasure through her.

'I love you,' she gasped. 'I love you so much.'

Through the fog of feeling, she could sense his restraint, how hard he was inside her as he kept up his rhythm. Taking a deep breath, she brought her hands to the sides of his face.

'I love you, James.'

He let out a strangled cry, and she bucked her pelvis, taking him deeper.

'Estelle—'

'I've got you. I love you.'

His gaze was overflowing with emotion, his muscles tensing tighter, his hips jerking faster. He looked anguished, as if he was trying to hold back, but locked into a rollercoaster.

'I want you to come.' She squeezed tighter around him. 'Come inside me.'

Her words were the last straw. He let go, pounding her into the bed, roaring with his release as his body shook above her.

He was fighting for air, clutching her to him as if she was the only person who could save him.

'I love you,' she whispered in his ear.

He took a shuddering breath, then covered her with kisses, murmuring how much he loved her, how perfect she was, saying her name over and over.

She clenched her jaw to keep tears from spilling out.

'Don't cry, baby.' James stroked her cheek. 'I want you to be happy.'

'I *am* happy, you numpty,' she sobbed. 'I've never been this bloody happy before.'

His eyes were shining as he rolled onto his side, taking her with him. His body was so big compared to hers that she felt safe and cocooned in his arms.

'Can I get you a tissue?'

She sniffed. 'For my nose, or the prodigious amounts of your come that's now seeping out of me?'

Throwing back his head, he laughed. 'Are we going to argue about who sleeps in the wet patch?'

She gave him a withering look. 'Do I need to remind you there's a shotgun under the bed?'

Her words only seemed to make him happier. 'You don't scare me anymore.'

'Really? How very disappointing.'

'Well, you failed to hit my nuts with the arrow, your attack-hounds humped me, and you missed the last time you pointed your shotgun my way. I think I'm safe.' He held her tighter. 'And I'd put money on the fact that you were more annoyed with the unicorn slippers than I was.'

'Humph.'

'I was wondering... What are you doing the week after next?'

She frowned. 'I suppose more of the festival debriefing and disassembling. Why?'

'Well, I've booked a five-night stay in a fancy hotel in Bognor Regis and wondered if you wanted to come with me?'

She sat up. 'What?'

'Well, you mentioned you'd like to go on holiday and suggested Bognor or Saint Barts. Unfortunately, I don't have another sports car to flog, so this year the Caribbean is out. However, I've learnt that Bognor is the UK's sunniest town and the home of sea views and coastal panoramas, where the natural backdrop and unspoilt charm inspire blue-sky thinking and bright ideas.'

'Where on *earth* did you learn that?'

'A website called, "Love Bognor Regis".'

She snorted.

'So, anyway,' he continued, 'I thought we could run it through the books as a team-building event.'

'Who's coming?'

'You, multiple times a day. And me, of course, to supply the orgasms.'

Estelle thought of all the work they still had to do. 'But—'

'It's fine. We can work next week on the urgent stuff, then leave Carly in charge. And I'm sure Molly wouldn't mind having Chester and Joy again?'

She squealed inside. When was the last time she'd been on holiday? 'Are you sure?'

'Ninety-nine per cent.'

'And the other one per cent?'

'Would rather we were in Saint Barts.'

She burst out laughing. 'Okay, I'm sold. Bognor Regis it is. Whose car are we going in?'

'The cleanest and most reliable.'

'Oh. So, I'd better get the Defender booked in for a full service and valet then.'

He grinned. 'Sounds like a plan. Although...'

'Ye-es?'

He pulled her onto his chest. 'If I'm with you, I don't give a shit about being seen in my car.'

'Really?'

'Yeah, I'm just going to call you "Barb" really loudly whenever we're in it.'

'Jamesy-boy, you're going down.' She pummelled his chest as he laughed.

He flipped her onto her back, caught her wrists and held her arms over her head, kissing her until she was moaning and writhing in his arms.

'I love you,' he murmured. 'I fucking love you.'

Spreading her legs, she angled her hips up and he pushed inside her.

His mouth found hers again and she rubbed her breasts against his chest, moaning with pleasure.

As their bodies moved together, her soul sang. This was a completeness she'd never known before, with someone who surprised and challenged her at every turn. For a man she'd thought was wrong on every level, there was now no doubt in her mind that for her, James Hunter-Savage was one hundred per cent right.

EPILOGUE

Estelle gazed down, utterly captivated, as a tiny hand curled around her finger and two dark eyes held hers. 'Just look at him,' she whispered to James. 'Isn't he perfect?'

The three of them were alone in the room, but James still glanced over his shoulder at the closed door.

'You want my honest opinion?' he asked under his breath.

'No, I do not,' she hissed.

'His face is all squished, he's too fragile for his own good, and so far all he's done is sleep and poop, sometimes at the same time. Imagine if I did that? You'd hit the roof.'

Estelle giggled.

'Our babies are going to be infinitely superior. I expect our first child to be born wielding a shotgun and reciting the periodic table.'

She snorted. 'Are you going to start playing Mozart to my belly the second I'm up the duff?'

'Well, something's got to balance out the Spice Girls.'

'Oi! They're the Jane Austen of pop.'

'Have you told Libby your theory?'

'Not yet, but I'm sure at the next living history tour at the manor, she'll get the punters dancing a quadrille to "Spice Up Your Life".'

James grinned. 'Now that I *have* to see.'

The door opened and Eveline entered the room. 'How's he doing? Still alive?'

'Yes,' Estelle replied. 'I haven't let James anywhere near him, so he's perfectly safe.'

Eveline gave her a look. 'Maybe James would like to hold him?'

He took a step back. 'I'm fine, thank you. I'll just admire him from over here.'

'Nonsense,' Estelle stood and held the baby out. 'Robert needs to get used to his godmother's boyfriend.'

James glanced uncertainly at Eveline.

'Go on,' she said encouragingly. 'Just support his head and keep him vaguely upright.'

James carefully took the baby, holding him in the crook of one of his massive arms.

Robert opened his eyes and stared at him.

'Hello, little man,' James said softly.

Robert cooed and waved an arm.

James held out a finger for the baby to grab, then kissed the back of his tiny hand.

Eveline sighed happily, and Estelle's heart and ovaries went into meltdown.

'Right then,' Eveline said. 'Now he's settled, Estelle, can you give me a hand bringing the tea things through?'

'You're leaving me with him?' James asked, sounding panicked.

'Four minutes, tops,' Eveline replied. 'Do you think you have the strength to hold him for that long?'

James raised an eyebrow and flexed his arms.

Robert giggled.

Estelle gasped. 'You made him laugh!'

'What can I say?' James replied smugly. 'I'm a funny guy.'

Eveline giggled.

Estelle rolled her eyes. 'Not you, too?' Taking Eveline's arm, she dragged her toward the door of the rectory living room. 'My godson was laughing *at* you, not *with* you, Mrs Doubtfire,' she called to James over her shoulder.

He winked at her as she left, and her heart flip-flopped in her chest.

'THANK YOU FOR LOOKING AFTER HIM WHILST I WENT TO the loo,' Eveline said to Estelle as they made their way through the rectory. 'Having a stress-free wee is such a treat.'

Estelle laughed. 'Now things have quietened down a bit, you can call on us for baby-sitting duties whenever you need.'

Entering the kitchen, Eveline flicked the kettle on. 'Thank you, but at the moment Jack is so hands on, I've been able to rest more than I thought I'd be able to.'

'Where is he now?'

'AA meeting. He'll be back soon.' Eveline took the lid off a plastic box to reveal a frosted carrot cake.

'Oh, yum,' Estelle said, her mouth watering. 'Did Jack make it?'

'Yes,' Eveline replied, a proud smile on her face. 'It's the same one that won him the "cake baked by a gentleman" category at the village fete.'

'Did you help?'

She shook her head. 'The only credit I'm taking is that it's my recipe.'

Estelle took plates from a cupboard and put them on a tray whilst Eveline made a pot of tea.

'Has baby Robert met his namesake yet?'

'Last week. We took him over to Foxbrooke Haven to meet Robert and Shirley for the first time.' Eveline's eyes filled with happy tears. 'We asked them to be official grandparents.'

'Oh, my god.' Estelle's hand covered her heart. The older Robert had lived a life alone and abroad, working on remote chemical plants. Now, a few months after moving into the assisted living facility at the edge of the village, he'd married one of the residents and had an unofficial grandson. 'Did they cry?'

Eveline nodded. 'We were all rather overcome, to be honest. The only person in the room who didn't shed a tear was the baby.'

Estelle wiped the corners of her eyes. 'That's beautiful.'

'It was.' Eveline sighed happily. 'My life is so rich with blessings.'

Estelle's gaze went to the kitchen door, imagining James down the hallway with Robert. 'As is mine.'

'Do you remember what you said to me before Christmas about your New Year's resolutions?' Eveline asked, putting the cake on the tray.

'No... And judging by your mischievous expression, I'm guessing that accidentally-on-purpose murdering my nemesis, now boyfriend, was at the top of the list?'

Eveline's eyes were sparkling. 'You told me you were going to get laid, and that James was going down. I'm glad to see that both of your wishes have come true...'

Estelle's mouth dropped open. 'Eveline Newton! You naughty girl! And that reminds me, I've got a bone to pick with you. Did you know what you were doing when you put me and James together at Sausage Saturday? All that "you hold the roll open nice and wide, and James, you can stick your sausage in" nonsense?'

Eveline picked up the tray with the cake and plates. 'I thought it might make you think about James's other attributes,' she replied with a grin. 'Can you carry the teapot?' Going to the door, she paused, a frown on her face. 'Although, were the sausages a comparable size? I'm assuming James's "BDE" is literal, not just metaphorical?'

'Will you behave?!'

Eveline winked. 'I'll take that as a yes, then.'

'JAMES! M'BOY!' ARTHUR CRIED. 'AND MY DARLING ESTELLE. Come in, come in!' He pulled them in for a hug as they passed through the front doors of Foxbrooke Manor. 'How's little Robert? Still as scrumptious as ever?'

'Gorgeous,' Estelle replied.

'I've given up eating babies, so I'm afraid I can't comment,' James said.

Arthur roared with laughter. 'Just wait till you have your own. God, I used to love their fat little legs. Summer was the chunkiest monkey of them all. We used to have to run a finger through her neck folds to look for food that had got lost.'

'What was that?' Summer asked as she entered the hall.

'Just telling them how deliciously squidgy you were as a baby, darling,' he replied. 'It only seems like yesterday.'

Summer rolled her eyes and glanced at Estelle and James. 'Run, whilst you can,' she murmured. 'Or he'll be hassling you for—'

'When are you going to give me grandchildren?' Arthur asked, a frown on his face, as if Estelle and James were setting out to offend him by not immediately procreating.

'Dad! We've been together—what? Three weeks?'

'And? Your Mom conceived you and Henry three *days* after we met. Chop chop!'

'I think we're going to wait a bit,' James said.

Arthur let out a frustrated huff, then went to answer the front door. 'Kev 'n' Bev! Come in! I was just asking Estelle and James when they were planning on giving us grandchildren.'

Beverley's eyes opened wide as she gazed at Estelle. 'Oh, babe, you gonna do it?'

'Shall we go through for dinner?' Summer asked brightly.

'Yes, great idea,' Estelle replied, dragging James down the corridor after her youngest sister.

'If you think you've got it bad, you should hear what Dad says to Henry and Libby,' Summer said in a low voice. 'He bought Henry an infrared lamp to shine on his bollocks to boost sperm production.'

'But they're not even trying for kids.'

'I know, but I think he's hoping the more annoying he is, the greater the chance they'll get pregnant just to shut him up.'

Estelle glanced at James. 'Sorry.'

'Don't be. Your dad's hilarious. Embarrassing your kids is one of the most important jobs for a parent. I'm taking notes for the future.'

They went through into the dining room, where Estelle's mom and mammy were, along with Connor, Leo, Willow, Henry, and Libby.

'Darlings!' Dervla darted forward to embrace them.

Estelle blinked as James hugged her mothers and siblings, remembering how he'd been public enemy number one only a few months ago.

'And Kevin and Beverley,' Vivienne said as James's parents entered the room. 'Welcome!'

Estelle hugged her twin. 'Infrared light for your balls?'

Henry sighed. 'I thought Eveline giving birth to Robert

might distract Dad for a bit, but it's made him even worse. I don't think he'll be happy until he's got so many grandkids he can't remember their names.'

He reached past Estelle to shake James's hand. 'I apologise for our father. Once he gets going, there's no off-switch.'

James's smile was affable. 'No need. My mum has been secretly ordering baby stuff online, but the boxes keep getting delivered to the office.'

Henry shook his head. 'They're relentless. Just make sure you don't accept any of Mammy's herbal teas. Either her eyesight's going, or she thinks magic mushrooms will miraculously make a baby turn up in the cabbage patch.'

Libby came to Henry's side and hugged him. 'Henry drank a cup a couple of months ago and spent all day giggling and pretending to be a squirrel.'

Estelle snorted. 'I'd pay to see that.'

Henry managed a rueful smile. 'It was an experience, and not one I'm intending to repeat.'

'Din-dins!' Arthur shouted. 'Take your seats!' Pulling a walkie-talkie from a patchwork bag, he pressed the call button. 'Foxbrooke One to the kitchen, over!'

There was a crackle, then Perry spoke. 'Roger that, Foxbrooke One. Red Leader on standby, over.'

'Roger, roger, jammy dodger, Red Leader. All present, correct and ready for nosh. Over!'

'Roger that, Foxbrooke One. Incoming. Over.'

Estelle took her seat next to James, and he reached for her hand. A current ran up her arm and fizzed through her body.

'I love you,' she whispered.

His smile made him even more heart-stoppingly gorgeous. 'And I love you more.'

'Where's Sophia?' Dervla asked. 'I thought she was coming too?'

Kev pulled a face. 'She's buggered off to an ashram.'

'Just for a month,' Bev quickly added. 'She needed a break.'

'I went to an ashram once,' Arthur said. 'Ended up in charge of the food. Had a bally marvellous time until they kicked me out for fornicating. In Puna, is she?'

'Nah,' Kev replied. 'The ashram's in the Caribbean.'

'Ooh! Very nice.' Arthur turned to Estelle. 'Is that where Isaac is? You know, the yoga chappie you used to fancy.'

Estelle gritted her teeth, mortified that her pointless crush had been so obvious. 'No, he's in India with his guru at the moment, but the ashram Sophia is at is part of the same organisation.'

'Ah, jolly good,' Arthur said, then stood as Perry entered, pushing a trolley of food. 'Let me help you with that.' He lifted dishes onto the table. 'It's cottage pie night, with sticky toffee pudding and ice cream for afters. Tuck in!'

Estelle was glad she and James were seated at the far end of the table with Henry and Libby, her siblings serving as a buffer between them and their parents. And as the food was always delicious, it ensured her dad was kept quiet for a few minutes.

'How are things going with BDE?' Henry asked them after they'd filled their plates and started eating.

'We're rebranding,' Estelle said quietly.

Libby leaned in. 'BDE?'

She nodded. 'Kevin's not happy because he's still got hundreds of t-shirts with aubergine emojis on them, but he's going to sell them to Dad at cost price to give away at his sex parties.'

'Sounds like the best place for them,' Libby said with a grin. 'So, what's the new name?'

Estelle glanced at James and he nodded. 'We've narrowed it down to two. Both are James's ideas. Either "Star Fox Entertainment", or "Savage Fox Entertainment".'

'Ooh! Love them! Which one's your favourite?' Libby asked her.

'Savage Fox. Because it's got something from both of us.'

James gazed at her and her face pricked with heat. He was looking at her as if he wasn't sure whether to recite a love poem in honour of her beauty, or throw her over his shoulder and carry her to bed.

Libby's eyes flicked between them as the air became super-charged. 'So, er, James, apart from the branding, how is the business side of things going?'

James blinked as if woken from an extremely erotic dream, then turned to her. 'Good. It'll take another successful festival to get it truly back in the black, but we've learnt so much from running this one, I'm confident next year's will turn a healthy profit.'

'And UberGraft are going to perform again?'

He nodded. 'All thanks to Estelle. Having them attached will help get other high-profile acts onboard.'

'Do you have any other projects for next year, apart from the Jane Austen festival in the spring?' Henry asked.

'A couple of small parties, but that's it. I want to focus on the festivals to make them the best they can be.'

'Austenfest is going to be amazing!' Libby said. 'And I've had another brilliant idea!'

James caught Henry's eye and a look of panic flashed across both their features.

'Er, that sounds wonderful,' Henry said, his tone conveying the opposite thought. 'What did you have in mind?'

'Well,' she began, her face shining with excitement, 'I want to build a buzz by getting people to consider whether they're Team Darcy or Team Wickham. I was thinking of hanging two huge banners on the outside of the manor with #TeamDarcy and #TeamWickham on them.'

Estelle glanced at her brother. He was scratching his fingers into his short curls as if worried.

'And would there be anything else on these banners?' he asked, clearly hoping his fiancée's answer would be 'no'.

Libby's cheeks pinked. 'You dressed as Darcy will be on one, and I was hoping James would play Wickham for the other.'

'And would that be the end of this particular thought? Or do you have any other ideas for us?'

'Um...'

'Who's better? Darcy or Wickham?' James asked her.

'Well...'

'Darcy,' Estelle said.

James looked affronted. 'So, Henry's got a head start?'

'It's not a competition,' Libby said quickly.

'Yes, it is,' Estelle said, a grin spreading across her face at James's frown and her brother's obvious discomfort.

James leaned back in his chair, manspreading to the max. 'I'll do it.'

'You will?' Libby asked, hope in her eyes.

'Yeah, on one condition.'

'Ye-es?'

'We're both wearing wet shirts.'

Estelle snorted with laughter as Henry dropped his chin to his chest with a sigh.

'Yes, yes, yes, yes, yes!' Libby squealed. 'This is going to be amazing!'

'How about it, Henry?' James asked, bringing his arms down and flexing. 'A little bit of healthy competition for a good cause?'

Henry mirrored his stance. 'I warn you, I've been working out more than normal. You might not catch me up.'

Estelle grinned at their peacocking, and the look on Libby's face as if she was on the verge of climaxing.

James reached across the table and shook Henry's hand. 'Challenge accepted.'

'YOU DON'T MIND PLAYING THE BAD GUY?' ESTELLE ASKED James as they strolled away from the manor a few hours later, hand-in-hand. The night air was warm, and the leaves glowed gold under the streetlights.

He shook his head. 'It's my chance to rehabilitate Wickham. Anyway, people love a reformed rake, and the greater their redemption, the more they love them.' He smiled. 'And bad guys are also way sexier than good guys.'

She smiled, her heart full. 'You're sexier now I know you're a good guy.'

He gazed at her, a look of utter contentment on his face. 'You know, I've been in Foxbrooke over a year now.'

Estelle thought back to everything that had happened since then. It seemed like a lifetime ago.

'I remember the first time I ever met you. You called me "Foxy lady".'

'Which, of course, you are. And you told me I had to stay away from your family if I knew what was good for me.'

She smirked. 'And look how that commandment turned out.'

James stopped and pulled her to him. Lowering his head, he grazed her lips with a kiss.

'I think it's all worked out perfectly,' he murmured. 'The perfect happy ending for ninety-nine per cent perfect people.'

'What's the one per cent we're missing?'

'I always like to give myself room for improvement.'

'You could make more of an effort to pretend to like the Spice Girls?'

He kissed her again. 'I'll see what I can do.'

'So, now we've had our happy ending, what happens next?'

He smiled. 'We have some more. Starting with tonight. How about we go home, and I give you a massage followed by multiple happy endings?'

She wrapped her arms around the back of his neck. 'Sounds perfect.'

'Just like you.'

Suddenly, James lifted her into his arms.

'What are you doing?'

'Reminding the residents of Foxbrooke that I am the strongest, most virile, and best boyfriend ever to walk the earth.'

She giggled. 'And modest with it. You do know there's no-one about to see you?'

'Dammit,' he replied, striding faster towards the manor's gates. 'I'll have to do a lap of the high street.' He smirked. 'And anyway, I'm in practice for Austenfest. If there's going to be a "carrying a beautiful woman through the countryside" race, then I'm intending to win it.'

'Do you always have to win?'

He pulled a face. 'Of course.' His features softened. 'Although I'm with Estelle Foxbrooke, so I've won already. Nothing can top that.' His gaze darkened. 'And "winning" doesn't always mean I come first...'

She smothered her smile. 'I don't understand.'

Pulling a set of keys from his pocket, he zapped the car unlocked. 'Give me fifteen minutes to get us home and I'll show you exactly what I mean.'

She sighed happily. 'Sounds like a plan.'

· · ·

The End

෨෩

Thank you so much for reading The Upper Crush! If you want to read Estelle and James's romantic **extended epilogue** at a very special competition in Poland, then join my newsletter list at
www.eviealexanderauthor.com/subscribe

෨෩

Isaac and Sophia's story is up next in The Love Position...

Get The Love Position in print, audio, or eBook format now from **www.eviealexanderbooks.com**

REVIEW THE UPPER CRUSH
WRITE A REVIEW & MAKE MY DAY!

Thank you so much for reading The Upper Crush! I hope you enjoyed reading it as much as I enjoyed writing it!

Even if just a few lines (or star rating), writing a review is the most amazing thing you can do! It helps people find my books, and lets them know what you loved about them.

You can review The Upper Crush at:
Apple
Amazon
Bookbub
Goodreads
Kobo
Barnes & Noble
Google Play

And any other storefront or platform you use!

And, if you want to share more about The Upper Crush on social media or your blog, please **help yourself to our library of graphics, elements and more by going to**

www.eviealexanderauthor.com/the-upper-crush/

Thank you!

Evie ♡

READ THE LOVE POSITION

Next up is Sophia and Isaac's story!

THE LOVE POSITION
His commitment to celibacy just got complicated...

Archaeologist Sophia Hunter-Savage's life is in ruins. After her groundbreaking work is stolen and her heart shattered, she turns to yoga to calm her anxiety. However, the irresistibly hot instructor leaves her breathless.

Isaac Hayward has it all figured out: yoga, meditation, and a firm vow of chastity. But his peace unravels when Sophia, the most distracting woman he's ever met, walks into his class.

Determined to stay on his spiritual path, Isaac runs to an ashram in the Caribbean. But when Sophia turns up, their forbidden attraction becomes impossible to ignore.

Stranded together as a tropical storm rolls in, with only one room – and one bed – can Isaac resist temptation, or will he break the biggest vow he's ever made?

The Love Position *is a sizzlingly steamy, forbidden-love, standalone romantic comedy with a shy academic bringing the hottest yoga instructor in the world to his knees. No cheating, no cliffhanger – just all the lols, all the feels, and a perfect happy ending guaranteed!*

Get The Love Position in print, audio, or eBook format now from www.eviealexanderbooks.com

NEWSLETTER SIGN-UP

Want to read Estelle and James's dramatic and romantic extended epilogue at a very special competition in Poland? Sign up to my newsletter to get it today, plus so much more...

In my newsletter you get Evie news before anyone else, as well as exclusive content and goodies.

Newsletter subscribers are my extra special friends, and get everything from bonus epilogues, 19,000 words of deleted sex scenes from Highland and Hollywood Games, free stories, free audiobooks, extracts from my current work-in-progress, and exclusive offers and giveaways.

Sign up now!

www.eviealexanderauthor.com/subscribe/

SEX INDEX
(AKA THE GOOD BITS)

There have been many great contributions to the world of literature. Gutenberg invented the printing press, Shakespeare invented romantic comedy, and J K Rowling invented Harry Potter. However, all of these achievements pale into insignificance compared to my contribution – the sex index.

Using this sex index, you can easily find the steamier moments from The Upper Crush. Enjoy...

Page 272 – Show me how you want to be kissed
Page 309 – Please don't shoot my dick off
Page 379 – It's time for my birthday present...
Page 475 – This is what love feels like

And if that wasn't enough, don't forget I've got nineteen thousand words of super-hot deleted sex scenes from Highland and Hollywood Games as well as Estelle and James's extended epilogue available exclusively for newsletter subscribers.

If you want some extra action, then sign up to my newsletter today!

www.eviealexanderauthor.com/subscribe/

ACKNOWLEDGMENTS

Whoop whoop! It's the acknowledgements! Here's the place I get to thank all the amazing people who have helped me get this book to publication.

This book is dedicated to Diana Hayward, who will be forever known as 'Mrs' Hayward to me. There's no particular reason why The Upper Crush is dedicated to her, however I always knew at least one of my books would be.

Mrs Hayward taught me at primary school and recognised I had a love of storytelling. When I was about eight, she gave me a notebook to write down all my stories and was the first non-family member to support and encourage my writing. At the time I didn't know how significant this would be, but I know now her belief helped me find the confidence to get to where I am today.

I stayed in touch with Mrs Hayward after she moved house and left our primary school. She came to my wedding and now knows my daughter. On our last visit she showed Elway the letters I'd written to her over the years, including one with a coin stuck on with sellotape for her to spend on her holidays...

We often don't know how the relationships we have with people will impact our lives, however Mrs Hayward's kindness to me as an eight-year-old helped me write this book, the ones that came before it, and the ones I have yet to write.

She is one of the kindest, sweetest people in the world and I am truly blessed to know her.

In terms of research into the organisation of festivals, massive thanks go to Will Angeloro, aka the 'Deli Llama'. He's spent many years as a musician, sound engineer, festival organiser and more. He very kindly gave up his precious (and extremely limited) time just before Glastonbury to tell me what goes into making a festival work and what can go spectacularly wrong. From exploding toilets to sinking stages, from fence jumpers to divas, he's seen it all and gave me so much insight and inspiration for this book.

Thanks as ever go to my alpha reader, Pash Baker, and my epic editing team - Margaret Amatt and Mike AF. Thank you to Matt Wellsted for designing this wonderful cover and Mark Karasick for taking such fabulous photos of me.

Thank you to my sensitivity readers, in particular Olivia Spring and the amazing Tori Ross, and thank you to Jude and Mark for checking my Italian!

My team at Emlin Press: Victoria, Mandy, and Liezl. Thank you for doing everything I can't, won't, or don't have time for. Thank you for tolerating my foul mouth, laughing at my unfunny jokes and sticking around.

Thank you to my husband—the best decision I've ever made, and to my daughter—the best luck I've ever had. I love you both to the ends of the multiverse and back.

And last, but by no means least, I want to thank my fabulous ARC team, the incredible online community of book lovers and, once again, YOU, the reader. Thank you for your continued support and for reading the third book in the Foxbrooke series. Each time you read my books, write me a review and recommend me in countless different ways, my heart gets a little fuller. Thank you!

Evie ♥

PS - I love, love, LOVE hearing from my readers, so please get in touch via email or social media to ask me anything or just tell me about your day!

hard truths. Can they find a future together, or will their love remain
a Highland fling?

Tropes

Small Town, Dark Secrets, Bodyguard/Actress, Forced Proximity,
Alpha-roll hero, Dating Game

MUSICAL GAMES

After lying to a Hollywood megastar, Sam needs Jamie to write an
album with her in just ten days He's got the voice of an angel and the
body of a god, but fame is the last thing on his mind. Will he help
make her dreams come true?

Tropes

Small Town, Grumpy/Sunshine, Male Virgin, Cinnamon Roll Hero,
Opposites Attract, Fish-out-of-Water, Forced Proximity

WEDDING GAMES

Rory and Zoe want to get married. Not easy when their mothers are
mortal enemies and Rory's step-father is a Hollywood star with a
death wish. Can they unravel the tangles in time to tie the knot, or is
eloping the only answer? Get ready for Scotland's wedding of the year!

Tropes

Small Town, Grumpy/Sunshine, Opposites Attract, Soulmates, Fish-
out-of-Water

CHRISTMAS GAMES

Having a baby's easy, right? Until wayward in-laws, an out-of-control
cow and mad Santa get in the way. All Rory and Zoe want is a relaxing
Christmas before their baby arrives, but straightforward is not their
style...

Tropes

Small Town, Grumpy/Sunshine, Opposites Attract, Soulmates, Fish-

❧

THE FOXBROOKE SERIES

ONE NIGHT IN FOXBROOKE

When chef Ben 'Kenobi' Walker gets the call to help save a VIP dinner at Foxbrooke Manor, he doesn't expect to run into old flame Leia Perry. She's all grown up and even more attractive than when they were teenagers – but she hasn't forgotten what happened ten years ago, and she *definitely* hasn't forgiven him. Will one night give Ben the second chance he needs to prove himself and win back Leia's heart?

Tropes

Small Town, Second Chance, Return to Hometown, Enemies-to-Lovers, Bet, Brother's Best Friend, Work Colleagues, Forced Proximity, First Love, Reverse Grumpy-Sunshine, Opposites Attract

LOVE AD LIB

Shy and reserved Lord Henry Foxbrooke needs a fake girlfriend. Free-spirited actress Libby Fletcher needs a job. But when they arrive in Somerset for Henry's birthday celebrations, neither are prepared for their reception. As friendship blurs and faking it starts to feel a little too real, disaster strikes. Can Libby and Henry stick to the script, or has their entire act just bombed?

Tropes

Small Town, Fake Dating, Grumpy/Sunshine, Opposites Attract, One Bed, Different Worlds, Fish-out-of-Water

AN UNHOLY AFFAIR

Gorgeous Jack Newton has fallen in love with Eveline Shaw. But she's a female vicar dreaming of marriage and kids, and he's a male escort heading out of town. Can Jack show Eveline heaven and keep his secret safe, or are they both headed straight for hell?

Tropes

Small Town, Forbidden Love, Love at First Sight, Sworn off a Relationship, Priest, Different Worlds, Opposites Attract, Dark Secret

THE UPPER CRUSH

James Hunter-Savage is a cocky city boy who isn't used to anyone else taking the reins. Lady Estelle Foxbrooke is a fiery country girl who's about to show him who's boss. Can they learn to fight for love rather than with each other, or will their love hate relationship destroy everything they're working for?

Tropes

Small Town, Enemies-to-Lovers, Alpha Hero, Love/Hate, Playboy in Love, Different Worlds, Workplace Romance, Fake Dating

THE LOVE POSITION

Beautiful academic, Sophia Hunter-Savage, has run away to an ashram to reinvent herself. Hot yoga teacher, Isaac Hayward, has left town to avoid the only woman able to tempt him off the spiritual path.

But karma sucks.

Now Isaac's teaching Sophia and they're finding themselves in all kinds of unexpected positions. Will their forbidden love bring inner peace and happiness, or end in a tangled mess?

Tropes

Forbidden Love, Opposites Attract, Teacher/Student, Sworn off a Relationship, Forced Proximity, Love at First Sight, Different Worlds, Fish-out-of-Water

CHRISTMAS OFF SCRIPT

Best friends, Leo Foxbrooke and Ella Chamberlain, have never been single at the same time. Until now... Playing Cinderella and Prince Charming in the Christmas pantomime, their on-stage chemistry kindles an unexpected spark behind the scenes. Can they rewrite their friendship this festive season and finally unwrap true love?

Tropes

Small Town, Friends-to-Lovers, Best Friend's Ex, Oblivious to Love, Unrequited Love, Fake Relationship

ONE NIGHT ONLY

Pop star Avery Taylor craves a break from her public life, and a one-night stand with a stranger feels like the perfect escape. A year later, while recovering from an injury, she's stunned to find her nurse is Connor Foxbrooke, the man who touched her soul that night. Avery is ready to break the rules for love, but Connor, who values his quiet life, fears heartbreak. With Avery set to return to the spotlight as soon as she's recovered, can they bridge their worlds and turn their one night into forever?

Tropes

Second-Chance, Mistaken Identity, One Night Stand, Different Worlds, Opposites Attract, Injury, Forced Proximity, Fish-out-of-Water, Celebrity, Pop Star, Small Town

RIGHTING MR WRONG

Mooning a party of nuns is bad for anyone, but for TV star Aiden Wilder, it's catastrophic. Enter Willow Foxbrooke, a quiet PR worker who's tasked with saving his reputation through a fake relationship. As Willow teaches him how to recover his image, they start to fall for each other. But how can true love grow from something that was never real to begin with?

Tropes

Small Town, Fake Dating, Grumpy/Sunshine, Celebrity, Opposites Attract, Different Worlds, Fish-out-of-Water

UNDER THE INFLUENCER

Sunny Summer Foxbrooke's career as an Influencer is over. Now she's forced to work with grumpy Finn Oakley, the man who's avoided her for years. Will Finn finally return her love, or will she always just be his best friend's little sister?

Tropes

Brother's best friend, Grumpy/Sunshine, Beauty and the Beast, Age Gap, Unrequited Love, Rivals, Different Worlds, All Grown Up, Small Town

By Evie Alexander and Kelly Kay

EVIE & KELLY'S HOLIDAY DISASTERS SERIES

Evie and Kelly's Holiday Disasters are a series of hot and hilarious romantic comedies with interconnected characters, focusing on one holiday and one trope at a time.

CUPID CALAMITY

Featuring **Animal Attraction** & **Stupid Cupid**

Patrick and Sabina have ditched their blind dates for each other. Ben's fighting a crazed chimp for Laurie's love. Insta-love meets insta-disaster in these laugh-out-loud Valentine's day novellas.

COOKOUT CARNAGE

Featuring **Off With a Bang** & **Up in Smoke**

Cute farm boy Jonathan clings to a love ideal, blissfully ignoring what the universe has planned, while keeping track of his pet pig. Posh Brit follows his heart into the American Midwest in search of Sherilyn, his digital dream love.

CHRISTMAS CHAOS

Featuring **No way in a Manger** & **No Crib and No Bed**

In Scotland, Zoe and Rory attempt to have a civilised and respectable rite of passage, but straightforward is not their style. In Sonoma, Bax and Tabi attempt to throw a meaningful Christmas celebration. But there are too many people involved and it's nothing like they expect.

Get Evie's books in all formats as well as special offers, early releases, and exclusive deals direct from her website:

www.eviealexanderbooks.com

ABOUT THE AUTHOR

Evie Alexander is a multi-award-winning author of sexy romantic comedies, blending snort-laugh humour and panty-melting chemistry into unputdownable stories that will steal your heart.

When she's not dreaming up swoony heroes and relatable heroines, Evie can be found in the beautiful West Country of the UK, where she lives with her ridiculously patient husband, miracle daughter, and two dogs who think they run the show.

eviealexanderbooks.com

www.eviealexanderauthor.com

instagram.com/eviealexanderauthor
facebook.com/eviealexanderauthor
x.com/Evie_author
bookbub.com/authors/evie-alexander
amazon.com/Evie-Alexander/e/B08ZJGLP29?ref=sr_ntt_s-rch_lnk_1&qid=1630667484&sr=8-1
pinterest.com/eviealexanderauthor

9 781914 473319